How to Cope with
Suburban Stress

How to Cope with
Suburban Stress

DAVID GALEF

THE PERMANENT PRESS
Sag Harbor, NY 11963

Library of Congress Cataloging-in-Publication Data

Galef, David.
   How to cope with suburban stress / David Galef.
      p. cm.

   ISBN 1-57962-131-7

   1. Marriage. 2. Family. I. Title.

HQ519.G35 2006
306.850973'091733—dc22   2006043557

The Permanent Press
4170 Noyac Road
Sag Harbor, NY 11963

I'm grateful to the artists' colonies Yaddo and Ragdale,
as well as the University of Mississippi,
for granting me the time and space
to complete a major portion of this book.

* * *

This novel is dedicated to my family.

Have not novelists and novel readers worked their way through one volume after another in order to stop with a happy marriage? And has not one generation after another endured the troubles and complications of four acts if only there was some likelihood of a happy marriage in the fifth? However, by these prodigious efforts very little has been accomplished for the glorification of marriage, and I doubt very much if by the reading of such works any man has been made capable of performing the task he set himself or has felt oriented in life. For this precisely is the pernicious, the unwholesome feature of such works, that they end where they ought to begin.

—Søren Kierkegaard,
Either/Or,translated by Walter Lowrie

So stay or go? Some men leave just for the sake of change. Didn't Kierkegaard propose the "rotation method" as a way of dealing with tedium? But you value continuity—you entered psychotherapy out of concern over your tendency to cut and run. And you know that in the end Kierkegaard recommended a different sort of rotation, not wandering but rather tending to one field and rotating the crop, which is oneself. The answer is not moving on but staying and altering perspective; limit yourself, Kierkegaard recommends, and become fertile in invention.

—Peter Kramer,
Should You Leave?

Chapter 1

"So, are you going to leave for good? Or for evil?" I wasn't addressing a confidant or the violin-chinned leprechaun on Alex's box of Lucky Charms, but myself. I sometimes speak that way when I'm trying to calm down. "You've lost your keys again—wonder what that means," I'll pronounce, or in a fake British accent when I really need to distance me from myself, "That makes three G & T's. Haven't you had enough, old boy?" It's the voice of my superego, whom I see as a fussy type named Martin. I took a scalding sip of tea and sloshed down the mug, leaving a blurred ring on the table. I was too rattled to consider the matter from a calm psychiatric perspective, though I happen to be a psychiatrist.

I was hunched over the table in our breakfast nook in our eat-in kitchen in our large, mortgaged house, steeped in the false calm of a weekend. My seven-year-old son Alex was at soccer practice, my wife Jane was engaged in a hot tennis match at the club, and I was surveying the ruins of breakfast. If we are what we eat, Alex should have been in his sugar-sweet phase, Jane was black coffee, and I was milk-tea with a scone from Price's Bake Shop—known as the Pricey Bakery.

I bit my lip and got up to look out the bay window that probably reveals us as much as it lets us observe the neighbors. Clapped on our neo-Tudor Victorian Colonial hodgepodge years after the original construction, the window looks like a see-through tummy, as Alex once described it. There I stood in the belly of the beast, watching the DiSalvas play bocci on their manicured lawn. To the left of the DiSalvas lived the Wallers, their Taurus minivan parked perfectly parallel to the Lexus Infiniti, though no one ever seemed to be home. I wouldn't even have known their name if some of their mail hadn't been misdirected to us, and I crossed the street to put it in the box labeled in cursive "*No. 116.*" The castle on the right with the topiary hedge was occupied by the Steinbaums, who had once invited us over for a cocktail party and then dropped us. Social sets in a suburb like Fairchester are like Venn diagrams: overlapping circles of employment, children's schools, church, and country clubs, with some odd intersections. We'd moved here from Brooklyn in 1997 and two years later were still getting settled. These days, Jane had a bunch of new sports friends, bronze-armed goddesses who did their shopping in tennis whites. Unless I wanted to be a ball boy, I was left out.

I ventured outside to get my bearings. The Indian summer of September, the last bit of warmth before leaf-change, had coaxed the pink asters out again. I waved to Gianni, the blocky patriarch of the DiSalva family, dressed incongruously in purple-striped shorts and a yellow polo shirt, and he conferred a genial nod. His teenage daughter, Carla, grinned as she took aim at the last ball thrown by her brother Michael, who was wearing his father's outfit upside-down: a purple-striped shirt and yellow shorts. Completing the *tableau vivant* was Louise the mother, coming out with a tray of glasses and lemonade.

So what made them tick happily along? "Happy families are all alike," wrote Tolstoy. "Every unhappy family is unhappy in its own way." But what the hell did Leo know about happy families? Happy families are happy because of wealth, warmth, welfare . . . the same list that can provoke unhappiness: a husband and wife whose money divides them, or a child who fantasizes about life outside the warm cocoon. So much for aphorisms, which at best are often half-true.

Besides, who said the DiSalvas were happy? Maybe Gianni was having an affair that Louise bore for the sake of the family. Both kids were in their teens, so I imagined a blossoming coke habit for Michael and bulimia for Carla, though she hardly looked undernourished. Still, appearances do count for something. Some families can't even put up a front.

I wondered how the three of us came across to others. Jane and I managed socially, but as my father used to say, we were on the skids. We quarreled loudly in front of Alex, which, as any child expert will tell you, you're not supposed to do. At those moments, I swear, we could have knifed each other if we weren't so damned civilized—and twisted the blades in the wounds. Then Alex would act out, crying "Mommy, I want my milk glass three-quarters full!" and accidentally on purpose knocking over the glass if the milk wasn't at the right level. If you confronted him about it, he'd go in the other direction: withdrawal. He either needed constant attention, or he wasn't there at all. He was in the TV room, absorbing scenes of animated violence and whining "Quit it . . . " if you interrupted his viewing. He'd become, in non-clinical terms, a real pain in the butt. Jane and I disagreed on how to cope with him. One day, Jane would play good cop and let him watch yet another episode of *Space Raiders*; the next day, she'd go on an anti-TV crusade as I protested, "Oh, c'mon, he's already done his homework."

"You helped him with it, didn't you?"

"You're supposed to for this assignment. It says, 'Ask a parent for assistance.'" I found the sheet and showed it to her.

She scrutinized the paper. "But that's your handwriting on the report. That's not assistance, that's *doing* it."

"No, he just told me what to write . . . ."

She marched off to the TV room. "I'm going to have him redo it. This can't be what the teacher wanted." I tripped her and sat on her till she begged for mercy. In my mind.

From the TV room a moment later came a familiar cry: "Quit it! *I can't see!*"

We could argue about anything. Anyhow. Anytime. A recent nightmare of mine started out blissfully on a desert island—until one of the palm trees started quarreling with me about the shape of its coconuts. I was reaching for an axe when I woke up.

Nights after Alex went to sleep, Jane would retreat behind a magazine in front of the TV, and I'd read a book in the living room or, lately, surf the Web. I found odd sites devoted to the world's biggest bugs, a candy warehouse in Topeka, and a forsythia plant named Dolores with a Web cam trained on her to record growth. Once after almost swatting Alex when he peanut-butter-and-jellied the kitchen wall with a sandwich, I checked the Web for advice on spanking, only to find something called an age-regression archive, with stories about grown men turned back into infants. Being back in diapers and unaccountable for your actions has a certain appeal. I wanted out, but not that way.

Anyway, none of this helped with real-time coping. The simplest coordination, from arranging dinner to agreeing on Alex's bedtime, led to drawn-out quarrels, the kind with no discernible end, the type that erupt over seemingly innocuous questions. We could never play bocci together like the DiSalvas, though we might derive some pleasure from knocking each other's balls off the field. As a take-charge executive, Jane had her own set of *cojones*.

"It's all about power," claimed Jerry Mirnoff, a psychiatric colleague and friend who was writing a book on the subject of suburban stress, updating Freud's focus on sex. "It's who gets to call the shots." Not that Jerry's marriage was idyllic: lately his wife Cathy seemed awfully vulnerable, as if anywhere you touched you'd leave a bruise. Maybe the whole dynamic of marriage was problematic: yoking yourself to someone else "till death do you part" seems medieval. We'd tried counseling twice, the first time with a balding man who kept matching his fingertips together and talking about creative compromise, the second time with a woman in a tailored suit who kept urging us to "prioritize our needs." I shouldn't badmouth a vital sector of my profession, but neither told us a damned thing we didn't already know. I had only recently begun entertaining a new idea: maybe I shouldn't put up with this situation at all. Get out before the suburbs swallowed me up forever.

I went back into the kitchen to clean up everyone's mess, then withdrew to my office. My consulting room is another addition to the house, accessible through the garage. But the interior is what counts, as I tell my patients, and the Eames chair, the lake-blue couch, and the lined-up issues of *American Journal of Psychiatry* are all conducive to therapy. A recent portrait of Jane and Alex on my desk, her in tennis garb and him holding her racket, looked accusingly at me, so I turned away. Gazing ceilingward, I reviewed the latest quarrel I'd had with Jane—over mayonnaise, but it had grown ugly quicker than you can say "marital crisis."

"I wanted the no-fat soy." She'd held the offending jar at arm's length as if it might contaminate her.

"But it doesn't taste good." When we're trying to justify ourselves, we often use our son as a pawn: "Besides, Alex likes Hellman's."

"Damn it, how about what *I* like?" And with a movement like an overhead serve, she slammed the jar down on the counter, but too hard because it smashed into white glop and glass shards. An hour later, after much tense discussion, I was the one who cleaned it up. I thought of mayonnaising her racket handle or substituting it for sunblock, but decided against it. Still, the images lingered—Jane losing her grip, Jane slathering herself with Hellman's—and when your main source of pleasure is humiliating fantasies about your spouse, it's time to reassess.

Pussy-whipped, sniped a heavy male mutter I listen to from time to time, a voice from my id that I call Snoggs.

That can't be it, I thought back. I'm a man of peace, a psychiatrist: I analyze things. Besides, we haven't had sex for two months.

You simply don't try hard enough, snipped superego Martin. Unfair as usual, and always demanding more than I could give.

But what exactly was the problem? It wasn't the mayonnaise or the childcare squabble from yesterday or the last, halfhearted sex we'd had in August. Jane had always been a type A personality, the kind who starts to tap her fingers on the counter if the take-out coffee is thirty seconds late. My last name is Eisler, but Jane kept her maiden name, and that's Edge. Suits her perfectly. I'm not exactly laid back, but I'm a psych type, more interested in process than result. If the coffee was late in coming, I'd wonder why the counterman took so much longer to perform the same task he does every morning—had something happened on his way to work that day? Was there a different inflection in the way he said, "What'll it be?"

For Jane, this kind of interest translated into attention paid to her moods, her daily travails. As for me, I don't like emotional clinging—I get enough of that in my patients. I admire a certain independence in a woman, and Jane could fix a flat tire in the time it took me to call AAA.

Once upon a time, what we felt for each other was love, which Freud defines as obsession and transferential neurosis. I let my gaze wander up to the highest bookshelf, where an earlier portrait of Jane smiled down upon my thinning brown hair. When we got married, we'd do little kindnesses for each other, from giving backrubs to cooking favorite dinners. We were both busy professionals, Jane as a rising corporate executive at Americorps, me cutting down on clinical work to expand my private practice. We'd had our rough spots, but we had a common goal: ourselves.

I remember Jane's moving up through the ranks, carrying back office anecdotes, like the personnel chief caught half-naked in the elevator with a subordinate and trying to pretend it was a necktie swap. I'd tell her about my more peculiar cases. And we relied on each other not just for an audience but also for sex—the sweaty, gymnastic kind since Jane liked strenuous positions. We both used our mouths a lot, and sometimes we played little S & M games.

But we'd been going steadily downhill since the time Alex was born. Here's a simplistic tracery: B. A. (Before Alex), we had reciprocal love and time for spontaneity. A. A., Jane was so worried about getting back her looks, as well as doing everything right for her offspring and working at the office, that I got left out of the equation. And lack of time and sleep ate up all our good will, to the point where I began criticizing everything Jane did.

"Will you *please* turn off the lights when you leave the living room?"

"But I'm coming right back in."

"That's what you said an hour ago. And while you're at it, wash your own damned coffee cup next time."

Or when we were driving anywhere: "Slow down, will you? I think we passed the sign for Route 90."

"I'm not going fast. Anyway, just check the map."

"Look, I don't know where we are now. Let's ask at that gas station up ahead."

"*No*, I'm not stopping here."

But who said what? Astute listeners will realize that I usually took the domestic, traditionally female stance—for instance, I always asked for directions on a trip, whereas Jane had been raised to see that as a weakness.

Moving to the suburbs hadn't helped matters. We'd both been raised there and saw it as a region to escape from, but when your child reaches school age, good public education and the safety of a small town sound seductive. Of course, the suburbs have their own pressures, with endless community activities, yet nowhere to really cut loose. Suburban angst?— that's what Jerry Mirnoff called it, and maybe he was right. To add to this mix, last year Jane jumped ship to a multinational biotech company called Haldome, which paid a lot more but was also a giant pressure cooker. That might have been one reason that Jane didn't want a second child, which caused a slow leak in my heart. Alex was a bright, lonely kid who could use a younger brother or sister.

"It's not so much good days and bad days," said an uncle of mine, now deceased, describing married life in large swings of his callused hands. "There are good years and bad years." But the thought of years like this was more than I could bear. Yes, yes, yes, the counselors we'd seen had plied us with the common sense we'd ignored, so we stopped the bickering. Until the next time.

You mean she turned into a bitch, muttered Snoggs. I'd ignored him so far, but now I wondered. At times just the sight of her retreating back after an argument was enough to keep me on edge for a day. Why did I put up with this?

Coward, sneered Snoggs. Maybe, but I'm no fool. It wouldn't be a clean break, it would hurt like hell, and the consequences would haunt me forever.

I am nothing if not methodical. I sometimes think I could have been an accountant if numbers interested me as much as defense mechanisms. From a drawer in my desk, I retrieved a list I'd made up the week before, a double column of pluses and minuses in our relationship, a cliché, but I sometimes advise patients to do this, since merely writing the list helps to clarify matters.

Under PLUSES was a short inventory, starting off with "stable home environment" and other non-romantic phrases. MINUSES was a far longer list, trailing from "atmosphere of distrust" to "constant irritation" and heavily annotated with recent examples, including the mayonnaise incident. But all I could do was stare at the paper as if written somewhere on it was the answer to my question: "Should you leave?"

I thought of how things used to be when I was single. Slurping take-out Chinese on the sofa, reading till late at night or going out to the movies. We still did some of that, time permitting, but it was different now. When I was alone and master of my own domain, I was never bored. Lonely occasionally, sexually frustrated, sure, but mostly working, socializing, itching and scratching, or just reading a book. I couldn't recall the last time I'd had uninterrupted reading time alone. I missed that.

What do you really miss? inquired Martin.

I miss me, sobbed Snoggs. *I miss the way I used to be.* That's what a client of mine, a middle-aged woman in a constrictive marriage, had said the other day. But when I asked her what she used to be like, she reeled off a description that seemed to fit her present self exactly.

Should you leave? In the end, the plus-and-minus list in my desk would tell me nothing. If I left, what would change? Not me, in which case I'd simply repeat the same behavior in any other relationship. Reaching over my head, I pulled down almost by instinct an old volume I hadn't looked at since my old psychoanalytic supervisor, Dr. Stanley Briggs, shoved it into my hands. Kierkegaard's *Either/Or*, if you can believe it. One essay in particular, "The Rotation Method," started out as a diatribe against boredom, intruded some unkind words about marriage, and then talked about crop rotation. There it was—I'd marked the passage: "My method does not consist in change of field, but resembles the true rotation method in changing the crop and the mode of cultivation." And later on, if one varies the soil, "then one must also constantly vary himself, and this is the essential secret." Don't leave for another patch of land, but stay and change what you grow. In another words: Physician, heal thyself. I thought of the DiSalva family out on their lawn, happily bowling away. Or maybe that was the wrong model, but I had to begin somewhere. The question was how.

Then, since I'd reached an impasse, I booted up the laptop computer I kept on my desktop, logged onto my AOL account, and typed in one of those wild-card searches that produces thousands of results: "CHILDREN + TOYS" because the holidays would be with us soon enough, and maybe I could avoid the cavernous hell of Toys R Us by going online. The first ten hits looked like sociology write-ups, but the second page had a few that looked vaguely retail, and I clicked on one that promised "boy toys."

The site took a while to access, but eventually a deep purple backdrop materialized on my screen. The second level of detail was an electric-yellow sign cautioning those under 18 to log off immediately. Pandora that I am, I clicked to enter.

The screen began to fill with a repeating pattern that looked abstract until I peered closer and saw that it was made up of boys: young boys in shorts pedaling bicycles, boys leaning back in pulled-down overalls, boys splashing about in bathing suits. When I waded through another disclaimer and clicked on "GALLERY," I got up close and personal. A graphic of prepubescent butt-cheeks spread wide, followed by a list of downloadable picture files: Jrnoshorts.bin, Jr-eatdad.jpg, Jrxpsd.gif . . . . "Input password," blinked a box in the lower right-hand corner. I sat there, transfixed by the list as the image burned a hole in my screen. Oh, I read the newspapers, and I knew this sort of thing existed. But to have it in my home, like a hand that had traveled through the sewer to reach for me from the sink drain, was something else.

My reverie, if that's what to call it, was interrupted by the crunch of gravel in the driveway. Jane was home, having picked up Alex from his soccer practice. I hurriedly exited the site, disconnected, and turned off the computer just as my family came in through the back door. Assuming a loopy cheeriness, I bounded into the kitchen, pretending to trip and eliciting a laugh from Alex.

"Watch out!" I told him. "The crazy DiSalvas are out there, conking each other with bocci balls."

"Really?" Alex looked wide-eyed toward the bay window, arms protecting his head.

"Well, we can all put on our bike helmets." Jane, aglow from tennis, smiled at me, spreading a balm. When she put her hands over her head, her taut bare arms made my pulse—and other parts—quicken. Jane had always been big-boned in a sloppy sort of way, but in the last six months she'd been faithfully attending aerobics classes during her lunch breaks. The results had trimmed her figure and put a bounce everywhere there'd been a sag. Those sleek thighs emerging from tennis shorts greatly increased my interest in sex. In fact, "good sex" was still in the pluses column, though balanced in the minuses ranks by "no sex lately." On the third hand, any action was impossible with Alex underfoot.

Still, hope springs infernal. I went out to the garage for our helmets, used on those rare occasions when we rode, and pretty soon we were eating tuna fish sandwiches, all prepared for the sky to fall. Alex's helmet sported a yellow Pokémon decal that soon had mayonnaise on it. Jane's fuchsia model gently bumped my white one as she bent to take a bite. One happy family, just the same as the DiSalvas, eh?

"So how was soccer practice?" I asked Alex, who shrugged. But fathers can be persistent. "Did you get a chance to handle the ball?"

"It's soccer—you don't *hand*-le the ball."

Jane concealed a smile. I couldn't help but retort. "Well, you do if you're playing goalie or taking a free throw."

"Um, yeah . . . ." He conceded defeat by looking away from me. He gave the table leg a kick, which he knew I hated.

"Look, I don't need all the lurid details—"

"What's 'lurid' mean?"

Jane suppressed a second smile on top of her first. "It means shocking, honey, or something terrible."

"Oh." Alex's lips moved soundlessly, trying out the word. "Can soccer be lurid?"

I intervened. "Maybe. Anyway, never mind the details. How about just rating it on a scale of 1 to 10?"

"Um, 4.75. Because it wasn't quite 5." He had recently discovered decimals and applied them everywhere, including telling time: *It's 7.5 o'clock, so get up, Daddy.* A bright, annoying kid, just like me at that age, so it was hard to complain. From Jane, he got his stubborn streak. He was definitely in my pluses column, though the endless arguments he spurred counted as a minus. And how would my leaving affect him? When he took another bite of sandwich, I turned to my helpmate.

"So how was tennis?" Equal time, equal phrasing.

"Oh, I'd have to give it a 9. Wylene and I creamed Frances and Mavis."

"Hm. Did they get to *hand*-le the ball?"

Jane has a lovely smile when it's not forced. And Alex, mouth full, didn't point out that mostly rackets and not hands hit tennis balls. Instead, Jane described the opposing team's shortcomings, including an inability to play the net when Frances was serving. All the women were friends off the court. Frances was a lawyer, Mavis a ceramicist, and Wylene the proprietress of Fairchester's independent bookstore, Between the Covers. We also knew the husbands socially, just two of them, since Wylene was a single mother. Tennis was just what they did for recreation. But it was lurid—or at least shocking—how competitive Jane had become over 30-love. I often felt left behind, another problem that needed addressing. Put it on the list.

After the tuna course, I cut an apple in sections, making Alex's a funny, wiggly shape so he'd eat it. "It's a fat snake," I told him.

"Yuk. I hate snakes."

"Okay, then, it's apple zigzag candy."

"Really?" He ate it in three quick bites. Jane toyed with her piece and left half of it on the plate. She wasn't much of a fruit-eater and did it only to please me. If she'd been Adam in Eden, she never would have been tempted.

Soon Jane went upstairs to shower while Alex and I left for his room to play a new game called Unicam about alien spy satellites. I decided to clean up later. In a few minutes, we were trying to head off three probes from Deneb 3.

Unfortunately, in preparing lunch, I'd left my "Should you leave?" list on the kitchen table.

Chapter 2

In the Yellow Room of his garden apartment, the man in gray slacks and short-sleeve shirt was taking careful sips from a coffee mug labeled "HOT STUFF!" Below the slogan flew a little pink devil that had taken the man's fancy at a yard sale. The man peered through the Venetian blinds at the rectangular front yard across Winfield Avenue, where two little boys were playing catch. One was wearing a green shirt the color of a plant stalk, his neck like a tender shoot. The other was all in red with a big, waggly smile. Four years old, five? They were at the bumbling age, and they missed a lot. Eventually, Green Shirt started missing on purpose, and when he flopped onto the grass in a sacrifice save, his shirt hiked up in back to reveal the delicate knobs of his spine. Then they went inside, the door closing as if the building were eating them.

Every once in a while, the man put down the mug to circle the room in the kind of measured tread learned in an institution. When the coffee was all gone, he brought the cup over to the sink, washed it out, and hung it upside down from the dish dryer. Then he exited to the Blue Room, where a Gateway Galaxy rested on a desk made from a door placed over two filing cabinets. The machine lay under a plastic dust cover like a sofa whose owner was concerned about scuff marks. With a twitch of the man's fingers, the cover came off like a shroud, emitting a ghostly *whoosh*. He booted up the computer, bringing it back to life, drumming his fingers on the arm of his swivel chair as the machine beeped and hummed, going through all its system-checks, from mouse to CPU to scanner. Before he began to type, he cracked his knuckles one by one, the big joints with a hollow *pop* and the smaller ones with a *ping*, as if tiny bones were being broken. Before sleep every night, he also performed this ritual on his toes.

The Blue Room's one window was covered up with navy Contac paper, the small interior divided in half. One section was the TV room, with an armchair, a television, and a VCR. The other part was the computer room, with a swivel chair and the homemade desk. The interior was mostly barren except for some old cardboard boxes along one wall, stuffed with manila envelopes, plump green plastic garbage bags, and stacks of video cassettes. The walls, floor, and ceiling were rolled with the same brand of cheap paint that made the Yellow Room yellow, illuminated by a strip of overhead fluorescent lighting. Emanating from nowhere in particular was an odd smell like sweat socks and sea water.

When the computer was ready, he linked up through his modem, keyed in an authorization code on his mIRC, typed in two more passwords to get into the Littl Boyz Room, and logged in as CandyMan. He was greeted immediately:

Hell-o! Back I see. That was CRater.

Can't see your back, he typed quickly. Wish I cud.

Here, I'm wiggling it 4 u.

Good, good. He thought a moment. U got a pic 4 me?

Wutchoo give fer it?

2 shower pix?

Ill give u 3! That was from CumAsUR, the total clown in the group.

Wait, CandyMan was 1st.

But I came 2nd!

Hey, whereza party? Chomper was always breaking in, rarely offering anything but talk. Two other people were in the room, HalfPint and Scumm, but they were just auditing. Funny how sometimes you thought you could hear them breathing.

Let's start over, he typed. I'm in the mood for love.

Da-da-da-dum.

So horny I could fuck Billy (goat). CumAsUR again.

u met my friend little willy? (Chomper.)

Usually this kind of exchange could stretch out for pages, but today he wasn't in the mood for it. He wasn't crazy about low epsilon types, anyway. He cut off CumAsUR and Chomper with a rude comment and quickly finished his arrangement with CRater. They exchanged anonymous account numbers, and he left the chat room. Leaving was like shutting a series of heavy steel doors behind him. After a few minutes, he checked his private e-mail account: there it was, a JPG waiting like a prize. He sent off his own part of the deal, two binary files, and downloaded the photo to resurrect later through QuickView Plus. Not now, but maybe after dinner. If he'd been a good boy. Compartmentalizing was important, as he'd learned in therapy. Putting off pleasure helped with self-control. It also increased the eventual payoff.

But lately, he'd been straying from his routine. His prescription for Dilantin was getting low, and he hadn't bothered to renew it. The succession of his days felt like a thread he'd been paying out for a long time, unraveling at times. Concentrating was harder, but the episodes were gone, and days without the drug seemed looser, more up for grabs. He was a free agent. He'd spent too long waiting for something to happen. Now he was ready to push things along. Yet for a while, he just sat there, staring at the blank azure wall in front of him. In the scuffed paint job were cloud shapes and a few other images that came to him. He wished he were a part of the wall, then one of the boys outside playing catch, then the ball itself. He soared, bounced, and was caught in a hot, sweaty hand.

He'd lived in the Ridgefield section of Fairchester for six months, an auspicious new start in the suburbs. Before this place, he'd lived lengthwise in a railroad apartment, and before that, in a cramped studio that overlooked a brick wall. (At one point, he'd resided in a hospital room with no window at all.) Now he could exist on a higher plane. His garden apartment had three rooms, not including the kitchen, and he was slowly expanding to fill the space. He'd once told himself that he could stay in a closet in Detroit or an underground bunker with the right electronic hookups, but he was growing restless these days. The suburbs extended their grassy lanes and shaded real estate in a promise of plenty. Children clustered like grapes at the elementary schools and the malls, ripe for picking. The hint of a spasm crossed his face.

Eventually he got up, patting his pants pocket for car keys. He left the Blue Room for the Yellow Room, which was really just the kitchenette, wondering for the hundredth time about the state of the Dungeon without actually going near the entrance. He was also putting that off. The Dungeon was dark and enclosed, and this morning he wanted to embrace life. He exited through the back door to his waiting car, a graying Nissan Sentra. As he backed down the twisty driveway, he hummed an old Beatles tune, "Maxwell's Silver Hammer." Too much time indoors. All this summer sunshine in September made him feel like a kid again, and as he accelerated up Elm Street, he rolled down the window and hung his arm out. He was headed toward the nearest playground.

*

The man in gray slacks drove home early that evening, when the golden haze was transmuting to gray dusk. On the seat beside him sat something like a cake box but misshapen, as if someone had sat on a corner of it. From time to time he patted it like an animal he'd just picked up from the vet. He also had something in the trunk that excited him. The radio was tuned to WHAB, a Golden Oldies station stuck between the Beatles and the Bee Gees. The back speakers blared out the lyrics to "YMCA" as he hummed and tapped along on the steering wheel.

The playground had been more than fun, and as he replayed it all in his mind, his eyes glazed over. Ridgefield was a good spot for crowds. Too bad they'd outlawed jungle gyms and seesaws as too dangerous. Still, he'd glimpsed some lovely views down the slides and up the swings. As to what he'd picked up behind the box-hedge, that was truly a find. His thin pink tongue licked the edge of his lips.

The dog ran into the middle of the road as he crested a hill. Its eyes suddenly shone in the sunset like a cat's, its black coat backlit in a warped halo. The man had just time to slam on the brakes or swerve, but he did neither. It was as if he were viewing another scene in a hole through the present, lit at the center by flickering images that urged him on. He spasmed slightly and couldn't focus. He simply drove down the tunnel with a canine mouth at the center.

The dog hit the front bumper with a thud. The man braked, backed up, and stopped the car. Getting out, he saw the dog still quivering on the pavement, bleeding but paralyzed. Its eyes, still reflected in the headlights, were wide with hurt and terror. The man watched the dog for a bit, unable to move himself forward to help. Slowly his own spasms subsided. He saw pain and wanted to put an end to it, to absorb it himself if he could. One of the dog's ribs was sticking through the thick fur in a gout of blood. He closed his eyes against the scene, mumbled something to himself, and finally got back in the car. With numb precision, he slowly ran over the dog with his front right wheel, this time feeling the crunch of bones. At the moment he did it, he was the driver and the car, the dog and the pavement. He did it once more for good measure, though there was only a subsiding bump this time. Then he drove the rest of the way home, his hands gripping the wheel so tightly that white ridges formed on his fingers. He was so rattled that he almost turned into the wrong apartment complex half a block down—there were two on Winfield Avenue and almost no others in all of Fairchester. When he finally turned off the ignition, the hush was deafening. He sat there for several minutes before climbing out, box in hand. By taking a few deep breaths, he cleared the mists from around himself. He felt better, shaken but restored. For now.

In the yellow kitchen, he placed the box on a stool as if it could observe the proceedings while he prepared a simple meal: Spaghetti-O's warmed up in a saucepan, and half a cucumber on a plate from the refrigerator. Sitting at the kitchen table, he flipped open the *Fairchester Guardian* from that week and scanned the front page. The town planning committee was looking into a bond issue for a new municipal parking lot; the high school football team, the Chargers, had beaten their rivals the Edgeville Eagles, 18-12. In the back pages was an article on elementary school field trips, which he read closely, paying particular attention to the destinations: the Pound Ridge Nature Center, the Museum of Natural History in Manhattan, the Circle Line Ferry. The one accompanying photo showed a second-grade class standing in front of a bus in a fairly even row with the blonde teacher at the end like a fence post.

One little boy, second from the left, was wearing shorts that showed off his knobby knees and thin calves. His hands were clasped in front of him as if to protect his groin, with a look balanced between surprise and chagrin. Had someone just kicked him? He was surrounded by two impish girls, who didn't interest the man, now focusing on a Greek-looking boy on the far right, with dark, expressive eyes and a heavy pout. He wore a white T-shirt tucked into belted jeans, his arms at attention. Smooth, oyster-skinned forearms. The man wondered what the boy looked like from the rear, his child's buttocks barely pressing against the denim—the back soft but straight, except where it flared at the shoulder blades, like recently severed wings. *Little angel*, he mouthed, and blew the boy a kiss.

The last boy the man looked at was Asian, his face smooth and calm, the nose upturned under a helmet of black hair. His arms were akimbo, his shirt ridden up slightly to reveal an appetizing sliver of belly between his pants and his shirt. But he smiled at the camera as if he had some hidden knowledge, as if he knew the photographer. It was the kind of expression that follows the viewer, and it made the man drop his gaze. He looked at the photo caption again, but no names were given.

As the Spaghetti-O's cooled, the man spooned them up and blew on them. He alternated a bite of pasta with a bite of cucumber for the difference between red and green taste, though the hot-cold variation hurt his teeth. Toward the end, he played a game with the Spaghetti-O's, seeing how many little O's he could get on his spoon without any dropping back into the bowl before they slid into his waiting mouth.

When he finished the paper, he sat there for a moment as if the reading and eating hadn't quite synchronized right. He cracked his knuckles one by one, reaching seven before a few failed to give. Finally he got up to make coffee and get dessert, a large chocolate-chip cookie from a baker's white bag marked in blocky black letters, **"Price's Baked Goods."** He rose to take his plate and cup into the Blue Room, but first he opened a kitchen drawer for a scissors and neatly cut out the class picture from the newspaper.

He filed the picture in a manila folder marked "Kidz R Us," which was already overflowing with similar clippings, and slid it back into a drawer. But when he faced away from the desk and walked forward, the Blue Room became the TV room, marked by an armchair, really a castoff stunted love seat, not quite big enough for two. In the other corner of the room was a distressed 22"-screen Sony, on top of which sat a black Minolta VCR like a squared-off hat. Videos sat stacked in a crate, including a large variety of Disney features. Yesterday, he had rented a video on three-day loan, a semi-documentary called *Streetwise* about vagrant kids in Seattle. He started the film, concentrating on the gamin who skateboarded up and down the streets, but soon he grew restless, half-embraced by the chair and idly kicking at the armrests. Filled with food, he felt as if he were expanding beyond his natural contours, like an amoeba in slacks. The image of the dog had evaporated, though it might rain down later. Right now, he was really just waiting to open the box he'd received, but kept putting it off for the right moment.

One last swallow of coffee, and he shut the video off. Maybe a visit to the Dungeon was in order. Opening a small door in the Blue Room, he pretended he was descending to the basement. The Dungeon was really just the bathroom, a surprisingly large but otherwise dank sector that smelled of mold and cold sweat. In the bathtub were castoff parts from a home gym with some odd homemade harness-like attachments. Fastened to the adjacent wall were manacles at child height. He breathed deeply, taking in the atmosphere. Crawling into the tub, he strapped himself in, pulling the last leather thong tight with his teeth. Balanced on his knees, he could almost dangle. If he closed his eyes, as he did now, he could be the Asian boy, scrawny arms upraised in helpless surrender, smooth armpits where fingernails could be dug in, soft belly buttoned down by an outie navel. A penis small as a hummingbird.

As his eyes adjusted to the lack of light, his gaze moved to the Slurpy Seat, a small wood-and-leather chair with a circle cut in the seat and the legs bolted to a mat. He craned his neck, imagining his head under the chair, sticking his tongue into someone squirming above. But he also flipped in his mind to feel himself on the chair, childlike and frail, with something wet and probing underneath. Half his fantasies were bodily projections, his desperate wish whenever he had an attack.

He made an animal face like that of a hyena, then a pig, then a wolf. It was part of an old game called Wild-Child that his aunt had taught him: one person made the expression and sounds while the other person guessed the animal. Part of him grunted while the frightened child squealed. Then he stuck out his wolf's tongue.

His head bobbed and weaved, his tongue protruding, his pelvis arching within the limits of the constraints. When he'd had enough, he freed himself by yanking at a quick-release buckle that occasionally stuck. After the whole meandering day, he felt better, as if some slothful flaccidity had been disciplined through hard exercise. Pain had a bracing, even clarifying, effect. He gripped and regripped his arms as he walked out, feeling his new body.

Back in the yellow kitchen, he washed the dishes thoroughly, lingering on each plate-face with sponge and soap. Everything had to be set in the drying rack at the correct angle. Only then did he turn to the box on the stool. Prolonging the moment, holding off, he tried to practice patience like a martial art.

Carrying the box as if it were crystal, he brought it into his bedroom, where the faded wallpaper was blocked out by posters of pastel airplanes, trains, and cars. A twin-size bed, its stippled coverlet neatly turned down, flanked the far wall. The Mickey Mouse clock on the night table showed just before ten, but the man generally went to sleep early. He laid the box down gently on the bed and undressed quickly. Carefully folded under his pillow were a pair of gray Goofy Gus boxer shorts and a tentlike baseball shirt, his grown-up pajamas.

The return address on the package was from a post office box in Minneapolis, just as the sender knew the man only as an anonymous post office box in Fairchester. He used his mother's old scissors with a blade like a bird's bill to cut the brown paper wrapping. There it was, swathed in several plastic bags: a complete set of boy's clothing, from little khaki pants to a crew-neck short-sleeved shirt. The prize was the boy's underwear, stained with a trace of urine and a little brown-rimmed sweat—delicate, almost tart, as different from the acrid reek of a man as lamb from mutton.

One last night-time routine before sleep. He padded to the bathroom adjoining the bedroom, snapped on the light, and peered at himself in the mirror. His face was pale and unlined, childish but for the growing thickness of age at his chin, the bluish moons under his watery eyes. He tried a smile that came out as a grimace and turned into a yawn, his mouth widening until it claimed half his face. Stop—no wolf this time. He smiled again, and this time it was a success: the lips parted expectantly with just a hint of the upper teeth, his eyes friendly. He patted himself. Good boy.

Back in the bedroom, he turned on his white-noise machine and set it to ocean waves, lay down, and draped the underwear across his face. When he stared into the cotton weave, he saw a boy running on the beach, little thighs straining against the fabric, the smooth arms above swinging from side to side. *My darling angel*, he murmured. He massaged, then stroked himself, finally gripping himself like a tennis racket and pumping hard. He came onto the sheets, swabbed himself with a tissue, and lay back spent.

Just as he was about to drop off, he realized that he'd never unpacked what was in the car trunk, but it didn't matter now.

Chapter 3

I was halfway to Mary Rohrenbach's house before I even thought about the list, and then I engaged in such a pocket-patting frenzy that Alex, seated in back and slapping the hell out of a Gameboy, cried out, "Daddy, watch the road!"

"Better keep your eyes on the space invaders," I told him over the *bleert-bleert* of some game called Star Lords, I think. "You're about to lose a battle cruiser." All right, I'd look for the list later. We got to the Rohrenbachs' in one piece, minus a few scout ships, where Mary popped from behind the screen door like a girl eager for a date—except that Mary was Alex's baby-sitter for tonight. We were going to a dinner party at the Mirnoffs'.

"Hi, Alex!" Mary naturally slipped into the back seat with Alex, though she was smart enough not to interrupt his final moments of concentration. She wore the standard-issue T-shirt and jeans, along with that year's black platform sandals.

"Hello." Alex rewarded her with a little boy's scowl, his whole face tilting downward. In fact, he liked Mary. She was imaginative: on her last visit, she'd improvised a game under the table with Alex called Cave that he still asked for. And she was responsible: not the kind who'd make out with her boyfriend on your couch after putting the kid to sleep.

"You're not mad at me, are you, Alex?" She screwed up her face in mock concern.

"N-no . . . ." *Bleert-bleert.* "I'm just trying to get this last alien." The car swerved at the intersection. "*Daddy*, you made me miss it!"

"You're right, I take full blame."

We drove through the twilight filtering down through the trees, great maples and oaks that almost met over the center of the streets. Minivans and sports utility vehicles lined the driveways. Fairchester is a pleasant suburb, just twenty miles from New York, with a reputation for affluence well before the term *bedroom community* was coined. Nothing prefab, few ranch houses in sight, and the older properties have grounds rather than yards. Ridgefield happens to be a poorer section of Fairchester, bordering Hillside, and that's where we live. The houses are more cracker boxes, and the elementary school isn't quite as well-equipped as the other four in the area. But the quality of education is high, just as lofty as the real-estate prices (and property taxes) that drive the system. It's a forty-five-minute commute to Manhattan for Jane, and Alex can walk to his school, Ridgefield Elementary.

When we got home, Alex jumped out of the car and dared Mary to catch him. She dashed after him into the house. When I entered the kitchen, I found my list face-down on the table, as unassuming as Poe's purloined letter—or as blatant as an unpaid bill. Had Jane looked at it? I didn't know, and now I couldn't ask. No more slip-ups this time. I went back to my office and slid the list among some other papers in the flat middle drawer of my desk, which has a puny lock with a key stuck in it. Then I went upstairs to our bedroom, where Jane was in the shower. When she's going out, she always prepares until the very last moment, depending on some internal clock that gets her out the door precisely ten minutes after we should have left.

Me, all I had to do was shave, which I never do on the weekends except for this sort of occasion. I needed my electric razor, which happened to be in the bathroom. If I were married to a man, I could have simply walked in and shaved in front of the wall mirror. But Jane and, I gather, most other women have a desperate need to be alone when performing their toilet and resent any intrusion. I don't know whether it's the preservation of Eleusynian mysteries or tweezing eyebrow hairs, but there's something about a woman in the bathroom that says KEEP OUT, even if you've been married to her for a decade.

On the other hand, if I didn't get to the goddamned shaver, *I'd* be late. So I waited until I couldn't bear it any longer, then tapped politely on the door. "Excuse me," I mumbled as I slid in, averting my eyes from whatever the hell I wasn't supposed to see.

From behind the shower curtain, where the water had just shut off, came a pained sigh. Out of the corner of my eye, I saw one perfect bare arm rise to the blurred head. "Why is it—" began the litany I knew all too well.

"Look, don't start. I just had to grab my razor. I'll shave in the other bathroom, okay?"

"Can't I ever have a moment's privacy?"

I should have flicked away the curtain: my chance to see a naked Gorgon. We used to have this routine where I'd pretend to surprise her, and she'd—but never mind. The really painful part now is how well-worn the grooves of our arguments are, and how inevitable.

I stuck to literalism and common sense, neither of which works in these situations. "'A moment'? Christ, you've been in here for almost half an hour—"

"So what?"

"—and it's not like I'm taking over your theater of operations. I just need my razor. There's no other way to get it except by boring a hole through the wall."

"I don't see why you can't wait."

"I'm *always* waiting for you." Which is true, though she claims she's always waiting for me. "I don't see why we can't share. You know, *sharing*? What we're trying to encourage our son to do?"

Silence. Then: "Have you got your razor?"

"Yes. But I don't see why we can't just—"

"Do we have to talk about this now?"

"No," I said as I took the razor and cord, which trailed behind me like a dead snake. "Never's okay with me."

Which explained why we were driving to the Mirnoffs' in stony silence half an hour later. The Mirnoffs, Jerry the fellow psychiatrist and Cathy the children's book illustrator, have a house in Dovecote, the swankest district in Fairchester. I've known Jerry since our residency at Brooklyn Downstate. Jane and Cathy came later, though the two of them get along fine, and in fact Jane has always made sure to buy all Cathy's books.

We graveled up the driveway, lit by imitation Japanese stone lanterns. The house was an attempt at Frank Lloyd Wright but succeeded only in being vertically challenged. It did have a wide wing span—probably over 5,000 square feet. We parked by blocking off two Chevy Suburbans in the driveway and got out still wordless, Jane cradling a bottle of Beaujolais like the second child we've never had. We exchanged frantic "be nice" faces at the doorstep.

The doorbell was one of those multi-tone affairs, something like the tune from *E.T.* We were met at the door by Cathy, wearing an orange-and-yellow caftan in an era that long ago bid goodbye to that kind of garment, along with Nehru jackets. She had always been plump, but now looked as if her body had shifted somehow, though it was hard to tell through the caftan. I could tell that Jane, dressed in an ice-blue sleeveless pullover and navy skirt that showed off her tennis muscles to best advantage, was thinking, *What's next, a muu-muu?*

"Michael! Jane!" Jerry waved effusively from the wood-paneled bar, which fit the rest of the retro look. A Hawaiian shirt hung from his wiry frame. He was involved with a cocktail shaker, a giant chrome container that looked like something NASA would send on a moon trip. "You know everyone here"—Francis and Frances Connolly, a high-salaried legal couple who Jane once dubbed "Mr. and Ms. Lawyer." Blue jackets for both, upright posture. They had two perfect children who already sounded litigious in the classroom. Frances was usually Jane's losing tennis opponent. Over on the far end of the sofa sprawled Mavis Talent, a ceramic artist, Frances's tennis partner, and the reason they usually lost. Scrunched up next to her was her husband, Arthur Schram, a financial consultant. Together, they had three screwed-up kids from three marriages. They wore shirts, skirt, and slacks in bright, primary colors and had the hunched-over posture that comes from hours of kiddie patrol. But this evening clearly wasn't for children. The Mirnoffs' bratty daughter Samantha, three years older than Alex, had been exiled to the den with a made-for-TV movie about delinquent teens or something.

Jerry solemnly filled the shaker with Bombay gin, vermouth more in name than substance, and a fistful of ice cubes. Then he hopped up and down, first on one leg, then the other, in a sort of alcoholic rain dance. The results were poured out and distributed, and took effect immediately. Something about an ice-cold martini freezes the forebrain, numbing the nerves that control inhibitions. There were niblets on the coffee table, including a black-bean-and-corn salsa that everyone was serving that summer, and I dipped a nacho chip into it to anchor myself.

Jane started talking tennis with Frances and Mavis, dissecting the match from this morning. I'd heard this replay already, though not so charitably phrased. The way Jane put it now made it sound like an accident: "Oh, sometimes you just get lucky," she announced, shrugging adorably. God, she could be sweet sometimes. *Treats her friends nicer than she does you*, sniped Snoggs. So put it on the list, I told him wearily. Anyway, it wasn't my conversation. I turned to Francis, sitting next to me with his arms folded.

"So how's business?" I asked because I couldn't think of anything else polite to open with. "Sue any widows?" seemed contentious.

"Never better." Francis took a satisfied sip from his martini glass and reached for a celery stick. "Frances and I are working on a way to turn last month's vacation in Mexico into billable hours." Only a slight upturn of his mouth told me he might be kidding.

Mavis asked Jane how the rat race was going. "It's tough, but incredibly fulfilling," I heard my wife say with astonishment (mine, not hers). *Jesus, if I have to deal with one more stupid male exec today, I'm going to murder a village*, was more along the lines of what she told me. She helped herself to a jicama slice from the plate of crudités and crunched with satisfaction. As the discussion broadened, Jerry launched into an appreciation of the Hippocratic oath, and Mavis said something New Age about art and self-actualization. Some competition came from Cathy about whether illustrating children's books was more fulfilling than glazing pots, but that's not the point. Self-deprecation was out and self-affirmation was in—or hypocrisy. When we moved on to the subject of kids, the one-upmanship continued.

"Oh, gosh, I can't even keep up with them these days." Mavis swiveled her head to emphasize this point. "They go in so many different directions." Mostly away from home, I'd heard. One of their kids had recently been found at a bus station in Buffalo, trying for Canada. In fact, as soon as the conversation passed from Mavis's spot, I saw Arthur nudge her with his foot.

"Daniel just started taking piano lessons," chimed in Frances. "I think music is so important for enrichment."

"What pieces can he play?" Cathy took my empty martini glass and passed it to Jerry, who handed it back full as new.

"We don't quite know yet," muttered Francis, proving that he at least had a sense of sarcasm, if only about his children.

I thought of saying something but decided against it. The alcohol had loosened us up only partly. People's postures tended to be relaxed and yet vigilant, as if the couch were situated over some invisible fault line. Halfway through the second round of martinis, Jerry rose importantly. "Okay, time to grill the steaks. Anyone who doesn't like it rare, confess now."

Frances raised a hand, mumbling something about bacteria. Francis smiled and shrugged, as if to dissociate himself from his wife's fears. Jerry shrugged in sympathy and departed. After a few more minutes of listening to stories about kids and community affairs, I got up to talk with the chef. I found him out on the back porch, ministering to a Weber grill the size of a trailer, with three tiers fed by canisters fit for jet propulsion.

"Yep," said Jerry, patting the side of his black-anodized beauty, "this thing'll char a whole steer with room left over." He fiddled with a dial in front.

I didn't ask him what the hell he wanted to do that for, just as I no longer ask people why they want to ride around in a Chevrolet Suburban. It's the suburbs, after all.

"So," I asked after he'd ignited the first rack with a whoosh, "how's the book coming?" Jerry was one of the few authors who *liked* to be asked about the progress of his work. His manual on suburban stress wasn't exactly therapy or self-help, but it had a catchy title: *How to Cope with Suburban Stress*. One of the chapters, "Housing Anxiety," had everything a homeowner could worry about and had already appeared as a magazine article in *H&G*.

"Oh, coming along. Almost finished a chapter on minivans that says volumes about power and anxiety in the American family." He reached for a platter of sirloins on the landing strip attached to the grill. "Of course, it's hard relieving stress when your own family contributes so much to it."

"What do you mean?"

Jerry lowered his voice so that the squirrels in his back yard couldn't hear. "Cathy's developed irritable bowel syndrome—makes her rush to the john a lot." He clenched and opened his hands as if he were her sphincter. "For a while, she was on something called Bentylac, but they recently took it off the market. Colon cancer risk. So now we're worried about that, too. These days she's on some medication that makes her retain a lot of fluid. And it doesn't even work."

So that explained the bloating. "Must be hell. Has she considered surgery?"

"Not really, unless she wants to walk around with a bag for the rest of her life. We're seeing another G.I. guy in Manhattan next Friday. I don't blame her for being in such a foul temper, but it's been tough on everyone."

I nodded. What could Jerry do about the situation when it had nothing to do with the suburbs? I thought of a cynical saying my father the banker used to quote, or maybe he made it up: "The family that stays together pays together." Or maybe I mean the other way around.

After Jerry distributed the meat evenly on the grill, I tried to change the subject. "At least the Connollys are the same as always. Now there's a united front."

"You think?" The flames shot up through the grill. "I heard that Francis is having an affair."

"Her?" I gestured with my martini glass perilously close to the fire.

"No, him."

I considered this notion for a moment. Both looked as if they didn't get out much, but somehow I'd have preferred it to be her. I brought up the one remaining couple. "Well, I know Mavis isn't doing so well, what with the kids and all."

"I don't know." He turned toward the house so that his cooking apron showed its motto: GRILL O' MY DREAMS. "You could ask Arthur."

Happy families are all alike; every unhappy family is unhappy in its own way—that damned Tolstoy line again. Who really knew what the hell was going on? Beyond the yard lay other back yards concealing equally dispiriting secrets. But I could guess at them all too easily. One point a psychiatrist learns early on is the sameness of neurotic misery from person to person. I kicked the deck in dull frustration.

"You okay, Michael?" Jerry pointed his spatula at me with concern.

"Not great, but don't grill me."

That got a grin. He performed the rest of his cooking ceremonies in silence (except for a few obscene jokes we traded to reassure ourselves that we were still all right). By the time we wended our way back to the long table in the dining area, it was almost dark. Four large sirloin steaks lay in state on a bloody platter, the product of Jerry's trial by fire. The platter was laid reverentially at the head of the table, and the guests were called in from the living room to admire the sacrifice before Jerry stabbed the meat with a carving knife big as a saber. On the table already were a spinach salad with crumbled bacon and blue cheese, as well as a zeppelin loaf of what we used to call peasant bread.

Were these really ailing people? I couldn't help but admire Mavis's wrist action as she cut into her slab of meat. She was a tall woman, even seated, able to apply plenty of leverage with her utensils. Her large, uneven white teeth bit and tore and chewed. Her strong potter's hands ripped a piece of the tough peasant bread as if it were tissue paper. When she reached for her glass of wine, she encircled the globe. Then she began to attack her salad.

There's something about a woman who really eats that I find exciting. Those who push away their food half-untasted are likely to perform that way in other activities, as well—men as well as women. Not that Jane was abstaining, having commandeered the salad bowl twice. Frances got her well-done piece, retrieved from the grill after an extra five minutes. There was a brief tussle with a piece of gristle, chewed and then quietly deposited at the edge of her plate. Does she do that when she goes down on Francis? I wondered. But she seemed not to hear my dirty thoughts.

"Daddy!" Four daddies looked up, but it was just Samantha calling for Jerry before she went to sleep. She was dressed in puma-stripe pajamas, a hint of her sleek tummy showing, and when she bent forward to whisper in his ear, it looked as if she were attacking her prey.

Jerry nodded importantly and uttered the universal parental put-off: "Tomorrow." It could have been anything from another video to a loan on her allowance. Samantha protested but was sent off to bed anyway. Soon after, Cathy excused herself to go to the bathroom and didn't come back for a while. Jerry kept on talking to Arthur about the soft bond market, which seemed somehow callous when his wife was probably in spasms on the toilet, but what was he supposed to do? Should he really feel Cathy's pain?—get sympathetic diarrhea the way some men mimicked their wives' symptoms when pregnant?

So much appears innocuous at these suburban gatherings. What were we all doing here, anyway? In the suburbs, I mean. Over dessert, a British trifle thick with ladyfingers soaked in rum, raspberry jam, and real whipped cream, Frances spoke wistfully about dreams she had of moving back to the city.

"Had it with the 'burbs, huh?" Arthur, who'd grown a spade beard that summer, probably to mask that he was a financial consultant, smiled knowingly. "Fancy a little *pied-à-terre* in Soho? Or are you more the Upper West Side type?"

"The suburbs are *boring*." Jerry placed his hands on the table as if folding in a poker game. His smile was rueful. "But that's where we live."

Mavis speared a ladyfinger. "I know. The kids."

Francis raised a sort of objection. "*I* grew up in the suburbs."

"So did I," said Cathy.

The assents were subdued but in chorus.

"It was different then," began the first nostalgic voice. Jerry looked dreamily toward the middle distance, probably sometime in the 1970's. "You could ride your bike practically anywhere." I saw Jerry on a Sting Ray, pedaling furiously to the candy store.

Jane spoke up next. "We could go to the movies alone. Kids could get in for a dollar." My mother-in-law once told me that, as a teenager growing up in Norwalk, Jane would do anything to get into an R-rated film.

"There wasn't as much money floating around." Arthur rubbed his hands together not in a bill-counting movement but more in a cash-divesting gesture. "The castles people build for themselves these days, and the real-estate prices!" Odd, coming from a man whose business was money.

"I remember the Fourth of July parade, when some boy scout always used to faint in the heat." Cathy wiped sweat from thirty years ago off her brow.

"So," said Francis, summing up for the prosecution, "was it as dull then as it is now?"

"It was different, that's all." Jane, sensing a trap, was on the defensive. "I mean, nowadays I wouldn't let Alex go to the video store alone."

Then I had to put my foot in it—or on it, depending on which metaphor you think I'm using. "Things aren't the way they used to be and probably never were," I said, quoting a source whose authorship is lost to me. "C'mon, weren't you ever told not to get into strange cars?"

Jane gestured as if swatting a gnat in midair. "Please. At least they didn't have car-jacking back then."

"You can't even let kids go trick-or-treating alone on Halloween anymore!" Jerry half-rose from the table. "Hell, I used to stay out till midnight."

"I would've spanked you," said Frances calmly, sending a slight shock through the group. Did she really believe in corporal punishment for children, did she mean something sexual, or both? Jane had told me she wielded a powerful backhand.

Francis's expression was inscrutable.

But I couldn't let go of the argument. When the time was right, I mumbled something about coat-hanger abortions back in the good old days.

"You're not a mother—you wouldn't know." Jane leaned forward, scowling at me. She always pulls the maternal role, I notice, when Alex is safely elsewhere. I wanted to hate her for this stupid rut we always got in, yet I couldn't help noticing her body as she hunched forward, her short blue skirt hiking up her muscled thighs, her calves trim. The taut spot between her legs bruised my poor eyes.

"It's the schools I worry about," declared Cathy. "I have nightmares about someone shooting Samantha."

From there, it was a short bridge to the education system around here, which Mavis seemed to have done extensive research on. Apparently, a high percentage of kids in a high percentage of suburban schools have done a high percentage of drugs by the time they've graduated or whatever it is they do. Jerry offered people Rémy Martin while gently herding us back into the living room area, but the conversation soon languished upon the shoals of repetition.

Soon afterwards, Francis motioned to Frances, they both got up to go, and the evening ended surprisingly early. Everyone had something to do on Sunday, had a sitter to get back to, or was really tired. Jerry looked a bit hurt, Cathy rather relieved.

As we were walking out to the car, I said something bantering about what different suburbs we must have grown up in, my White Plains, New York, versus her Norwalk, Connecticut, how limited what we specifically remember as opposed to what actually happened—but all Jane replied was "Do we have to continue this?"

"No," I said, starting the engine. "I guess we don't."

So we drove home in silence, as well. Damn this argument, this whole situation, this darkness between us thicker than night. As I steered along the curving suburban streets, I would cheerfully have pressed the passenger-seat eject-button if our Subaru station wagon had been properly equipped. Suddenly, about five blocks from home, I hit a black dog lying in the street. I slammed on the brakes.

"Jesus, Michael!"

"Jesus *what*? What was I supposed to do?" But when I got out, I saw that the dog was already dead. From the look of its caved-in chest and the flies buzzing around, it had been that way for a while.

I told this weird news to Jane, and that shut her up for a moment, but only a moment. I still should have been driving more safely, and didn't I know there were children around?

Here we goddamn went again. Riding in a car with another driver, as I emphasize to my clients who bring up their marital tensions *vis-à-vis* automobiles, is a matter of trust and control. Or as one of my clients put it, "You mean I shouldn't say anything when Harry goes into one of his seven-point turns?"

So I said nothing. Easier said than done. But I did it, which probably wasn't the right response because it made me seem sullen. That's the point about these arguments: they can't be won, only repeated in mind-numbing variations.

Physician, heal thyself. That was Martin again, my superego, urger of caution and scold to the king. He said this a lot.

Can it, doc. My id Snoggs, also already introduced.

Did Jane have a little girl inside her? She used to, I think. When we got home, she played Big Mommy, interrogating Mary as to how Alex had been.

"Fine," said Mary. "We played a game called Wild-Child and watched one Inspector Gadget video. He went to bed at nine."

I counted out eighteen dollars (Jane would have made it an even twenty) and told her I'd drive her home. She sat where Jane had been, the seatbelt strapping her in, cleaving across her breasts. It made me think of those stories—you know, husbands putting the moves on sitters. Tempting but idiotic, and such a cliché. To take my mind off the subject, I kept a strict watch out for dogs.

When I got back, Jane was upstairs, moving about. That's what I call it, at any rate: putting her magazine down, fiddling with something at the bathroom sink, walking out again, peering through the bedroom window, then returning to her reading. She does this when she wants to avoid something. I picked up my bedside book, a Robert Parker thriller whose ending I'd already guessed a third of the way through. Neither of us spoke. Not another night like this. So I broke in.

"Hey, what's Wild-Child?"

Jane smiled. "I don't know. I was going to ask Mary that myself."

"I think it starts at the back of the bra, like this." I reached around and tweaked the clasp, not quite undoing it. "Then it moves downward . . . ."

"Hey, stop."

"'Stop' means 'go' in Wild-Child, right?" I cupped her breasts. I nibbled her neck.

Jane rolled her head, which in this game either meant "This is silly" or "Do my shoulders, honey." I chose the second sense, pressing my thumbs into her shoulder blades, where some move she executes in tennis always makes her sore. She sighed gratefully. Maybe we wouldn't have to talk at all. When I pulled off her shirt, I could see new definition in her biceps, or was it triceps? I squeezed and stroked those arm muscles past the vulnerable crook of the elbow, across the flat expanse of forearm, all the way to her fingertips. I bent to kiss her ear lobe, collar bone, breast, belly button, and pubic patch.

When she finally turned around, she ran her fingertips down my chest. Then she cupped my face in her hands and kissed me. As I lay back, she bent down to tongue me, then clenched me hard in her fist. By the time she swung her long legs onto the bed, I was ready.

"*Aairrrt.*"

Jane sat up. "What the hell was that? It sounded like it came from downstairs."

"Probably just the house settling." It *was* like the creak of a hinge, as if someone had trod on a board. I reached out and had her half-horizontal again when suddenly—

"*Aairrrrrrt.*"

This time we both sat up. I got out of bed, put on my underwear, and cautiously headed down the stairs. Marriage has certain unwritten rules. One of them is that the man has to take out the garbage. Another is that he has to investigate any strange sounds in the house. Halfway down the stairs, the sound came again, and I froze. Now it sounded like a cross between a cat and a creak from the basement. "Who's there!" I shouted into the void.

Nothing.

I crept farther down the stairs, flicking on the lights as I reached the bottom.

No one.

I looked around, checked the doors, even tried imitating the sound once to see if that would somehow help.

"Michael, is that you?"

"No, it's the Beast of Sexual Frustration."

"Very funny. Did you check in the basement? Or maybe the garage."

By the time I came back to the bedroom, I was annoyed at the whole situation, and Jane was—with magnificent illogic—tired of waiting. She had changed into an ice-blue nightgown and was reading a magazine. We didn't talk much about it. It was all too clear.

Half an hour later, Jane was ensconced in the sheets, sleeping on her side away from me. We could have spooned, but the spooner's arm always falls asleep before the rest of the person. Besides, it's more a post-coital gesture. Instead, I watched the slow rise and fall from her breathing. It was nearing midnight, the moon peeking through the window like a voyeur.

I couldn't sleep. Eventually I got up. Almost making love had solved almost nothing, and we would bicker again tomorrow and the day after that about everything and nothing at all. What had happened to my resolve for change? I stared at the moon, which told me I had to solve my own problems. I didn't want to do this night after night, I couldn't, I wouldn't, I'd leave first, and I didn't want to do that, did I? I shook my head.

I crept back to bed, and when Jane shifted toward me in her sleep, I fitted myself against her. I cradled her back against my chest even as my arm grew numb. It was settled: I would stay but change myself, complaining less, for a start. I would be—and here I forced a smile—nice.

Chapter 4

From off Route 22, the Westfield mall beckoned like a giant ship, a three-tiered luxury liner moored in white concrete. The man in gray slacks turned off at the Court Plaza intersection and drove his Sentra at a perfectly even ten miles per hour into the largest lot, north of the main entrance. He circled for a few minutes before settling on a space halfway down the far row, in between a Ford Explorer and a Taurus minivan. Before entering the mall, he slipped on a pair of yellow sunglasses. They made him feel important, as if he were on a mission, and they also prevented anyone from getting a close look at his eyes. He had stopped his meds over a month ago and felt rather suspect.

One hundred steps to the side entrance, marked by a triptych of gray steel-and-glass doors. He chose the one on the right, which opened with a *whuff* of escaping air. The interior didn't have the stale popcorn and bubble gum odor of cheaper malls, but instead a hint of something floral and green, maybe money. On this Saturday afternoon, the upscale crowd circulated in a Brownian eddy, moving from Nordstrom's to Zany Brainy, Disc-o-Rama, the Kaffee Shoppe, Gap Kids, Godiva, Victoria's Secret, Lechter's Housewares, all along the triple-decker esplanade and back again. Among the shoppers were adults with children in strollers, kids on shoulders, toddlers in their stiff-legged walk, and older ones shrieking and running away from their parents, up the escalator, down the stairs, begging for ice cream and crunching on snacks. A lot of the men were dressed like boys in cartoon colors, the women in stretch pants. The man in gray slacks actually smiled at the boylike men, the expression an odd sight, like a lizard extending its facial muscles. And when he breathed in deeply, he was like a creature from under a rock finally re-experiencing the sun.

It was his day out.

A little shock-haired boy of five or six, in retrieving a blue rubber ball, almost ran across the man's feet. A girl who had to be his older sister followed right behind him, snatching away the ball and holding it over his head.

"Give it back!"

The girl just laughed, stretching her arm ceilingwards so that her shirt followed, revealing a belly button like a toy balloon nozzle. As he jumped for the ball, she danced away.

"Teresa, stop that!" A tall woman in a GUESS sweatshirt came bearing down on the two of them, and the girl threw the ball at her brother.

"There—he just can't catch, that's all."

"Mommy, she wouldn't let me have it!" The boy's cheeks were puffy and red with indignation. The man in the gray slacks looked on appreciatively.

"He dropped it, so I picked it up."

"I did not!"

"Did too!"

"All right, *both* of you stop it." The mother placed her hands on her hips. "Now, I have one more place to go. I need a new pair of sunglasses from Opticks. Do you think you can behave for that long?"

"Yeah, if she doesn't take my ball."

"Can't catch, can't catch!"

"Teresa, that's enough! Mark, stop whining." Taking the middle and clamping one of their hands each, she marched them away. Since Mark's stride was so short, he had to take two steps to match every one of his sister's and mother's, his little legs pumping furiously. The man watched them recede from view and suddenly disappear, like a popped soap bubble, around a bend in the hallway.

The man drew back, remembering his mission. With studied care, he reached into his jacket pocket—not the bulging lefthand one—and pulled out a crumpled shopping list. "Socks," he murmured to himself, though loud enough for others to hear. "Duct tape, underwear, batteries, rope . . . ." As he pretended to read, slowly moving along, he gazed lovingly at the crowd. Halfway down the vast hall, he dropped into a candle store and bought a beeswax cylinder so he'd be carrying a bag, like most of the other shoppers.

Coming out of F.A.O. Schwarz was a chunky boy with a heavy scowl underneath a mixing-bowl haircut. "No, no, *no* . . . " his father was lecturing him, in a speech that had something to do with choosing one, and only one, toy. Seven years old, maybe eight, thought the man, focusing on the boy's sturdy buttocks in heavy brown slacks. Just the right age. When the father stopped to examine a tie in the window of Haberdasher Heaven, the man paused as if trying to remember an item not on his list. Those little-boy legs, he thought, squirming away from him but not quite escaping. That sweaty little butt-hole. But father and son soon left the mall by one of the side exits, and the man moved on. A lot of the women clumped along in retro platforms, and a phalanx of old men strode by with that aggressive side-to-side motion peculiar to mall-walkers. But not the man in gray slacks, whose soft brown loafers almost glided across the polished floor like a hovercraft. It wasn't his ward tread but a walk learned years earlier, now second nature, so as not to wake a foul-tempered father. Seeing the mall-walking men reminded him again of the old bastard: the bloodshot eyes that pierced right through a small boy, the sour whiskey breath, the hairy arm that held him off the floor.

Old bastard, huh? He stopped in front of the plate-glass window at T. J. Maxx and saw—himself. Maybe it was just the fault of the lighting, but his features looked slightly gray and drooping. It occurred to him suddenly that he was now the same age as his father had been when . . . when he had still been his father. Whenever he thought of him, which certainly wasn't often these days, he saw an ancient green Plymouth driving away, trailing a plume of blue-white exhaust, his mother gripping him tighter, holding him back from the screen door. Twenty-five years ago?

Without really thinking where he was going, he found himself entering Nordstrom's mezzanine entrance. Racks of shirts and slacks loomed ahead like twisted, beclothed windmills, and a pile of folded sweaters rose to block his path. But he was still blinded by the pain of recall, and it wasn't until he saw a slack-jawed man headed straight for him that he stopped—right in front of a mirrored column.

"Excuse me," he muttered to his likeness and circumvented the obstacle.

Checking the floor plans by the elevator, he located the boys' department and moved in that direction. He bought nothing, just looked at the displays of socks and tyke-sized jeans. When a clerk saw him circling for the fifth time and asked if he could help, the man said he thought not. But it bothered him to be taken for a loiterer, so a few minutes later in the men's department he purchased a reversible brown-and-black leather belt with a good, strong buckle. With the sales clerk's approval, he slipped off his old braided belt and put that in the bag. The new belt felt good coiled in his hand and then cinched tightly around his waist. He grinned and pulled it in another notch.

"Teach those pants a lesson, eh?" joked the sales clerk.

"Right, right." But the man's expression tensed, and he walked stiff-legged out of the store, not in his usual glide at all.

At ChildQuest, he bought a pair of toy handcuffs while contemplating a little boy in a blue track suit that mimicked his father's. "No, I'm not going to buy you another baseball bat," said the father. "You've got two already."

"But mine doesn't hit well."

"That's not the bat, that's you." The father swung an imaginary Louisville Slugger with the practiced ease of an ex-jock. "Practice, practice, practice. Maybe we'll hit a few after supper, okay?"

"No. I want a new bat."

"No way, pal. You heard what I said?"

The little boy said nothing but looked at the floor and bit his lip. The man in slacks unconsciously bit his lip, as well.

"Look, this is stupid. What'd your mom say?"

The boy said nothing, having turned into a juvenile statue.

"I'm leaving soon," said the father after another awkward pause. "You want me to go without you?"

Yes, please, telegraphed the man in slacks.

But instead, the boy suddenly ran out of the store. The father glanced at the assembled adults with a sympathy-begging look, then tore after his son. He caught up with him by the circular fountain in the center of the mall and hoisted him high in the air as the boy struggled and kicked. The man in slacks looked away.

When he advanced in line to the register, acting on some obscure impulse, he asked to have the handcuffs wrapped. He checked his watch: three o'clock already. Why was he wasting his time here, anyway? He could be elsewhere, doing—what, exactly? Accessing boys on the Web? Fixing up the Dungeon? His future opened before him like a narrow corridor that stretched along featureless and without end. Or maybe it ended in a small black door, but no one was behind it, he knew. He had to find someone before it was too late.

From the opposite direction came a delicate-looking boy seemingly alone, and the man's pace quickened. Today might be just a dry run, but he could have brought a rag in his pocket soaked in anaesthetic and sealed in two zip-lock sandwich bags. In the left side pocket, maybe two Hershey bars with Darvon injected through a pinhole. In fact, he'd once tried making chloroform from a recipe on the Web and some mail-order chemicals. But the result had stunk so badly, even double-wrapped in plastic baggies, that he'd had to throw it out. He did have a whippet of nitrous oxide, but that was in the sock drawer of his bedroom dresser. He lifted his head as if to get a breath of fresh air from some higher-altitude zone in the mall, but really to keep track of the new boy.

The boy weaved his head back and forth as if it were too heavy to hold upright. His eyes were half-closed, his hands fluttered like fledglings, and he was humming to himself. His lips described a perfect cupid's bow—the man imagined the little jaw prised open and sucking hard. Like a kite let off the string, the boy wandered on with no connection to anyone else. He was headed across three lanes of human traffic, straight for the man in gray slacks.

The man stuck his hands in his pockets, pretending to be interested in a bosomy Victoria's Secret mannequin.

The boy kept walking in a slanted line, as if in a trance, and finally bumped gently into the man. The man reached out to steady the boy. And waited.

"Alex?" A slightly rumpled man in black jeans and a plaid shirt made his way through the crowd, looking for his errant son. "Alex! There you are." He reached out to grab the boy's shirt.

"I'm blind, Daddy." Alex turned his face upwards like a sunflower. "I can't see where you are."

"All right, but you can hear me, right?" The father made sonar sounds from his cupped mouth. "Now come this way." He led his son toward Nordstrom's, stopping every ten paces or so to check the progress of his submarine boy.

The man in gray slacks tightened his fists in his pockets, biting his lip. Everyone was attached, the parents so damned worried these days that a casual pickup seemed impossible. But it could happen, he knew that. He'd heard stories over the Web, like CRater's story about a fat boy at a local Dairy Queen. He'd come close himself once or twice. It might be just a matter of biding his time.

He walked around each level of the mall a few more times, seeming to window-shop but really using the storefronts to glimpse reflections of any youngster who tickled his fancy, as his mother used to put it. "There," she'd say, trying to cheer him up, "maybe this'll tickle your fancy"—and she'd really tickle him, reaching for his armpits and belly with her long, manicured nails. He'd struggle helplessly, lovingly, under her strong hands.

"Stop that right now!" A heavy woman in a blue parka grabbed her son's hand just as the boy was about to thump the side of the escalator again. The woman reminded him of a systems analyst at work, mostly in her moon face and powerful heft. The boy squirmed and pouted adorably. The man pouted back just to see what would happen, but the two had already moved on.

The idea that this outing could turn into a mission still excited him. He imagined himself talking loudly with a boy whose hand he was holding, saying, "Now, Johnny, if I've told you once, I've told you a million times . . . ." And even if the boy struggled in his grasp, everyone would think he was the father. He held hands with himself and twisted his own wrist experimentally. Come along. He began pulling himself toward the side entrance.

Suddenly, a stocky boy in brown corduroys cantered by him. The father, a short man wearing a heavy scowl, called out to him. "Jerry!"

The boy turned impatiently. "I hafta *go*."

"Jesus, why didn't you say that before we left?"

The boy sighed as if being asked to defend gravity. Eight or nine years old, the man in the gray slacks guessed. "Because I didn't hafta go then."

"All right, all right." The father frowned. "Short or long?"

"*Long.*"

"Okay. I'll wait for you in the car." He gestured toward the main entrance, beyond which lay the parking lot, and began moving in that direction. As he walked, he unfolded a newspaper from under his arm and began to read.

The man in gray slacks pursed his lips. His eyes widened. Here was a chance out of the blue, an opportunity falling into his lap. All the ambient noise in the mall, the random motion of other bodies, faded away. With only a dim idea of what was next, he followed the boy about twenty feet behind.

The public restrooms at the mall were situated at the center of the main floor along the end of a corridor. This late in the afternoon, more and more people were leaving, and the area was nearly deserted. As he neared the corridor, the boy started jogging again, so the man in the gray slacks picked up his pace, too, trying to look as if he weren't hurrying. At the end of the hall, the boy entered through the wide, white entrance marked by a stick-figure man. The door thumped back in place. The man in gray slacks arrived a moment later. He took a deep breath, made a wish, and walked in.

The bathroom area was empty. The row of urinals stood by the far wall like porcelain sentries, giving off a reek of disinfectant over stale piss. The mirrors by the sinks, having nobody to reflect, looked blank. Three toilet stalls jutted from the corner, and a boy's sneakers were barely touching the floor of the one nearest the wall. The man sighed: his wish had been granted. The question was what to do now. In his job, in his everyday existence, he was such a careful planner, always adhering to design, but fantasies were his release from the pattern. Now here was a fantasy come true. He cracked a few knuckles, then realized how loud the sound was in the tiled room, and stopped abruptly.

Okay. He entered the adjoining cubicle, which featured a crude pen drawing of a penis between a pair of tits. Now what? The boy next door grunted a bit. Do something, damn it. But improvisation wasn't one of his strengths. Luckily, the stall divider had over a foot of clearance between its bottom edge and the tile floor. He pulled down his slacks noisily, trying to make his wallet fall out and slide underneath the divider. When it stuck halfway out of its pocket, he grabbed it and skidded it along the dirty tile floor.

"Oops!" he announced brightly. When no response came from the other stall, he decided to take matters further. "Ah, hell!" He put his hand under the divider, extending his reach in order to grope. But the toilets were spaced wider apart than he'd calculated, and he found himself up to his shoulder before he touched something. The boy had said nothing so far, and yet here was the cold porcelain surface of the toilet, and there was a smooth thigh—

"Hey!" The thigh shifted abruptly out of range, pulling the man's hand with it through sympathetic attraction. All at once, he was halfway under the divider. Now he could see into the other stall: a frightened boy cringing, half off the toilet seat. "What—what are you doing?"

"Me?" The man tried to sound authoritative, despite his absurd position. "Whaddya mean? You've got my wallet!"

"No, I don't!" The boy leaned to kick it forward, exposing his hairless scrotum. "There!"

"Now you've done it." The man slid the rest of his body under the divider and stood up crookedly in the boy's stall. "You shouldn't, you can't just kick other—other people's property." He bent to pick up his wallet, his hair practically brushing the poor boy's knees. The corduroy pants around the boy's ankles acted like an imprisoning band.

"I'm—I'm sorry." The boy was confused to be in the wrong so quickly. His eyes beseeched the man half out of his gray slacks to just disappear. But the man advanced.

"You didn't take anything, did you?"

"N-no."

"Because you know—you know what happens to little boys who take what's not theirs?" Now he was almost on top of the boy, ready to claim a forfeit. The boy was practically against the wall, his shirt riding up to expose his little belly, just as in the man's dreams. He was deciding on his next move when the outer door thumped open with the sound of two adult male voices.

"Christ, I gotta take a leak. Three hours at the register'll do that to you."

"Yeah, try waiting on fifty customers who all want the sale price from last week."

The man froze. The little boy did, too, but he was clearly about to open his mouth.

So the man beat him to it. "Listen, Jerry, next time, wipe yourself, huh?" He pulled up his slacks. The kid simply stared at him. The man was half out the cubicle door when he remembered that his wallet was lying on the floor. He reached back to scoop it up, and as he did, he couldn't resist: he rested one hand on the boy's thigh, which felt like upholstered ivory. "C'mon," he breathed, "your father's waiting for you." And he exited the stall, letting the door bang after him. He rolled his eyes for the benefit of the two guys and trotted outside. In the corridor, the trot turned into a controlled run, but no one stopped him, and nobody even yelled from behind. People and shop signs passed in a blur. Then he was out the door and halfway free. Only after he got to his car and belted himself in was he hit by the full import of what he'd done.

He felt exhilarated and horrified, amazed at himself and terribly upset. On the way back, he saw the evil black dog by the side of the road and rode over it again. When he finally reached home, he stayed in the car for a while. Finally, he reached a hand into his front pocket and took out not a chloroform gag or a stun gun but a toy top and two red Matchbox cars.

Chapter 5

On my third day of being nice, the Metro section of the *Times* was nastier than I could bear. It's as if they piled all the arson, rape, and shootings into a few pages for maximum effect. Mother of three shot by boyfriend in Bronx. Arson suspected in storefront blaze. *Look,* the section blares, *this is what goes on in New York. You don't like it? Get lost, buddy.* I've even caught them smuggling violent stories from other regions into that section, like cyclones from Kansas, to achieve some critical mass of disaster. Even Jane, usually a systematic reader, sometimes skips those pages, especially if small children happen to be involved. "Now that I'm a mother," she's told me, "I take these things personally."

Contrast this reportage with the town section of the local paper, the *Fairchester Guardian*, in which nothing ever happens but real-estate developments and zoning disputes. Aldermen approve bond issue for park expansion. 24-hour leash law to be enforced, says police chief. This week, since school had recently started up, page five featured a squib about child abuse and other threats. "We recognize that our students are at a vulnerable age," proclaimed the superintendent of schools, Sid Weinstein, in a speech that started on page 1 and continued below the weekly school lunch menu on page 7. The photo showed a short, sharp-beaked man with a pair of no-nonsense horn-rims. Jane and I had once met him at a party and found him polished but metallic, as if his sense of humor had been surgically removed and replaced by a chrome plate. "In an era of drive-by shootings, Fairchester is particularly fortunate to have less crime than most other communities. But we must still be vigilant." In a related move, he set up a committee dealing with student locker inspection.

But I couldn't get anxious about that with so many other problems to fret over. I took a sip of my overbrewed tea and let the tannin stiffen my tongue. Tuesday mid-morning, and Jane had yet to pick up on my grand plan for marital revision. She had already left for the office, fuming about something I'd said, a response to a crack she'd made—starting from my innocent comment about Alex's breakfast and quickly getting out of hand:

"Not those deep-fried French toast sticks again."

Jane shrugged. "He likes them."

"I want him to eat better, that's all." My mistake: escalation.

Jane placed her hands on her hips. "What about the garbage he eats when he's at the mall with you?" Contrapuntal counterattack.

"It's only on Saturdays, and it's just fruit-wrap. It's still better for him than Tost Stix."

"You mean Too Stickies!" the old Alex would have piped up, but this Alex just pushed away his breakfast. "I'm not hungry anymore," he said, and left the table.

A small dagger wiggled its way into my chest. "We really shouldn't bring this up in front of him, you know."

"We? You're the one who dragged it out!"

Ad hominem (or feminam), ad infinitum, ad nauseam. And here I was practicing to be kind. What Jane practiced was aggression. She picked up her briefcase, slammed out the door, and backed out the driveway with gravel-pitching speed. I still loved her determination and verve—if only I were her job.

"Daddy?" Alex had asked last night. "Why do you and Mommy fight so much?"

"Hmm." I pretended to ponder the question. "What do you mean by fight?"

"I don't know . . . arguing, shouting."

"It's not always arguing. Sometimes we just disagree, that's all."

"Oh." But he didn't seem convinced, and later I heard him asking Jane the same question. She hesitated, then tried a statistical approach: the number of arguments wasn't really that high; it just seemed that way because no one counted all the times we agreed on things.

"Like what?" asked Alex.

"Well . . . like . . . " and here she floundered. "Daddy and I agreed on what to have for dinner last weekend. We ordered pizza, remember?"

"Yeah, but Daddy wanted pepperoni and you didn't."

"Okay, so we compromised, half and half." Jane settled into her maternal mode, stroking Alex's hair to make him accept the sweet logic of the situation. "Compromise is what life's all about."

Alex looked up so quickly that Jane's well-manicured fingers almost skewered his eyes. "I thought you said love is what life's all about." He looked betrayed.

"It is, sweetie—before marriage."

Con or not, there are times when I wish my head were in her lap, her long fingers smoothing away all distress. She used to do it sometimes, too, back when I was her boy. But there's no getting around the Oedipal stuff. Love isn't so divisible, and Alex stole her heart.

Not that he was satisfied, either. Alex's growing depression showed first as withdrawal: not sitting at the table for meals, probably figuring that Jane and I would argue about which end of the hot dog he should bite, or something. "Can I eat alone?" he'd ask hopefully.

"*No,*" Jane and I pronounced in unison. We'd both read the children's manuals that talk about the importance of the family meal.

"Please . . . ."

"Listen to your father," said Jane.

"Listen to your mother," I said.

Then came the little hindrances, like hiding Jane's tennis racket during a pre-game quarrel. That actually had the desired effect: Jane stopped lynching into me for messing up her schedule and transferred her annoyance to the missing object. The racket magically reappeared when she stopped arguing with me. Alex found it right under our bed, where it must have crawled.

As for his parents' behavior, which at times would disgrace a seven-year-old, what was there to say—or do? Should we establish time-outs for parents? Or blame Alex as a flash point? The truth was that our bickering predated Alex altogether. Unfortunately, it had grown from an annoyance to a behavior pattern. Hence my twelve-step program, or whatever it was, to lead this marriage back to happiness. I looked outside the kitchen window: a squirrel was running down a tree, looking nervously over his shoulder. He was followed a few seconds later by what might have been the squirrel-mate, chittering angrily. It's a romantic mistake to read your backyard wild-life as a pattern of your existence, I know, but they looked so much like a married couple that I flinched.

Maybe it shouldn't be happiness we strive after. After all, Freud claimed that therapy simply replaced neurotic misery with everyday suffering. Maybe we should just try for contentment or peace and not risk disappointment. People nowadays think that happiness is guaranteed in the Constitution, but it's not. Only the pursuit of it is. It had now been confirmed that the oldest Talent-Schramm kid, Dalton, a sixteen-year-old with a scowl tattooed on his lips, had recently taken this precept to heart by running away to Canada—or at least Buffalo, where they turned him back at the border. "He doesn't know his own mind," Mavis interpreted for us, and Arthur tried to ground him by taking away all car privileges for a month. But how do you rein in a kid who's convinced that happiness lies elsewhere? I retained an image of Dalton standing hopefully on the side of Route 95 North, thumb outstretched. The other two Talent-Schramms were a twelve-year-old boy named Andover, unsure of whether to ape Dalton or run from him, and a bright ten-year-old girl called Brearley, who wisely kept her distance from her two brothers.

On the other hand, Alex's best friend, a sickly but sweet little boy named James, never went anywhere, yet seemed reasonably happy, especially with his head in a book. He was this shrunken seven-year-old with a wisp of a nose almost too frail to support his glasses, which protected his weak, watery eyes. His body always seemed to shift an awkward second after he decided how he wanted it to move, and as a result he was always picked last for any games, or left out entirely. As a psychiatrist, I don't believe that suffering purifies the soul, but James was at times beatific. "Do you ever pray, Dr. Eisler?" he once asked me.

"No," I told him bluntly.

"Neither do I," he told me solemnly. "And I think an awful lot of people are going to be disappointed."

I thought of him as a positive influence on Alex. Lately, he'd been out of school—sick with something lingering.

My tea had gone stone cold. I checked my watch. As Alex would have said a few years ago, the little hand was on the ten and the big hand was almost at the twelve. Right now he was in school, probably bored with arithmetic. I was in between clients, during a half-hour I'd been unable to fill. But now it was time to return to the office.

I cut through the garage, as usual. My clients proceed by a flagstone path around the side of the house, camouflaged by shrubbery. That way, we don't meet outside the context of the therapy, which is more important than you might realize. Imagine how taken aback Freud's Dora would have been to see the good doctor with his jacket off, chowing down on cold *Rindfleisch*. The traditional double door to the office also ensures privacy, though at certain times I can hear Alex playing with his electric train set in the basement.

My 10:00 patient was—well, let's call her R. Mid-thirties, well-spoken but with a rueful air, as if she regretted even words like "hello" and "yes." At precisely on the hour, I emerged from my *sanctum sanctorum* and beckoned her inside. Adjoining my office is a bathroom-sized waiting area furnished with two wicker chairs and a low table displaying copies of *The New Yorker*, *Harper's*, and *Time*.

"Good morning." I gave her my therapist's smile, reassuring yet noncommittal.

"I suppose," she ventured. R was not unattractive, though depression makes most people mousy. She may once have had a sense of humor, but if so, it had long been buried underneath layers of gloom. Her best feature, depending on what kind of person you were, was either her analytical mind or else her shoulder-length red hair, worn loose when she felt unencumbered and coiled in a librarian's bun when she was tense, which was most of the time.

She worked as a corporate librarian and had been married for three years to a man who sold bonds for a living. They had no children and not much else between them. The silence at home had gradually thickened and twisted. A list of his faults included the usual series of male impedimenta, from inattention to a few gross habits, including belching out of context.

She was wearing an embroidered white blouse and sweeping skirt today, looking ready to be persuaded that she was in a good mood. But sartorial cues can be confusing (do you wear bright clothes when you're happy or to cheer yourself up?), and no sooner had she sat down in the armchair aslant to mine than she started complaining about her husband. "I know I should let the small things ride, but Dwight left the toilet seat up again. I nearly fell in when I got up in the middle of the night."

I permitted myself a real smile. "You think he was being hostile?"

"I don't know—sure—maybe." She hunched forward, her hands grasping at nothing. "But we've been over this so many times."

"What did he say?"

"He told me to dry up."

"And?"

"I told him to go to hell." She pressed her lips into a line. "That pretty much did it."

"Hmm." I leaned back as if to reach for an interpretation. "What happens if you make light of it?"

"Like what?"

"Oh, I don't know. Posting a funny sign or shaking yourself off."

"Are you saying I'm the one who should bend?"

"No, you're in the right . . . but what good does that do? Maybe you can make him change and maybe you can't. You've got to work on strategies for coping with the person you love." I looked at her closely. "If you still love him."

She fell silent for a moment. In truth, the list of her faults neatly complemented his: unresponsiveness to his needs, over-sensitivity to her own—the typical narcissism of our age that adds up to a feeling of entitlement. Love me not in spite of my flaws but because of them. Which is okay with one narcissistic person in the relationship, but not with two.

Finally R, looking toward the window at Jane's rhododendrons, said "I do" with true wedding conviction. So we worked on ways of reforming her husband without threatening him and maybe, just maybe, taking his thoughtless acts a little less personally. Should she leave? No, not at this stage. We talked till 10:50, and then it was time for her to resume on Thursday. I watched her drive away in her sensible Saturn.

There was no time to do anything much in the ten minutes between R's departure and my next client at 11:00. I once compiled a list of ten-minute activities I could fit in between clients, including reading a short-short story, making a phone call, and writing lists. But my "Should You Leave?" list stayed in the flat middle drawer of my desk, as untouched as a will. Adding to it right now would only depress me. I could have started a Web session, but was still wary from my recent experience with the pederast site. So I spent the time staring out the window at the Steinbaums' home, which looked somehow aslant, or maybe I was on the bias. It was a unicorn of a house, with one turret and windows like glazed-over eyes. The inhabitants, whose children were grown and departed, kept pretty much to themselves. The cocktail party we'd attended lo these many months ago had been semi-pro: the husband was in sales for Nabisco, and the wife did some sort of philanthropic work, so a bunch of business types flanked by trophy wives talked about stocks and gardening. We were probably their charity case that afternoon. But that was it for us, or them—we never got around to reciprocating. Now we were barely on nodding acquaintance. That perfectly manicured lawn . . . I noticed with satisfaction that their mailbox, like ours, had been whacked askew, no doubt by some teenage marauder in the night.

Then the ten minutes were up, and I got up from my chair with a creak. Promptly on time, I let in S, a big-shouldered guy who scowled a lot and at times seemed like R's crumbo husband.

"Hey." This was his standard greeting as he slouched into the chair recently vacated by R. Like most other therapists, I do have a couch, but that's for psychiatric surgery, the deep stuff.

"Hey. How's it going?" It relieves some clients if you lead off with their speech patterns.

"Christ. More trouble with Sheryl—it's always something, it's endless."

"Hmm." One day my pursed lips will turn into a snap-clasp Kelly bag. "How did it start?"

"Oh, I left the damned toilet seat up, and she got on my case about it."

"Huh." *Déjà vu* is the bedrock of marriage—or neurosis. I laced my fingers behind my neck. "You think it was a hostile act?"

"Hell, no!" S ground his dirty clodhoppers into my clean carpet. "It's just not something I think about, you know?"

"Maybe if you—"

"But I *have* been thinking about it since then, and you know what I think?"

"What?" Just call me Mike the straight man.

"I figure it's a question of effort." S squinted meanly at the rhododendron bushes. He did analyze things, though often with nasty results. "If I gotta take a leak, I have to raise the seat. So why shouldn't she have to lower it?"

"Hmm, I see your point"—a point that Jane and I had settled years ago by my giving in. And Alex had been taught the same etiquette. "Did you tell her this?"

"No, but I think I'm gonna." S raised his hands, which clenched midair into fists. "Why the hell do we spend so much time on this crap?"

So we spent forty more minutes on this excremental subject, finally deciding it had something to do with control. And if he would cede on this one matter, she might give in on others. Should he leave? Maybe. He was the type who liked a good lay but didn't want to pay for it with compromise. As for love, he rarely mentioned the word. "Care for" was as close as he got.

Was the world made up of R's and S's, and me trying to be supportive to both? Some days I feel that all I am is a glorified marriage counselor. In classical psychoanalysis, the old therapists with thick Viennese accents tore down their patients to rebuild them later, but everyone these days wants quickie feel-good results. Pursuit of happiness again. Maybe I should keep a supply of lollipops in my desk drawer.

Time for lunch. Back in the kitchen, I found some old rye bread losing its seeds and slapped two pieces onto a plate. Then I rummaged around the fridge for a package of smoked turkey, which is as close to lunch meat as either Jane or Alex will eat (I remember when you could get tongue at the deli, and it was all called "cold cuts"). I sliced some Jarlsberg cheese, which is just designer-Swiss.

While putting together a sloppy sandwich, the only kind I like, I got a call from Jerry Mirnoff. "Hi. Patient referral. You interested?"

"Um, yeah." I slathered mustard on one slice of rye and clapped it onto its mate. Beneath a cardboard art project that Alex had abandoned in the kitchen, I found a leaky green pen. "I guess."

After his first magazine article appeared, Jerry had become identified as the man to consult on suburban stress (his coinage), and his projected book on the subject was only part of the aftermath. (One recent chapter he'd shown me, "Leaving in the Morning," had to do with commuting and marital fidelity.) The other part of the effect was a practice burgeoning so quickly, he had to turn people away. Hence the referrals. I had a few slots to fill on Monday and Wednesday afternoons.

"Okay. This is an interesting case, in fact . . . ."

They're all interesting, intelligent individuals. The referring physician always makes a pitch like that.

"She's actually quite intelligent."

So why didn't you make room for her yourself? sniffed superego Martin.

". . . depressed a lot lately, thinking about divorce . . . ."

Should be happier about that . . . growled Snoggs.

"I'm not sure what her schedule is, but I think she's free Monday afternoons."

Bingo! Worth a consultation, anyway. "Sure," I told Jerry, "sounds like it might work." My sandwich was beginning to stare accusingly at me, but after I'd jotted down the particulars, I couldn't just hang up. And Jerry clearly wanted to talk further. His sentences, usually clipped, just trailed off instead.

"So how's Cathy doing?" I prompted. "Bowel-wise, I mean."

"A mess. She's thinking of walking around with a cork up her ass. The doctor at Sinai couldn't recommend a thing."

I clenched my rectum reflexively. The last time I had the trots on a large scale was in Mexico, on a family vacation in Acapulco. Jane had escaped unscathed, and so had Alex, who thought it particularly funny that Daddy was racing to the toilet every ten minutes. Little brat. But when I thought of Cathy squeezing her broad buttocks together, I saw his point of view and allowed myself an inward leer. "You know how conservative some of these G.I. specialists are. Might be for the best," I platituded along. "You don't want to take chances with this kind of condition." I paused a beat, and I could sense that I hadn't quite finished with this transaction, as my former supervisor Briggs used to put it. Jerry was always so frank about everything. Try a touch of humor. "I take it Samantha hasn't caught it."

I could hear Jerry *hmm*-ing. "No, but these things can be hereditary. Actually, I worry that she's acting out in response."

"How?"

"Well, with Cathy trying so hard to be anal-retentive, Samantha's turned anal-expulsive. She's running with a gang, I think."

"Samantha? Hell, she's only—what, ten?"

"And a half. But she's precocious. Anyway, they start early these days."

"How can you tell?"

"Oh, she came home with some ghoulish fake-tattoo on her arm, and her friend Marcy said something about initiation rites."

"You sure it's not just Girl Scouts?"

"One of the things she mentioned was ransoming a kid's knapsack."

"Huh." I stole a glance at the frost-white clock over the refrigerator. 12:50. Ten more minutes till I had to be back at the office. "So, um, what are you doing about it?"

Jerry was vehement. "Make it seem uncool. Confront her if I have to. It's all in my book: a chapter called 'The Suburban Delinquent.'" He gave me a brief outline. It sounded like common sense repackaged with New Age therapy-speak.

I don't buy guidelines to life, but plenty of people do. If Jerry ever completed his book, he'd have a bestseller—at least at the suburban malls. I finally hung up five minutes later, inhaled my sandwich—getting mustard up my nose—and ran back to my office. But my desk-clock read 12:50. Then I recalled that the clock in the kitchen is in a different time zone: it's set five minutes fast so Jane won't be late walking out the door. Now I had time on my hands, as well as a little mustard.

This time, what the hell, I decided to do a little Web-surfing. I booted up my faithful Gateway Solo laptop, clicked on Internet Explorer, waited for the homepage to appear—and instead saw a wide-angle picture of a little boy mooning me. It wasn't just a cute Coppertone shot, either. In fact, it looked like an outtake from that boy-toys Web site I'd accidentally accessed a while ago, come back to haunt me. I tried to click on the Close key, but it had receded into the background. In fact, the picture seemed to block out all the usual controls. I tried Ctrl + Alt + Del, which usually shuts everything down, but I was still being mooned. Finally, I reached down to turn off the machine, which you're not supposed to do, then turned it on to see what damage I'd done. As the messages onscreen scolded me for improperly turning off the computer, I waited for it to check its drives and perform general housekeeping tasks, or whatever the hell it does. Then I tried Internet Explorer again.

Same picture. This time, I clicked everywhere, even between the little boy's spread cheeks, where a reddened area looked a bit like a Windows STOP button. No go. Shit. Was this some kind of virus? My punishment for accessing that site? And if I called Norton Anti-Virus, how would I explain the situation? "Someone made me the butt of a joke . . . ." As I stared at the screen, I could swear the little boy did a slight wiggle. Great—an X-rated screensaver.

I heard the door of the waiting room open and shut, and I realized it was one o'clock. I turned off the computer, collected myself as best as I could, and strode to meet my responsibility. The first after-lunch patient was relatively new, a middle-aged woman I'll call T who ran her own graphics design shop on the Web. Lately she'd soured on the business (I gathered it was mutual), and she'd also had an extramarital affair, which her teen-aged daughter but not her husband knew about. We were working on what social workers call "sorting out your priorities," but it was more compli-cated than that. For one thing, I'd recently discovered that her mother had also embarked on a fling or two. The disconcerting aspect of T, who origi-nated as a referral, was her way of starting and ending *in medias res*. "I just didn't know what he meant," she began when she'd settled down in the chair opposite mine.

I smiled helpfully. "What who meant?"

"Harry, after that last incident."

"Ah." Did I mention her vagueness? And non sequiturs? Half the ses-sions were taken up with requests for clarification. But we kept gamely at it, like two Scrabble players with different sets of tiles, trying to piece out an interlocking vocabulary. When her fifty minutes were up, and we'd established that her husband Harry may have misunderstood her, she left with a cryptic "So maybe Cindy will come back tomorrow." Cindy was her daughter; that much I knew.

In the ten-minute interval between 1:50 and 2:00, I didn't go near the computer. That I'd deal with later, somehow. Instead, I stared at the Steinbaums' house again, speculating on the evergreen topiary by the side of the house. From front on, it resembled a hedge of five-foot bowling balls, but from my side-view, it looked more like giant artillery ammunition. I'd seen a gardener clip the row last June and July and then periodically prune it as it grew into a blockade. All it lacked was a large hanging placard reading, "KEEP OUT."

Precisely at three minutes to two, my second patient of the afternoon let himself in. He was late middle-aged when I first started seeing him and had been worrying about his relationship with his wife. He was slow and deliberate and probably that way even in his youth. I'll call him Z—no other letter more appropriate. We'd originally been working on his fears of intimacy. That was seven years ago. Now he was retired from his importing business, his long-suffering wife had suffered a fatal stroke two years ago, and we were dealing with his fears of loneliness and death. Near the end of his life, Freud wrote an essay called "Analysis: Terminable and Interminable." Unfortunately, Z's treatment was turning into the second kind. We usually picked up right where we'd left off, going over the same dull ground of avoidance and worry. But something new had entered the equation since last week.

"So how did your date go?" At my urging, he'd gone out with a widow whom he'd met at the supermarket.

He raised his hand as if testing the breeze. "Okay, okay. She seems like a nice lady."

"What do you like about her?"

"Well, she doesn't nudge like Marilyn." He sighed, recalling his partner in sickness and in health. "But this one wants me to come over for tea on Saturday."

We were back to fear of commitment. But he generally avoided talking about avoidance.

At 2:50, I ushered out Z and turned from Dr. Eisler into Daddy. Some therapists remain Daddy in their practice, as well, but I don't think that's advisable. Anyway, I had to be home when Alex got off the school bus, which let him off at the corner of Garner and Somers a little after three. Then he straggled the two blocks home, his knapsack listing at an angle of 45°. The whole bus routine was silly, really. It was all of seven blocks from our doorstep to Ridgefield, yet some bizarre zoning regulation put us on the school bus route. A parents' group from our neighborhood walked a bunch of kids to Ridgefield in the mornings, but Alex preferred the bus. "I like to look out the window," he said when I asked why.

"But isn't it better to be outside with no window at all?"

He shook his head. "It's different."

I didn't pursue the matter. Alex was bookish, as I'd been at that age, which meant that he liked stories better than real life, and indoors more than outdoors. I still had to fight against that tendency myself. Jane got impatient sometimes—she wanted to take on the whole world.

Alex also liked routine. I placed a small plate on the kitchen table and arranged seven, count 'em, 7, pretzel sticks on it. On bad days, he got upset if there were eight or six or even if one of the sticks was slightly deformed. Did I mention that the positioning was significant? One triangle and one square.

Anyway, here came Alex, progressing steadily down the sidewalk until a candy wrapper snagged on a bush made him look up. It was a sunny

November afternoon, and the way the slanted light caught his upturned face, that promising blossom connected to a sturdy little stem of a body, *my* boy, spurred a rush of love for him that caught me right in the chest. It melted away anxiety, making me feel that everything would be all right as long as sons and fathers lived on this earth.

But Alex didn't stop at 117 Garner Road, which happens to be our address. He walked right by the flagstone path that meanders up to our doorstep. I couldn't tell whether his behavior was purposeful or just oblivious. His expression was unreadable.

"Alex!"

He kept walking.

"Alex, where are you going?"

He glanced back at the shouting father. He looked at the sidewalk stretching in front of him. "Oh."

I smiled. "Forgot your way back home?"

"No. I was just . . . thinking about things."

"Like what?"

"Never mind."

Since pursuing this line leads nowhere, I said nothing. I just held open the door and waited for Alex to tromp-scuffle in. Inside the entryway, he dropped his coat and knapsack on the floor, though I'd told him a hundred times not to. I wearily picked them up as he made his way into the kitchen. When I got there, I found him staring at the pretzel sticks as if they were something poisonous, like carrots.

I paused a beat. "What's the matter?"

"I'm tired of pretzels."

"Great! What would you like instead?"

"Well . . . ." He bit his lip. "Something else."

We went through crackers, corn chips, Melba toast, and popcorn before I lost my temper. "But I don't know what I want!" he cried as I sent him to his room for a time-out.

During my son's incarceration, I nibbled at his pretzel sticks. There were five left.

Since we never laid a hand on Alex, we had to deal with his bad behavior somehow. I'm not crazy about the phrase "time-out," which conjures up the image of some hockey player in the penalty box, but that's what you're supposed to call it. Actually, the whole point is that you're not punishing the child (God forbid), just giving the kid a breather so he can pick up where he left off.

Three pretzel sticks left.

Some psychologists even suggest that you shouldn't hold time-outs in the child's bedroom because of negative associations that might build up. I thought of my mother, who relied on the stock phrase "Go to your room, young man!" And it worked, sort of, though eventually I *liked* going to my room, which had all my books and toys, and when my mother found that out, she started sending me to the basement.

No pretzels left anymore.

Was Alex starting to like his room too much? Awfully quiet up there. Ten minutes later, I called out, "Alex, you can come out now!"

No response.

I called him again. When I still heard nothing, I began to worry. What if he'd accidentally plugged his finger into a socket or something? Had he climbed out the window? I ran up the stairs two at a time and burst into Alex's room.

He wasn't there.

I looked under his bed and in the closet. I checked the bolt on the window and was just about to shift into high-gear panic when I heard "Surprise!"

Behind the door, the oldest trick in the book. I should have been furious, but he was giggling, and Alex's laugh is extremely infectious. Pretty soon I was hauling him down the stairs, and we ended up in the kitchen again. "Are you ready to behave?" I asked him.

"I'm ready to eat my pretzels." He looked at the empty plate. "What happened to them? They're gone!"

"I'll get you some more."

"No, I wanted *those*!"

"Alex, I—"

"*Where are my pretzels?*"

The second time-out lasted fifteen minutes while I finished the newspaper, and there was no hiding when I entered his room. He was kneeling in front of his bed, putting together a brain-teaser puzzle on the Amish quilt Jane had bought for him. He didn't look up.

"Okay." I tapped him on the shoulder. "Time's up. You can come downstairs now."

He turned his head minimally. "Daddy, I'm *busy*."

So I left him there. What would have been the point in making him move out of his cell now that he had done his time? But it bothered me that he wasn't more apologetic. Absorbed isn't the same as penitent.

Of course, the afternoon wasn't over yet. I knew I wouldn't get much work done between now and dinner. I was supposed to make a few calls: get back to a patient about rescheduling a session, confirm some information about Jerry's referral, that sort of thing. I'd just gotten downstairs when I heard a plaintive "Daddy!"

"What?"

"Will you play Monopoly with me?"

This had been one of my arguments for having another child: a playmate. Someone for whom passing Go and collecting $200 was a fresh experience. But Jane, who like me was an only child, said she didn't want double the responsibility. I thought of one possible escape: "Why don't you call James to play with you?"

"He's sick."

So that's how I ended up buying Park Place at 4:30 in the afternoon. I was feeling put upon, so I didn't go easy. By 5:00, I owned half the board and was cleaning him out. After forcing him into bankruptcy, I let him watch the Cartoon Network channel as I went to prepare dinner. I'm the one who cooks in the family—Jane merely follows recipes occasionally—and I thought tonight I'd do something with chicken breasts, onions, and green peppers. Maybe add a little lemon and curry and serve it over rice. I'd never be a house husband, but I could be domestic. When Jane started working longer hours at Haldome, we set up Alex with an after-school program at the local Y that took him right through 5:30 on Mondays, Wednesdays, and Thursdays, but that still left two weekdays of father-son bonding. Or whatever this was.

"Daddy, can I have my pretzels now?"

"No."

"Why *not*?"

"Too close to dinner." I hate the clichés of parenthood but find myself repeating them anyway.

Jane called just as I was chopping onions to tell me she'd be running a little late that evening.

"How late?"

"Oh . . . I'll be home by seven, I hope."

Which meant seven-thirty or later, but I just said okay and hung up. At six, I gave Alex his separate dinner of fish sticks, rice, and corn. Afterwards, I helped him with his homework, which involved locating the country of Andorra on an orange-peel map of the world. Then he read an assigned book to me, *I'll Have Spaghetti, Freddie*, looking up from time to time to see whether I was paying attention.

"Did you like the book, Daddy?" he asked after reading "The End" with great finality.

"I liked the way you read it." It was too easy for him. He was already reading on a seventh-grade level, but his teacher, Ms. Hardin, kept feeding him spaghetti. So we supplemented where we could. I left him on the couch, reaching for a library book called *The Secret of Treasure Cove*.

At seven-fifteen, I ate some of the dinner I'd prepared and left the rest in a covered pot. At eight, just as I was putting Alex to bed, Jane breezed in, smelling from the scent I term Attar of Executive, which combines a faint floral smell with a whiff of power. Alex was already in his pajamas, but he flew downstairs, crying, "Mommy! Mommy!"

Parental cliché #5: That's the thanks I get.

Jane kissed and hugged him while taking care not to muss her Armani suit. After Alex went to sleep, she changed into slacks and came back into the kitchen. "God, the office was jumping today. Max said all the paperwork for the Singapore branch had to be in by December 1st." She removed the pot lid from what I'd left on the stove, releasing a fragrant cloud of steam. "Hmm, smells good. Curry?" She didn't wait for an answer but instead rattled on as she went to get a plate. Max Liederman was her boss, if that isn't too antiquated a term for a horizontal hierarchy like Haldome. He was tall and broad, and his tailored suits made him look like a well-dressed wall. But he was always in motion, which had made Jane more kinetic, as well. Even her vocabulary had shifted: the office was always *jumping*, *hopping*, or *crazed*, with just time to *grab* lunch or *hit* the barricades. Liederman was in charge of all overseas operations, with Jane *spearheading* the Asian *advance*. The biotech industry was easier to run there, with cheaper labor and fewer FDA regulations.

"Max is revving up for a party, a bunch of Singapore businessmen next Friday at seven—mark your calendar, okay? I'll be home late. Oh, and on Saturday, you'll have to take Alex to soccer practice. I've got a tennis match at nine."

And how was *your* day, dear? Go ahead, ask me.

But Jane ignored my attempt at telepathy. She sat down at the table and took a few bites of chicken, chewing elegantly. She put down her fork. "You know, driving home, I saw that black dog you almost ran into, remember? Only it was *dead*."

"Really?" Something about that canine made me shiver, even if it wasn't alive anymore. Especially if it wasn't alive.

"Uh-huh. Someone must've hit the poor thing, and then everyone else ran over it." She wrinkled her nose. "Sanitation should clear it away. It doesn't look good for the neighborhood."

So that's what bothered her. Nothing like roadkill for bringing down property values. I didn't say anything. Instead, I focused on a tiny smear of curry sauce on her chin, which I found oddly endearing. I let her go on for a while, then interjected: "Alex is getting obsessive again." I told her about the pretzel-sticks incident. "I don't think the time-outs are working anymore, either."

"Oh?" Jane carried her plate to the sink but left it at the edge. Washing up rarely occurred to her.

"He likes staying in his room. He's also started hiding again."

She rolled her eyes. "You mean when you call, and he's suddenly not there? I hate that."

"And the fake asthma, have you heard *that*?" Alex could make himself wheeze spontaneously. Then he'd gasp for air and keel over. The first time, I was almost on the phone to the ER when he started to laugh.

"No, God no." She sighed and came up with parental cliché #3: "Maybe he's just going through a phase."

"Maybe." I tightened my grip on the table edge. "But I think he should see someone."

"Alex? See a shrink?"

I've never liked that term, and she knew it. "No, not a *shrink*," I pronounced primly. "A child psychiatrist. I know several practicing in Fairchester."

"But he's not—" Jane broke off, unsure how to put it. Disturbed? Bats? "In need of therapy," she offered finally.

"Look, it's not a bad idea . . . ."

"Well, sure, you're in the business!"

"So what? It might help him."

"No!" Jane seemed to grow taller when she was being emphatic. From my seated position, she looked positively Amazonian. Her thighs tensed, her bare arms flexed and swelled, and her eyes seemed to flash green.

But I'd seen all this before and wasn't cowed so much as annoyed. I was just about to contradict with a strenuous "Yes!" when I remembered my vow to be more agreeable, to change this stupid cycle of arguing. It might as well start now. I took a deep breath.

"All right," I nodded.

"What?" Jane looked at me suspiciously. I had deterred from the standard line.

"I said all right. We'll hold off on that." I pressed my lips into the semblance of a smile to show acquiescence.

Jane was uncertain about such a quick victory. "Okay . . . good." But
a paucity hung in the air, a hole that the quarrel would have occupied. We
both circled it for a moment. I half-felt I should fill the void with *Nice day,
eh?* or *Read any good books lately?* In the end, Jane decided on active
avoidance. "I'm going up," she volunteered. "I think I'll soak in the tub. It's
been a long day."

"I'm sure it has," I offered agreeably. I cleaned up the dinner dishes and
then followed her upstairs. I read my murder mystery on the bed while Jane
returned to the primal aquatic state. I could hear a few contented sighs from
the bathroom. When she finally came out, she was all rosy, wrapped in the
terrycloth robe that every woman owns.

"Ahh, that was wonderful." She lay down alongside me languorously.
And since we were getting along for a change, she asked me to perform an
act I hadn't done in a while. "Michael? Would you rub my back?"

"Sure." She flopped on her stomach and I straddled her with my thighs,
reaching down to start at her neck. Soft grip and release, again and again,
slowly working my way down to her shoulder blades.

"Ohhhh . . . ."

"Good?"

"Mmmm . . . ."

I was sitting on her buttocks as I kneaded her spine, especially the
upper area that carried the weight of her breasts. I was being a nice guy,
but I was also getting aroused. I let my fingers trail down to her lower back
and traced the flare of her hips, feeling the heat emanate from her loins like
some fleshy blossom. I heard another sigh.

Should I press my advantage? Would we finally get to what had so long
remained unconsummated? I stroked her more and more softly until my
hands were barely touching her, then bent down for a tender kiss.

"Mmm—*smghh* . . . ." A gentle snore issued from her barely parted lips.
I swore inwardly but managed to remain composed. Agreeable. I covered
her with the blanket, lay down on my side of the bed, and picked up my
murder mystery again. I had yet to reach the climax.

"*Smgh—gghr* . . . ."

Whatever you say, dear.

Chapter 6

The start of the work week always made the man in the gray slacks apprehensive. He woke up at seven-thirty, having shaved the night before to save time. His first view was always the Mickey Mouse clock on the night table, sometimes cheerful, other times mocking. The rest of the room slowly came into focus: the poster of Peter Pan on the far wall, the three-drawer bureau topped by a marble maze, the closet door that always looked as if it were opening into a secret passageway. As autumn progressed, the days grew cold and gray, and the bedroom sometimes felt like a cell. But buried somewhere in his dreams was a memory of mornings like an endless meadow, when the distance between breakfast and evening was longer than a trip to the moon.

Not these days. His parents had split up when he was seven, and he and his mother had moved to Albany to be with her sister. The two women worked in a beauty parlor that smelled of floral rinse and burnt hair. It was a latchkey childhood, punctuated by angry visits from his father, who finally disappeared. To keep himself occupied, he devised a game in which he located a pattern—the stripes on a shirt, the checkerboard linoleum squares in a hallway—and had to carry it in his head until he matched it to the same design somewhere else. When he was thirteen, he ran away from home and got as far as Rochester before he was yanked back like a piece of elastic: his mother had called the police.

In high school, he was so out of touch that he didn't even have a group to be alienated with. He was bright enough, good at math, but classes bored him. He was the kid who sat at the back of the room and didn't say much. Girls frightened him. At Clarkson in Potsdam, he discovered an interest in computers, whose programs resembled an endless array of patterns. He liked number sequences, designs, anything that promised a stable structure. Halfway through college, he fell apart and spent some time at the Binghamton Psychiatric Center, something he didn't like to think about. That was when the spells had started. He went back and was pursuing a degree in computer science when he simply dropped out, getting a job at a short-lived software company called Input. He'd changed jobs three times since then, never anything too demanding, and now he worked as a disaster recovery planner for a commercial insurer named Mutual Fidelity. When his mother died from cancer in his early twenties, he had another seizure and was put on Dilantin. While away from work, he began hanging out at a nearby playground in the mornings. Children soaring on swings, their little legs pumping hard; kids climbing up ladders and stamping across the sandbox—including a sandy-haired seven-year-old boy named Jeffrey who liked to ride head-first and bellywards down the long slide. The descent caused his shorts to pull halfway down, revealing pert white buttocks. Jeffrey performed a number of other tricks, including a violent side-to-side motion on the sling-swings that hiked up his shirt and showed his pinched-in navel. When Jeffrey's mother got angry and simply plucked him from his perch, her strong arm wrapped about his middle, the man in the gray slacks was enthralled. That was when the fantasies started. Or maybe they had always been there, waiting for something to shove them into motion.

That night, he dreamed he was swinging toward Jeffrey, colliding in midair but so gently that it was like two balloons bumping. Their two swings merged into one as Jeffrey pumped higher and higher. The man in the gray slacks looked down and saw the sand on the ground flying towards them. He looked up and saw himself framed between Jeffrey's thighs as the boy's coquettish smile grew wider and wider. He hadn't played with himself in a while, but the next morning he awoke all sticky. For three days, he was greatly upset, but then he had another, similar dream and then another. Other boys began figuring in the fantasies, as well, and when he walked by a playground or a school, he would stop to sightsee.

The hands in his mind would reach out and fondle the little boys' bellies and buttocks and sometimes their fledgling penises. But it was puzzling: half the time, he wanted to poke his head between their innocent thighs, penetrate their buttocks, or just stroke their limbs. Other times, he wanted to *be* them, wearing boys' elastic Jockey briefs and a polo shirt the size of a toy kite, running joyously toward recess. Even after he returned to work, he went back to the playground on weekends. Jeffrey was no longer around, but Billy was: a frail little boy with pale white limbs like something aquatic washed ashore. Billy would shut his eyes tightly, raise his arms and spread his legs, as if waiting for some strong wind to blow him aloft. The man in the gray slacks imagined himself as a gale of leaves, a gust of blue-white air fluting through Billy's arched groin, up his backside and circling his delicate neck. But he never made any advances, even when Billy's older sister ran off to play with her friends. He was still the kid who sat in the back of the room without saying anything.

That all changed with Bobby, a truck-like boy who marched right up to where the man in the gray slacks was pretending to read his magazine. He tapped the man on the shoulder. "Hey, mister, would you push me on the swing?" Bobby didn't seem to have any parental support close by, and the man decided to risk it. With even, measured strokes, the man pushed away at Bobby's firm rear. But Bobby was frisky, sticking out his arms and laughing with a gap-toothed mouth like an inviting red cave. When he pumped too hard, he arched back into the man's arms. The man prevented him from dropping by clutching him under the armpits, which just started Bobby laughing again. Finally he fell off altogether, and the man stumbled in the sand, overbalanced with the weight of a sixty-pound boy. The man hit the ground with Bobby landing on his chest, winding him. As he lay there, half-stunned, half-enraptured, his view of the sky obscured by a dancing swing in its final throes and the striped-shirt stomach of a boy, he knew what he wanted to do. Bobby's denim-covered crotch was within a few inches of his nose. Fortunately, unfortunately, Bobby's sister returned at that point, apologized, and yanked him away. The man went home to his bare apartment and masturbated three times that night.

He thought of bringing Bobby back to his place for the evening, imagining how they might share a bath like father and son. Running the bar of soap up, down, and around. Maybe a tablet of Percodan dressed up as candy would keep the boy compliant. A dim memory of his own father bubbled up . . . those strong hands that held him in place, the whiskey voice that breathed, "Don't move." But the man blocked out the ends of those episodes. He was back at work now and couldn't go to the playground when most of the children were there. But he also couldn't stand not being there. He was a junior programmer then. His hands twitched at work and mistyped, his eyes focused on an inner screen. He drove back to the park during overextended lunch breaks and sometimes mid-mornings, but he saw Bobby again only once, playing a game of boxball with his sister and her friends. Then one day he could go to the playground all he wanted because they let him go at work.

He tried nonchalantly asking a few boys on the swings if they wanted a boost. A few accepted. But a mother took her son away, a father scowled at him, and the next time he surveyed the swings, he noticed a patrol car idling by the chain-link fence. He needed a new job, a new life, but he also knew what was possible. After a few weeks, he found a data-processing job at an insurance company. He moved twenty miles away to an apartment remarkably like the one he'd left. He tried staying away from the objects of his desire, but that only increased the urge. The only measure that helped was a soul-deadening routine, with every activity mapped out in advance. Where and when to shop for the same foods; what to wear every day of the week. The patterns held and consoled him. The seizures faded into the background, except for one or two spasmodic surprises over the years. They seemed to coincide with a spike in sexual activity.

At times he would break free. He found an adult bookstore in the city with a section just for him. When the Web started spreading its strands across computer networks, the man found some hot sites, as well as chat rooms and a support group. There were others out there, offering pictures, clothing, and a lot more. With the right cyber-handle, he could even achieve his dream of being a little boy himself, a cocky preadolescent named Owen who liked to sit on men's faces. And he got suggestions from his group, including the mini-dungeon in the bathroom, and an idea for an abduction plan. Malls on the weekend became his new sightseeing spots. He was thirty-three by now and ready for the next step.

But until then he took his usual refuge in ritual, the repetition of pattern over time. He owned five identical pairs of gray slacks, and underneath he wore cotton Jockey briefs emblazoned with Atom Boy, procured from a Japanese *anime* Web site. His job at Mutual Fidelity had lasted over a year, landing him the title of assistant manager and a few co-workers who almost knew him.

*

Breakfast. He was in a three mood today. Three scoops of coffee into the coffee maker three minutes ago, and now the machine gently beeped three times. He poured the steaming contents into his Big Boy mug, stirring in three pours of milk and three scoops of sugar. Then he took a large cinnamon bun from a white baker's bag marked "Price's," put it in the center of a plate, and cut it into thirds. He turned each piece into three precise bites, each ending in a sip of coffee. He checked his Dennis the Menace wristwatch: two minutes to eight, so he waited until the big hand was on the twelve. He poured the rest of the coffee into a Flintstones mini-thermos and took it out to the drink-holder of his car.

He knew none of his neighbors in Fanshaw Garden Apartments, though he'd once said hello to the Asian woman in #1, and the guy in #5 seemed to stay around most of the day. Late nights, he'd seen gay porn on the guy's

VCR through the window, and the guy had caught him looking, but that was the extent of their relationship. They avoided each other.

Backing the Sentra out of his space, he drove straight for three blocks, then turned onto Crest Hill. On a sudden impulse, he veered to the side of the road just to see if the black dog was still there. It was, but its furred rib cage had been flattened into a black mat, the head a pulped mess with a dark purple tongue protruding. He slowed to a standstill. Nosing the car ahead, he ran over the carcass once more for the sensation it gave him: power and helplessness at the same time. He shut his eyes for a moment, feeling something expand and collapse inside him. Leaving the scene, he didn't look in the rearview mirror.

Soon he reached the access ramp to the Saw Mill River Parkway as he maneuvered through the morning rush-hour traffic to Mamaroneck, where Mutual Fidelity maintained its corporate headquarters. The suite of offices was located along Route 1 in a business building slanted away from the road behind a moat of a parking lot. At 8:25, he deposited his Nissan in one of the three spaces equidistant from the two entrances. The stainless steel elevator rode him to the third floor, where the new receptionist named Connie doled out a smile as he passed by. Inside was one of those office environments designed to create an interconnecting, sharing atmosphere, which the man in the gray slacks had done everything to frustrate once he had his own cubicle. A barricade of books and papers was his interior line of defense, with his portcullis a children's latticed gate to block the entrance, mercifully tolerated as a joke. His nameplate, TED SACKS, was artfully concealed behind a Jetsons digital clock. A street artist's drawing of a wide-eyed child stared from the corner.

At 8:30, he booted up his IBM power station, logged on, and started checking his e-mail. A few after-hours memos from Client Records, which he replied to cursorily. For over six months, he had worked on revising the encyclopedia-sized manual of contingency planning: what to do in case a fire destroyed some data tapes, how to cope in the event of a massive power failure, how to recover the system if a worm burrowed into the e-mail system. A sign on the far wall of his cubicle summed up his job: "1) PREVENTION. 2) MITIGATION. 3) REDUNDANCY."

But something was always shifting: upgraded telecommunications, a new vendor. Back to writing more code and running simulations: the phone lines down, the data center crashed. *And what if a fucking asteroid hits Mamaroneck dead on?* he asked himself. The latest plan for Client Records was what he had to deal with today, and it involved a cold site set up in

Arizona with a three-day readiness factor. It was comfortably dull, dependable work, except for the personnel factor, which always made him nervous. He had to contact others and ask them questions, and in turn respond to what they told him. He had to issue memos making everyone aware of upcoming events—"FLASH! There will be a simulated shutdown at 5:00 A.M. next Sunday, lasting approximately ten minutes"—contingencies that everyone ignored. Still, it was better than data analysis, which itself was a step up from the trained monkeys who typed and typed and typed. He occasionally used office equipment for his own purposes—who didn't?—but not for anything serious, and he wasn't so stupid as to get caught.

"Hey!" That was Rod, who considered himself a computer cowboy, though he was in fact junior to the man in the gray slacks.

"Morning." He nodded in the direction of Rod's cubicle. Rod was a data analyst who spent his days reading flat file across the screen and number-crunching to make bar graphs. A while back, there had been an embarrassing incident when Rod had approached him in the men's room. But that was long past.

When another man in gray slacks walked by, his face a bit puffy, Ted swiveled his head to murmur hello: Don Feinstein, the other disaster recovery planner at Mutual Fidelity. He was good at what he did, which was write a lot of code. He was particularly adept at dealing with Ted, which meant being cordial while keeping his distance. Ted knew from casual conversation that Don had been divorced a few years ago and had a small daughter named Leah. He had coffee-colored eyes and spoke in a strong, gruff voice. When Don helloed him back, Ted felt the word vibrate into him as if he were a sounding board. In a way, Don reminded him of his father, but he also knew enough about himself to limit his interaction to brief conversation. Or business-related matters. They generally divided up the tasks of risk-management categorically: Don, natural disasters; Ted, electronic mishaps. When they had to coordinate, as in a presentation or a report write-up, they behaved like well-coordinated twins. He was senior to Don by a month, but Don was older and Ted would defer to his judgment. Don also had what others in the firm called people skills. For that reason, Don was usually the main interface between disaster recovery and management.

"I'm going to get the new safety parameters from the guys upstairs this morning. The new vendor's causing a headache. Gleason wants everything plugged."

"Yeah. Okay. Wonder if Gleason knows a firewall from a fire escape."

Don favored him with a grin as he turned to leave. Ted turned his chair to view Don's bulky retreating figure until he sensed that Rod was watching.

He savagely pushed himself back within his stronghold and began to stab at his keyboard. Rigging up a simulation took real concentration, and it didn't help when some fruitcake was staring at him. This morning, according to his calendar, he was supposed to be testing a data overflow mechanism. The new parallel processors could handle up to five gigabytes /sec. without a blip, but above that level, the queuing system got confused. He spent till mid-morning pushing through dummy figures and watching "ILLEGAL OPERATION" notices flash onscreen. The problem seemed to have something to do with uneven data columns.

The breaks in his routine were invariant. At 10:00, he left his cubicle to get some coffee from the giant dildo of a thermos by the Kodak copier. At 10:30, he made a trip to the men's room, taking the far way by the windows. He would always retrace the same route back, glancing surreptitiously at others' work stations to see whether anything had changed since the day before. Pattern and difference, continuity and change. Sometimes a setup altered in the time it took to go to the bathroom, but you had to be alert to catch that.

The window route brought him past the work areas of the three systems analysts. Solly Watchnik, the senior guy, had a setup like a wallpapered sty. The backdrop was 3D computer graphics taped to beige Contac sheets beginning to curl. His cubicle was littered with Post-its, stacks of printouts, multiple coffee mugs, stupid framed mottos, and a desk caddy with paper clips and cheap pens. Ben Ashoka, by comparison, was a neatness freak. His sole wall decoration was a business calendar with items carefully crossed out, and his desktop was clean enough for the Formica surface to be visible. His desk drawer, which Ted had once been privileged to see open, had a roll of Scotch Magic Transparent tape, a child's scissors, a container of Liquid Paper, and a mini-stapler arranged in a row. Ted admired Ben's precise arrays, but nothing much ever changed there, whereas Solly's squalor had the appeal of a litter box.

The cubicle in the corner belonged to Myra Connor and was somewhere in between her colleagues' extremes. Myra made periodic attempts to clean up her space, but she liked to keep what Ted's mother had called doohickeys: a tiny plaster elf, a souvenir key chain, a polished lump of blue glass, and a series of snapshots in chrome and gold frames. Today he noticed a new photo on Myra's desk, showing a toothy little boy in blue shorts with his limbs wrapped around a fireman's pole.

Ted allowed himself only the usual glance on the fly. That was part of the game, and besides, Myra was right there. But the picture stayed with him when he entered the men's room, and he craned his neck to get another glimpse of it on the way back to his cubicle. Back inside his own domain, he was still bothered. He closed his eyes to see better. The boy couldn't be more than seven or eight, with a half-smirk that reminded him of someone, though he couldn't quite place it . . . but of course he could. It was Bobby, or some recombinant version of him: the same solid build, the same hint of illicit fun. Christ, he hadn't thought about him in years. After that, it was difficult to regain his concentration. He stared at the screen but just registered numbers floating by until he found that he'd typed "bobby bobby bobby" in the lower window.

He was supposed to confer briefly with Don before the meeting at 11:00. At 10:45, he made the extraordinary divergence of getting up to glimpse Myra's photo again. He had an ostensible errand, getting a refill for his Tintin coffee mug, but he lingered a bit too long by Myra's cubicle on the way back.

"Hey, Ted." Myra didn't stop typing as she flashed a look that identified him. She wore too much eye shadow and had a big soft middle that rubbed against her desk. "Want something?"

"No . . . thanks." Then he decided to risk it. "Hey, who's the kid in the new photo?"

"Oh, him. That's my nephew, Donald. Eight years old. Cute, isn't he?"

"Yeah." He wanted to know everything about Donald but could think of nothing except blunt questions like "Where's he live?" Finally, he asked, "You see him much?"

"Nah, he lives upstate. But I bring him something whenever I visit. Once I gave him a set of rainbow markers." Myra shrugged. "I didn't realize they were indelible. His folks threw a fit."

"Yeah?"

"Uh-huh. So last time it was a toy drum." She grinned. "I guess I don't like my sister that much."

"Hm." He took the opportunity to peer more closely at the picture. The legs around the pole, maybe that was it. Squeezing and being squeezed. But he had run out of conversation, so he ended the way he always did, "Well, gotta run," and moved on to Don's cubicle. He wanted to masturbate, the urge fighting through his concentration. Last weekend's incident at the mall, which he had sealed off in a rear compartment of his brain, kept rustling about back there. His hand retained the felt memory of a twitching thigh. He thought about going back on Dilantin but decided against it. Without it, he felt more alive.

The meeting with the suits went all right, not great. The asymmetry of the conference room, a stunted trapezoid, always made Ted nervous.

Gleason, the fatboy in charge of financial operations, kept pressing them to come up with an interim report. "Look, why don't you guys just write up something we can show the clients? PR'll work it over."

Don, ever the diplomat, spread his hands in a conciliatory gesture. "I understand. But isn't that what we gave you last month?"

Gleason dismissed the last four weeks with a wave. "That was okay as far as it went. But we want some reassurance that we can handle what happened to AOL—you know, if someone tries to flood us with data."

That was related to the problem Ted had been working on, but he said nothing. Don interpreted for him. "Well," he temporized, "you can say we're investigating the situation."

"Hmph." That was Weller, another big guy in pinstripe shirt and suspenders, who was head of bank transactions. "Sounds weak."

"Yeah," seconded Gleason, "why can't we at least say something more positive?"

"Because everything'll crash and burn," Ted snapped back before Don could intervene. These M.B.A. types never understood squat about tech problems. But clearly Gleason and Weller didn't want to hear this.

"Really?" Gleason seemed to grow taller as he bobbed forward on the toe-caps of his polished black wingtips. "Don't we have a fire escape or something? Isn't this what we pay you for? We need to tell our clients that we'll be fine in an emergency."

"After all, we're an insurance company," joked Weller. It was a line that Ted had heard before, but he applied a smile to his face—*like a crack in shellack*, his father had once said. After a few more admonitions, they were dismissed.

"There's no solution to that problem, you know." Ted was staring at a spot on the elevator wall that looked like a coffee spill.

"I know." Don placed a fatherly arm around Ted's narrow shoulders. "Just run some more tests. I'll write up something."

At noon, Ted left his computer on doze and went out for lunch. For the last few months, he'd gone to the McDonald's five blocks away and purchased a kid's Happy Meal, which was really all the food he wanted. This particular McDonald's had an indoor tube-slide playground, so he'd sit on a nearby bench and watch the kids crawl on their tummies from one level to another. Every day, he'd locate one boy who took his fancy and offer him the toy that came with his Happy Meal. Today, it was a *Star Wars* spinoff, a small plastic rocket that came in two sections. Through the blind of a computing magazine, he watched one little boy intent on doing everything in reverse: digging in with his sneakers, he would climb up the twisting yellow

slide, then travel backwards down the red ladder, over and over again. Four
or five at the most, guessed Ted.

"Eric!" called out the boy's mother, a woman whose frown looked
heavy and permanent. "We have to go soon. And why don't you go *down*
the slide for a change?"

"I don't *want* to . . . ." He simpered at Ted, or at least it looked that way.
Eric wore a little rugby shirt over blue sweat pants, and the way his rear end
wiggled down the slide opened a small gash in Ted's chest. Ted wanted to
stand underneath the ladder and squeeze *here* and *there*.

After a few minutes, he got up to offer his toy rocket to Eric. "Please, I
don't want it." The mother's frown relaxed only slightly.

Eric pouted. "Then why'd ya get it?"

Ted ran through his standard explanation about a man with a small
boy's appetite, and Eric snatched the prize before he could finish. Holding
the rocket in his hand, he zoomed it around and around.

"Eric, say 'thank you.'"

"Oh, that's all right." Ted made a dismissive motion. "Kids, you know."

But Eric zoomed back to where Ted was seated, cried, "Thank you!
Thankyouthankyou!" and gave Ted a kiss on the cheek. The hard kiss was
almost like an attack, and it thudded Ted's head against the wall.

Eric's mother glared. "That wasn't nice, Eric. Say you're sorry."

Eric danced back. "But I said thank you!"

"We're leaving. *Now*." Eric's mother gathered her purse and coffee
cup. As she got up, she turned to Ted. "You're okay, right?"

"Me?" Ted brushed his cheek where the kiss still glowed. "Never
felt better."

*

Back at the office, Ted remained distracted. It was as if small boys
danced down the corridors of Mutual Fidelity, peeking in at him, flashing
from his monitor screen. The tingling in his groin almost forced him to go
whack off in a toilet stall, but he held off. That was something he could
enjoy at home. Meanwhile, he'd already checked his e-mail twice and taken
two circuits about the office, though he was supposed to be working on a
new data-transmission test. Don approached him around 1:30, coming over
to his cubicle. Certain conversations, as they both knew, probably shouldn't
show up onscreen anywhere. Don leaned over the lattice gate without stepping in. "Look," he told Ted, "why don't you run a simulation with a mile-
long queue and just keep each file—well, not too big?"

Sudden bulk was what jammed the system. This would be more sequential. Ted considered the point. "It's not what they asked for," he finally said. "Fuck that." Don did and didn't meet his eye. "Give 'em what they want to hear." He walked away noiselessly, his measured tread disappearing between the rows of cubicles.

Ted sat for a moment, deciding. When one of the ghost-boys on the monitor winked at him, he cleared the screen and began to type. It wouldn't be too hard to rig up, but it had to look better than it was. In his mind, a thousand loaded freight cars rumbled down the data superhighway, all trying to squeeze out a two-lane exit. But by tagging each and ordering them, he could move them along at a slower rate. He stuffed each file with junk data from the records dump, no more than . . . oh, 100KB apiece. Then the ghost of Eric blew in his ear, and he got up for another walk around the office.

He lingered by Solly's cubicle and took in the latest addition: a drawing of a dog with duct tape around its muzzle, captioned "Mut(e). Fid(e)." Solly was on the phone and barely looked up, his short legs bent at the knees and angled outwards. Ben's desk on the other side of the divider had a simple yellow Post-it stuck to the desk top. It read "OUT."

Myra was also somewhere else, so Ted took the opportunity to gaze long and hard at the photo of Donald around the fireman's pole. But she came back unexpectedly.

"Visiting, huh?"

"Uh, just leaving." He hurried away, stopping off at the men's room. The door to the corner stall was invitingly ajar, and was that a pair of boy's sneakers rooted to the floor? He blinked, and they were gone. At the sink, he splashed some water on himself to get rid of the cobwebbed feeling across his face. He'd been told that was a symptom of Dilantin withdrawal. He'd gone without those little green pills for over a month now—what was he doing? Running three fingers through his thinning hair, he felt his mother nearby, but a stale breeze from the ventilation system blew her away. Leaving the bathroom, he felt as if he were entering another phase of his existence, emerging from a cocoon all sticky and raw.

But he still had unfinished business onscreen. It was hard to concentrate when he felt so twitchy. He set the simulation time for 6:30 A.M. Tuesday, though it should have been earlier in the morning. When Mickey's big hand was on the 6 and the little hand was stroking his cock. Shit, gotta focus. What time was it now, anyway?—after three. Put in a shutdown routine in case things got hairy. Should be automatic anyway. He cracked his thumb knuckles with a sound like *splunch*. His mouth felt dry. He went to get some more coffee and spilled half of it on the way back when Ben Ashoka almost

bumped into him. "Hot soup!" cried Ben, darting by. Ted threw some paper
towels on the spill and swabbed up most if it. By the time he got back to his
cubicle, he'd forgotten where he'd left off and had to scroll upscreen. Eric
blew him a kiss from somewhere behind his monitor. Concentrate on the
goddamned screen. Taking a big swig of coffee, he burned his tongue.

For a moment, he shut his eyes against the setup on the screen. This
problem had cropped up before, but not so bad and not at work. The last
of his meds were at home, tucked in the bathroom cabinet. He should just
finish this job and go back to his apartment. What had Don said? The files
shouldn't be too big. He went back to resize them—it looked like they were
off by a factor of ten. His fingers like claws, he typed some more numbers.
He froze in front of the screen, not moving for no telling how long. Finally,
three frames deep, he clicked his mouse on the START button and exited
the sequence.

Then he shut down his system, picked up his jacket, and walked out.

"You're leaving early," chirped Connie the receptionist.

"Really?" He licked his dry lips. He felt achy and unwell. "Feels
awfully late to me."

When he reached home, he went into the bedroom and masturbated. He
watched TV for half an hour, then made himself a dinner of macaroni and
cheese. He felt better now, or at least different: more resolved to act on his
desires, which had been submerged too long. Groping in the bathroom, he
found the rest of his pills and flushed them down the toilet. The Dungeon
beckoned, but he ignored it. Instead, he went into the Blue Room and
started surfing. Time to learn more about his own community. "Fairchester"
and "schools" led down a few boring avenues until he happened upon the
elementary school category. Hilltop, Pinewood, Ridgefield . . . . The photo
from Ms. Hardin's second-grade class appeared on the screen, and Ted sat
up intently. He reached for a pen, took down some names, and started running a few searches.

By the time he went to bed, he had begun to form a vague plan. He felt
stronger and more confident already. But his day at work continued to bother
him, and in one of his dreams, he was being chased down the hallway by
Ben Ashoka brandishing a giant countdown clock. "The simulation! You're
in hot soup!" Ted woke up in a panic, wanted his meds, but then recalled
what he'd done with them. He set the noise machine on "seashore" and tried
going back to sleep. The sheets were twisted somehow, and he couldn't get
comfortable.

It was too late, anyway. His phone began to ring at 6:35.

Chapter 7

"Got your purse?" I asked Jane as we hurried out the kitchen door.

"Yep."

"Car keys?"

"Uh-huh."

"Glock 9 mm?"

"I thought *you* were going to bring that."

"No, I'm good for the stun gun. You're in charge of all firearms. Check the list."

"Don't *go* . . . ." Alex was hunched over in his chair like a red-faced gnome, unwilling to interact with Steffie McHale, our second-string baby-sitter. You recognize the type: not so bright or child-friendly but responsible enough to trust for an occasional evening out. Ignore the nose-stud and the spider web tattoo. Unfortunately, Steffie didn't know how to play Wild-Child, and she'd cut Alex's pizza into squares without asking. He demanded triangles. Steffie was trying to convince him that squares were hip, and to do that she reached over and ate one of them, but that just worsened the situation.

"I want it back!"

"C'mon, Alex, I can't do that." She rubbed her stomach, which showed in a sexy strip between her jeans and sweater. "It's in here already."

"Then you have to get it out."

Jane was tapping her foot on the threshold. Time for Mr. Nice. "Alex, look." I poised a knife at the edge of a pizza square. "You know geometry. What's a square made out of?"

He peered so closely at his food that he got a dab of tomato sauce on his nose. He drew back suddenly. "Two triangles!"

"That's right. Now, here . . . and here and here . . . ." I quickly slashed all the squares on the diagonal, then handed him the fork.

He stared at them suspiciously. "Are they equal?"

"Of course, or they wouldn't make up a square. Now eat." *That's right, feed the little monster*, muttered Snoggs. Oddly enough, Martin uttered the same words.

And we were off, telling Steffie we'd be back around nine. A dinner reservation? A film we'd been dying to catch? No, Open House night at Ridgefield Elementary. We'd done this last year, so it wasn't entirely unknown territory. We'd been through Principal Levy's boilerplate spiel about a community of achievers and stood in the first-grade classroom to be led through the morning routine. But tonight was second grade: multiplication, journal-writing, and harder books.

In the entrance hallway, we saw Francis and Frances Connolly, dressed as if they'd come directly from work. I'd heard they had 24/7 nanny care, just in case something came up at the office. "Hello, you two!" called out Mavis Talent to them, before any of them saw us. She was wearing a black sweater and skirt that looked vaguely as if it had been through the kiln. Arthur Schram was wearing subdued financial consulting clothes and a bemused expression, as if he hadn't a clue how he'd got there. He almost always looked that way. Yet there had to be some occasions where he looked sharp and in the know, or else how would he inspire the confidence of clients?

As always, Francis shook hands tightly all around. I had the feeling that he performed that ritual even in the bedroom. After all, they call it pressing the flesh. But Frances's reaction was different. She smiled alluringly at poor, abstracted Arthur and reached over to remove a piece of fluff or something from his jacket. No one else was watching, and her hand lingered by his lapel. When he looked up, she held his gaze. I saw her slowly lick her upper lip. Arthur shifted from bemused to entranced. It was like a reprise of the recent dinner party at the Mirnoffs—except without the Mirnoffs. Samantha attended Pinewood Elementary in a ritzier district of town.

"I don't like these back-to-school gatherings." Mavis pulled at Arthur. "I always worry they're going to tell me that Brearley flunked gym, or something."

"Sue the bastards," said Frances so quietly, it took us a second to realize she was kidding. At least I think she was. Anyway, it was time to enter the gymnasium, which doubled as an auditorium and theater with bad acoustics. We heard a repeat of Principal Levy's speech from last year, and then we set out for Room 17, the domain of Ms. Hardin, Alex's teacher.

Ms. Hardin greeted us at the door and told us to take a seat at one of the miniature desks. We'd met her before, but only briefly. She looked like an aerobics instructor: short but springy-looking, as if someone had sewn a steel coil up her spine. Bright blue eyes, reddish-brown hair, early thirties. She spoke in an emphatic tone, leaving no room for ambiguity about what she meant. But her smile seemed to extend almost beyond her cheekbones.

Alex had told us with mild astonishment, "She has the *biggest* mouth, but she *never* raises her voice."

When was the last time you saw the inside of a second-grade classroom? When *I* was seven, the room was large as a field, with space for cubbies, desks in rows, a trestle table in back, three bulletin boards and a blackboard, and five-cubit-high windows to gaze out when you wanted to be elsewhere.

Now the desks were Formica with a molded plastic shelf underneath. No inkwells or lids that closed. As in first grade, the alphabet ran around the room, looking like the key to civilization, only now it was in script, with sample words alongside. Bookshelves lined one wall, filled with paperbacks. A math sphere, something like a soccer ball but with multiplication and division on its pentagons, hung over the long table in back, alongside a mobile of the planets. Since it was still October, Halloween witches and ghosts were crucified with staples onto facing bulletin boards across the room. The blackboard had been replaced by one of those plastic dry-marker boards, and I couldn't recall that Macintosh computer being there when I was, but otherwise it looked eerily familiar. I didn't know what I had expected, but I sighed as I sunk into a sturdy blue plastic chair built for a dwarf. Jane perched gingerly on the seat next to mine.

I don't know what the other teachers were doing—afterwards I heard that Mavis and Arthur had to endure a short history lesson, and the Connollys had to crane their necks to view an overhead projection of geography. But Ms. Hardin just gave a brief speech about what the class was learning these days. "When we have Parent-Teacher night, I'll be meeting with each of you to discuss how your child is doing. In the meantime, please find your child's cubby and look inside. Each of them put together a little project for you tonight. Also, feel free to look around the room."

So we did. We ducked under a pendulous "READ" poster with an angelic-looking boy and girl sharing a book. Over by the *faux* milk crates were a double row of cubbies, peg-holed and labeled. "ALEX EISLER" was third from the right, with a large manila envelope leaning against the back.

The front read "FOR MOMMY AND DADDY" in inch-high green crayon. Jane reached out and professionally slit open the flap with the sharp nail of her forefinger. Inside was a card of folded construction paper with a house enclosing three lopsided faces. By the house, in a Dali-esque touch, a tree hung with hearts thrust its branches skywards. Inside the card was a little essay titled "What I Like about School." Thank God Alex wasn't one of those wayward kids who liked recess and lunch best. Instead, he liked "higher mathematics, reading *Charlie and the Chocolate Factory*, and the way rain looks when it slides down the classroom windows." That last point, if it hadn't been ventriloquized, made me think of Alex as a budding poet. As we walked about, Jane struck up a tennis conversation with Wylene Wilbur. Whereas Jane worked on her powerhouse slam, I gathered that Wylene preferred a sneaky placement game. The two made for a vicious doubles team. I could hear their laughs as they dissected the playing style of someone low on the club ladder. I felt alone, maybe as Alex did at times like this, and looked around. I vaguely knew a woman at the corner desk, a plump stay-at-home mother whose son was the star of Alex's soccer team, and whose husband coached it. I vaguely waved and she half-waved back. A short, sad-looking couple, the woman clinging to the man for support, trudged about on a tour of the bulletin boards. I realized with a start that they were James's parents. Hello, James's parents—what *was* their last name? I walked over to where they were stooped, peering hopefully at a fat cutout pumpkin. Mrs. James's mother brightened when she saw me.

"Oh, hello." She had one of those smiles that looks all the more endearing for being slightly crooked. Her hair was in a fragile nimbus of a bun. She wore an old-fashioned blouse and pleated skirt cinched in at the waist. Mr. James's father, wearing a vest under his jacket, nodded in a slight bow. I remembered his graying walrus mustache from when I'd picked up Alex at James's house a few months ago.

Thank God for name tags. There'd been a stack of them at the front of the classroom, with a Magic Marker for you to label yourself. Mrs. James's mother, I saw with relief, was Ellen Ottoway, and Mr. James's father was George Ottoway.

"Learning anything?" I gestured around the classroom.

"Yes." Ellen said nothing more, and I felt as if I should draw them out a bit.

"Alex misses James, you know . . . ."

"I'm sorry he hasn't been in school lately," she apologized, as if it were her fault.

"Is he all right? Alex said he was sick."

"That's right." George stepped forward. "We're not sure what it is. The hospital said they'd run some tests to find out whether—." But at this point, his wife squeezed his hand, and he shifted in mid-sentence: "to—to find out what was wrong."

"I see." I hung on an understanding smile. "Well, I hope he gets better soon. Tell him Alex says hello." What else could I say? I glided away with a small valedictory flourish.

At the back of the room, Jane was still verbally volleying with Wylene, now joined by a third woman, who cackled at the end of her sentences. I kept my distance. It wasn't that I disliked Wylene, with her overbearing manner and incurable habit of interrupting—okay, I found her a pain, but I admired her. She ran the only decent bookstore in town, and she was a brave single mother, and I *wanted* to like her. But if you needed a book and went to Between the Covers, she peppered you with so many suggestions ("Ever try Brookner? How about Murdoch? You know, her first novel is really her best.") that you finally felt like ordering the damn thing in blessed silence on the Internet. And her daughter, Lily, a chubby eight-year-old who often hung around the store after school, was still in the phase where she was trying to be just like Mommy.

Straying over to the Macintosh in a nook by the cubbies, I took a look at what was on the screen. Above a class picture floated yellow block capitals: "MS. HARDIN'S SECOND-GRADE CLASS." You could click on a desk icon for STUDENTS, which I did. Steve Bonnati was matched up with his picture, age, and a one-sentence soundbite of his interests. "I like skating and TV." Lisa Chen liked to draw pictures. And there was Alex Eisler, staring slightly away from the camera as if he didn't want to meet my gaze. "I like to read." Stacey Gewirtz, who looked as if she were about to blow me a kiss; James Ottoway, who said he was interested in everything . . . all the way to Lily Wilbur, who said she liked to sell books. Click on the bulletin board for "DRAWINGS AND PICTURES"—none by Alex that I could spot. Other hot buttons included the markerboard ("WHAT WE DO IN CLASS") and a fish tank ("CLASS MASCOT"). There were also links to the school library and the two other second-grade classes.

I looked up to see that Jane had detached herself from her tennis group. I had just rejoined her when Ms. Hardin, circulating like a hostess at a party, caught our eye. "Have you got a moment?" she asked. "Why don't you come up front?" Exchanging nervous glances, we moved up the aisle as a couple. We stood by the side of the teacher's desk as if expecting a reprimand.

She paused as if searching for the right words. "It's about Alex."

Jane nodded for both of us. "How's he been?"

"Oh, Alex is a very bright boy." Ms. Hardin's smile widened. "As I'm sure you know. He excels in both language arts and mathematics. Cheery, too. He started out this fall with such promise." Her smiled narrowed. "But he hasn't really been himself lately."

Jane tilted her head. "How do you mean?"

"Well, he acts out a lot . . . ."

"You mean misbehaving?" Jane realized her mistake at once: it was like saying *cripple* or *mental retard*.

"Well, let's just say he gets cranky. He'll whine about his lunch or complain that someone's blocking his view. He'll argue about anything, and sometimes he knocks things over." Ms. Hardin cleared her throat. "But then he mopes a lot. Sort of withdrawing."

"Hmm," I said.

"Really?" said Jane.

"He even tries to hide occasionally." Ms. Hardin pointed to the space between the computer and the last cubby. "Usually he's right there, but twice he's wandered out of the classroom."

That boy needs a leash. Who said that?—Snoggs? Martin? How did they handle errant executives at Haldome?

Jane put on a concerned look. "What would you suggest we do?"

"Well." Ms. Hardin leaned forward. "This is always a difficult question to ask, but is everything okay at home?"

Jane and I barely exchanged glances. "I . . . *think* so," I replied, a psychiatrist making a considered judgment.

"Good, then maybe it's just a phase." Her teacher's smile assumed its former width. "You know, he's usually a fun kid."

After a few more comments, including praise for Alex's reading ability, we were dismissed. We milled about a bit more, examining the bookshelves. I found *The Lonely Rabbit* particularly poignant.

Poor us, poor Alex. *Hasn't been himself lately?* I heard Snoggs muttering. *Well, who's he been?* I looked again at Alex's card, which I'd nervously creased in half. When I turned it over, I realized that the back was written on, too. In the left-hand corner, in tiny lowercase letters that practically sat on top of one another, was a little sign that read "What I Don't Like about Home." And underneath that were two words: "fights" and "arguing." When I showed that to Jane, she looked as if she'd been punched. Me, I felt like the man proved right who wishes he'd been wrong. We'd gotten what we came for, I guess.

On the way home, I drove, and neither of us said anything for a while. It was like burrowing through a tunnel. Finally Jane said in a small voice, "We've really got to be more careful." Always a good start, "we."

"Yeah." *Why couldn't we have thought of this earlier?* sniped Martin, but I was going to be agreeable. "Hey, at least he's not flunking math. I wonder what the other parents were told."

Jane's competitive spirit took over. She snorted. "Ms. Hardin probably wasn't too happy with Lily. Wylene told me she's been misbehav—I mean *acting out* lately. Used an indelible marker to write the phone number of Between the Covers on a whole shelf of books."

"What about Risa?" A gangly kid whose pigtails looked scrawny, too. Whenever I took Alex to Davis Park, we saw her there with her mother, trying to reach the sky by wildly pumping on the swings.

"I think she has a learning disorder." Jane paused as if about to deliver a non sequitur. "Her parents are getting divorced."

"Hmm." I thought of my years in White Plains and Jane's upbringing in Norwalk. "Genetics or environment? Were we like that?" I reached out for Jane in the dark and caught her shoulder. "Tell me, aren't you the kid who hung upside-down from the jungle gym and showed everyone her underwear?"

"Maybe. Were you the one who told on me?"

"No," I lied. "I was the one with the toy binoculars." In fact, at six years old, I did see an older girl named Mary Beth display herself that way. She was said to be slightly crazy, but she seemed to be having a good time. I was kind of grossed out by the spectacle and told everyone about it, though it also half-excited me. It still did. Thank God Jane wasn't overly modest.

And then we were home. It was after nine, but Alex was still up. He and Steffie were watching a Japanese animated feature on Cartoon Network. A giant cyborg was laying waste to a metropolis with his ray-gun eyes. All four of us watched as the windows of a skyscraper melted and flowed down the sides of the building like tears. Then came a commercial for Hostess snack cakes, and I reached over to shut off the set. "Bedtime," I announced before anyone could protest.

"Was he good?" asked Jane hopefully.

"Oh, yeah. He got kind of cranky for a while, so I gave him an extra dessert. No problem-o, right, Alexis?" She tickled his belly, which I knew he didn't like. Yet he didn't complain—maybe he was just glad of the attention. He didn't seem that happy to see us.

Steffie was just old enough to drive, but not at night, so I had the honor. She lived in the Highmeadow district of Fairchester, where the houses still looked like milk cartons because no one had remade them into McMansions. Sitting in the passenger seat, she smelled vaguely of peppermint and patchouli—this generation was rediscovering India. Her long white arm snaked around the back of my seat like a make-out queen, but I figured it was just how she sat in a car. Anyway, Steffie had a punkoid boyfriend named Chad, far more pierced than she was.

As we approached her street, I saw that most of the mailboxes had been knocked half off their stanchions. One or two were twisted upwards, as if to receive junk mail from the clouds. A punks' holiday in Fairchester? Probably some high-school kids who wanted to express themselves. Pathetic, the limits of suburban vandalism. I turned onto Steffie's block.

"This one, isn't it?" Second or third milk carton on the right, the one with the perfectly intact mailbox in the shape of a shark, and a winding path to the front door, though it was only five yards.

"Yup, Mr. Eisler. Know what?" Steffie leaned toward me, her lips a breath away. For a moment I thought I was wrong and I was about to get a goodnight kiss.

"No, what?" Steady on.

"Alex is like the brightest kid I've ever babysat. But I don't know, something's bugging him lately."

"Really?" A typical psychiatric interjection. If I'd been seated behind my desk, my hands would have been clasped together and my brow lightly furrowed. In the car, I had to content myself with leaning on the steering wheel.

"Yeah, he said the oddest thing tonight."

"Really?"

"He told me that you're not his parents."

"Huh?"

"Yup. He told me that his real mommy and daddy were gypsies."

Ah. Dressed in rags by the roadside, poor but humble, yet exotic— and deliriously in love with their offspring. What Freud called the family romance: the persistent conviction that the lunkheads in charge of your childhood couldn't possibly be related to you. Only in this case, Alex wanted parents who didn't think so much of themselves and argued less.

"Well," I temporized, "Alex's maternal grandmother may have had a little Romany in her."

"Yeah? That's so cool!" Steffie got out at that point, patting the shark mailbox as if it were a pet and sticking strictly to the winding path all the way to the front door. I didn't drive away until she was safely inside, an adult custom I used to resent bitterly when I was her age—what did they expect? A molester hiding in the bushes?

By the time I got back, Alex's bedroom door was closed, and Jane was also upstairs. I went back down to the fridge and picked at the leftover pizza, now cut into tiny stars. Steffie's idea? The kitchen scissors was propped in the sink with tomato sauce on its blades. I ate three stars and brought the last one up to Jane on the one silver-plated tray we own, an inheritance from my grandmother, who was no Romany.

Jane was already in her nightgown, reading *Forbes* in bed as part of her professional obligations. She accepted the pizza cutlet on the tray as the half-joke it was. "Mm, thanks."

"Alex," I told her solemnly, "thinks his real parents are gypsies." I explained as I undressed for bed.

Jane sighed, shrugging helplessly. "That's probably what Ms. Hardin thinks, too."

"I thought gypsies argued all the time."

"That clinches it, no?" She gave a Jane-smile, compounded of pleasure and complicity.

It stirred me, and I bent over to kiss her. She pulled me in closer, her bare arm wrapping around my neck. When I leaned in, she slid back, pulling me with her. In a moment, we were both horizontal on the bed. I caressed her shoulders. She sighed, much better than a hiss of annoyance. But one of the problems we'd had was not understanding each other's needs. So I asked as I stroked her arms, "Is this okay?"

"Hmm . . . yes."

Over to her neck, trailing lazily down to her breasts. "And this?"

"Fine. Listen, you don't need a signed permission slip."

"Just checking." Her nightgown seemed to slide magically open as I teased her nipples erect. I gripped her hips and squeezed. As she slid her thighs against mine, I reached down with my thumb and began to rub gently.

Then I remembered placement. I wanted to please. "A little higher?"

"No, s'fine."

"How about now?"

"Yes, I told you."

"Not over to the right?"

"No."

"Harder?"

Her thighs closed abruptly, squashing my hand like a blossom in jam. "Michael, this is supposed to be sex, not an inquisition."

"Sorry." She graciously permitted me to continue. After a minute, I figured I'd be even nicer and lowered my head to below her waist. She must not have washed down there since her morning shower, and an acrid cat-and-fish odor gloved my face. But Mr. Nice is capable of anything, and I started to tongue her.

"Oh, you shouldn't . . . " she murmured. "I'm probably yucky down there."

"Thaphth aw ri'," I began, my voice muffled against her.

"What?" She half-levered herself upward.

I tilted my head up. I wanted to be nice and sincere. "That's all right. You know, it really doesn't smell that bad."

"Thanks a lot."

"That's okay." I was about to return to my spelunker work when she swiveled away. "Now what—"

Her sigh was like steam escaping a fissure. "We'll try some other time, all right?"

"I guess so." We eventually retreated to our separate sides of the bed and fell asleep.

Non coitus tristus est.

*

"Where's my blue umbrella? Alex, Michael—have you seen it?" Jane was getting ready to leave for work, an accelerating process that started out calm and usually ended up frantic. It was a fifty-minute commute to the giant Haldome offices on 34th Street, including the drive to the train station and the walk from Grand Central. That much was a given, and she could have planned accordingly. But no matter how early she got up, some internal fly-spring adjusted her pace so that she moved faster and faster until, propelled by haste and the schedule of the Hudson Valley Line, she rocketed out the door. I'd always maintained that she built up this drama to get herself going. She admitted I might have a point, but that changed nothing.

The question I had to face was whether my strategy was working. My agreeability seemed to mollify Jane temporarily, but sometimes it derailed her. The Friday before, as she was headed to that Haldome soirée with the Singapore set, she held up a mid-length dress so deep blue it was black, peering doubtfully at herself in the mirror. Then she asked the question all husbands dread. "What should I wear tonight?"

Usually I ventured an opinion, sometimes going so far as to suggest a different color or cut. That always got us into an argument about men's poor taste, and who was I to lecture her on style? Not this time, baby. "I think," I said, weighing my words, "that you should wear whatever you like."

She snorted. "Don't give me orders, all right?" And she stalked into the bathroom.

This is what a well-worn routine will do to you. I was trying to change all that. Occasionally, I longed for a life in which Jane was a prostitute and I was insanely jealous, or I stole to put bread on the table and Jane lived in fear of my going to prison. Those kind of relationships seemed pure and passionate, or at least no one could accuse them of being trivial.

Preparing my office for the first patient of the day, I straightened the Andes throw rug and shut the blinds. The view out the window, though just the Steinbaums' topiary hedge and the side of their castle, could prove distracting to patients who should be concentrating on their own problems.

Hell, what about my problems? Was I changing myself or just practicing accommodation? A behaviorist might have argued that actions are the same no matter what the motive, but I couldn't agree. In any event, the more I practiced agreeability with Jane, the more it bled over into other areas where it didn't belong. My patients, for instance.

R appeared promptly at 10:00, as usual. She looked physically happier—shoulders less slumped, hair more buoyant, mouth curling slightly upwards. What they call a risible expression. Recalling one of Jane's grievances, that I rarely complimented her, I opened with "Well, you're looking fine, I must say."

R looked around as if to see who I was talking about. "Maybe it's the light," she ventured. Low self-esteem. Normally, I would have commented on this behavior, asking why she felt she didn't deserve praise. Instead, in my new complaisant role, I followed it up.

"No, it's the way you hold yourself . . . ." *Damning with faint praise*, I could hear my superego Martin snipe. He was all in favor of the niceness project—thought it would improve me—so I went further. I scooted my chair forward and smiled. "You know, you really are a most attractive woman." But this remark seemed only to make her more uncomfortable. She sat back and spindled her hair with a forefinger.

After my ten-minute buffer came S, who swaggered in like a bullying male in a china doll shop. I gathered he'd somehow got the upper hand over his wife, but brutality was exactly what he had to watch out for. "Well," he grunted, once he'd settled himself heavily in the armchair vacated by R, "Sheryl's started cooperating more."

That must've taken some doing, remarked Snoggs. "Great, great!" the new Michael enthused, slapping his knees.

"You think?" S cocked his head, squinting at me.

"Well, maybe—why not?"

"I dunno." S placed his hands on his thick thighs and leaned forward. "I mean, is she doing it because we're hotsy-totsy again or because she's gotten afraid of me?"

I smiled disarmingly, as if to ask what woman could resist him.

This back-and-forth went on for a while longer, me being fatuously agreeable, until S cut in with "You know, doc, you're acting like one of my ex-girlfriends. Annie. Wasn't anything I could say she didn't agree with. I finally started contradicting myself just to see her squirm."

Unfortunately, that afternoon my charming attitude also didn't help T, who seemed to be claiming that her fifteen-year-old daughter either was or would never be pregnant. And poor Z described his tepid Saturday tea, only to have his analyst embarrassingly whoop it up for him.

*

That Saturday was Alex's fifth soccer game, which took place at the Ridgefield Elementary School field. I used to wake up with him every Saturday, but for the last two years he'd risen by himself to watch early morning cartoons. The soccer had been Jane's idea. After breakfast, I watched him don his black-and-yellow jersey and shorts—his team was called the Dragonflies—and struggle with his cleats. He looked, to put it bluntly, non-athletic, not heavy or soft but slow and dreamy. Given the choice between absorbing a book on the couch and kicking a ball, Alex preferred to read. Which is why his well-meaning mother had pushed him towards soccer, hoping to make him more active. It made him more sullen, really.

Since Jane wasn't exactly a soccer mom, I pitched in, driving Alex the seven blocks to the game and pacing the sidelines while shouting, "Go, Alex!" When we got there, the coach, the husband of the plump woman I'd seen at Open House, waved a paw at me. An ex-jock named Gordie who'd seen better days, he was already at the ten-yard line, flanked by his enormous Adidas duffel bag, stuffed with extra balls and uniforms, an air pump, a first-aid kit, and the all-important after-game refreshments. His wife, a stay-at-home mom, had probably stayed at home. Good for her.

"Hey, Alex!" Gordie snapped a smile at him, then turned his attention back toward three Dragonflies advancing on the goal. "C'mon, fellas, teamwork!" He was putting the kids through a little drillwork, having them pass to each other and shoot at the net. Alex joined them reluctantly, as if saving his energy for the game. The Dragonflies had no real practices, as other teams apparently had, just these warm-ups. I gather that Gordie, whose dot-com business was headed for its IPO, didn't want to be bothered with the extra time commitment. His son, a sandy-haired star named Mark, could dribble and shoot with real accuracy while the rest of the team was, to put it mildly, uneven. In fact, the Dragonflies were not the winningest team around, but in the true spirit of today's permissive parenting, it wasn't supposed to matter.

Like hell it didn't. In his book, Jerry had a chapter on suburban sports, which he called "the theater for acting out." Alex didn't have much invested in the game since there were fourteen boys on the team and he wasn't rotated in too often. But some of the mothers and most of the fathers acted as if they had bet the farm on the outcome. Another woman from Open House, an ex-model striding tempestuously up and down the field in spandex knickers and retro Seventies platforms, looked like she wanted to kick the opposing team in the balls. What came out of her mouth was more invective than cheers—colorful expressions I'd never heard before, the mildest of which was "Goathead!" Her name was "Juan's mother." Juan's father was never there, though occasionally his grandmother appeared, a Barbara Bush type with the build of a linebacker. Something about the set-up hinted "single mom," a guess confirmed when I asked the grandmother about Juan's paterfamilias. "Juan has no father." She squared her shoulders. "Court order." Grandma wasn't around that day, but Juan's mother was there, digging holes in the turf with her chunky three-inch heels. By the far goal, a man in gray slacks stood nearby, shifting his weight from one foot to the other and cracking his knuckles.

The Dragonflies were matched against the Pinewood Stingers, who looked more prepared than the home team: casually passing practice balls on their end of the field, the result of the drillwork that Alex's crew was still attempting. Watching Alex trot around in front of the goal reminded me of my own soccer games when I was growing up. They weren't all that different—that same mob pursuit up and down the field—but we had nothing like the equipment these kids had. Even the grass looked greener now, as opposed to the field that we called Old Baldy.

My parents had never particularly encouraged me toward sports. My father was busy banking, and my mother was interested in taking me to the city. We'd go to the Museum of Natural History or a Broadway musical. We had all the cast recordings at home, and I memorized the lyrics to *Guys and Dolls* by the time I was ten. I also had flare-ups of asthma, which went away with adolescence but crept into my personality. I like books, and I've never had much use for jocks. Alex was turning out the same, including some medium-strong allergies. We spent a lot of time indoors, especially at the public library, where the librarians all knew Alex by name.

I checked my watch. The game was supposed to start at nine, but the referee, a high school guy named Doug, hadn't shown up yet. Juan's mother whipped out her cell phone and offered to chew him out. But nobody had his number—no one even recalled his last name. A lot of collective shrugs. Finally, Gordie jogged over to me.

"Hey, Michael, you used to play, right?"

"Yeah . . . ."

"Well, it doesn't look as if Doug's gonna show. And these kids are waiting." He cocked his head. "Whaddya say you be the ref?"

I stepped backwards like an army recruit unvolunteering. "Um, I don't know . . . ."

"C'mon, it's just a kids' game. You know all the rules. I got a whistle and a stopwatch in my bag."

I looked at the two teams and all the parents milling about the field. I saw Alex, my own Dragonfly, gamely trotting after a ball, his thatch of brown hair falling over his eyes. I remembered I was supposed to be agreeable.

Ten minutes later, I was jogging after a muddy ball with a score of kids strung after it like the cords on a parachute. The main action went something like this: Stinger #7, big as a ten-year-old, kicked the ball forward in a low arc, blocked by Dragonfly #2, Gordie's son Mark. Then the ball veered out of bounds. I blew my whistle and pointed downfield, wearing my agreeable smile. "Stinger throw-in." The throw-in bounced off Stinger #5's head and was kicked across the field. A flying wedge of kids raced after the ball, but Stinger #7 passed the rest of the group, terrifying our goalie before a high leftward shot made the score 1-0. Gordie's son Mark kicked the goalpost in frustration. Juan's mother stomped the sod and called someone a dickhead.

The whole game went like that. By the third quarter, I was winded from following the ball around, but the importance of my office kept me going. The one time the ball rolled toward Alex, I don't know what the hell he was dreaming about, but he bent down and gently scooped up the ball. The sharp *wheeeet* of my referee's whistle blasted him out of his stupor. "Foul!" cried Daddy. "Free kick for the Stingers." Alex dropped the ball as if burnt, and I won't forget his look of betrayal.

In the final minute, the Stingers swarmed around me and the ball, and one of them kicked me right in the shin. Christ! The pain thrummed in my leg like an anvil hit by a hammer. I couldn't see who'd done it, so I just put on an awful grimace and hobbled about until I blew the whistle to end the game. By now, my shin was throbbing like a second pulse. Gordie thanked me, and I found Alex in the back of our car, already seat-belted and on the last page of his new mystery, *The Secret of Slippery Slope*.

"Look," I told him, "I'm sorry I had to blow the whistle on you."

No comment. He kept reading.

"Hey, I'm talking to you. I expect a response."

"What." But he still wouldn't look up, so I reached over and grabbed the book away. He seemed genuinely surprised.

"Why'd you do that?"

"Because you weren't listening."

"Okay, Daddy. I'm sorry." He seemed repentant, and I counted the scene a victory, if not a triumph of niceness. But as I was about to walk over to the driver's side of the car, he held out his hand. "Can I have my book back now?"

We drove home in silence. Jane usually came out to the car after Alex's games for what she called a debriefing, but not this time. After an awkward wait, we trudged inside: the menfolk back from the field. My shin was still aching, so I went for an ice-pack from the freezer. Alex walked in after me, climbed the stairs to his room, and shut the door. I sat at the kitchen table and nursed my leg. I felt like calling a foul on everyone in the house—but that wouldn't be agreeable. Give everyone a free penalty kick, and you can start on me.

From upstairs, I could hear Jane on the phone. "No . . . *yes* . . . sure, drinks would be *lovely*." Her voice had a strange yet oddly familiar lilt. At first I couldn't place it, and then I remembered: that was how she talked when we were first going out together. "*Uh-huh*, eight's okay . . . *no*, I don't *care* what we eat, I'll be *starved* by then." Or "*Sounds* good . . . what kind of party *is* it?" Giggle. "How'll I recognize you?"

In fact, we'd first recognized each other at a drunken gathering in a Brooklyn railroad apartment hosted by a friend of a friend in common. It was slightly confusing because everyone there seemed to know each other, except for us. "Mikey-boy, this is Jane, I think. Say hello," said our Hawaiian-shirted host before darting away for another bottle of vodka. So we started talking. I was still wearing hospital chic, a green scrub shirt over chinos, but she'd lost every trace of corporate America in a pair of jeans and a striped sleeveless blouse that showed off her arms—those strong round limbs that I still loved.

"So," she smiled, shaking my hand firmly, "do all your friends call you Mikey-boy?" Only at parties like these, I told her. Then both of us confessed that we didn't know anyone there. She caused me to spill my drink when someone jostled her from behind, and she gallantly got me another. I was enchanted. I've always liked assertive women. When the noise in the tiny living room got too loud, we stood chest to chest in the narrow corridor and asserted ourselves for two hours. I thought she was high energy; she thought I was smart and cute. We started dating. Later, I'd call her from Downstate, where I was doing my internship, and she'd practically jump into my ear. At the time, she was a junior vice president at Amogen, scheming and dreaming of a way to climb over her superior. We'd meet in the Deluxe Coffee Shop on Linden Boulevard because I couldn't go too far on my breaks, and hold hands and sometimes other parts under the table. Once she even went back to the hospital with me, where I managed to locate an empty bed. Another time, she held me down with her tongue for half an hour. We took turns being at each other's mercy.

But I hadn't heard that tone of voice in a while. Who was she talking to upstairs that way? I craned my neck as if I were an electronic ear on a stalk, but she'd already hung up. Was this the start of an office affair, or one already in progress? Was I supposed to be Mr. Nice Guy about it? Should I just leave now and avoid a messy confrontation? How many questions could I pile up without any answers, all on the basis of a half-heard telephone call? In my imagination, I was already heading toward the door. *Wait*, counseled Martin. *Yeah, stick around*, gravelled Snoggs. *This might be good.*

Then I recalled my resolve. The old Michael might have been accusatory when she appeared, or worse, said nothing about it—then gotten involved in some argument that was a substitute for the aggression I really felt. The new Michael wouldn't fall into that trap. So when she came downstairs, radiant from whoever the hell she'd been talking with, I launched into a description of the soccer game. I made light of my shin injury. "I tried to please everyone," I shrugged as I tried to balance the ice-pack on my extended leg. "Mr. Nice Guy, you know."

"I know." Jane came up behind me to rest her arms on my back. She rubbed my shoulders for a moment, then let her hands drop. "Michael, you know what the problem is?"

"Um, no."

Jane shook her head wearily. Then she spoke in what was clearly the sum-up of many days. "You know, being a nice guy is one thing, but you've turned into a wimp."

She was right. I couldn't have agreed more.

Chapter 8

Three weeks after the disaster, the disaster-recovery planner hadn't yet recovered. He spent almost all his time indoors, sleeping on and off as a form of withdrawal. When he got up, he'd make himself a sandwich and walk around the apartment, picking things up and putting them down in different places. His Winnie the Pooh coffee mug grinned at him from behind the sofa, and he couldn't find his razor. Except for food shopping, he had no real reason to go out, no place to be at any particular time. When his severance pay ran out, he should go look for another job, or probably before that happened, but he couldn't think clearly. Being completely off his meds seemed both good and bad. He no longer felt the restrained sleepiness he associated with Dilantin, which had become a way of life for him, but instead he felt dislocated and apprehensive. He slept poorly and woke up at odd hours. Now it was around noon, he figured, judging from the last time he had looked at a clock. He stood by the window and peered at not much. The dingy white crescent of leftover snow on the lawn looked chewed at. The gray fringe of a few January clouds was tinged with anger. Well, some of the bosses at Mut Fid might still be furious, but maybe he should be, too.

He still wasn't quite sure what had gone wrong. That awful wake-up call at 6:35 A.M., the data-processing supervisor screaming in his ear, shutdown, shutdown! His simulation had somehow gone haywire, the whole system clogged with gigabyte feeds the size of skyscrapers. And everything crashing. It had taken him and Don until ten A.M. to get operations back to normal, to cease data processing and set back the computers. They'd lost a ton of data, time, and money. He remained convinced that the situation wasn't entirely his fault, though he couldn't think who else to blame. Then there was Gleason, who'd made some extremely unkind comments about Ted's job. "Contingency planner, hell—what we need is someone to protect us against people like you!"

Weller mentioned ominously that they'd calculated the morning's loss at $1.3 million. "We want you out of here by Wednesday."

"Are you firing me?"

Gleason stepped forward. "Let's just say we're asking for your resignation."

And that was it. No more job. The next day, he came in to clean out his cubicle, bringing a few cardboard liquor boxes and a green 30-gallon garbage bag. He'd always thought of his work area as having only the amount of clutter necessary to carry out his job, but he was amazed at all the stuff he'd accumulated: outdated manuals, old printouts, a whole drawer of paper clips and Post-its in varying sizes, a Posture-Perfect wedge pillow still in its bag, three brands of anti-static pads, a crooked column of phone directories, a whole file drawer of Mut Fid corporate brochures, and on and on. Then there were the doohickeys—why had he ever saved a plastic Taco Bell coffee stirrer or those three empty soda cans? It was as if he were viewing the remains of another individual, someone terribly akin to him, yet already receding into the past. What should he do about the few kid-photos he had taken during a lunch break with a disposable Kodak? A guy from Security was supposed to check through his belongings, but no one was worried. They all knew that Ted Sacks was a fuck-up, not a saboteur or spy. In the end, it was too wearying to think about what should be discarded, so he scrounged two more boxes from supplies and just crammed everything in.

No one said much. Ben and Solly kind of avoided him, though Myra was kind enough to ask how he was feeling. She seemed to mean it, so Ted answered her.

"I don't know." He tried for a smile, but it didn't come out right. "I haven't felt normal in a while."

"Well, I hope things get better." She gave him a totally unexpected hug, soft and firm at the same time. "Take care of yourself, Ted."

There was a brief message from Rod, scrawled on a Mut Fid memo pad. "So long, pardner. Happy trails!"

But the oddest response came from Don, who came by his cubicle to talk with him before he started packing. "I'm sorry this happened," he said quietly, curling his big-knuckled hands about the top of Ted's cubicle divider. "I feel partly responsible, in a way."

For some reason, this hadn't occurred to Ted. He'd been so steeped in his own funk that he'd practically forgotten the original circumstances. What if he hadn't done as Don said? What if he'd gone his own way, what if . . . but the line of possibilities didn't extend that far, really. The pattern didn't fit somehow. "Thanks," he said finally. "But I'm the one who rigged it up. I guess I was . . . distracted or something."

"Hmm." Don looked him up and down with his clear brown eyes, as if picking up the patterns Ted had never told anyone about. "What were you thinking of?"

And since Ted didn't want to say anything about little boys, or seizures, no matter how understanding Don might be, he fell back on what he'd told Myra. "I don't know." Only this time he looked away. "I just don't feel normal these days."

At this, Don came forward, laying one of his big hands on Ted's bony shoulder. The hand felt even heavier than it looked, with veins thick as pencils, and its grip was solid. It rooted Ted in place as Don delivered a little speech on finding satisfaction in an unsatisfactory world. "You know, most people aren't normal. That's okay." His grip on Ted increased, to the point where it almost hurt. It felt paternal somehow, that combination of strength and comfort and pain. Don's breath smelled of coffee and doughnuts, overlaying something flat and stale. His face was creased around the upper lip where a mustache might have once grown, and his mouth didn't move much when he talked. The hand was now vaguely massaging his shoulder.

Ted only half-listened to the speech, which he knew was intended to make him feel better about himself despite being such a geek. He was distracted again, wondering what kind of father Don was. He seemed both right and horribly wrong for the role. "Yeah," he told Don during a pause, "I guess you're right."

"Of course I am," said Don. "I'll tell you something else. I'll bet you get another position real soon. You see if you don't." He reached over with his free hand to deliver two hard pats to Ted's other shoulder. For a moment, Ted felt held, guided, and eight years old. As if no harm would ever come to him except through those very same hands.

And then the moment was over, and Don was walking away. The sturdy back of his gray trousers swung around the corner.

Days afterwards, Ted could still feel the hand on his shoulder. If he stood very still, he could also re-experience the cushioned support of Myra's hug. The first sensation was the same as the second, though opposite. And both were gone now. Life as a bunch of failed patterns. He had to do something about himself, he knew that, though he still wasn't sure what. Meanwhile, he had his severance pay, which topped $10,000, and the likelihood of another job when he was ready to try again. As long as he felt like only part of himself, he wasn't yet at that stage.

He turned away from the window. The job had provided a pattern for him to follow, and without it, he felt random and aimless. Yesterday, he'd been so scatterbrained that he toasted the same slice of bread three times. The yellow warmth of the kitchen drew him in, though right now he couldn't remember specifically what he'd come there for. He'd started talking to himself lately for company, but the replies were too one-sided. His mirror told him he was depressed. Talk to someone else, maybe, but who? He remembered the afternoon his mother died, and there was no one to tell. His aunt was now just an address in Idaho.

His head was still cobwebbed from sleep. Every night, he turned the sound machine to "rain" and tried to lose himself in the pattern. Lately, he'd been having dreams about his parents: his father buckled to the Slurpy Seat while his mother attended to her customers in a row of hair dryers, all in surreal undersea silence; or seeing his mother drink endlessly from a bottle in which his father was imprisoned. But thinking about his father always made him dizzy. Maybe he was hungry.

He reached for the white paper bag from Price's Bake Shop, but shook out only crumbs. Empty-handed, he walked into the Blue Room and sat down in front of the computer. The first few days at home, he had spent in front of the screen, surfing the Web. It was like a floating indoor universe: bulletin boards, satellite news, the Daily Gardenia site, chat rooms, sixty-colored animated graphics that invited him in, restricted domains that couldn't quite keep him out, a data base in the shape of a giant human face, online shopping, forms to fill out for the rest of his life. For some reason, the activity on his usual boy channels was muted these days—a nasty virus had taken over one of them, and he only narrowly avoided it himself. On the other hand, the Web site of the Ridgefield Elementary School provided some voyeuristic thrills. When he grew tired of the Web, he played adventure after adventure of a new game he'd installed called *Karate Boy*. It wasn't so much the pleasure of delivering roundhouse kicks to his opponents as that the hero looked all of ten years old and acted it, right down to the prepubescent voice calling out, "*Ichi, ni, san!*" Finally he switched to videos, running through his limited collection that included *Asteroid Boy* and *Band of Brothers*. He also played the swimming hole scene from *A River Runs Through It* over and over again. The way the golden light fell on the boys' bodies made him want first to be another boy, then the water, then the dripping shorts barely clinging to their waists when they emerged.

He also worked out in the Dungeon, mostly just strapping himself in for fun. For short intervals, it made him feel *alive*. It made him feel potent, and if that wasn't a common need, what was? Most people aren't normal, he recalled Don telling him, and that's okay. He mentally removed the hand on his shoulder and substituted Myra's hug.

But by now the walls in his apartment had grown too close together, and neither staged nor virtual reality sufficed. Was this how the guy in #5 felt, at home all the time? He'd seen the guy jerking off again—why didn't the idiot angle his blinds?—and been seen observing, which just made everything more claustrophobic. "I've got to escape," he announced to himself. Anyway, he was running out of food again. He made a list of items he needed, from Spaghetti-O's to coffee. Destinations: the supermarket, the park for sightseeing, and maybe Price's Bake Shop. He went to the front door and stuck his head outside. It was balmy for January, so he decided to take a chance and walk part of the way. The day looked promising rather than threatening. And when he stepped outside, the air blew about his face like a wreath. Perfect for some time at the park.

The supermarket shopping went quickly, automatically. Price's Bake Shop came next, and that was within easy walking distance on Douglas Street. It was the one upscale store in Fairchester that he liked, partly because of their frosted cinnamon buns and partly because the people who worked there were nice to him. The absentee owner employed high school kids who were vaguely hippie-dippy, the kind who might dye their hair orange or skateboard to work. One in particular, a girl named Steffie with a nose stud, started chatting with him about computers once she found out his job. Or what she called "the soul of the machine," which was silly, but he didn't mind. She had an awesome spider web tattoo on her midriff, which you could see whenever she reached for anything behind the counter and her shirt hiked up. She had the pale, unfocused skin tone of an eight-year-old boy, which he risked telling her once, though it confused her. "That's good, right?" she asked, wax-papering three cinnamon buns before sliding them into a bag for him.

"Sure." He leaned forward to see where the inky blue lattice of her tattoo disappeared down her left hip. Then he smiled and came close to giving himself away. "Depends on what you like."

Too bad she had this dorky punkoid boyfriend named Chad, who liked to hang around the bakery. He had five piercings in each ear and something metallic in his right eyebrow, but the real problem was his low, flat stare, which he practiced on Ted, as if he could see all the way back to Ted's secret history. When Ted walked in this Saturday, ringing the jingly bells on the entrance door, he was relieved to see Steffie behind the counter and no sign of Chad. Not that no one else was in the shop. Price's hadn't yet decided whether to become a café, and simply set out a few tables for people who liked to sit with a cup of coffee or hot chocolate, also available at the counter. A man and his young son were at the first table, but Ted diverted his eyes only slightly. It sounded as if they weren't getting along.

Steffie gave Ted a regular's greeting. "Hey, computer guy." Today she was wearing a T-shirt that read "DYSLEXICS OF THE WORLD UNTIE." Her black jeans hung low on her hips, revealing more of the web than usual.

"Hi, spider lady."

Behind the glassed casing were an array of baked goods, all a dollar-fifty and higher: banana-walnut muffins with broad-brim tops, currant scones, peach-preserve Danishes, chocolate-filled croissants, tollhouse cookies big as Frisbees, and a double row of his favorite item, looking like lined-up little buttocks. There was also an assortment of breads, pies, and cakes, but no one ever seemed to buy them.

Steffie favored him with a crooked grin. "Three cinnamon buns, right?"

Ted nodded haplessly. "I should be less predictable, huh?"

From the front table came the little boy's voice: "No, no, that's too much! It's not what I said."

Steffie shrugged. "You should do whatever makes you comfortable."

"*Oh, no, I shouldn't.*" The words were out of Ted's mouth before he realized he'd said them aloud instead of just thinking them. But Steffie didn't seem to notice. For one thing, her boyfriend Chad had just skated in the door with a jangle of bells. He executed a 180° stop just before the counter.

"Surf's up!"

"You know," came the father's voice from the table, "it's not so easy cutting .85 of a muffin. Why don't *you* try it?" The man got up and walked to the counter. "Steffie, can I borrow a knife?"

Chad was eyeing the cookies as he stowed his skateboard under the counter. While Steffie reached for a bread knife, Ted followed the man's route backward to the table, where the boy was seated. He looked like an elf and more than a little familiar, as if Ted had seen his picture somewhere. Suddenly, the boy darted behind the far side of the counter, where a curtain separated the front from the back of the shop. He sat down in back of the curtain and, to all appearances, vanished from sight.

"No, you can't have a cookie," said Steffie to Chad, following his gaze. "I got in trouble last time for that."

"All right," said the man, returning to the table with the knife, "where are you, Alex? Remember what we said about hiding."

For a moment, nobody moved or said anything. Ted thought for a moment about changing patterns and broke the silence himself. "Tell you what, I'll buy cookies for the . . . *boys.*" He stretched out that last word till it was almost two syllables. He reached for his billfold. "You want one, Chad? And that little guy—he's hiding behind the curtain—he can have one, too."

"Um, thanks, man," said Chad, helping himself.

"A cookie!" cried Alex, bursting from behind the curtain like a star attraction. "That's even better than a muffin!"

The father frowned. "I'm sorry, that's kind of you, but not when he misbehaves like this."

"*Please* . . . ." The boy stopped himself and started again. "Please can I have a cookie?"

"No."

"Please *may* I have a cookie?"

"Alex—"

"But I asked nicely." The boy looked adorable when he begged, his button nose turned up ever so slightly.

"That's not the point." The father began to turn away.

At this juncture, Ted made a blunder. "How about if I buy one for him, and you take it with you? He's a cute kid."

The father peered at Ted, then dismissed him. "Sorry, no cookies from strangers. Family rule." He gathered up his and the boy's coats, leaving the decimated muffin on the table, and started hustling his son out of the shop.

"But, Daddy . . . ." The little boy was windmilling his arms about, trying to stop the inevitable.

"I said no." The man stopped at the door and turned. "Look, sorry if we were rude." And they were out the door.

The jingles slowly faded in the growing stillness, which was interrupted by Steffie. "I babysit for him occasionally," she said. "He's cute, but he sure is high-maintenance."

Chad, his mouth full of tollhouse cookie, nodded in acknowledgment. When he finished chewing, he held up what was left. "Hey, this is really good," he told Ted. "You want a bite?"

A few minutes later, Ted was back at his car, still upset but also put out. As with his lost job at Mut Fid, he was slowly replacing hurt with anger. Who were these people to always make him feel so wrong? Rich suburbanites with 1.7 children and 2.5 cars. People raising little boys without understanding their treasure. From time to time, he'd accessed the North American Man-Boy Love Association site, and though he didn't like the philosophy, he was glad to see that people out there were on the same track. Anyway, he'd never raped a kid. Right, right? For one thing, half his fantasies were about him as the boy. He liked identifying with the victim. He laid his white bag of cinnamon buns in the back seat and sat there for a moment, watching the Saturday traffic go by. Each time a minivan went by, the *whoosh* of air rocked his car.

At one o'clock, he drove to the park, or rather, ten blocks before it. He stopped at Garner Street by a house that looked like a castle, complete with a surrounding hedge like a battlement. Who lived in these places, anyway? Guys like Gleason, maybe. Obeying a spiteful impulse, he drew closer to the hedge and surreptitiously broke off a branch. So there. As he headed down the block, he noticed that someone had whacked half the mailboxes in the neighborhood, a prank that he had once played when he was a teenager.

Now he was headed for the park, but at the base of the hill between Delaney and Sycamore, he realized that he was near the remains of the black dog. He detoured just to see it, wondering exactly what he intended this time. He wouldn't stomp on it, would he? A decaying pattern. Up the rise, over to the right . . . but the corpse was gone. Maybe he'd missed it. He looked closer. A dark, greasy blotch marked a spot by the curb, all that was left. Someone must have finally flipped it into a dumpster or called the town's waste disposal unit. He hurried on without looking back.

Now here he was, seated on a bench at Davis Park, Ted Sacks, an employee in the area?—on his lunch break. Or since it was Saturday, maybe he was just enjoying the same sunshine that everyone else in Fairchester was entitled to. In fact, look, he'd brought a sandwich and the newspaper, okay, the supermarket circular, whose pages he ostentatiously shook out so they rippled and rattled in the breeze. The play area showed a dozen kids on the slides and swings and running after each other with their jackets open like flapping birds. The asphalt had chalked-in boxball courts and hopscotch squares, but somehow no one ever played an organized game like that outside of school recess. *I'll* play with you, thought Ted, and if you're good, I'll give you a cookie. If you're really good, you can sit on my face.

He took a large bite of his salami sandwich and chewed vigorously. A few shouts from behind the bushes turned into three boys chasing after a soccer ball. The boy in the lead, with close-cropped curly black hair and a Roman nose, faked to the left, then kicked it hard sideways—past a pudgy red-haired kid on his right and almost into Ted's lap. Ted smiled. They walked right by, one of them showing his middle, soft and white, undoubtedly leading down to a cute little scrotum. Close enough to reach out for. It was the nearness, the idea of availability, that he found so appealing. There'd be others. He finished his sandwich and reached again for the circular that the ball had just missed. Despite the torpor of the past week, he felt a strong erection coming on. Without phenytoin, all things were possible. His penis pressed against the front of his jeans with pleasant urgency. No matter what Dr. Kohlberg had said, his sexual responses always seemed the most natural thing in the world. He needed release. After all the time he'd spent being good, that seemed only fair.

He knew he should go back to the car and do it there. Or better, just drive home and cut loose back in the apartment, the scene of countless unrequited love trysts. But the idea of returning so soon to where he'd just spent so many vague days nauseated him. The privacy of the Blue Room suddenly seemed like a tomb. The sunshine was warm. And the boys were right here, that was the point. He touched his bulging fly and *wanted it now*. Maybe when no one was looking? He giggled, thinking how, at Mut Fid, he would first need to construct a contingency plan. Locate a hot site in Arizona. Build a hierarchy of people to call in case of an ejaculation.

But the fact remained that here he was on a bench with more than time on his hands. Damn it. *Was* anyone looking? Difficult to tell from his vantage point. He stood up and peered both ways, as if he were trying to determine the whereabouts of a small child. No one in the immediate vicinity. So he contented himself with spreading the food advertisements over his thighs and fondling himself. That helped a bit. Maybe a little more. He zipped open his fly. More . . . maybe the Asian kid with the mouth—those sullen lips wrapped around his dick, the kid's thick black hair *fff-fff*-ing against his thighs. *Ahhhh.* The underside of the newsprint was now stained with cum, the pungent salt odor strong in his nostrils. He looked up—and saw a tall woman no more than ten feet away, leading a Labrador retriever and staring fixedly at him.

"Just what do you think you're doing?"

His first instinct was to cover himself, which he did by clasping his hands over his groin in a little dome. But the pages fluttered to the ground, and when he automatically bent to pick them up, his ugly red penis popped out like one of those spring snakes in a can. Shit, fuck. When he tried to zip himself up, he hadn't gotten himself all the way back in, and he caught the skin of his shaft on the steel teeth of the zipper.

"*Aaaah!*" The pain knifed through him. He bolted upright, but that just made it worse—and exposed him fully. He hopped in place.

"*What is going on here?*" The woman kept her distance, yet she was clearly not going to run away. He'd have to get the hell out of here, and fast. But the zipper had formed into a little metal claw that dug into him, and he couldn't run. He couldn't cover himself properly. He couldn't even think of what to say. All he could do was take small, halting steps as he gingerly tugged at the problem.

"That's disgusting!" Though there wasn't a cloud in the sky, the woman carried a stiffly furled umbrella, which she now brandished at him. As if on cue, the Lab snarled a bit, exposing its teeth. And by now, a few other people were beginning to take notice. As he moved back, she bore down.

He managed to spread two limp pages across his front. Awkward as a walking tent. Out of the corner of his eye, he thought he saw someone reaching for a cell phone. Better do something, and fast. Finally, he gritted his teeth, shut his eyes, and yanked hard. The pain level shot up like a gong, but he'd torn free. He zipped himself up—steady!—dropped the circular, picked up the flapping pages, and hobbled off. Not too fast, or that would look suspicious, too.

The dog-woman waved her umbrella again. "We don't want you here!"

"I'm going, I'm going."

"Next time, I'll call the police."

Half a block away, he ventured a look back and saw her figure shrinking in the distance. He fancied he heard a last cry and a bark before he rounded the corner. Two bitches.

Maybe they were still tracking him or something. Once past Delaney Street, already blocks from the park, Ted stopped, refolded the pages as best as he could, and *regrouped*—a verb that Don at work had used a lot. Just to be cautious, he decided to take a circuitous route back to his car. He ended up taking Black Dog Hill, as he classified it, but from the other side of the street. Five more blocks, and he was back on Garner Street to retrieve his car. The castle house and hedge loomed large, as if about to swallow his vehicle. The branch he'd left on the sidewalk was still there, and he thought about whacking a mailbox, just for luck. Then he noticed a father and son playing on the lawn right next door.

The father was kicking a soccer ball toward a boy who let it go by. "C'mon, Alex, chase after the ball," he called out. And then, as the boy bent to pick it up: "Now no hands, okay?"

"Can't we play something else?" The boy looked as if he'd rather be indoors. His narrow shoulders slumped with fatigue and resentment. With a start, Ted realized it was the boy and his father from Price's Bake Shop. Great. Just get in the car, damn it.

But it was too late. With a running start, maybe just to get back at Daddy, the boy kicked the ball into the street. He couldn't have aimed better at Ted if he'd tried. The ball rolled to a stop right at his feet. He couldn't pretend it wasn't there and step over it. Okay. Just get it over with. He picked up the ball and tossed it back at them.

"Daddy, it's the cookie man!" Alex was clearly delighted. "And look, *he* used his hands!"

"Yes." The father muttered thanks, looking annoyed. But when Ted moved toward his car, the father came forward. He said nothing, but stood by as Ted got into the Sentra and started up as quickly as he could. He drove forward sluggishly till he realized that the emergency brake was still on. By that time, the father was at the curb, and I just know he wants my license plate number, thought Ted. The perfect end to the perfect day. Fuck Fairchester.

When he got back to his apartment, good and rattled, he brought in the *Fairchester Guardian* and tossed it onto the kitchen table. Then he went back to retrieve the cinnamon buns he'd forgotten in the back seat. They went on the counter. Only then did he remember that he'd gone shopping, and the bag of groceries was still in the trunk. He had a habit of leaving items there.

Calm down, he told himself. Here, read the newspaper. He bent down to look at the headlines. Pre-election campaigns heating up . . . budget shortfall expected this year . . . oh, *Christ*. He looked closer at the article that began in the lower right-hand corner and continued on page 6. Residents of Bronxville petitioning town officials to relocate a paroled sex offender who'd just moved in. Parallel with Megan's Law, danger of repeat offenses—"This is something we shouldn't have to put up with"—angry mother of two school-age children, joined by other parents in the neighborhood . . . though no legal basis for eviction. A lawyer for Community Watch rebutted points made by the ACLU. "The question isn't whether he's paid his debt to society . . . ." Ted felt his balls crawl into his belly. He hastily finished the article, which also mentioned chemical castration, then folded the newspaper in half, in quarters, and finally in eighths with an effort. He sat at the kitchen table for a while, cycling through fear and anger like some overheated appliance. They're always out to get you; they never let up. He wondered whether being fired at Mut Fid had any connection to who he was rather than how he'd screwed up. Probably not, but you never knew. Eventually, he got up and slowly began unpacking groceries, storing them away as if for a siege. He didn't think he'd be going out for a while. His contingency plan was to take good care of himself, since no one else would.

Later that evening, the computer beckoned, as did the stack of videos and the door to the dungeon, but instead he sat down at the TV room sofa with a book. It was an old copy of *Peter Pan*, given to him by his mother.

He read and read and finally took the book to bed with him, finishing a few last pages while propped up on his pillow. Ah, the Lost Boys. Before he turned out the light, he turned on the sound machine to "waves." (Why was there no setting called "oblivion"?) Then he did something he hadn't done in years: he tucked himself in and kissed himself goodnight.

Chapter 9

When the UPS guy delivered the Re-Flex, I was a little concerned. All these boxes for one exercise machine? Would I be able to assemble it on my own, and where would I put it? Why hadn't I thought of the space problem earlier? In the house where I grew up, someone could have stuck a contraption like that in the basement, behind the door in the furnace room or somewhere in the shadowy mildew of the cellar. But now we had a finished basement with carpeting, fluorescent lighting, and an unused ping pong table, not to mention a hoard of Alex's games. The basement in my lifetime had turned from a site of fear to a place for fun. Hell, maybe I could stash it somewhere in my office and pass it off as an eccentricity.

The UPS guy thrust an electronic clipboard in my face. "Sign here." He looked trim in his loam-colored uniform—all that outdoor work, or maybe just good genes. But what people haven't inherited they can often get by hard work; hence, the Re-Flex, one of those home gyms for work on the abs, pecs, biceps, triceps, quads, and five or six other muscle groups listed in the brochure.

Acting like a pushover certainly hadn't worked with Jane. After the soccer game, I knew that being docile was a mistake. How could I have so miscalculated? Jane was a corporate executive, for Christ's sake, dealing every day with people who wanted to eat her for lunch, and a boss who defined the term *alpha male*. She was bound to go for boldness. Right now, I was working on acting tough—screw you, pal—but it had to be physical as well as emotional. Building muscles would be part of my strong new image. The trick was not to let Alex or Jane see what I was up to.

I had just seen my last patient of the morning, so I was alone for a while. Alex was involved in a winter pageant at school (at Thanksgiving, he'd been chestnut stuffing). Jane was busy working on a deal to market Haldome's vitamin-enriched rice in southeast Asia. They thought so globally and so far ahead that she seemed to be living in a different time zone. Me, I had an hour to kill between now, lunch, and more patients in the afternoon. I'd also planned a trip to Home Depot—a manly place to go. How long would it take to put together my fitness machine? And then how long would it take to get fit?

I reached down to pick up the first box, which was damned heavy. That was reassuring in a way—the product I'd bought was solid metal, by God—but I practically got a hernia hauling it into my office waiting room. I lugged the other two boxes there and sat back in the wicker chair to catch my breath. From the chair, I got a view of a potted rubber plant, a cream-colored wall, and a framed reproduction of Picasso's *Three Dancers*. The wall ended at the double-door that psychoanalysts use to block any sound-leakage from the inner sanctum. Sometimes I wondered what I was missing from the other direction. What did my patients do as they were waiting to see Dr. Eisler?

Not that there was much room to move around. My waiting room was only seven by ten, but through artful arrangement of two chairs, a coffee table, and a halogen lamp, it managed to look complete rather than cramped. I even had a Japanese screen to partition off an alcove where I kept extra paper towels. And that, I realized, was where I could stash my Re-Flex.

I got a box-cutter, a pliers, a screwdriver, and a crescent wrench and set to work. My father had been a banker Monday to Friday and a home-repairman on weekends, the kind of guy who'd tinker with the toaster and either fix it or break it completely. I'd acquired some of his fix-it drive from watching him. I had a similar success rate, too. A replaced garage door pulley went in perfectly, but our dual-tone doorbell had never quite recovered from my tinkering. Somehow in rewiring it, I'd reduced it to a single tone, omitting one sound rather than emitting two. People who remembered the old bell often stood puzzled on the welcome mat for a moment, as if waiting for the other shoe to drop. Just part of living in the suburbs and the joys of home ownership. Alex owned a toy tool chest with two screwdrivers and was growing into the Eisler family tradition.

I cut open the boxes and began lifting out equipment. I started by bolting the main frame to the stabilizer bar. The Re-Flex was bigger than I'd realized, with a three-by-four L-shaped stand and a six-foot-high stan-chion that might have doubled as a crucifix. At least the instructions were clear, with illustrations of smiling male and female androids assembling the contraption and working out on the finished product. Terms like "floating lever arm pin" and "leg extension attachment" didn't faze me when I could see where they fit in the illustration. My memory went back to my father's heyday, when instructions came on fuzzily mimeographed sheets in frac-tured English from Japan. Given such hazy direction, he often put together a lamp or a bicycle with a few pieces left over—and the thing worked fine. Of course, today's computerized technology means a lot less to fix. You can't tinker with a microchip—all you can do is trash it.

That's one reason I liked the Re-Flex, a brute apparatus with all parts visible. For twenty minutes, just inserting and tightening bolts made me happy. When I'd finished, standing in front of me was a shiny black armature next to a stack of heavy rubber weight straps in varying resistance, from 5 to 100 pounds. The foam-pad bench beckoned to me: "Come on," it murmured, "just a few reps on the lats and maybe a curl or two. You know you want it, boy." *Go for it*, chorused Snoggs.

I sat down on the bench and reached for the weight straps, hooking up 50 pounds of pull to the biceps curl. Like so many thirtysomething types, I'd been in decent shape once. I'd even been on the psychiatric softball team at Downstate. But that had been ten years ago. In the interim, I'd grown kind of slack. Now I curled the load upward, a stretched rubber-band feeling in my forearms as I let it down each time. Ten, eleven . . . twelve. Good. Then I rearranged the bench for two sets of Roman chair sit-ups, which hit me right in the pit of my stomach.

I should have stopped then, but I wanted one last exercise to grow on. I scanned the list of possibilities in the brochure: lat pulldowns, bench presses, squats, crunches . . . . I felt powerful just pronouncing them. I finally settled on twelve reps of the butterfly, which consisted of forcing two bent-metal levers from my shoulders towards the middle of my chest—like flapping your wings if you happened to be made of cast steel.

This time I could really feel the strain in my pectorals. I'd probably overloaded the weights, and it was a struggle just to finish one set of twelve. I ended with my chest on fire. And I could tell that it was already later than I'd intended. Even after I stopped, I continued to sweat, and I had no time to change. I staggered down to the basement to find an old blanket we once used to make a teepee for Alex, and threw it over the Re-Flex like a lopsided shroud. The Japanese screen blocked most of the view, anyway.

What exactly was I hurrying for? On Thursday afternoons, I used to drive to Mount Faith Hospital in the Bronx, an escape from the manicured suburbs and the well-mannered neurotics who inhabit them. I had latched onto a Department of Social Services grant for aiding welfare cases too ill to work. I could meet other people in the profession on a working basis, often around a chipped seminar table in Room 123b as we discussed whether Mr. Gonzalez was ready to go off medication. Working at Mount Faith was useful, too, on the rare occasions when I felt someone should be admitted to a hospital. No wait, and they'd cut through most of the red tape. I'd quit half a year ago in favor of paying patients, but I still felt the pull. So all I did before my 1:30 patient was drive over to Home Depot and check out the tools. I bought a needle-nosed pliers because I felt I had to bring back something, and then I came right back.

As I turned back into our driveway, I noticed that our mailbox, a black-metal bread loaf tube, had been whacked. The stanchion on the curb had remained more or less upright, but the box now slanted upward, its mouth ajar like some imbecile gaping at the sky. I collected the mail—bills, catalogues, personal letter for Jane?—and tried to twist the box back onto the level. *Should do that to your clients*, advised Snoggs. *They're off-kilter, too.* I nodded curtly: act tough.

I was done with my afternoon caseload by 5:00. Alex would be carpooled home from an after-school program at the Y by six, and then I had to make dinner. But maybe that was too servile. Besides, Jane wouldn't be home until after the dinner had grown cold. I walked straight into my office and booted up my laptop. I had about half an hour, and I needed to check my e-mail. That much I might accomplish. Without my doing anything in particular, the screen-freeze problem had magically gone away, or so I first thought. In fact, it had turned unpredictable: sometimes I got my icons all lined up on the screen, from ViewPlus to Waste Disposal. Other times, I got a little boy's buttocks in my face. And the image *always* came back on when I tried to access the Web, as if suspecting the worst and punishing me in advance. So what would it be this time? Heads . . . ? No, tails. The crack of doom, I'd taken to calling it. All right, time to act. My father would have taken a screwdriver to the machine. I took a deep breath and phoned tech support.

After listening to an automated menu, I heard the inevitable recorded announcement: "All of our agents are currently busy. Your call is very important to us. Please stay on the line, and a representative will be with you shortly." What's so eerie about these messages, not to mention annoying, is that they share the same wording, as if they all came from one giant company. The clichés of our era are corporate.

After a musical interlude of seven minutes, I was connected to a live person. "This call may be monitored for quality assurance." Great—so my embarrassing problem might achieve wider scope than I knew.

"Hi, my name is Phil. How may I help you today?"

I imagined some clean-cut tech type in Utah. I explained the problem as briefly and elliptically as I could.

A pause, while Phil consulted his manual or filed his nails or whatever they do to pass the time in Utah. "Have you tried shutting off and rebooting the computer?"

"Yes."

"And it keeps reappearing?"

"Yes, yes, yes."

"Well, it may be the sign of a virus. What does the image look like?"

"It appears to be"—no. Let's just forget I called. Wait. "It, uh, looks like twin pink planets. Sort of side by side."

"Sheesh, that's not one I've ever heard of. Do you want to download our latest anti-virus software?"

"I can't download because the screen's frozen."

"Oh, right."

Still, he wasn't entirely stupid. After declining to purchase a new hard drive, I paid Fed-Ex rates for sending a special housecleaning CD, one that should mop up this mess. I turned off my computer and strode into the kitchen. Thinking evil thoughts about pederasts, I began to cut up stew meat.

At a little before six, I heard a car pull up to our house. I looked out the window and saw Alex get out, minus his knapsack. What was he thinking? Luckily, someone reached out and handed it to him. He took it but didn't look back to thank whoever had passed it on, and hoisted it with one strap as if it were a lopsided suitcase. He carried it right by our house, in a reprise of what I'd caught him at last time. The carpool van had moved on. He was halfway down the block, God damn it, when I ran out of the house, waving my meat knife.

"Alex! *Where* do you think you're going?"

He looked up wonderingly, or was it slyly. "Daddy?"

"That would be me."

"Did somebody move our house? It doesn't look in the same place anymore."

"Hmm." I guided him back to our path, pulling on his knapsack strap as if it were a toy balloon. "Home is where the heart is," I proclaimed at our door. Somewhere in the basement is a cross-stitched sampler embroidered with that sentiment. It was sewn by Jane's mother, whose home is still in Norwalk, though she's getting old and her heart isn't what it used to be. She rarely visits.

"I know," said Alex. "You've told me. But this is a house, not a home."

"It takes a heap o' livin' in a house t' make it home—"

"I know, I know! Daddy, stop." He dropped his knapsack on the rug and headed for the TV room. The coat slid off halfway there. "Anyway, I still think the house has moved."

It was time to get tough. "Alex."

No response. I heard the TV go on.

"*Alex.*" Some days, the lag in response is uncanny. It's as if we're each standing in a different time zone.

"Yes . . . ."

"C'mon. Pick up your knapsack and coat. *Now.*"

Another gap, punctuated by a commercial for Hot Wheels.

"*Did you hear me?*" At one point, Jane actually thought he was going deaf, so we took him to an audiologist. At least then we knew the problem wasn't with his ears. Though maybe between his ears. I strode into the TV room. "I'm tired of picking up after you."

"Daddy, you're blocking the screen!"

He looked like a little pasha sprawled on the sofa, and I felt my jaw set into a strange new position. A black, iron rage had hold of me. I put down my knife and shut off the TV. "I. Want. You. To pick up what you dropped."

"Turn that back on!"

"Are you going to do what I said?"

"Not unless you turn the TV back on first."

"That does it!" I rushed at him, grabbing his legs and flipping him over at the same time. Clamping him between my thighs so he couldn't move, I gave him five, count 'em , 5, hard smacks on his rear end. Or I intended to. But then I kept going. I hit harder and harder—so furious at the boy who just. *Whack!* Wouldn't. *Whack!* Listen. When I finally stopped, he was so surprised and fearful, he just looked at me. It was like when a toddler stumbles on the playground and for a second doesn't cry because he hasn't settled on a response.

Then Alex's face collapsed into a bowl of misery. He howled for a quarter of an hour.

I'd never done anything like that before. At first, I tried to sit next to him on the sofa, but he crawled away. When I attempted to apologize, he just bawled louder. "Yoo-hoo h-hit me!"

"I know, and I'm sorry." I reached out to pat him, but ended up patting the sofa cushion instead. He wouldn't look at me. Stupid parent-clichés ran through my head. "It's for your own good." "This hurts me more than it hurts you." "You got exactly what you deserved." Which is to say that plenty of parents swat their kids, but we never have. And this was more than a spanking. It's not a suburban problem. I'd never heard Jerry mention it as part of his book.

All the while Alex was wailing, I wondered who was right. The truth is, when I hit my son, it felt good. A clean and justified act. But it also felt awful—and damn it, why wouldn't he stop crying already? I got up to stalk around, then sat down. My shoulder hurt again, maybe from the exercise that morning. Would it have been better if I'd just gone blindly after Alex? Or announced in advance, "You, sir, deserve a spanking"? In his absentee way, my father had left the disciplining up to my mother, who smacked me just once. That was when I threw a tantrum—and then threw a shoe at her—because she made me stop watching TV.

The sins of the fathers . . . . I don't know what Jane's parents had done. Maybe not enough. Go blame Dr. Spock. Who divorced his wife of almost fifty years to marry someone else. Or was that Dr. Seuss? There's an awful lot of material around to clog and confuse the minds of parents.

Alex had mostly stopped whimpering by now, except for an occasional sniffle. Had I scarred him permanently? I looked for signs of incipient juvenile delinquency but saw only his small, neat features, his lips pressed together in a perfect pink Cupid's bow, his blue eyes focused elsewhere. "Listen," I told him, getting up from the sofa with a *whoomph*, "I've got to prepare dinner. You all right?"

"I . . . guess."

"Good. Mommy will be home—oh, probably late, as usual." I retrieved my knife from beside the TV and began the trek to the kitchen.

"Daddy?" The restored voice pierced me as I tripped over his knapsack in the hallway. "Can I please watch TV again?"

Let's just say we reached a mutually satisfactory agreement. After the knapsack and coat were hung over a chair, Alex got to watch a cartoon about the adventures of a sponge and a starfish. Back in the kitchen, I chopped up meat, potatoes, onions, green pepper, carrots, and mushrooms, sliding everything off the cutting board into a glass casserole dish. Tough guys ate stew, right? Then I dumped a can of cream of tomato soup on top (an old family recipe) and set the microwave for fifteen minutes. While it was cooking, I cracked a beer from the fridge. I would have preferred a good glass of Beaujolais, but it didn't fit my current image. I took a deep swig and brooded about fatherhood.

When the microwave beeped, I yelled out, "Dinner!" No one came. The TV was still blaring, or maybe Alex's selective deafness was to blame. But when I went in to offer him an engraved invitation, the sofa was empty.

Christ, not again. "Alex, are you hiding?" I looked in all the obvious places, including under the sofa. "Alex, *where* are you hiding?" That was when I noticed the basement door was ajar. I descended the stairs two at a time, in no mood for this kind of behavior. Most of the area below was warm and dry, a carpeted room with space for shelves and the ping-pong table we kept meaning to use. But the adjoining room, really a cell, was the primeval cellar. It housed the furnace and the fuse box, and the floor was a cracked green linoleum that mildewed in summer. A frosted casement window near the ceiling was its only contact with the outside world. In fact, the window looked oddly askew—shoved out of place by a frozen ground-swell or something. I'd have to get someone to fix it one of these days.

Alex was huddled by the furnace, wrapped in a ratty beige blanket as if it were a cloak of invisibility. He looked up in disappointment as I came in. "How'd you know I was here?"

I waved my hand theatrically. "Fathers have eyes in the backs of their heads." This was an old line that had beguiled Alex till the age of four.

"That's not true."

I sighed. "Look, why were you hiding? We've talked about this before." I began to pull roughly at his blanket, which didn't look like something we owned.

Alex shrank back. "Are you going to hit me?"

Sure, cackled Snoggs, *give him a hiding for hiding!*

"No," I told him. "Now just come upstairs, okay? Your poor father has worked hard to put dinner on the table."

Jane was late, of course, so we had a stag meal at the kitchen table. "This stew is tough," complained Alex, putting down his fork after one mouthful. "Can I have a peanut-butter-and-jelly sandwich?"

"Try the potatoes or some of the vegetables." Wouldn't you think a kid who's just been spanked would be . . . chastened somehow? Not only wouldn't he tell me about his day, but apparently they'd given out prizes at the Y for some kind of swimming event, and he didn't get any, so could I give him one?

"Why? You haven't been behaving at all lately."

"I know. But I still want one." I started giving him a lecture on award-winning behavior, but he interrupted me. "If I eat a potato, will you give me a prize?"

I banged the table. "No prizes, you understand?"

He shut up after that. For a while, his mouth was full of peanut-butter-and-jelly sandwich. Which I made for him because—because? How much of this family was held together by love, and how much by guilt?

We shouldn't award prizes for either. But when Jane came home at eight, she dug into her purse and handed Alex a model car she'd bought that day. He was ecstatic and went to bed just as Mommy asked.

"What'd you give him that for?" I asked later. I'd set out a bowl of stew, which Jane had tasted before putting her fork down.

"Michael, do I need a reason for everything? I just saw it, figured he'd like it—and he did." She got up to get a glass of wine. "You heard him, right? 'Mommy, I love you *so* much.'"

"I think he's got too many toys already."

"So get rid of some." She waved her fork dismissively: the corporate executive telling a subordinate to dump shares. "Look, this isn't a problem, as far as I'm concerned."

"All right. Have some stew." What's the point in being a tough guy when your spouse has the edge in that department? Or maybe I'd just have to be tougher. Tomorrow.

Jane pushed away her bowl politely but firmly. "Sorry, I'm just not hungry. Harry brought in some sushi at the office, and I nibbled at that all afternoon."

"Harry?" I thought I knew the roster at the office, but every once in a while I realize that all I know is what Jane tells me. "Who's Harry?"

"Harry Laker. The new director of communications. Max brought him onboard a few months ago." She smiled reminiscently, almost sexily. "He's funny. Last week, he made a paperclip chain twenty feet long and lowered it out the window with a sign attached: GREETINGS FROM THE 25TH FLOOR."

I snorted. What a guy. Was he the one she was going to have drinks with—had already drunk with? Linked arms with as she downed a second G&T—Jane could always hold her liquor, which made her one of the boys. Isn't that how office affairs got started?

We needed to talk more. That was the problem. But when we talked, we got into arguments, so maybe we should talk less. I reached over with my fork and took a bite of her stew. She took a few forkfuls herself.

"It's not bad," she allowed. "The meat's a little tough."

"It takes a tough man to make a tough stew. I could have cooked it longer, but I had to make up for lost time. Alex and I had . . . an incident this afternoon. He didn't say anything?"

"He said . . . you . . . spanked him." She spoke slowly, not looking at me, choosing her words carefully. "I was . . . wondering if . . . you were going to mention it."

We'd agreed on no corporal punishment when Alex was born. But when I explained the situation, she nodded. "All right. He can be infuriating, I know. Anyway, he certainly doesn't seem traumatized by it." She ran a hand through her hair, which I noticed was thinning a bit on top. "Know what he said about the car I gave him? That it was his prize for being good."

"Huh." I rested my arms on the table. I leaned forward till I was practically on top of her. "So what do *I* get for being good?"

She seemed to consider my point seriously. Then she asked, "*Have* you been good?"

The question brought me up short. After all my plans to remake myself! I'd been a goddamned angel. But she wasn't supposed to know about any of that, really. Finally, all I said was "Yes."

For a second, I thought she was going to reach into her purse and give me a prize—a small puzzle to solve in between patients, maybe, or a token redeemable for a day of domestic bliss. Instead, she just sighed and shook her head. "Not recently." She left the kitchen. I followed her partway, but stopped. As she climbed upstairs, her hips did that flare and roll which makes almost any woman seductive.

She's been bad, remarked Martin. *What you get for trying to please your wife*, said Snoggs. But I couldn't help myself: I followed behind her, tongue hanging out a yard or more. She was still wearing her blue business suit, but this one had an unaccountably short skirt I hadn't seen before. Blue tights and semi-heels emphasized her sculpted calves, her thighs extending upward to merge into that tight bottom. God, it had been a while. The exercise this morning had gotten my juices flowing. No: even though I was horny as hell, I'd tough it out. While she took a bath, I lay spreadeagled on the bed, clenching myself. Make her beg for it. I just hoped it wouldn't take forever.

*

But two weeks later, I began to think I had competition. In a testosterone-fueled rage, I found myself at my wife's workplace, banging at the gate.

"I don't care if she's not in," I told the receptionist unreasonably. "I'll wait."

"But look, Mr.—"

"Eisler. I'm Jane Edge's husband." *And I have reason to suspect that my wife is having an affair with some gentleman in these offices.* You mean she's boffing him. *Or he, her.* Who said that—Snoggs, Martin, or me, Michael? Probably all three at this point—we were furious. Tough guys don't take things lying down. We storm the barricades. We take the bull by the horns. We get to the bottom of the matter.

The receptionist, a dyed blonde in a tailored jacket and skirt, spread her well-manicured hands. "All right. But she's not due back till later this afternoon. She's having lunch with a client."

"Really."

"Yes."

"Really?"

"I just told you." She twisted around in her seat, probably wondering whether she'd need to call Security. The suite of offices at Haldome headquarters in Manhattan was typical high tech, with a lot of recessed lighting and low-nap carpeting. Poster-sized color photos of rice-planting, coffee-growing, and other agricultural activities around the world hung on the maize-yellow walls. On one side, three clocks showed the time in Tokyo, New York, and London. Hanging above the receptionist's desk like the sword of Damocles was the corporate logo, a vertical wedge of stainless steel letters spelling out "HALDOME," with the "H" bestriding a globe. One press of a button below her desk, I felt, and two beefy guys in dark glasses and suits would emerge through the nearest doorway. They would escort me peaceably but firmly off the premises.

So I backed down a bit. "Sorry. Let me explain."

But where could I begin? Should I mention the phone calls I'd heard Jane receive lately, where she spoke in a livelier voice than in recent memory? And though she often arrived home late, tired and ready to crawl into bed, for the last few weeks she'd come back with a sort of secret inner exhaustion, as if someone had plumbed her depths. Was it necessary to bring up our marital problems, which dated back long before these suspicions? Item #7 on The List stated clearly: "Won't share her inner life." Item #11 said more or less the same about her sexuality. Where *had* this all started, anyway?

Maybe the jump-off point was this morning, when I saw Jerry Mirnoff's new referral for the first time. She was a tall woman with striking good looks, the kind who, when she crosses her legs, draws the attention of all the men in the room. "So tell me . . . " I began as I ran down what little Jerry had told me, and so she began. She was a suburban-based executive for Revlon in Manhattan. Married ten years, school-age child, loved her husband—but thinking of having an affair at work. The guilt was turning her into a nervous wreck. I decided to take her on as a patient, though uneasily aware I was putting my own life on the couch. The description ran so close to my worries about Jane—minus the guilt, perhaps—that I started growing agitated myself. But since tough guys don't turn into nervous wrecks (why must all wrecks be nervous?), I got hot under the collar instead. By the time she described one brief fantasy, I was steaming.

I needed an outlet. Right after my referral departed, I tromped over to the Re-Flex and loaded up the bench press with one hundred pounds of

resistance. Lying on my back and staring at the ceiling, I began the first of
three sets. Up . . . down . . . *uhh!* Up . . . down . . . *uhh!* With the proper
timing, including a one-minute cool-down period, I could fit two routines in
between patients. The first time I'd tried this, R had surprised me by coming
into the waiting room early. "Just working out . . . *uhh* . . . some problems,"
I'd muttered. "Be right with you." But it wasn't apt for the therapeutic situation, and I was thinking of lugging the apparatus, concealing screen and
all, to the garage.

R this morning hadn't helped matters. She was beginning to worry that
her husband was having an affair, and it was all I could do to avoid snap-
ping, "Join the crowd!"

In between R and S this morning, I went at the lateral crossovers with
a vengeance, figuring my tough-guy patient would take a little sweat in
stride. But I was still distracted, unable to concentrate on what S was saying.
Maybe she'd come around. That's what S was saying, I think. A good doctor
always listens to his patients. S had problems.

"Yeah," gestured S from his perch on the chair, since he wasn't the kind
of guy who sat comfortably anywhere, "Sheryl's gone back to the way she
was before. Kinda high-strung and bitchy." He slapped the side of the chair
as if it were an animal he was scolding. "I guess some days are just better
than others."

"Yeah?" I eyed him narrowly. The old Michael would probably have
eased in with "Really? Why do you think that might be?" The Nice-Guy
version might have made sympathetic clucking noises. But that wasn't me,
or at least not anymore. I had my own problems, buddy. I drummed my
fingers a little too hard on my own chair arm.

"Uh-huh." He waited uneasily for me to interject. When all I did was
stare him down, he looked away and began again. "I don't know, maybe I'm
doing this wrong. She says I make her nervous, like she's always waiting
for the other shoe to drop." S tried a smile, which made him look like a
sympathetic ape.

I didn't smile back. "Tough. What're you going to do this time?"

At this, S's face caved in. "*I don't know.*" He fumbled for some invisible object in the vicinity of his pilling black sweater. "She says she's really
gonna leave if this keeps up."

But this morning's confessions of marital infidelity, consummated or
planned, pushed me to the ropes. I imagined Jane sharing a drink with whatsisname, Harry-something, the new director of communications. Funny guy,
Harry. Was he married? Maybe he made dumb-husband jokes. A couple of
comments could lead in all sorts of directions. I stared out the window at the

Steinbaums' bulletproof hedge and saw images in the shrubbery. I imagined
Jane at her desk—under her desk—no, she wouldn't be so crude—maybe
he had an apartment not too far downtown. This was becoming intolerable.
When my last afternoon patient called to cancel, I knew what I had to do.
I left the office early and drove into the city. Alex wouldn't be home from the
Y till almost six, so I figured I had time for a head-to-head confrontation.

Now I was at Haldome on Park and 34th, having spent half an hour
trying to find a space for the Subaru (tough guys don't use parking garages).
I was here, but my wife wasn't. I felt stupid. Meanwhile, the receptionist
was waiting for me to explain. I shifted from foot to foot, wishing I hadn't
done so many leg lifts this morning. Time to improvise. "I, uh, was supposed to meet my wife here at 2:30. Maybe I got the time wrong."

"That's too bad." The receptionist reached for her phone. "I can contact
her assistant, if you'd like."

"Assistant?" I'd forgotten that she had one, but sure, some nebbish
named Bruce? Or maybe he was the one servicing her needs. So of course
she wouldn't talk much about him.

The receptionist was giving me the fish eye again. You're not Jane
Edge's husband, you're just some jerk trying to cause trouble. Why had
I never visited Jane here? We'd planned a lunch in the city once, and a
pre-theater dinner and show, but the lunch had been canceled, and I ended
up meeting her downtown for the theater. Like so many suburban couples,
we didn't enjoy the city together enough, Jane because she worked there,
and me because I never seemed to find the time. And I never called her at
the office. The truth was, I knew very little about what went on in Jane's
daily corporate world. Standard couples counseling advice is to show some
interest in your partner's work.

"Oh, right. Bruce, uh . . . ."

"Bryce Carlson. Let me just give him a call." *And get you out of my
hair*, I could hear her thinking. When I got on edge like this, I became tele-
pathic. While waiting for Bryce to show up, I picked up a copy of *Esquire*
from a low table fanned with magazines. Scanning the table of contents, I
noticed one article in particular: "How to Tell If Your Wife Is Having an
Affair." I furiously flipped toward page 86, where the piece started. The first
sign was odd gaps in her daily schedule. There were six other signs, and I
was just about to continue on page 125 when the receptionist cued me. "Mr.
Eisler? Bryce Carlson is here."

A puppyish guy in a chalk-striped shirt had materialized to the right of
the receptionist's desk. He held out his hand. "Michael, right? Jane's told
me so much about you."

I nodded immodestly. But of course she had. *On the other hand, she's told me nothing about you.* Just what does an executive assistant do, anyway?

"You're probably wondering how I find the time to fuck Jane." No, I lip-read badly. What he actually said was "You're probably wondering where Jane is." He smiled reassuringly: she's out there somewhere! "I checked her planner, and she's with a client from our Singapore group until three. Were you supposed to meet her before then?"

"Well . . . not exactly." I was supposed to confront her like a jealous lover, shoot her husband—no, make that the other way around—and get back to the suburbs in time to greet my son. All in a day's work. "Maybe, uh, maybe we just got our wires crossed."

"Do you want to wait in her office?"

What I wanted was to catch her out. But maybe her office would show certain clues . . . a condom carelessly flung into a corner—all right, not that, but an item in her datebook, or something stuffed in a desk drawer. So I told Bryce, "Sure, let me go in there. I'll wait for a bit, and if she doesn't come back in that time, I can always leave a note."

"Right. Follow me."

I trailed behind Bryce as we navigated through two corridor crossings, with office doors ranging from cozily ajar to shut firmly. It didn't look too biotechnical—where were all the men in lab coats? One invitingly open door was marked "Max Liederman, Executive Chief of Marketing," but he didn't appear to be in. It occurred to me that he was another candidate for the role of Jane's lover, if you can imagine my frame of mind. We ended up at a far door marked "Jane Edge, Vice-President of Marketing." Bryce knocked perfunctorily and walked us in.

After he left, softly shutting the door so it wasn't quite closed, I counted to fifteen. Then I got up for a look around, as if admiring the view. On my way to the windows, I ran my hand wonderingly over the desktop, which felt as slick as it looked. I decided to try out her chair, which was both springy and comfortable. Once I was behind her desk, I took surreptitious glances at everything on it. The Post-its were mostly in Jane's forceful print, with its dominant diagonals. Many were self-explanatory, like "Bring prod. rpt. to Tues. mtg." or "New expense sht. –> Max?," though a few remained opaque: what was "2@4 sess." or "dem/mkt/grp"? The Post-it on the chair simply read "Pick up dry-cleaning. Hyper @ 6." Hyper was the gym where she worked out. The point is, I didn't find any notes on the order of "Set up tryst this aft. w/ loverboy." And I was touched by the family snapshots on the outer rim of the desk, including one of me in a bathing suit some ten years ago, posed by a dune in Cape Cod. I'd forgotten that I could look—or feel—that way. When I checked under her desk, I saw one of those ribbed wooden footrests to massage the soles. I pictured her here, take-charge above but shoeless below. Talking on the phone while wiggling her toes— *that* was the Jane I married.

And inside the desk? I took a deep breath, checked the door again, and slowly eased out the middle drawer. It was full of not much, mostly stationery items and an address book that told me nothing I didn't know. The side drawers were even duller, though one had a suspiciously deflated bag of M&M's.

I knew when to admit I was getting nowhere. Best to decamp, though Bryce was bound to mention my visit, so maybe I should leave a note. Since another Post-it would just get lost in the yellow swarm, I rummaged for a large piece of scrap paper. I found a scrawled-on piece of corporate stationery in the wastebasket and began composing a message on the other side.

Dear J.,

Had a canceled patient this afternoon and thought I'd pay you a visit. Should've called ahead—sorry. Next time, huh?

See you at home.

Love,

M.

I was about to place this somewhere prominently on her desk when I began to have second thoughts about the tone. Too conciliatory for a tough guy? Actually, I found staying in tough-guy mode difficult, even more so than being completely agreeable. Still, the whole note was a bit odd. It needed a better explanation. So I reached into the wastebasket again for another piece of scrap paper, and that's when I found the two ticket stubs to the Museum of Modern Art.

Well, well, observed Martin. *Just like a broad*, said You-Know-Who. "Huh!" I said aloud. The tickets were dated yesterday afternoon, when Jane was presumably at her desk. I visualized a clandestine meeting by the sculpture garden, followed by a cab to—I don't know where, just follow that cab. It leads to sin, just off Broadway. Item to add to the list: infidelity.

I sat down heavily in Jane's chair, ready to write an entirely different note. I penned the opening, which began, "Damn it," and said she had some explaining to do. I told her I'd be at her gym tonight. Because I wasn't a total renegade, I scribbled, "P.S.: I've got a sitter for Alex."

Of course, I had to make some arrangements in a hurry. By now it was past three-thirty. Luckily, I knew our babysitters' phone numbers by heart, and I dialed Mary Rohrenbach from a Starbucks one avenue over from Haldome's offices. One of these days, I had to get a cell phone. Jane had two. Unfortunately, Mary was booked that night. So I called Steffie McHale, and lo and behold, she had a free evening. I told her where to find the spare house key we'd stashed in the garage, and that we'd be home by nine. If she hadn't been available, I'm not sure what I'd have done—maybe driven all the way home to Fairchester, picked up Alex early from the Y, hauled back to the Hyper fitness center, and tried to leave him with a sports attendant or someone while I had my chat with Jane. The logistics of childcare these days make army maneuvers seem primitive by comparison. I don't recall my father getting in such a tizzy over such matters, possibly because he left all the details to my mother.

Anyway, once I'd settled that, I had some time to kill before my date at Hyper. Since I was at Starbucks, I bellied up to the barrista and ordered a double espresso. I nursed it for a while, but you can't take too many sips from an espresso before it's gone. All around me were men and women quaffing and stirring as they typed into laptops, chatted with friends, or just stared out the plate glass window at Lexington Avenue. Most customers looked as if they were there for a long haul: one woman was poring over a chunky paperback edition of *War and Peace*. I didn't have to be headed anywhere until close to six. So I went back and this time ordered a Sumatra venti, a 20-ounce brew of liquid tar that I carried carefully to the armchair where I'd staked my claim.

Even in my rush to the city, I'd brought along the black nylon bag I use in place of a briefcase. It had a pen and pad, some notes on patients, a bag of salted peanuts, and a few other items useful in a pinch, including a tiny halogen flashlight and a half-read copy of *Sister Carrie* that had been a godsend during a two-hour flight delay six months ago—though I hadn't gone back to it since. Luckily, I'd also packed a sheaf of paper that Jerry had sent me the other day, a draft of his latest chapter on suburban stress. "Like your opinion on this," he'd penned across the front page. I took a pull on my Sumatra venti and began to read.

Choking, I spat out a mouthful of coffee onto Jerry's first page. The heading read, "Suburban Affairs." My God, was everyone abreast of this topic but me? I swabbed at the manuscript with a paper napkin, but the angry brown corona remained, so I just read around it. "The motives for an affair seem obvious: boredom with your situation, a desire for freedom, pru-rient curiosity—but always, always, some disconnection from your spouse. The suburbs aggravate this problem because of their own disconnectedness:

people don't work where they live, and the safe but limited surroundings prompt thoughts of being somewhere else, perhaps with someone else, as well." There was a lot more in that vein, interspersed with colorful case histories. One of them, about a woman who chucked it all for her Mexican gardener, I found a little farfetched, but others had the depressing ring of truth. I took another gulp of my coffee, almost down to the bottom now. When I looked up, I caught the gaze of a cute woman in cashmere who was writing in a notebook. Or had been. Now her gaze was wandering, as if she were contemplating an affair.

It was almost time to leave, anyway. I shoved Jerry's chapter into my briefcase. But the megadose of caffeine had given me the jitters, and all that liquid made me practically slosh when I got up from the chair. It was the thick of rush hour in the city as I podged crosstown and downtown to the gym. Everyone seemed to be headed in the opposite direction. I was practically forced to the edge of the sidewalk as hordes of commuters headed back home, their eyes focused on that 5:47 local to Larchmont or the 6:00 express to Fairchester. Clickety-clack, back to the 'burbs, and who were they leaving behind? They all looked so well-dressed, too. Just what were they hiding? I'd managed not to brood too much after my visit to Haldome, but now a caffeine fury began to get the better of me.

Fortunately, the Hyper branch Jane used was on Lexington and 23rd, only ten blocks away. If I'd walked much farther the way I felt, I might have started pushing pedestrians off the sidewalk. Entering the gym through the heavy double glass doors had the effect of canceling out the urban world. A waist-high counter curved around the reception area, manned by a perfectly tanned and toned guy in a Hyper polo shirt. When I mentioned Jane's name, he nodded coyly and told me I could wait inside if I wanted.

She wouldn't be having it off with a fitness trainer, would she?

Get a grip. Since I was about ten minutes early, I decided to take a look around. From down the hall, I could hear the steady chant of an instructor against a post-disco beat. When I looked in, I saw a cadre of fifteen determined women engaged in step aerobics. At the end of the hall were sauna and massage rooms. The main workout room was massive, like a ballroom that someone had strewn with treadmills and exercycles, slant boards and free weights. Some of the apparatuses I recognized as Re-Flex stations grown large, but others looked alien—like a machine with a padded strut that one guy was pushing against with his neck. An indoor running track girdled the walls fifteen feet up. The lone woman jogging up there in a thong-and-leotard combo offered a breathtaking view of—

"Like what you see?" Jane was standing there, holding a gym bag.

"Um, nice place." I didn't want to be on the defensive. She was the one who should be on the ropes. "Where do you want to talk?"

"You know what? It's been a rough day, and I need to work out. I've got an extra tank top and shorts. Why don't you join me on the Stairmaster?"

Tough-guy was back, and he had only one response to a question like that. "Sure." We both went to change. Good thing I'd worn walking shoes. I also took the time to relieve my poor bladder in a seemingly endless stream. And I still felt bloated. By the time I re-emerged, Jane was already climbing ever upwards and not panting at all. In fact, she looked foxy as hell in her sports bra and Lycra shorts. I felt desexed in a baggy tank top and a pair of floppy fuchsia shorts, but I gamely hopped on the Stairmaster next to hers. Too bad I'd done all those leg lifts this morning on the Re-Flex. My thighs dragged, and the liquid inside me was still sloshing around.

"All right," said Jane after a minute, "what did you want to talk about?"

I paused in mid-step. "I don't know how to put this . . . "

"Hey, Jane!" A hunk in gray sweats waved to my wife, who was clearly everyone's property.

"Hi, Ralph." She didn't introduce me but waited until he'd passed on to the leg press machine. "Don't know how to put what?"

Maybe a lead-in would help. I gritted my teeth and stepped up and up. "Look, I know we haven't been getting along so well lately."

"True. What's your point?"

"Well . . ." *up, down, up, down* ". . . that doesn't mean . . . ." I still couldn't say it. *Look, my good woman,* Martin would put it, *are you carrying on with someone else?* I was wondering whether to go with my superego when I felt something else competing for my attention. *Slosh.* "I've got to go to the bathroom. Be right back."

Jane arched an eyebrow. "Okay. If I'm not on the Stairmaster, I'll be up on the running track."

I nodded weakly and made a beeline for the bathroom. Jane was doing laps above me when I returned. For a moment, I thought she'd simply vaulted upward—then I saw the narrow stairway access in the far corner of the ballroom. When I got up there, I began to trudge along, waiting for her to catch up with me. None of my Re-Flex work had done much for my lungs, and I was breathing hard. Two other joggers, a man and a woman, passed me effortlessly.

Jane ran with excellent form, her stride graceful, her arms like pistons that helped propel her forward. I didn't know how long I'd last, so as soon as she reached me, I began to speak. "Look, I know we've been having some problems . . . ."

"You said that." She began to pass me on the left.

"Right, but—." The distance between us was increasing. I had to say something before the gap got any wider. "Jane!" I shouted at her feet disappearing up ahead. "Are you having an affair?"

If the world didn't freeze for a second, at least it hiccupped. The other two joggers swiveled their heads, and a guy on the main exercise floor stopped in mid-arm-curl. Jane slowed down. "*What?*"

I motioned her to come around, and she did, thereby lapping me. Which meant I was behind her yet also with her, something I would think about later that night. Meanwhile, I had a wicked stitch in my side and some explaining to do. Or was that Jane's job?

"All right, what are you talking about?"

I stared at my feet. I didn't want to meet her eye yet. "How about," I began, and stopped. Judging from the exercisers who'd stopped exercising, we had a small but growing audience. It was a see-and-be-seen kind of place. "How about if I drive you home, and we'll talk about it on the way?"

"Fine."

On the way out, I used the bathroom again. The attendant at the refreshment bar offered me fresh carrot juice, Evian, and coffee, but I declined with thanks. We said nothing on the way to the car, which I'd parked all the way over on 10th Avenue. But once we were inside with the doors closed, I started again. "Okay, call me crazy, but I thought you might be playing around."

She snorted. "Where would I find the time?" She gestured in the vague direction of Haldome's offices. "You saw what it's like up there."

It bothered me that she protested lack of opportunity rather than her love for me. Anyway, I still had a few bones to pick. "Sure, enough time to see a museum exhibit on Tuesday afternoon."

"An exhibit? Oh, you mean at MoMA. One of the Singapore execs wanted to see what a Jackson Pollack looked like up close. So I took him." She shook her head. "How'd you know about that?"

"Um, Bryce mentioned it." I hurried on."So these guys from Singapore, what's their connection with Haldome?"

"They're part of a consortium that might help fund our Asian division."

"Ah." It was annoying how everything got explained so plausibly. I thought of one last point, the one that had gotten me started. "And those calls at home, where you're practically giggling into the phone, is that someone from Singapore, too?"

"Huh?" She thought for a moment. "Oh, you mean Harry Laker? He's just a funny guy. We were trying to coordinate our schedules for a meeting."

"So there's nothing between you?"

"Harry?" It was a banner night for snorts. "Harry shares a huge loft with his lover in Tribeca."

"So?"

"His lover's name is Frank."

"All right, I get the idea." I started the engine and began the crawl down 23rd Street. It was still the tail-end of rush hour, and it was going to take us a while to get home. At this point in the film, the repentant spouse is supposed to murmur, "Honey, I'm sorry I ever doubted you." And I *was* sorry about that. But mostly I was sorry about us: that Jane was so busy, she no longer had the time for me or Alex. Or that Harry seemed to have a rapport with Jane that I lacked. As Jerry had written, maybe the problem was disconnection.

"By the way, I didn't realize you had an assistant named Bryce."

"We hired him last August. I know I've mentioned him before." She looked out the window at all the traffic trying to reach the F. D. R. Drive. "You're not jealous of him, too?"

"No, I don't think so. I just never hear about these things."

"You're not supposed to bring your job back with you, isn't that what they say?" Maybe remembering that I did most of my work at home, she added, "Anyway, you're wrong. I tell you plenty. You just never listen. Or ask."

"Hmm."

"Haldome could be peddling hashish, for all you know."

"Is it?" Always willing to learn. "See, I'm asking."

She didn't answer the question. Instead, she sighed. "That's the first time you ever saw my office, isn't it? I wish you'd let me know ahead of time. We could have—I don't know, maybe gone to a museum together."

"I think I'm jealous of Haldome."

"Then get over it. It's what I do for a living."

"And what do you do for your loving?"

"Argue with you? Oh, Michael . . . ." She reached over to tousle my hair, and that helped a bit. We spent the rest of the car ride talking about subjects we did have in common, people we knew. Someone had spotted Francis Connolly entering a Days Inn motel off the Hutchinson Parkway at noon. Cathy Mirnoff was doing better on a drug called Lotronex, but now the Mirnoffs had other worries: Samantha and her girl gang had just been given a warning for shoplifting. Arthur and Mavis had put out an alert for their son Dalton, who apparently had given up hitchhiking but now seemed to disappear for long periods in the afternoon and sometimes the evening, as well. He wouldn't talk about where he went or what he did. Mavis was half-afraid that Andover and Brearley would soon follow suit.

It wasn't as if we were the only family with problems. It just felt that way. And I dreaded what Alex might turn into as an adolescent. I tried to visualize him elongated over five feet, with a hint of a mustache and an angry CD collection, but he refused to remain in focus. We'd just have to wait six or seven years.

We got home by eight o'clock, or would have, but I dropped Jane off at the Fairchester train station so she could retrieve the Volvo. I got back first and heard loud crunching noises from the TV room. I advanced stealthily till I was almost at the threshold. Steffie and Alex were sprawled on the couch, legs entwined, each with a bag of Cheetos between their thighs. "My turn," declared Steffie, reaching into Alex's bag and moving her hand around till he was writhing in tickle-torture. While he was gasping, she calmly removed her hand and ate the one fat Cheeto she'd pulled out.

"Now mine!" But instead of reaching out, Alex put on a Wild-Child expression—the boar, it must have been. He reared up and snuffled headfirst into Steffie's bag.

See, no hands! crowed Snoggs. *Told you he'd learn.*

"Alex!" Steffie reflexively clamped her legs together, trapping his head between her thighs.

"*Mmmphgh!*" cried Alex the boar.

"Hi," I announced. Steffie bolted upright and Alex freed himself, his face crusted in orange.

"Daddy, go away! We're playing a game."

"It was his idea." Steffie began brushing herself off. "He wouldn't eat the carrots he asked for, and these were orange, too—"

"That's what *I* said."

"But then he wanted some from my bag . . . ." Steffie shrugged as only an adolescent girl can: Go figure. Whatever. Look at my midriff.

I could have been annoyed or offended. But it had already been a long, outrageous day, and I was too damned hungry to care. "Go ahead, sit down again." I commanded in my tough-guy voice. "With the bags." They did as I said. "*Now,*" I proclaimed, swooping down with both hands, "*my turn!*"

And that's how Jane found us when she came home a few minutes later.

I removed my hand from Steffie's crotch. The spider tattoo on her hip was showing a lot of web. Alex pointed to the bag between his legs. "Want a fat orange snake, Mommy?"

"Um, no. But thanks." She turned to address me, her expression frosty. "Maybe we need to talk some more. But first, I think I'll drive Steffie home. Why don't you put Alex to bed?"

"No, no, no . . . !" Alex's whining always showed a flair for the dramatic. He bounced off the couch to prostrate himself at Jane's feet. "I want you . . . !"

"That's nice, honey, but I have to drive Steffie." She stepped backwards so Alex couldn't hug her legs. "It's late. You should be in your pajamas already. *And* brush your teeth." Having issued her orders, she escorted Steffie outside.

"Is Mommy mad?" asked Alex after the back door slammed.

"Maybe. She's had a rough day." *Weren't no picnic for you, either*, put in Snoggs.

"Huh." He detached a last Cheeto from the couch and crunched it. "I didn't like my day, either."

"Why not?" I began cleaning up a bit. Crumbs were everywhere.

"Ms. Hardin . . . said I made some 'unfortunate choices' at school today. She said I had to consult with my parents."

"She what?" Only after he repeated it did I figure out what she meant. Ten years ago, it would have been "acted up." In my day, "misbehaved." What the hell—in my tough-guy mode, I felt like calling a spade a shovel, not a digging implement. "So you did something wrong, huh?"

"That's not what she said . . . ."

"But that's what happened, no?" On such a crazy day, maybe my seven-year-old son was having an affair. I made a last, futile swipe at the couch. I'd get the mini-vac later, though right now I felt like making a little boy suck up all the debris himself. "Look, just go upstairs. Brush your teeth. Put on your pajamas. Get into bed. I'll be there in a few minutes."

"But it's still early."

"It's already past your regular bedtime."

"But it's dark up there."

"So turn on a light."

"But—"

I held up a traffic-cop hand. "Just do it. *Now*."

He saved face with his patented slowdown routine, moving away in baby-steps and dragging his feet up the stairs, but he did it. Five minutes later, I was picking my way through the minefield of toys on his bedroom floor. I skidded on a piece of Hot Wheels track and narrowly avoided crunching an orange space capsule. I sat down heavily on his bed.

"All right. Now tell me what happened."

"It was at recess." Alex looked away from me. "I pushed someone. She started crying."

"Huh? Why'd you do that?" My son can be maddening, charming, stubborn, clever, insubordinate, you name it, but he's not violent. He's not even particularly physical, as his soccer teammates could attest.

"I don't know."

"C'mon." I laid a hand on his shoulder, which felt frail inside his Space Ranger pajamas. "There's got to be a reason."

He wouldn't speak for a moment. Finally, in such a small voice that it seemed to get lost in a fold of the blanket, he mumbled, "Because I like her."

"Oh." As I surveyed my son, trying to make his way in this world of males and females, I felt I should offer some advice, but what? *That's tellin' her*, said Snoggs, but I filtered him out. Should I have pointed out that most girls like a boy with push rather than being pushed themselves? Should I have advised him to clean up his act or "To thine own self be true"? In the back of my mind, I recalled a little girl named Linda in second grade, whose red cap I snatched away because she wasn't paying enough attention to me. That changed things, all right—she became furious. I sighed. "Did you apologize?"

"Yeah," he mumbled. "Ms. Hardin made me."

"All right." I got up from his bed. "Just remember, the next time you want to impress a girl, there are better ways to do it."

He nodded as if he'd already thought of a few. "Okay. Good night, Daddy." But when I kissed him goodnight, he reached out to hug me. "I love you," he murmured, and kissed me hard on the lips. I stumbled out of his darkened room just as Jane pulled into the driveway. I hurriedly tromped downstairs in time to greet Jane as she walked through the door. The glint in her eye had muted to weariness.

"Look, about the Cheetos," I began gruffly, "it was just a game."

"I know. Steffie told me." Jane slumped into one of the plastic chairs at the breakfast table. "That's quite a tattoo on her left hip. I don't know why I never noticed before."

"She's also got a boyfriend. Some dork named Chad. He skateboarded into the Pricey Bakery when we were there on Saturday." I told her about the incident with the man who seemed interested in Alex. And the gray car parked right by our yard.

"As long as he brings him back by six." She gave a half-laugh. "No, I shouldn't joke. You can't be too careful these days." She was still in her gym clothes, and when she extended her legs, her Lycra shorts stretched my imagination. "I'm starved. Any more Cheetos left?"

"Lots." I brought over the bag from the counter. "You know, we eat too much junk food in this family."

"Sure. Now give me some."

"Don't you want to know how the game's played?" I held the bag at arm's length.

"Michael, just give me the damned bag."

I pushed it between my thighs, and she reached for a handful, I squeezed my legs together.

"Hey."

"What?"

"It's been a long day." She tried to free her hand. "I got accused of adultery and my husband tried to make out with the babysitter."

"But I explained." Jane tried to yank herself free, but I squeezed harder. At least the Re-Flex had been good for something. "Anyway, it's you I want."

"Let me go."

"Make me."

That was stupid. Jane's hand turned into a fist. The sudden pain spread down to my knees as I hobbled to a chair. "*Aaahhhhh . . . .*"

"Michael, I'm *sorry*. I didn't mean to—all I wanted was for you—let me get something for that."

"*Ahhhhhh.*"

In a minute, my ministering black Lycra angel loomed over me, handing me a baggy with two ice cubes. "That won't help much," I said weakly.

"Give it a chance."

"No, I—"

"*Try it.*" She wrapped one arm around my shoulder to steady me. So I tried it, rather than risk further injury. I found her power erotic—or I would have under less painful circumstances. Did I mention that Jane is half an inch taller than me? Maybe there's not enough room for two tough people in one marriage.

The throbbing didn't subside until after midnight. Jane kindly offered to caress the area, but I declined with thanks. Instead, I lay on my back in bed, worrying how I should change next. You really need a sense of humor to appreciate the situation. Wait, I thought as I drifted off to fitful sleep, I've got another idea. This one'll slay you.

Chapter 10

The Sentra shimmered like a gray cloud by the school playground where the ice cream truck came in the summer. Pooling at the gate, the children separated at the fence and began walking in different directions. Some flowed like water; others sifted like sand. Parents accompanied some of them, but soon drifted away like smoke. The man scanned the crowd until his gaze settled on a blond-haired boy who just had to be named Billy, twisting his head to talk with an Asian kid who flapped his arms like a bird and soared off into the trees.

After Billy got in the man's car, the road disappeared, though a black dog barked at them from behind. But now the man was also the boy, alive in short, sweaty fingers that couldn't be pulled apart. The traffic light turned to blue. They got off the skyway at half past thirteen, and soon they were skirting a stubbly field like an unshaven face, fringed by overhanging trees with hairlike branches. The car went slower and slower until finally it nosed off the road and stopped. The man reached out and laid a hand on his own thigh. Now he was Billy alone, staring helplessly at the hand, big-knuckled and ridged with callus. A knuckle cracked. The forefinger tapped twice, like the neck of an animal extending to explore the range ahead. It crawled toward his jeans zipper.

He had eight limbs, like an insect. He pulled the underwear to his calves, kicking it off in a fluttery motion. Exposed, his penis looked like a featherless fledgling, nesting in its scrotum. His hands—whose hands?—settled protectively over it. He was also sitting on the toilet in the mall, pumping high on the swing, hanging on to the strap in the bathtub. He ran over the black dog with a bump and a grind.

Back and forth, up and down. When the ejaculation came, he started shuddering uncontrollably. Then everything froze into whiteness, and he woke to find himself half off the bed, clutching his pillow.

It was only five in the morning, but he couldn't go back to sleep. He held on a little longer, squeezing his eyes shut and feeling the phantom body plastered against his thighs. Soon gone. He blinked. There he was, back in himself again. The far wall was as close as ever. After staring at his Peter Pan poster for a while, he slowly got up and turned off the sound machine, which had been turned to "Summer Night," emitting a noise like crickets. Without even the artificial sound, the room became truly empty. He had nowhere to go; that was the worst part.

Staring at himself in the mirror, he thought for a minute of becoming someone else: a realtor, maybe, or a banker. He recalled what his mother had once told him: "You like what you're good at, and if you're lucky, you're good at what you like." But what was he good at? The disaster at Mut Fid had shaken him more than he cared to admit. It recurred in other dreams: a little boy flailing away at a keyboard that he could barely reach, a wall of data about to fall on him. His aunt had often told him, "Anybody can make a mistake," and she committed enough of them in the beauty parlor to almost get fired several times. "Don't quit," his father had lectured him, shortly before leaving the family for good. Maybe all of them were right. Anyway, his domain was still the electronic world.

Back in the bedroom, he dressed himself in a pair of ancient green corduroy pants that had belonged to his father. They didn't fit so well, sagging around the waist, but at least they weren't gray. He put on a Hawaiian shirt of black and gold, also a paternal relic, and entered the Blue Room as a new man. Whisking the dust cover off the computer, he booted it up and connected to the Internet. He knew a lot of databases and bulletin boards, and he began to check Web postings for jobs. Too many were for data processing and systems analysis, which he felt above. The online versions of *Disaster Recovery Journal* and *Decision Support Systems* had listings. Another idea: send an e-mail to Don Feinstein about job leads. He'd just gotten into his AOL account to compose a note when he was told he had mail. It was addressed to one of his anonymous addresses, and he knew who it was from even before he opened it, but couldn't help himself. CRater, wondering whether CandyMan had fallen through the hole in his bottom. Before he knew it, he had accessed the 24/7 chat room and was typing to Scumm, who seemed to have nothing but time on his hands.

Not just time but sticky stuff u wanna lick it off?

Scum on Scumm? he typed.

I know what boyz like . . . . Chomper was in the room, too.

Boys like Ben Dover? —Scumm. Then please Ben Dover.

Or Jack in the box, wrote Chomper.

Butt of course, replied Scumm.

What are little boys made of? typed a new guy, LidlBoyBlu.

Ted was considering an answer when he caught himself. He could spend an awfully long time in this non-space and get nowhere. In the end, he'd still be home alone, without a life. *Would he ever change?* He took a deep breath, logged off, and got up to make some more coffee. When he got back, he composed a perfectly normal e-mail to Don and sent it off, wondering what the response would be if he'd written it in boyz chat-room style. In a while, he ventured outside his apartment to pick up any regular mail that might have accumulated. His mailbox had been whacked, tilting up like a prize erection, and he straightened it with care. No mail, though.

By that time, it was after eight. He went back to the Blue Room and busied himself going through some of his collectibles, making a throw-out pile. Chutes and Ladders with one player's piece left, a toy drum without drumsticks, a whistle, seven Richie Rich comic books, a clip-on bow-tie . . . . As with his cubicle at work, it was hard to believe he'd amassed so much, but the evidence was there in profusion, from shrunken clothing and broken toys to love tokens and snapshots. In fact, there was the original Billy grinning upward in a photo Ted had taken on the sly.

When nine o'clock came, he envisioned the start of the workday at Mut Fid, and how the receptionist would give him a smile. At ten, he'd get up to walk by Myra's cubicle—and suddenly he had an idea. Rummaging around the cardboard cartons he'd brought home from Mut Fid, he located an office directory and dialed a number.

"You've reached," began the automated voice-mail system. "*Myra Conner*," put in Myra's recorded voice. "Leave a message after the beep," the male voice-mail voice continued. "If you need to speak with an operator, press zero now."

Ted would like to have spoken with Myra right now, but he left a carefully worded message after the tone. In a surprisingly short time, she called back. He picked up on the second ring.

"Hello."

"Ted?" The syllable hung in space like a balloon waiting to be popped.

"Myra. Thanks—thanks for getting back to me." He paused. He could see her now in her cubicle, her kind face angled toward him. "I was just . . . thinking about you."

"Really? That's nice." She made a sound almost like a chuckle. "I think about you sometimes, too. So how's life after Mut Fid?"

"Oh, it's . . . not bad." *No, it's awful*, he mouthed to himself. "I'm doing some freelance work, pursuing a few job opportunities." They talked for a few more minutes, at the end of which Ted cleared his throat and took his life in his hands. "Listen, I was wondering . . . ."

"Yes . . . ?" She seemed almost to know what was coming.

"I was wondering if you'd be interested in getting together. For lunch, I mean."

"Sure, why not?" Her warm voice eased through the constricted line, unfreezing some blocked area in his brain. "When and where?"

Those were questions he hadn't considered. Today at Burger King wouldn't do, he knew. But Myra was able to help him out. They eventually settled on Thursday, noon, at a restaurant called Elena's, not too far from Mut Fid headquarters.

"Well! I'm looking forward to this event." She gave another semi-chuckle. "So tell me, how will I recognize you?"

Ted thought a moment. "I'll be the one in gray slacks," he said. He looked down at himself. "Or maybe green corduroys."

Myra laughed at that, pleasing him immensely. He hung up soon afterwards, but for a while didn't move. He felt potential gathering inside him, like a dry cell recharging, providing the capability for some future force.

Lunch at Elena's on Thursday. It was a start, anyway.

*

Ted arrived at Elena's fifteen minutes early and just sat in the car, peering out at the blue-and-white awning of the restaurant and biding his time. In fact, he had driven around for a while beforehand, having left his apartment at eleven to make sure of being punctual. He had brought along the latest *Fairchester Guardian* as part of a vague plan to connect more with the community. But the newspaper remained folded up on the front passenger seat like an unopened invitation. He was too nervous to read. For the tenth time in ten minutes, he cracked each of his knuckles twice. When his new Casio watch showed 11:59, he got out of the car and made his way into the restaurant.

The lighting inside was subdued, with a black-clad hostess hovering by a desk and asking if he had a reservation.

"Um, no, I don't think so." He gazed into the seating area and counted fourteen tables but no diners. A lone waiter at the back of the room was counting silverware. For a second, Ted felt the victim of a put-up job.

"That's all right," smiled the hostess. "I think we can accommodate you. How many in your party?"

"Oh. Two." He looked over his shoulder. "But I'm a little early. She may not be here yet."

The hostess comprehended everything with the briefest of nods. "Not a problem. Would you like to be seated now or have a drink at the bar while you wait?"

This was a situation he hadn't anticipated. He didn't care for a drink, but if he went ahead and sat down at the table, it might seem rude. Luckily, Myra showed up at this point, entering as if on cue. He recognized her slate-blue coat, though she looked somehow different from how he remembered her.

"Ted!" She came forward and gave him a peck on the cheek, which surprised him. "I figured you'd be absolutely on time. I hope I'm not late."

Ted's watch showed 12:00. "No, you're fine," he said seriously. "Let's go in."

Elena's was a white-tablecloth joint, as his father used to say. Not quite uncharted territory, but Ted hadn't been to a place like this since an ill-fated date in high school. The hostess led them to a spot near the rear. "Would you like to check your coats?" she asked.

"No," said Ted just as Myra said "Yes." They exchanged glances. "Sure," he corrected himself as Myra changed to "That's all right."

Myra shrugged humorously. "I guess we're fine as is," she told the hostess, who, with a smile of complicity, gracefully withdrew. Ted hung his green windbreaker on the back of his chair, with the empty sleeves hanging down like an extra pair of arms. Myra neatly folded her coat in thirds and lay it next to her on the seat cushion. Now that she had her coat off, he could see a slightly different image from the systems analyst in the corner cubicle. She was wearing a short navy skirt and an open white blouse, sharply reined in by a broad black belt with a silver buckle. The amethyst eye shadow she always wore, but it was her hair style that had really changed. Growing up with a mother and an aunt in the beauty parlor business, Ted had learned something about what his mother termed "coiffure." Myra's usual mousy bangs had been highlighted with accents of lemon and swept to the sides. It didn't look bad, but it required a mental readjustment on his part.

Then again, he had also made a few minor concessions. Rummaging in his closet, he had come up with a blue button-down shirt, marked only by an irregular brown stain that was probably just coffee. When the shirt was tucked into the loose green corduroy pants, which it mostly was now, you could barely see it. The reversible belt that he'd purchased at the Westfield mall roughly bisected the blue and green regions.

For a moment, they sat as stiffly as the folded cloth napkins on the table. When the waiter came by a moment later, he handed them lunch menus handwritten on one page.

"Would you care for something to drink?" he asked them. He was young and blond, but with a mustache that Ted thought was a mistake. "Sure, it's more festive." Myra glanced at the wine list. "I'll have a glass of the Oakwood Merlot." She grinned at Ted. "How about you?" He shrugged in what he hoped was a devil-may-care fashion. The windbreaker behind his back echoed the gesture. "Why not? I'll have the same." All he really wanted was water, but he did wish to please her, and the symmetry of the double order felt right. So what if he rarely drank? He was off his meds, and this was an experiment.

"I like this place," Myra confided, leaning back after the waiter had gone. "It's chic but not fancy."

"I know what you mean," said Ted, who didn't. He'd been getting ready for this lunch since Monday when he'd called her. Why shouldn't he eat out with a friend? Without admitting it to himself, he felt the occasion was a chance at normalcy. In the past few days, he'd been altering little aspects of his home life. He'd reorganized the boxes and bags in the Blue Room and already thrown out a lot. Since a therapist long ago had taught him "A new broom sweeps clean," he bought a dust-buster and used it to vacuum everywhere, even the Dungeon. On Wednesday, he'd gone for a morning walk that might one day aspire to a jog. It was just four circuits around the block, but it fulfilled a pattern. He regularly read the *Fairchester Guardian*, though he hadn't yet got to this week's issue.

Now he scanned the menu anxiously, wondering what to order. His tastes ran toward the extremely plain: omelettes, hamburgers. Would it be all right to ask for a sandwich? He felt he should take advantage of a place like this, and he didn't want to impress Myra as a hick. As the waiter approached with their wine, Ted fastened on a pasta dish that he hoped was close to Spaghetti-O's. Myra ordered the grilled chicken salad.

"So," announced Myra as she lifted her glass, "to life after Mut Fid."

"Right." He took a sip to mimic hers. It wasn't much to his taste, but he could handle it. Then he thought about what she'd said. "Are you thinking of quitting?"

"Me? Oh, only every other day." She made a face. "You know how Gleason is, though he's not the worst. Anyway, maybe it's different if you're a systems analyst. I know Solly's looking around. The work there is just so *deadening*."

"Oh. I . . . liked it."

"To each his own." Myra took a larger sip of wine. Ted again followed suit. They both paused again, and Myra shifted in her seat as if to regroup. "Well." She grinned. "*You* look a lot better since you left."

"I do?"

"Definitely." As her grin widened, she leaned forward, her thick waist pressing against the edge of the table. Her breasts strained against the front of her blouse, her bra line visible. Ted noticed these details with neither arousal nor distaste. In fact, she looked somewhat like his mother, an aspect he found comforting, but imbued with the predatory look of his aunt, which unsettled him. His aunt had not been a nice woman. Unconsciously, he shifted backwards and found his arms embracing the sleeves of the windbreaker.

Time to change the topic, maybe. To Myra herself, for instance. He knew so little about her, he suddenly realized—so little about anyone, really. It was as if everyone in the world lived in labeled metal containers, and he had no way of penetrating, no idea of what was inside. He had to start from outside. Her full, soft lips and kind brown eyes were a good place to start. "You look nice, too," he told her.

"Why, Ted Sacks, you say the kindest things!" She said this with a false southern twang, accompanied by a giggle.

"It's the truth," he said with some truth, though admiring his own diplomacy. Unsure of how to proceed, he decided to start at the beginning. "Where were you born?"

"Me? Chappaqua."

"What school did you go to?"

"You mean college?" Her eyes widened. "SUNY at Purchase."

"What was your major?"

"Communications, actually—but why all these questions?"

Ted considered the matter. "Because I want to get to know you better."

Her expression softened. "Okay. But you have to tell me about yourself, too." For the next few minutes, they swapped data. She was thirty-four, currently unattached, and lived in a studio apartment in Mamaroneck. She liked old black-and-white movies, Chinese food, and going to the beach. Trying to come up with some equivalents, Ted ventured that he was thirty-three and single. He mentioned his garden apartment in Fairchester and his fondness for videos. Thinking of his recent perambulations around the block, he added, "I've just started an exercise routine in the mornings."

"Really? Good for you. I try, but"—here she sighed heavily—"it doesn't last." She patted her plump upper arms, snugly encased by the sleeves of her blouse. "The problem is, there's too much of me."

"That's silly," he told her. "You're just right for who you are. You're Myra."

"Hmm." She stared at him curiously, as if pondering what lay behind that statement. *Your move*, she seemed to say, though all she did was purse her lips.

Ted himself wondered what to say next. Should he start asking more questions? Luckily, their food arrived at that point, providing a welcome distraction. Myra's salad was something to look at, a loosely woven circle of greens with four strips of chicken laid lengthwise on top. Ted admired the symmetry, which Myra soon violated with a stab of her fork. "Mm, this is good. Would you like some?"

"Um, no, thanks." He was uneasily appraising his pasta, which consisted of slim strands coated in a green-flecked sauce. The spaghetti was too thin for his liking, and the sauce didn't look at all tomato-ey. Still, he had ordered it. He twirled some on his fork, rather skillfully, he thought, and took a bite. It tasted green. And the spaghetti wasn't soft enough. Back in college, a guy in the dorm who cooked for himself used to fling a strand of spaghetti at the wall: if it stuck, it was done. This stuff wasn't done. He took a few more bites, then put down his fork. "Here, have some of mine," he offered gallantly.

"I shouldn't—all right, just a taste. Here, you can put it on my bread plate. But then you have to try some chicken." Myra directed the exchange with mock gravity. Though he'd refused just a moment ago, Ted was now grateful for the handout. At least it was plain chicken, though not as good as the chicken strips from Popeye's. He reached for the bread basket and put two wedges from an Italian loaf on his bread plate. He slathered them thickly with butter, ripped off a piece, and began to feed. In preparation for today's lunch, all he'd had this morning was half a frozen waffle.

"So," began Myra when he was halfway through the bread basket, "where are you trying for jobs?"

Ted looked up from his latest hunk of bread. Actually, he'd done little but start a list. He had yet to send out a résumé, and Don hadn't replied to his e-mail. On the one hand, he desperately wanted a means to fill his vagrant days, and he would soon need some money. But he rather doubted his prospects and in his gloomier periods thought he might be reduced to data processing. On the other hand, he hadn't risked rejection so far and could therefore enjoy his potential. One place he was considering happened to be Mut Fid's main competitor, Trust Consortium, and he mentioned the name to Myra.

"Really?" She put down her fork and sat up straighter. "That's a place I've thought of myself."

He tried to sound nonchalant. "It's possible I might be interviewing there."

"Well, in that case, you could use my help." She cocked her head in assessment. "I can act as your clothing consultant."

"What do you mean?"

"Ted, Ted . . . " she sighed. "If you're going to interview at Tru Con, you shouldn't, well . . . "

"Shouldn't what?" She was beginning to alarm him.

"Okay. Here." Her belly pushing against the table, she reached across the short divide between them. With a gentle but firm touch, she tucked down one of his collar ends that had been sticking up like a rabbit ear. Up this close, her eye shadow looked pasted on, and he could smell her breath in a whiff of stale mints. But he was quite taken by the smooth white skin of her forearm, exposed through the tug on her blouse sleeve and an inch away from his cheek. Her action was pure and yet strong, pulling him in, straightening him out. She lingered in front of his vision a moment longer, her hand resting on his shoulder, then withdrew.

"It's not just the collar, you know," she continued as if she hadn't laid a hand on him. "Please don't be insulted, but I think that shirt is stained."

"Hey, I take my clothes to the laundromat."

"Hm. How often?"

"Every three weeks." Ted was definite on this point. It was every third Saturday.

"Men . . . ." She rolled her eyes theatrically. "Anyway, all I'm saying is that you're a handsome man, and you should play that up. Who knows? The person interviewing you at Tru Con might be a woman."

Ted rather doubted that—the whole enterprise, he reminded himself, was iffy—but he wasn't immune to compliments. He exposed his teeth much wider than in his usual crack of a smile and sat up taller in his chair. When Myra reached for her glass of wine, he picked up his. Through the reddened lens of the glass as he drank, he saw her head weirdly distorted and on fire. Some of the wine went down the wrong way, and he started to cough. Trying to swallow just made it worse.

"Ted, are you all right?"

He tried to choke out that he was fine, but the words got caught in his throat. Myra got up from her chair, but before she could pound him on the back, he managed to clear his airway. Still, he was touched by her solicitude. He took a careful sip of water and thanked her.

The waiter appeared a moment later to ask how the food was. "Fine," answered Myra, and Ted nodded grudgingly.

"Would either of you care for dessert?"

"No," said Ted as Myra said "Maybe."

"I really shouldn't," said Myra as Ted said "Okay."

"Why don't we split something?" she suggested, and after a brief consultation with the waiter, ordered a slice of chocolate mousse cake. Ted also
asked for coffee.

Myra arranged her hands as if laying her cards on the table. He liked
her fingers, which were small but well formed. He recalled how they flew
over the keyboard. "How long have you been living in Fairchester?" she
wanted to know.

"Me?" asked Ted, as if several other men were seated behind him. The
restaurant was still mostly empty. "A little over half a year."

"Do you like it there?" she asked in a tone implying he shouldn't.

"Oh, I don't know . . . ." He thought of the streets full of houses that
would never include him. "I think it's better if you're a family. It gets lonely
sometimes."

"I know *exactly* what you mean."

As her hand slid forward, he thought to ask about her nephew. The
image of the boy wrapped around a fire pole had stayed with him.

"Oh, Donald? How sweet of you to remember! I just sent him a card
for Valentine's Day. Of course, he's a little young for me." She giggled,
a completely different sound from her throaty chuckle. When her hand
moved again, his involuntarily darted the other way and knocked over his
wine glass.

"Sorry, sorry . . . " he mumbled, getting up to dab at the spreading stain
with his napkin.

"That's all right." She touched his arm. "Next time, we'll just have
club soda." When the coffee and cake came, he busied himself stirring the
right amounts of milk and sugar into his cup. "May I?" said Myra, and
began picking at the cake. Ted joined her, but only to be polite. He did like
watching her eat. Those mobile lips, those full cheeks. What if he were the
fork in her hand, Ted imagined, moving toward her mouth?

Finally, Myra checked her watch and wistfully remarked that she had to
get back to the office. Ted nodded, depressed by having no place to go. His
garden apartment seemed like a desert island. He had a sudden fantasy of
her taking him along, perhaps shrinking him down to doll size and packing
him in her handbag. He could be one of the doohickeys on her desk. When
the check came, he offered to pay.

"You're the one who's unemployed. I should spring for this one." When
he protested, she shushed him. "No, I enjoyed this."

"Me, too."

"Then we'll have to do it again, and soon. Two lost souls in the suburbs." Before they parted, she ripped off a piece of Mut Fid notepaper from her handbag and scribbled her home phone number on it. "Call me."

Chapter 11

"Stop me if you've heard this one," I told Alex, interposing myself between the couch and the TV. It was the best way to get his attention when he was watching. That is, short of laying hands on him, which I was not, repeat not, going to do again. Cross my heart and hope to die, stick a finger in my eye. Or is it "needle"? Anyway, he laughed when I told him that rhyme. Only now he wasn't listening again.

"*I said*, stop me if you've heard this one before."

"How will I know until I've heard it?" He leaned to the right in a pathetic attempt to see around me. The Cartoon Network was replaying some old *Road Runner* shows, which I've never thought were that funny. Too predictable. Like other adult males I've talked with, I'd like the coyote to shove a stick of dynamite up the road runner's tail-feathers one day and have done with it. Alex and I agreed that Bugs Bunny rated a lot higher. But TV was better than no TV, I guess, and nothing much else was on around weekdays at noon. Usually at that time, Alex was occupied being bored in school, but today he was home sick with a cold and a fever. Wadded-up tissues that I kept asking him to pick up littered the area around the coffee table. Since I was technically home while at work, I agreed to watch him as Jane gratefully flew out of the house that morning.

"Don't worry yourself sick!" I told her when she strode toward the Volvo. My new strategy was to be funny. Mr. Agreeability and Tough Guy were all very well—all right, they weren't. My Re-Flex was now in the garage, flanked by similarly unused bicycles. Anyway, the main element missing from our recent relations was humor. That was something we'd once shared, witty asides and recent jokes we'd heard, and I wanted it back. I gave her a mock salute as she shot out the driveway, already perilously close to missing the 8:07. She didn't return the gesture, but I hoped she appreciated it.

My son, on the other hand, was a captive audience. Yesterday, I'd arranged his afternoon pretzels into a smile face, and when he objected, I turned them into a frown. I recited a comic poem by Ogden Nash about a crocodile who eats a professor's wife. "A cold like that," I chided him gently him when he blew his nose for the tenth time in two minutes, "is nothing to sneeze at."

"I'b biserable," he mouthed, both nostrils temporarily clogged.

"Laughter is the best medicine," I told him, echoing my father, who used to quote bits from *Reader's Digest* around the dinner table. I tried to recall some of the chestnuts the old man was partial to. "Let's see . . . what do you call a steam engine with a cold?"

"I don't care." Alex blew his nose through another tissue and dropped it on the floor.

But he mostly liked Funny Daddy, or he would have if he were feeling better. So I persevered while still blocking the TV. "C'mon, think. A steam engine with a cold." I smiled winningly. "Want a hint?"

"No. *Ah . . . ah-choo!*"

I clapped my hands. "That's right, *ah-choo* choo train."

"Oh." He looked puzzled for a moment. "Where are you getting all these jokes?"

I waved my hand to indicate ubiquity. "Around." Actually, now that my browser was fixed, I'd gotten most of them off comedy Web sites. "Some I've heard recently. Some I heard when I was your age."

"How many do you know?"

I waved my hand in a different direction to show infinity. "A lot. I thought I'd cheer you up while you're sick."

"Thanks. It does help, a bit. Now can I watch TV?"

Not the audience reaction I wanted, but I squelched an impending scowl. Instead, I smiled genially and withdrew. That was the point, really: not to slay 'em in the aisles but just to make light of things. If our situation wouldn't change, at least we could laugh at it.

Put that way, it sounded like therapeutic advice. The results with my patients had been mixed. When I'd seen R yesterday morning, she'd been steeped in gloom. She slumped so low in her seat that I wanted to be like Alex's teacher Ms. Hardin and chant, "Posture, posture!"

"Dwight and I had a huge argument last night," she sighed into the chair. "He thinks I'm a lousy housekeeper."

"What brought that on, do you think?"

"It was early. He got home around five-thirty, and I didn't have time to clean the dishes. He grabbed a glass from the sink and poured some scotch in it." She paused a beat. "There was still bourbon in it from the night before."

Normally I would have repressed a smile. This time, I chuckled. R looked narrowly at me, which should have been a warning.

"Then, when he walked into the hallway, I'd left the vacuum cleaner there, and he tripped on the hose."

"You're kidding." I thought of the rich comic possibilities buried beneath this domestic dust-up. "That's great."

"What do you mean? He smacked into the wall. Then he started yelling."

"Hmm. Let me put it another way. What if he'd slipped on a banana peel?"

"Then he'd have blamed me for—I don't know. Mismanaged fruit disposal."

"Hey, good line."

"That's easy for you to say. You weren't there." Her lips compressed into one line, and it was hard to pry them open after that.

So I varied my approach with S. For one thing, ever since he'd flinched under my tough-guy act, I felt we'd reached a new plane of disclosure. But when he started complaining about what a rotten housekeeper Sheryl had become, I didn't sneer. I didn't smirk (though it was hurting me not to).

"Yeah, she's pissed off I won't hire someone to come clean." He rolled his eyes. "So now she's, like, withholding. Sexual favors, I mean."

With some women, it's no favor, put in Martin, a voice I hadn't heard from in a while. Snoggs pointedly said nothing.

"You don't find this humorous, I take it."

No one could scowl more heavily than S. "What's so goddamn funny?"

"Nothing, that's the problem." I laced my fingers over one knee. "Only sometimes a little humor helps. You know, like 'Women—can't live with 'em, can't live without 'em.'"

"'S'what my father used to say, and he went through three wives. Anyway, what's so funny about that? It's true."

Now it was noon, time for me to quickly make lunch for two and get back to the office. I decanned and heated up some chicken soup that I knew Alex wouldn't eat, but it was the right parental move. I was just troweling some hummus on pita bread for myself when I got a phone call from Jerry. As usual, he wanted to chat, but seemed a bit rushed.

"Look," I figured out, "I'm one of your ten-minute breaks between patients, right?"

"I . . . wouldn't put it that way. How's that referral I sent you?"

"You should hear all the nasty things she said about you."

"What? Oh, you're kidding."

"Right, I'm kidding." Put pita on plate. "So how's Cathy?"

"Same."

"That's shitty."

"Very funny. Look, is this a bad time to call?"

"Sorry. It's just that Alex is home sick. Never mind. Tell me what's going on."

"Did I tell you that Samantha's been grounded for a week?"

I guessed for something like shoplifting, but this was another variety of theft, stealing school lunches. She even had an accomplice, another girl who acted as the lookout while she rifled through the bags. She didn't eat what she took, but sort of flung it around at recess. A lot of the kids were afraid of her and wouldn't report her. But one boy did. Now Samantha had to go home right after school every day and make cookies for the children whose lunches she'd vandalized.

Funny? I didn't press the issue. For one thing, Jerry was also obsessing about his book, which lacked a suitable ending chapter. "What do you think about closure?" he asked anxiously.

"I'm in favor of it." I eyed my sandwich, which lacked only a tomato slice to be complete. "Look, I gotta run."

"Yeah, me, too. Catch ya later."

We hung up together. Should I have told him the one about the little farm girl and the traveling salesman?

The soup was boiling over, so I dumped it into a plastic bowl decorated with roosters. 12:30 already. I brought the bowl into the TV room for Alex, crying out, "Hot soup, hot soup!" I also brought an apple cut in an odd shape, each slice resembling grinning lips.

"What is this?"

"It's a happy apple. If you eat some, it'll put a smile in your cheeks."

"Hmm. That doesn't make sense." But he reached for a piece anyway, and when I looked in a few minutes later, I saw him feeling his face curiously.

After the pita and some coffee, it was time to return to the office. When I told some jokes to my after-lunch patients, they reacted as if I'd given them a rare treat. One told a few himself. Fine—I'd made a few individuals feel better today. In between, at a little before 2:00, I rushed back into the house to check on Alex. He was still on the couch, having switched back to TV. For some reason, he was watching upside down. "You doing all right?" I called out, on my way to the bathroom.

"I'b sduffed ub again."

"Sitting that way makes it worse, not better!"

"Oh." But he didn't move. At least he wasn't arguing. When I emerged from the office at 3:00, I checked the TV room. No Alex, just a bowl of cold soup and a ring of tissues. He wasn't in his room, either.

It better be funny, I thought. This time, I went right down to the basement, where I noticed the blanket had returned to the corner by the furnace. A box of cheese crackers and a flashlight anchored either side. Like camping out indoors. In the middle was an elongated lump that could be a small boy. All right, if he wanted this to be his hideaway, maybe it was someplace he needed to escape from parental squabbling. Once, when Jane and I had been bickering about—what was it? toilet paper, one- or two-ply?—I looked over at Alex, who was reading a book and had silently put his hands over his ears. This is how you form defense mechanisms as you grow up. They turn into neuroses when they persist long after the need has passed: if your thirty-year-old friends are quarreling in front of you, say, and your automatic reaction is to feign deafness.

But Alex wasn't in the basement. When I gently prodded the lump in the middle of the blanket, it gave without comment. Further investigation revealed a pillow and an olive-drab knapsack, which was packed as if for an overnight trip. The contents included a jack-knife and a dog-eared paperback of *On the Road*. Unless Alex had lately taken up Kerouac, we had an intruder in our house.

At first I felt violated, no other word for it. Someone, damn it, had broken into our unhappy home. Even odder: he'd entered repeatedly and stayed for a while, like some mysterious boarder. The cellar window had clearly been jimmied, maybe explaining those creaks at night. And all for what, to find someplace to sleep? I started looking through the knapsack for any identification, and it didn't take long. Sewed on an inside flap, sleepaway camp style, was a nametag: D. SCHRAMM. So that accounted for Dalton's periodic disappearances that Mavis had mentioned. Typical, I guess, though not every alienated adolescent goes this far—and some go a lot further, carrying guns to school. Looked at from that vantage, Dalton's behavior hardly seemed like a crime at all. I recalled the last time I'd seen him: a sullen presence stalking away from a dinner table, a wisp of an adolescent mustache accentuating a dark frown. I wondered whether Andover intended to imitate this latest stunt, if he even knew about it. And Brearley? Girls usually didn't behave this way, and I doubt she even cared.

The knapsack contained a banana, a pocket knife, a cigarette lighter, a pen, and a notebook with some free verse he'd written called "Against Parents." Of course, having a stepmother like Mavis Talent couldn't be easy:

treating the family as a flawed work of art and more concerned about her clay pots than getting dinner on the table, while Arthur closely watched the stock market. By this point, I had swerved from wanting to call the police to wondering whether I should let anyone know at all. What the hell, who was it hurting? *It'll be our secret,* I could hear myself (or was it Snoggs?) saying to the frightened face of Dalton, the ratty green blanket pulled up to his neck. I carefully reburied the pillow and knapsack.

And what about the parents? sniffed Martin. *Don't they have a right to know? Come to think of it, where's* your *son?*

"Alex!" I stumbled up the basement stairs two and a half steps at a time. "Where are you?" I ran into the garage, smashing my shin on the Re-Flex, right where the anonymous Stinger soccer player had nailed me during Alex's last game. I hopped around in pain for a minute and finally had the wit to check the last place I'd have guessed.

In my office. Seated in the waiting room, reading a magazine. He must have gone in just after I came out, like the old switcheroo in a gag routine.

I advanced into the room. "Very funny. What? Are you doing? In my office?"

He looked up at me. "I'm sick."

"I know, I know. But do *you* know that I've just spent"—I checked my watch—"almost twenty minutes looking for you?"

"Sorry." He blew his nose. "But I'm not feeling so good."

"So?"

"Don't you help sick people?"

I sighed. "Alex, you know very well—"

"It was a *joke*, Daddy."

"I see. Now go." I pointed to the door. "But don't get lost."

He got up. "I just wanted to find out what it felt like. To be one of your patients, I mean." He lowered his voice as he turned away. "You care more about them than about me."

"Alex!"

"What?"

"You really believe that?"

He sniffled. Hard to tell whether it was the cold or a stifled sob. I remember once, when my busy banker father didn't pay any attention to me, I wanted to go hide in the vault where he worked. Not that I ever did, but Alex might've.

"Okay, get on the couch."

"Why?"

"I'm going to treat you. Just like one of my patients."

"Really?" He lay down full length on the couch, this time on his belly.
"Um, is this going to hurt?"

"It shouldn't." I stepped back to my Eames chair, favoring my left leg
because my right was still throbbing. "All right. Now tell me what you
dreamed last night . . . ." I went through the whole Freudian routine, from
free association to dream analysis. The one dream memory he dredged up
featured him as Daddy, disappearing down a hole that led to an office where
Mommy was waiting. I ignored the Oedipal implications and told him it
sounded like Alice in Wonderland. I also asked him about school and home
life. James was sick again, back in the hospital. This clearly bothered Alex
a lot, but he wouldn't talk much about it. He was also evasive when it came
to relationships with his parents. In fact, he showed real discomfort, so I cut
the session short. "Alex, I'm afraid our time is up." The whole business had
taken all of ten minutes.

"Thank you, Daddy." He got up and sniffed experimentally. "I feel
much better." Then a moment later: "You promised me a joke."

I had, hadn't I? Too bad I couldn't think of one. After all the material
I'd heard and told today, my mind had gone blank. Probably every comedi-
an's worst nightmare. "I'm sorry, I just can't think of any right now."

Alex put on one of his crafty smiles. "I've got one for you, Daddy."

"Really? Let's hear it."

"What goes away when you get up?"

An erection, that's what. "I don't know."

Alex looked delighted. "Guess."

I tried to visualize the setup, but the coffee from lunch was wearing
off. And I'd been roused from bed at six this morning because Alex had
been breathing like a steam engine. What goes away if you get up too early?
Your patience.

"I don't know. I really don't. Just tell me."

"You didn't even try!"

"That's enough," I told him. "I'm going upstairs to take a nap. I'll come
down later to cook dinner."

"*But I want to play Monopoly.*"

At times like these, I wanted to walk out of the room—or opt out of
parenthood. "You can still play," I told him as I made for the stairs, "just not
with me."

"All right!" he yelled at my retreating back. "I'll play by myself."

And that's apparently what he did, though I wasn't there to watch.
Instead, I lay spreadeagled on our queen-sized bed, trying to catch sixty or
more winks, but that proved difficult. Guilt lay on me like a heavy quilt. It

wasn't really Alex I was tired of—I was tired of my mistreatment of him. He was a good kid, an imaginative boy. My poor son, who had to bear me as his father. At least my old man had an excuse as the main support of our family. I squirmed—this bed was impossible to get comfortable in.

From down the hall, I heard the sound of dice landing on a playing board, and markers being *tump tump tump*-ed around the squares. "Are you going to buy Park Place?" I thought I heard him say at one point, and "You owe me twenty-eight dollars."

I thought again of the riddle that Alex had posed to me. I still had no answer. The question sounded vaguely familiar, like something I'd heard in grade school, that vast mountain of childhood I'd mostly put behind me. Until Alex. He made me relive those years from a new, awkward angle. How did it go again? "What gets away when you go up?" No, that wasn't quite right. "What goes away and never comes back?"

Ghostly dice rattled from the far room. A child's voice chanted, "One, two, three, four, five."

I turned onto my side. "Why don't I have the same get-up-and-go that I used to?" No, no, what really gets me these days . . . .

Somebody sneezed, but it barely registered. I was still lying on the bed, and either it had expanded or I had shrunk. When I looked around, I saw my son approaching, a giant who had taken over my life. He loomed above me. His hands, his fingers were reaching out . . . . He tapped me on the shoulder.

"Daddy? Daddy?" He peered at me closely, his eyes huge. "Were you asleep?"

"Huh?" I drew back in fright before realizing who we actually both were. I must have drifted a bit. "Asleep?" I yawned. "Not quite."

"Sorry. But the game's over."

"Who won?"

"Me." He studied the bed post. "Can I have my pretzel sticks now?"

"No, too close to dinner."

"It's not fair!" he cried, and stomped off to his room again. Why couldn't I be nicer? In a minute, I heard mumbling and the rattle of dice again. I hoped I wasn't pushing him toward anything weird. Alex wasn't the type to have an imaginary playmate, but you never knew.

"I want to apologize," I announced as I walked into his room.

He looked wary. "What for?"

"For being, I don't know, not so nice lately." I couldn't meet his eye.

"That's all right, Daddy." He said this so understandingly that for a moment I thought he knew all about my marital strains, which in a way he did. When he offered me a *Mad* magazine to look at, I suggested we read it together. We sat together on his bed and alternated reciting a page of greeting card take-offs. Soon we were howling.

"'I heard that you were *ill* . . .'" Alex sang for the third time.

I took over. "'But I have had my *fill* . . . .'"

The phone rang just as we got to the last line. I sprinted down the hallway to reach the phone in the bedroom. Jane. "I'm calling from Grand Central. Just wanted to let you know I'll be home for dinner on time for a change. How's the boy?"

"Better. He's all yours tonight." I tried to end humorously: "Though I'm almost positive he's half mine." I hustled back to Alex's room and sang a few more choruses. Then I left for the kitchen to start cooking, just spaghetti and salad. For a bit of whimsy, I stirred into the sauce some green food coloring left over from last Easter, but the combination of red and green turned it almost black. So I added some more coloring, but that just made things worse. Too bad I couldn't undo the damage by stirring backwards. I tried a spoonful: it tasted fine. My family would just have to grin and bear it.

I had just put the pasta water on to boil when Alex clattered downstairs. You could usually tell his mood by the timbre of his footsteps. His elfin face poked into the kitchen. I hastily covered the pot of sauce with a lid. He stood at attention to recite from memory. "'You probably shouldn't take this *pill* . . . '"

"'But I suppose you always *will* . . . .'"

"Now I'm hungry," Alex announced after we reached the end.

"Good. So am I." I frowned at the stove. "Hey, what was the answer to that riddle?"

Alex shook his head. "I'm not telling yet. It won't mean as much if I do."

"Ah, c'mon."

"Uh-uh."

The gravel crunched loudly in the driveway. Jane was home, and Alex ran out to greet her, leaving the door open. Looked like Mommy wasn't in a good mood, though. She let Alex carry her black nylon briefcase, since he liked to pretend it was his, but his performance was unsatisfactory. "You're dragging it. You've got to hold it up higher"—she tried to grab it from his hands—"like this." But Alex wouldn't let go, and they walked in the door sideways, both holding onto their half of the briefcase.

The problem was that he was only four feet tall, and Jane never recognized this fact. Maybe all sons are larger than life to their mothers, or maybe she thought he wasn't living up to his potential. She was in a captious frame of mind. Time for a few laughs to bring her down.

"Hi, honey! You're home." I waved exaggeratedly. "Early, too."

Jane dropped her part of the briefcase onto the kitchen table. "God, what a day! Everything's falling apart. I finally decided to skedaddle and pick up the pieces tomorrow."

"Make like an egg and beat it, eh?"

She looked at me slant-eyed. "Something like that." She shifted her gaze toward the stove and the empty box of spaghetti. "Pasta again?"

"I made a new sauce." I beamed at her. "See what you think of it."

"Right, okay. Let me just change out of my suit."

Alex tugged at her tailored gray jacket, Chanel West 9 Dior, or something like that. As she once explained to me, if you work for a high-cost corporation, you dress expensively. Alex tugged again, threatening to rip a seam. "I'm hungry. Let's eat *now*."

So we sat down to that most hallowed of institutions, the family dinner. More honored in the breach than in the observance, ranging from anticlimax to minefield. It didn't start out well. Distracted, I'd let the spaghetti cook for too long. Too mushy, which at least was how Alex liked it. "Who is this guy Al Dente?" I said for Jane's benefit, but maybe she didn't hear me. Then I unveiled the sauce.

"Eeewww!" That was Alex's contribution. Simmering had only deepened the color. "Why's it black?"

"Maybe it has squid-ink in it," put in Jane semi-kindly. "That was big in restaurants about ten years ago."

Alex put down his fork. "I'm not eating squid."

"There's no fish in it. Only food coloring. It was supposed to be green." I clenched my teeth in the semblance of a grin. "Just try it." Miraculously, I got everyone eating, one family indivisible, with pasta and salad for all. I poured two generous glasses of California Merlot and one cup of hormone-free milk. Jane complained about her day in between bites. Bryce had called in sick, leaving her shorthanded, and then it was discovered that the paperwork for the AsiAm deal hadn't been properly filed . . . .

"Mommy, look at me!" Alex was twirling his spaghetti into a big ball on his fork.

"Wait a minute, honey." She took a sip of wine. "Anyway, the server went down at precisely 4:02, and I know that because—"

"Mommy, you're not watching!"

"In a minute."

I was trying to pay undivided attention to Jane, seated across from me, but most parents possess a primitive form of sonar. To my right, I could sense from peripheral motions that Alex was building up to something. When I finally turned to look, he had twirled a huge bolus of spaghetti onto his fork and was about to shove it into his mouth.

"No, that's too big!"

"It'll fit." It just about did, with a few black-dripping strands trailing from his mouth that he slowly sucked in. We all breathed a sigh.

Then Alex sneezed. It started with a premonitory *"Ahhh . . . ,"* but there was no time to move. He simply exploded. Out came gobs of blackened sauce and fat worms, hurled in a broad spectrum but mostly at Jane's outfit. It didn't mix well with the white silk blouse or even the gray jacket. My reflexive gesture, just before the wave hit, was to fling out a hand—which knocked over Jane's wineglass, adding a deep red to the mixture.

"Alex!" Jane was shouting at him, getting up from the table, futilely swabbing at her front with a paper napkin. He began to wail.

Quickly, before the incident could escalate into Greek tragedy, I tried to bring things into proper perspective with a little humor. "Alex, this is a fine mess," I lectured him. "Pasta point of no return."

Alex looked puzzled. Jane was livid. "Why are you making stupid puns when he just ruined a seven-hundred-dollar outfit?"

I held up my hand. "You're right. We'll expunge this. Alex, get the sponge."

He flapped his arms. "But it was an *accident*."

Before he could dig himself in deeper, I got him out of his chair and propelled him in the direction of the sink. After Jane had gone upstairs to change and come down wearing a baleful look, I tried to explain. "I didn't mean to make fun. I just thought a little laugh would help."

"Ha ha."

"Well, it's true. Everything's so damned grim." I looked at their faces, which were looking at me. Suddenly the room was too confining, the air chokingly thick. Since this was Jane's night with Alex, I should be at liberty. Normally, I would have dived for the computer, but that wasn't removed enough. Old-fashioned though it was, maybe I needed a stroll around the block. I got up and started for the coat closet in the hall.

"Where are you going?" asked Jane.

What I said next didn't come out right. "I think I'll go for a week."

"What?"

"A walk, I mean." Freud said there are no mistakes. "I need to get out. I'll be back in a while." As I left, I couldn't catch what Jane was saying, but

I did hear Alex protesting again that it was an accident.

The evening wind at the start of March felt good against my face. A hint of woodsmoke wafted toward me. It wasn't that chilly, but if people buy houses with working fireplaces, they like to use them. Meanwhile, commuters were still coming back from work, most humming along in minivans but some walking from the station. I walked around, trying to peer into houses whose windows didn't show much. I crossed Chester Street and started along Jefferson Lane, where the sidewalk petered out and the lawns were hemmed in by cobblestones. The sky seemed to be expanding upwards as it darkened, higher and higher above the elms and oaks. This was still Ridgefield, but an earlier section of Fairchester, with more modest houses and older trees. The Talent-Schramm ménage lived at #41 in a dark-shuttered Tudor knockoff, and as I neared their address, I thought again of Dalton. All the Lost Boys in hiding . . . it sounded like a line from *Peter Pan*. I should really be laughing this off, or at least not taking it so seriously. When I arrived at #41, I noticed that only one car was in the driveway. I debated whether to knock on the door. But who would answer, and what would I say? I didn't relish the role of a policeman. *Stop being a parent for once*, I thought. Comforting clichés crossed my mind: *boys will be boys*, *where's the harm*, *it's just a phase*. Eventually I blundered onto Winfield Avenue, a drab stretch with ranch-style houses and what looked like cottages for rent. I turned around at a middle-aged maple tree and headed for home.

By now, the air had thickened into night. The green of the suburbs had turned to black, just like my spaghetti sauce. I took a looping route back, but avoided Crest Hill when I realized it would take me through Dead Dog Drive, as I mentally tabbed it. The carcass had to be gone by now; still, something about the site lingered unpleasantly. Consequently, I approached Garner Road in the opposite direction from usual. The houses loomed like familiar but somehow strange presences: I didn't know what was inside them. Who belonged to that clapboard house, the Delanceys, was that their name? Hadn't there been an Asian family occupying the beige stucco on the corner? We didn't know that many of our neighbors, not like when I was growing up, and the whole block of kids would organize games like Bombardment and Tag. Life was funnier then: even the ice cream vendor we swarmed after was called the Good Humor man. Or take Halloween, which used to be a night for kids to be mischievous away from their parents. Now everything's chaperoned. Kids still played pranks—I couldn't help noticing how many mailboxes on our block had been whacked—but that wasn't the same. If I ever caught that son of a bitch, I'd—I didn't know what I'd do.

When I reached the DiSalvas's red brick villa, I paused. The house featured an invitingly large dining room window. The interior was lit by a chandelier over a long table, and the DiSalvas all sat around the polished oval, eating whatever Louise had cooked for them. No black sauce for them. A real family dinner on show for the neighborhood, though they all seemed to be angled in one direction. I craned my neck to see better, and that's when I spotted the large-screen TV on a wheel-in dolly. Is that what it took to get everyone together? They were all eating in slow motion, synchronized by whatever they were watching. Their performance added new meaning to the slogan "Get with the program." I tiptoed away, though no one was likely to hear me.

I repressed my impulse to kick the Steinbaums' impregnable bushes. Their children were all grown up, so now they had shrubbery. Or snubbery. Did they squabble in the evenings over the right method of pruning and what kind of mulch was best? The houses were strange only because I didn't know their interior lives, but I could guess: fights about money, about his needs versus hers (not to mention the children's). Was it romantic of me to think that happy families existed somewhere?

I finally stopped back in front of our house, whose interior I knew all too well. From the outside, it looked cheerful and well lighted, but the thought of what lay inside was paralyzing. Were they waiting for me? I'd never be Superdad, but I was a pretty good father, and a husband more accommodating than most. So why did I so often veer between anger and guilt? I don't think my father was consumed by doubts, but then, it was a different era. And besides, I never asked him.

Hand on the doorknob, I had a sudden urge to move to New Zealand and raise sheep. They would *baa* and not say, "What about me?" or "Daddy, I hate you, " eat grass and not ask for pretzel sticks. But that would be leaving the situation behind, which I had concluded was wrong. Now I wasn't so sure. Maybe *they* had changed without telling me. Alex was growing up semi-sullen. Jane was so businesslike these days. Did we even have the same sense of humor anymore? Another item for The List.

Then I heard noise from indoors. Mother-son sounds. They were probably having fun. I should be, too. The point was to keep trying. I should have called Jane up at the office this afternoon when she was frenzied and done my imitation of a telemarketer. I entered quietly by the front door, resisting the impulse to cry out, "I'm home, honey!" From upstairs came the clack of dice. It sounded as if Jane had been coopted into the Monopoly game I refused. Nice Mommy. Daddy's gone for a walk. Or a week. Maybe I wasn't even home yet.

The idea that I might not be there excited me. And then I did something curious. I took off my coat and shoes and padded up the stairs, silent as the cat we've never adopted. Near the top of the stairs is a corner of the hallway where you can see partway into Alex's room without being seen. In fact, I couldn't take in much because the Monopoly game was over by his bed, but I could hear everything. If I wasn't a voyeur, I was an auditor.

The dice rattled. Alex counted out his move and announced that he'd landed on his own property. The dice tumbled once more. But instead of Jane's move, it sounded like Alex's again. Did Mommy indulgently let him push along her marker, was that it? I sneaked a peek by creeping forward five or so feet just as Jane finally got her turn. Aha. It looked like the Monopoly game was set up for three players, with precocious Alex as two of them. That way, I suppose, he could play by himself and also include someone else. Talk about a monopoly. Or was I the absent second person? They didn't seem to miss me.

Were we having fun yet? Any moment, I was going to yell, "Surprise!" But the seconds ticked into minutes, and I just watched. From my covert vantage, it seemed as though Jane was letting Alex win, a common parental ploy. (On the other hand, my father simply gave me a handicap—seven points in ping pong, a rook in chess—and went full bore.) Anyway, the game was soon over. At which point Alex demanded a joke.

Jane laughed. "Sorry, honey, I can't think of any right now."

"But Daddy tells them." Alex crouched over the board, a petulant figure in pajamas.

Did you hear about the boy who threw his alarm clock to make time fly? I sent this by telepathy to Jane, but she didn't receive it.

"I'm not Daddy," replied Jane. A bit grimly, I thought.

Alex got up, standing apart with his hands on his hips. "I want a joke."

Jane had been half-lying on the floor, propped up by one arm. Now she crawled toward him like a predator. "No, no jokes tonight . . . but I can make you laugh!" She pounced, wrapping her arms around him to lift his body backward onto the bed. In an instant, he lay splayed out on the coverlet, his legs pinned by Jane's calves, his arms held down by her hands. Quickly, she moved his arms together so that she could grip both his wrists, leaving her one free hand. "Ah, ah, *ah* . . . ," she grinned. Her index finger hovered over one defenseless armpit as he squirmed in anticipation.

"Ha ha—no, Mommy—ha ha ha—stop!"

"Stop what?" Jane waggled her finger above his belly. "You mean—*this*?"

"No-ho ho . . . *ahh!* . . ." His face, what little I could see of it, was contorted in painful bliss. When he writhed, she squatted more heavily to keep him from escaping. The finger went in and out, from his clamped-down neck to his wriggling thighs. Only after reducing him to paroxysms did she let him up, and then he just lay there, exhausted.

I crept downstairs just as she told him to go brush his teeth. I opened the front door and slammed it shut. "I'm back from my walk!" Fifteen minutes later, Alex was in bed, ready to recall the scene for his therapist some twenty years hence. Jane and I were in the living room, settling down to the remains of the day. Jane was flipping through magazines. I was seated in the armchair, holding a book over my groin. I felt in the mood, but I knew from frustrated experience that I couldn't just put the moves on Jane. She seemed frosty, for some reason. Maybe I could tickle her fancy.

"So how was your walk?" she asked without looking up.

So that was it. I'd deserted the family. Time to amuse. "Oh, I got off the leash a few times, but nothing I couldn't handle." I paused. "Do you know, the DiSalvas all watch a giant TV screen at dinner?"

"Hmm. Maybe we should do that with Alex." She mimed swiping off her front. "That outfit is ruined."

Try again. "You know, one of my patients thinks he's a standup comic. He's actually not that bad. You want to hear—"

Jane held up a hand. "Please, no jokes. You know, you've been acting awfully . . . funny lately."

And that was how the evening went. I could have gone on, but for what purpose? Eventually Jane yawned, and I followed suit. The one high point was when I got up abruptly from the chair, and the book clattered to the floor.

What goes away when you get up? Your lap, of course.

I felt like tiptoeing into Alex's room and triumphantly whispering the punch line into his sleeping ear. Instead, I lay in bed an hour later—we were all tired—as I pulled the blanket up to my chin. Why is a bed like a free nightclub? There's no cover charge. But my captive audience lay faced away from me, as if she weren't present. "I know you're out there," I mumbled in homage to countless second-rate comedians. "I can hear you breathing."

Chapter 12

973-4856. The scrap of Mut Fid notepaper with Myra's phone number was stuck to the refrigerator with a Goofy Gus magnet for a while, then transferred to the kitchen table, then the computer room, then under a pile of papers. He had thought occasionally of calling her, but each time he was on the cusp of telephoning, he felt a tremor of hesitation. The hesitation developed into a pause, during which he'd stare at the phone as if it were a box with something dark and mysterious inside. He liked Myra, he was fairly certain of that, but he also knew he couldn't follow through. She saw something in him that wasn't there: an available man, a romantic interest. He'd been in this situation once before, when he worked as a programmer at Input. A mousy data processor named Nancy had gone on two dates with him, one his suggestion, the other hers. It hadn't worked then, and it wouldn't now. They would just buzz around each other like two flies trying to get out a window but hopelessly stuck.

He thought about it during his morning walk, which had expanded from a vague stroll to five brisk circuits around an eight-block rectangle. He had newfound health, and it seemed to expand his horizons. After a few weeks, the houses along the way had metamorphosed from large, anonymous dwellings to homes with distinct personalities. Across from Fanshaw Garden Apartments were twin giant milk cartons, one painted yellow, the other gray. The yellow one was the home of a little boy who liked to play catch on the front lawn—with himself, if he couldn't enlist another child or grownup. Ted thought occasionally of becoming a catcher or catchee himself, but the boy was at school during the morning walk. Half a block down was the other apartment cluster, but it had no kids at all and was therefore uninteresting.

In the afternoon, he'd drive to Modesto for a part-time data analysis job he'd snagged, but now he had a while to kill before lunch. Sometimes he spent half an hour or so in the Littl Boyz Room, but he was growing tired of that. Guys like Chomper and CRater, whoever the hell they really were, got on his nerves after a few exchanges. Too jokey and stupid when he wanted—what, exactly?

He wanted a friend to confide in, yet he didn't want to tell anyone any-thing. He was even tired of talking to himself. He desired a naked young boy to sit down heavily on his chest and adorably refuse to move. That seemed out of the question, though it was never far from the edge of reason. But he also needed employment; hence, the flex hours at Modesto. He still had to get a real job.

*

On Sunday, he purchased a Sunday newspaper at a 7-Eleven, away from the main clutch of downtown stores, in a five-store mall where the youth of Fairchester hung out on Saturday nights. This morning, the Indian clerk was reading a letter and listening to something classical on the radio. He nodded to Ted over the transaction as if they were conducting secret business. Then on to Price's Bakery for someplace to sit.

From a distance, the bakery looked like a boutique. The bells on the door tinkled prettily to announce his arrival. Steffie wasn't working that day, but the girl behind the counter showed a sad, sympathetic smile he liked. Her straight brown hair hung down to her shoulders and swayed like a pendulum whenever she moved. He took the table by the window and glanced at the headlines: President to Meet with Chinese Premier; Dollar Falls against the Yen; Lawsuits Pending for Tobacco Companies. As his father had once commented, no one made news on the weekend. He searched through the stack of sections till he found the employment ads, then spread out the paper. It was an old-fashioned source, but it comforted him. Nursing his latte and cinnamon bun, he began jotting down notes on a faded yellow legal pad: headhunting.com, database administrator @ 60K+, senior programmer analyst, Novel/NT guru, Java application architect, data center manager, junior programmer . . . how low should he go?

He'd just circled "CICS system programmer" under an oblong ad when he looked up to see that boy and his father entering the store. The father was carrying a big plastic sack that he plopped down on a table.

"Alex!" the man called out to his errant charge already zooming to the counter.

The boy—Ted recalled those pouting lips—smacked sideways into the glass case display, cried "Ouch!" and abruptly sat down on the floor. "That hurt," he complained, rubbing his arm.

"Then why did you do it?" The father frowned. "Particularly when we've talked about this ten times."

Alex curled his lip. "No, we didn't."

"What do you mean?"

"It wasn't that many times." He got up to peer at the pastries on display. "Anyway, I want a cinnamon bun."

The father shook his head as if heavy weights were attached. "You've already had breakfast."

"So? I'm still hungry." He shifted from one leg to the other, his button nose barely clearing the top of the counter.

Ted pressed down on the edges of his newspaper as if it might fly away from him. The tension between the little boy and his father was building inside him, as well.

"Can I help you?" asked the girl behind the counter, smiling and bending to address Alex. Her hair shifted its angle again, making her face look off-kilter.

Before the father could intervene, Alex spoke. "You're not Steffie," he proclaimed.

"No, I'm Angela. Steffie's not working today."

Alex folded his arms across his chest. He had the elfin look of a changeling, his chin narrow, his ears poking out, and his eyes almost unnaturally bright. "Why not?"

"Well, I guess she has a day off."

"But she's usually here."

"Alex," intoned the father behind him, "give it a rest, okay?"

The boy made a noise like "Hmmph," but retreated from the counter. He marched over to the table next to Ted's and sat down heavily. Meanwhile, the father ordered a cup of coffee and a glass of milk. "And a sourdough loaf—just put that in a bag." Then the father sat down and erected a wall of newsprint. When Alex saw no one watching, he pushed on the chair again until it was too late. The slatted back hit the floor with a *whap*. Alex yelped and rubbed his bottom.

"Alex." The father stood up. "I want you to sit upright—"

"It wasn't my fault!"

"—in that chair for five minutes. Let's see if you can do that, okay?"

"I'll try . . . ." This was said without much conviction. Facing the counter, he announced to no one and everyone in particular, "I'm *bored*." When he slid down the chair under the table, his shirt hiking up past his outie belly button, Ted was fascinated. Noiselessly, Alex crawled over to his father's running shoes and began to untie and retie the laces. When he finished what he was doing, he glanced sideways and caught Ted staring at him. He smiled slyly and raised a finger to his lips. Ted nodded in complicity.

What he didn't expect was that Alex would come crawling to his table, where he settled underneath like a friendly dog. When Alex pushed against Ted's chair, all Ted could think of doing was to pat his head. "Nice doggie," he whispered.

Alex gave a canine whimper. He licked Ted's hand.

The touch was electric. Just then the bells on the door jingled, and Ted pulled back at once. A woman in high-waisted blue slacks entered, followed by a chunky preteen girl dressed the same. It was the local bookstore owner. Ted browsed at Between the Covers every once in a while and recognized the mother-daughter duo. The woman had the deep-socketed, high-beaked face of a disapproving bird, the kind who looked down upon Ted. Had she been one of the adults in the park that disastrous afternoon? She didn't know him, of course, but she said hello to the father. They chatted for a moment—something to do with tennis—while the daughter wandered to the counter.

Alex nuzzled Ted's leg. "No . . . bad dog," Ted murmured, drawing away. When the boy came forward again, Ted broke off a piece of cinnamon bun in desperation and held it out to him. "Now go, please."

When the girl turned toward her mother, she spotted the boy under the table instantly. She saw what he was doing and started to say something, but Ted shook his head hugely, and she closed her mouth. As she walked toward him, Ted had the sudden worry that soon she, too, would be under the table, feeding from his hand. Instead, at the last second she skipped away between the tables and waltzed back to her mother.

Alex had gobbled the piece of cinnamon bun and was just emerging from beneath the table when his father spied him.

"Alex! What are you doing under there?"

"Nothing."

Alex's father rose from his chair and started toward his son, but he didn't get too far. One foot somehow tripped the other, and he toppled to the floor. His shoelaces had been tied together. Alex giggled, but not for long. What happened next was almost too fast for Ted to follow. One tied shoe was wrenched off, Alex was sailing through the air in his father's arms, and he was crammed into his original chair. "And stay there! Don't you *ever* do that again." The father's face was blotched with anger. "You've got a long time-out, is that understood?"

Alex rubbed his arms. "You *hurt* me!"

"I did? Well, I'm sorry, but it serves you right." The father felt his shin.

Alex started to cry. "I hate you."

The bookstore woman was at the counter, carefully looking elsewhere. Ted held onto the edges of the newspaper so tightly that he poked holes in the sides with his thumbs.

"But, Mom . . . " protested the daughter.

"Quiet, Lily. Let's just get what we came for." She instructed Angela to pack up three croissants while Alex wailed and the father grimly retreated behind his newspaper. She and her daughter left soon after in a flurry of bells. Before the door closed, Ted had followed them out, clutching his newspaper and notes. It had become difficult to breathe in there, the edges of his vision growing hazy. All the way back, he took deep gulps of air, as if traveling through an atmosphere too thin to sustain him. When he got home, he sat in his armchair until he had calmed down. Then he read through the entire newspaper, from the front-page headlines to the arts columns, which took upwards of two hours. The accounts of foreign summit meetings and lifestyle articles were magnificently irrelevant, but they took his mind off boys and dogs and tongues and snuffling noises.

In the evening, after Spaghetti-O's and a doughnut, he brought a cup of coffee to the Blue Room and accessed the Littl Boyz Room. CRater, Chomper, and HalfPint were present, like three guests who'd never left the party. They were discussing how to best grab a boy's attention.

Offer him a sugar daddy heh heh—Chomper.

HalfPint begged to differ. Nah, thats too old, I use matchbox cars.

The doors are too small on those models! I just wedge 'em in the back seat of my buick, wrote CRater.

Ted waited until the debate had subsided into complete nonsense before typing in a rejoinder. So tell me, do any of you have REAL experience getting a boy?

The cybernetic equivalent of silence ensued. For almost a minute, the rest of the screen stayed blank.

Finally, CRater weighed in with a question. Um, candyman, r u a narc in disguise?

Nope. He paused for a moment. Just someone getting tired of all this role-playing.

Hey its sposed to be fantasy, typed HalfPint.

We got boyz on the brain, added Chomper.

Ted took a deep breath. Well, he wrote, today I had a boy eating out of the palm of my hand.

You dont say?—Chomper.

I do. He got down on all fours and licked me.

This little confession spurred a fifteen-minute discussion that wasn't so illuminating, except for what it revealed about the guys in the chat room. The one point on which they were adamant was that CandyMan had done no wrong. **Thanx for your support**, he finally wrote, and exited the room. But that night, he dreamed he was eating his way through a giant cinnamon bun, only to meet another gnawer halfway through.

Serendipitously, the next day he was offered a full-time post at Modesto with his own cubicle. He accepted. Joan, the heavy-browed sysop who worked in the adjoining space, had a picture of her seven-year-old son on her desk, a cute tyke named Ramsay who for some reason Ted found not at all appealing. He cast his mind back to Myra's nephew Donald, who'd always seemed to be sharing a secret with Ted. He left the office late, humming a tune his mother had taught him: "Take good care of yourself, you belong to me." That night, he dreamed that Donald was riding piggyback on him but suddenly swiveled back to front so that his groin was pressed against Ted's face. The scene felt so real that Ted woke up mouthing his pillow. He walked before work, passing all the children on their way to school, and spent his first full day of work in an excellent mood.

Two days later came the deluge. The *Fairchester Guardian* ran a headline that bugged out his eyes: "LOCAL SEX OFFENDER SOUGHT IN RELATED INCIDENTS." "Responding to complaints from Fairchester citizens, police are searching for an adult white male in connection with a series of suspicious events involving minors. Given the pattern of appearances, police conjecture that the perpetrator resides within the township. Parents are advised to keep a tight watch on their children, especially in crowded public areas such as parks and shopping malls."

"Shit, shit . . ." he murmured. The print began swimming into a river of black, so he put down the paper and sat down in his armchair before he faded out. Slowly the scene in his apartment came back, the walls around him achieving solidity and depth once again. Had the kid talked to his father after that stupid scene in the bathroom?—or maybe that damned lady in the park had filed a complaint. When he felt a little calmer, he reached for the newspaper, spreadeagled on the floor like a broken kite, and read some more. One description of a confrontation in a public restroom might have been him.

"'This is no reflection on Fairchester,' said Detective John Slavian of the Dover County Vice Squad in an interview yesterday. 'It can happen anywhere these days.' Given the public data available under New York's version of Megan's law, however, it appears that the would-be assailant may not be someone with a criminal record ." The rest of the article went on about the nature of such crimes and the percentage of recidivism, with a few soundbites from a forensic psychologist named Chadwick.

"But I'm clean," Ted proclaimed to the nearest wall, which didn't deign to respond. It was only six o'clock in the evening, yet already it felt like two A.M. and he was wrapped around the warped, scummy edges of a nightmare. Only he had no other place to wake up into. For a while, he burrowed into his chair as anxiety gave way to resignation and then a pang of hunger. Finally he headed for the kitchen, where he heated up a macaroni-and-cheese TV dinner. He could let the newspaper story terrify him, or he could get truculent about it. Or try to see the funny side—what funny side? For his own amusement, he spelled out something obscene with fifteen macaroni elbows before shoveling them into his mouth.

In the ensuing week, the story spread around town. The bird-beak woman who ran Between the Covers put up a notice in the window display about unattended children, alongside a book titled *Sexcrimes: True Stories.* On his morning walk, skirting the park, he saw what looked like a girl gang, except that it was composed of nine- or ten-year-olds. They were chalking body outlines on the asphalt and chanting:

Strawberry shortcake, cream on top,
How many children will you stop?

Then they squirted what looked like strawberry jam on the outlines before an adult came out from a nearby house and they ran away. Ted himself hurried off before anyone could focus on him. But someone must have snapped a photo of the chalk drawings because two days later, the Fairchester chief of police came out with a public statement in the *Guardian*: "The chalk images in the park were just a childish prank. Please—the last thing we need here is mass panic. Rest assured, our primary concern is the children, and we are taking every step possible to ensure their safety." One of the effects was that many more parents now walked their children to school.

*

"Hey, stop pulling me!" cried one recognizable boy to his father as Ted rounded Edgewood Street, a block from Ridgefield Elementary. It was the dog-boy from the bakery. Ted hung back so that neither would see him.

"Then stop dawdling behind," said the father. "I have to get back to see a patient soon."

"What's 'dawdling'?" The boy stopped when he asked the question.

"It means hanging around, wasting time." And the father gave another yank, which started the protest all over again.

Ted took another route to bypass the school, a detour that brought him past the site of the dead dog. Or rather, where the carcass had once been, nothing left but the stench of memory. When he got back to his apartment, he saw a teenager skateboarding off in a hurry, disappearing south on Winfield. Then he noticed that his mailbox was bashed on the side, tilted at a sick angle with its tongue hanging out. Goddamned punk—yet he looked familiar, even from the back at fifty feet. Ted tried to ease out the dent and pushed the box back to horizontal. He was like everybody else, a part of the community, a mailbox victim. He had an idea who was doing it, but the image of the kid remained a blur in his memory that refused to focus. One of the high school punks who skateboarded around the 7-Eleven? As he drove to work, he entertained fantasies of laying a trap: electrify the mailbox, tape a silent signaler to it, or just pay out a line low to the ground that would send the skateboarder sprawling.

At Modesto, even though it was located several towns over in Larchmont, they were talking about the sexual pervert on the loose. Joan in particular was concerned about her son, Ramsay. "You don't know what it's like to be a mother," she told Ted, staring as if she could see right through him. "The idea that someone out there might be *after him*—I couldn't sleep last night."

"I don't think he's after *every* child . . . " began Ted, but Joan cut in.

"You know what I'd like to do to people like that?" She jabbed a pen into the fleshy part of her thumb. "Castrate 'em. It's the only way."

At the mention of castration, he pulled back violently and had to pretend he'd had a muscle spasm.

Then one morning, it was all over. "Did you hear? They caught him," announced Joan during the first coffee break of the day, at around nine-thirty.

Ted reached for a cruller from a communal box. "Caught who?"

"The child molester. You know, the guy they've been looking for." Joan looked strangely triumphant, as if she'd helped to nab him.

Ted bit his lip—hard—in the middle of chewing his doughnut. "*Ow.*"

"What did you say?"

"Nothing. I mean," he temporized while swallowing, "that's good news, I guess."

"Darn right it is. People like that make me sick." Joan took a swig of milky coffee and began to deliver a diatribe on sex offenders.

Since Ted had heard it all before, he simply waited glumly until she had finished. He did have one question, though. "How do they know it's the right guy?"

"Oh, they know." Joan waved her hand flatly. "Fingerprints, DNA tests—they check all that stuff."

When he drove home that night, he first straightened out his mailbox, which this time the whacker had slammed practically sideways. Two pieces of junk mail dribbled out. On the doorstep, the *Guardian* was waiting for him like a cross between a loyal pet and a furled umbrella. Now was the right moment. Even before he unlocked the door, he was unrolling the newspaper to see the front page. There it was, in 30-point type: "SEX OFFENDER APPREHENDED." After spending hours at the computer screen, he found himself reaching for an invisible mouse to scroll downward. Shaking his head at the miscue, he spread the paper fully and read downward in the fuzzy twilight.

"Police took a Greendale man into custody yesterday on charges of child molestation. The alleged assailant, whose identity has not been revealed, is accused of three separate counts of sexual solicitation of a minor. The incidents took place over three months in Dover county. The man in custody has pleaded guilty to two of the three charges and is awaiting further questioning. Scanning records from a database of sexual offenders residing in the county, police detectives were able to match up details with the alleged perpetrator. The suspect has a history of sexual assault, with previous convictions in Rockland county. Given the legacy of Megan's Law . . . ."

"They might just lynch him," muttered Ted, finishing the newspaper sentence. Further on was a brief description of the incidents, including one at the Westfield mall. Hell. Finally, he unlocked the door and let himself in. Dropping his knapsack-briefcase in the tiny hallway, he trudged toward the kitchen. Over a quiet TV dinner of fried chicken and mashed potatoes, he mulled over the news. Should he celebrate or be furious? He felt both let off the hook and convicted. At least no one would be looking for him. He mentally thumbed his nose at the guy in apartment #5, far more likely to publicly offend people. He studied his hands on the table, twitching slightly. Later that evening, he might cyber-chat with CRater about boys' underwear or strap himself under the slurpy seat in the Dungeon. But these were silly substitutes for what he missed at the playground.

He took a deep breath. Enough was enough. Was this how he was going to live for the rest of his days? That night, he dreamt that he shrank to four feet and was bumping into all the other boys in a sort of gymnasium. *Boing, squish, boing*. It gave him an immensely pleasurable feeling, and when he woke up, he decided that was what he wanted. In real life. And soon.

Chapter 13

My jaw aches just telling this. It started with another ugly breakfast scene, more tempestuous than usual. Alex was busily not eating the breakfast I'd put in front of him, Cream of Wheat so thick that it stuck to an upside-down spoon. That was the way he liked it, but for some reason this morning—the weather? the fascinating design of the tablecloth?—he was looking elsewhere. I knew from experience that as soon as it was time for him to leave, he'd whine, "But I'm still *hungry*." On the other hand (parenthood has so many hands), if I chivvied him about it, he'd just sulk and eat nothing. Jane was pointedly ignoring both of us, the dry toast on her plate untouched. She was trying to prepare for some presentation at work and taking a later train than usual. I had heated up a cranberry scone from the Pricey Bakery and put it on a plate for myself but had no time even to take a bite as I got Alex's lunch ready. God, I hate the smell of peanut butter at seven-thirty in the morning. I thought of sabotaging my son's sandwich by poking a hole in the middle or leaving on all the crusts, but reminded myself that I was above such pettiness. Still, we all have our fantasies, and mine that Thursday morning was to strap him down and force-feed him a ten-gallon vat of hot cereal. No more funny Daddy.

"Why isn't he eating?" asked Jane as she looked up from her sheaf of papers. She checked her watch. "It's almost time for the bus."

The bus swung by the corner of Garner and Somers at 7:45, and usually Alex just made it. Today looked iffy.

Alex looked up and came to a conclusion. "I've decided I don't want Cream of Wheat." He stared in my direction. "What else do we have?"

"Nothing—there isn't time," I announced just as Jane intervened with "What do you want?"

We exchanged glances and tried again. "I'll see what's in the freezer," I told him as Jane remarked, "Just eat what's in front of you."

Alex looked from one parental unit to the other, trying to figure out where the soft spot lay. The clock by the refrigerator shifted silently to 7:40. Finally Jane broke the silence: "Oh, hell, just give him a doughnut or something."

And that's how Alex came to be racing down the sidewalk at 7:44 with a cruller in his hand—until he tripped on a root protruding from a stately elm and went sprawling. I'd been watching from the doorway, and I ran out to help him up.

"Are you all right?"

"I . . . think so." He'd scraped both hands, though there was no blood. The unseen presence of the bus rumbled from somewhere up ahead.

"All right, good." I got him to his feet. "Now, hurry, or you'll miss your pick-up."

"Wait. I lost my doughnut."

"Alex, come on."

He shook his head vehemently. "I *have* to find it."

"We'll get you another when you come home from school."

"But I'm *hungry*." He folded his arms defiantly.

So I smacked him upside the head. I picked him up and shook him till his teeth rattled. I kicked him all the way down the block. No, I spent the next minute looking for that stupid cruller, which turned out to be caught on the low-lying branch of an evergreen shrub. And Alex missed the bus, which was driven by an old curmudgeon deaf to the far-off pleas of approaching children. Because I wanted to make this an object lesson, I insisted that Alex walk to school, though he whined for automotive transport.

"No. That'll teach you to hurry next time."

"It's not fair!"

"Look on the bright side: you can finish your doughnut on the way." I left him with that thought and headed home again. When I looked back, he was making his slow way schoolward.

Inside the house, I faced a far greater peril. Jane was still seated at the breakfast table, scowling at something—her report, or the toast from which she'd taken one cautious bite. Or maybe, I realized as she looked up, me.

"Did he manage the bus all right?"

"No." I sat down heavily in my seat and picked up the scone I'd intended to eat so long ago. It was stone cold. I took a mouthful anyway.

"What do you mean?"

"Imehethrippt."

"What?"

I finished my bite by chewing double-time. "I *mean*, he tripped. On the sidewalk. His doughnut went flying, and we had to hunt for it." As I spoke these lines, I realized how absurd they sounded.

"So he missed the bus? Why are you here now?"

"Because I told him he had to walk."

She shook her head ominously. "I don't think that's a good idea. He could be abducted or something."

"In Fairchester? I didn't think they allowed in that kind of people."

"Don't joke. It can happen anywhere. Last month, in Long Island—"

"All right, all right, he should never be left alone. He's halfway to school by now. Do you want to run after him?"

"No, *you're* the one who should do it. I've got work to finish here and a meeting I can't miss—"

"Yeah, and I've got a patient at nine." There she sat in her charcoal Armani suit, already in office mode, barking orders to her subordinate, Bryce whatsisname.

She slapped down her papers. "Listen, are you going to catch my train?"

"What is this, a game of 'my job beats your job'?"

"You don't get it, do you?" She shook her head pityingly. "You've got to learn a sense of responsibility. If you could just—"

"Knock it off."

"I said, if you could just stop acting like a child, we'd all appreciate it."

"You—." I stopped, looking for words and finding some I never used. But there she sat, Ms. Executrix, goading me. "You nickel-plated bitch."

A sharp intake of breath. "*What?*"

"You heard me."

Jane rose from the table, reaching her full height of 5'9½". Since she was also wearing heels, she stood about two inches taller than me—or she would have, if I'd bothered to get up from my chair. That put my chin on a level with the top button of her suit. She talked downwards. "I don't *ever* want to hear that kind of language directed at me."

That did it. I got up slowly from my seat and faced her. "*Cunt.*"

I barely saw her backhand, it was so fast. The next thing I knew, my jaw was throbbing. My mouth was filled with blood—my teeth had gouged my inner cheek.

She stood there, breathing heavily. She looked so damned self-righteous. I was so furious, I was ready to slug her, but she backed into a crouch.

"Go ahead, try and hit me," she barked. "Is that what you want to do?"

That stopped me. Being told how I'm about to act always makes me veer in another direction. I took a step closer just to see her flinch, but left it at that. "Goddamn it, you hit me."

"You started it."

"What, took a poke at you?" I reached out, but only to show an open palm. "You're the one who took a swing." But it hurt to talk. Jane backed away as I walked over to the kitchen sink to rinse and spit.

"I'm—I'm sorry. But there are certain things . . . ."

"I see." The cold water had helped. I was thinking like a therapist again. Part of me, anyway. "So when I get angry, I should just let go, too."

"I didn't say that."

The twisted path of this argument stretched before me like a dust-choked road. My jaw hurt, and I was about to get a mouthful of grit. The foretaste wasn't what made me wince so much as the desperate knowledge that I'd been along this road too many times. I just wanted to turn in the other direction. "Maybe I should leave," I thought, unaware that I'd said the words aloud.

"Maybe you should," retorted Jane. "It's on your list, isn't it?"

"What do you mean?"

She planted her hands on her hips. "Just what I said. That stupid list you wrote up—I don't know, back in September. With the two columns."

So she'd seen it: my much-embroidered, labored-over catalogue of sins and virtues. For a moment, the knowledge that I'd been found out thudded into me as if I'd been hit again. "You saw it." I shook my head dumbly. "You saw my list. That wasn't for you to look at."

"Really? Then don't leave it lying on the kitchen table."

I cast my mind back to that day, remembering what a close call I thought I'd had. "So why didn't you say something?"

She shrugged. "*You* didn't say anything. I figured you didn't want to discuss it. Anyway, I drew up a list of my own."

"Where is it?"

"In a safe place." She looked over her shoulder. "Where Alex can't read it. You know, he could have just picked up that—that document of yours and gotten all sorts of ideas."

Hell, maybe he *had* read it. That might explain some of his recent behavior. The thought of him with that knowledge, trudging along with such a burden every day, saddened me. It also made me angry at Jane, who was part of the problem. "All right, where's *your* list? I want to see what's on it."

She shrugged those bossy shoulders. "I'm not sure I should show it to you. It's kind of private."

"If you show me yours, I'll show you mine." I tried to grin as if this were all some big joke.

"I've already seen yours, remember?"

"No, it's changed since then." What was this now, draft #7? I'd crossed out "infidelity," added when I suspected her of having that office affair. But I'd added "bossiness." Anyway, the basic irritations remained the same. Unwillingness to share, for one.

She thought for an executive moment. "All right, I'll get my list— you get yours." When she went upstairs, I scurried to my office, where I unlocked the flat desk drawer and pulled out The List. Did I have time to edit out some of the more objectionable points? "Debit #3: Needs to get her own way. Debit #4: Often flies off the handle." My jaw began to ache again. To hell with it: full disclosure or nothing. By the time I returned to the kitchen, Jane was already back, a yellow folder on the table. I silently handed her my list, and she gave me the folder.

The first page was a computer-generated spreadsheet. In the column marked "DEBITS" was a list of ten items. Heading off the stack was "always arguing." I looked up to contest this point, but she was busy going through my list. Second was "fussy," with several subheadings: "controlling," "nitpicking," and "obsessive at times." Third was "not romantic enough." Fourth was "intellectualizes everything." Other items included "impractical"—*hah!*—"careless driving" and "weak chin." I stroked my jaw fiercely and moved on to the "ASSETS" column, which led off with "good husband and father," an item flagged by a question mark in parentheses. "Sense of humor" was up there, as well as her own touch of humor: "good sex (none lately)." No argument there. In fact, as I made my way down the page, I noticed that her complaints and plaudits were extremely similar to what I'd jotted down on my list. At the bottom was "love," but printed so that it seemed to belong in both columns.

The second page was a compatibility index, which compared various traits and came up with 72%. I flipped to the last page, which looked like some form of cost-benefit analysis, with long-term projections for growth. Accompanying the commentary ("investment in home," "domestic benefits include cooking") was a graph of happiness over time, an upward-sloping line that leveled off after three years and took a dip at 1992, around the time Alex was born.

"You know," began Jane just as I was about to start the same way, "you seem to have mistaken me for you."

"Or vice versa." I reached out to get my list back, as if it were flammable in the wrong hands. "Also, remember, you saw my complaints first. You copied me."

"Actually, that's one of my complaints about *you*. First you tried to match my workout schedule, then you acted like a junior executive . . . ." She expelled some air, one of those more-in-sorrow-than-in-anger sighs that infuriates me.

"I was trying to be nice, damn it."

"You have a funny way of showing it."

"All right, enough. I'm sorry I showed you my list—or I'm sorry you sneaked a look at it. Is that why you've been so annoyed recently?" (I meant "annoying.")

She looked appraisingly at me. "That's part of it, yes."

"So where does that leave us?"

Another shrug. "You tell me. You're the one who wanted to leave. Though God knows, I've thought of it, too."

For some reason, an image of the couch from my old apartment floated into my mind, badly upholstered in plaid and worn at the seams but comfortable. I was able to read for hours lying on the plump cushioning. Or snoring, Snoggs-like. Of course I could—no one else was around to disturb me. No female presence hogging the bathroom, no juvenile voice tugging at my attention. It was like a time capsule unearthed, a bubble of ancient atmosphere too fragile to endure the current climate. Then the bubble burst. A pinprick of conscience? I saw a little boy trudging glumly along to limbo.

"Wait a minute, what about Alex?"

"I know, that's a real issue."

"No." I rubbed my cheek, which was swelling up. "I mean, you said he might get waylaid on the way to school."

Jane checked her watch. "Jesus, it's a quarter to nine. Look, just drive to Ridgefield and check, all right? You're the one who let him walk. I've got an 8:57 train to catch."

"Why don't we just call Ms. Hardin?" So I was impractical, huh? I walked over to the kitchen phone, checked the general number for Ridgefield on the bulletin board, and punched it in. After being put on a two-minute hold by the principal's secretary, I was told that Alex Eisler hadn't shown up for class.

"Well, where the hell *is* he?" I barked into the phone. After apologizing to the secretary for my outburst, I hung up.

"He's not there, right?" Jane looked as if she might slug me again.

"No, he's not." But I had a feeling he was en route.

"Damn it, I told you—"

"I know you did, and I don't have time to argue." I grabbed the car keys from the counter. "I'm going out there to find him."

"Wait, I'm going with you."

Which is how we came to be jetting along Chester Street a moment later, the Volvo's wheels barely scraping the pavement at times. We squealed around the turns like a getaway car in the movies. Jane was at the wheel while I scanned the sidewalk for signs of our errant son. Our dear lost son, our poor misguided offspring—where had he got to? Had someone actually picked him up? What was I thinking of when I told him to walk? It was only seven blocks to school, but I regretted every one. Each Alex-less stretch was like a jab in my gut. *Pushed him away, did you?* insinuated Martin. What had I been thinking of? On the other hand, if I was right . . . .

"Stop the car!"

Jane trod on the brakes so hard, she almost activated the airbags. "What? What?"

We were just past Edgewood, the last street before Ridgefield. And there was Alex, knapsack slung awkwardly across his back, moving so slowly that he looked drugged. We pulled alongside him, and I yelled "Hey, Alex!" out the window.

He barely looked up. He was taking the tiniest of steps, his gaze fixed on the sidewalk directly in front of him. His adorable head bobbed slightly as he moved.

I jumped out of the car. I was so happy to see him that I could barely contain myself, so angry that the first thing to come out was "What the hell do you think you're doing?"

He finally looked up. "Oh. Hi."

"I said, what do you think you're doing?"

"Walking to school." He pretended to look puzzled. "That's what you told me to do, isn't it?"

"Yeah, okay, but why aren't you there already?"

He shrugged, with something of Jane in his gesture.

"Because you're taking baby steps, that's why!"

"Michael, lay off, okay?" Jane craned her neck out the window. "Let's just get him in the car."

I'd have accused her of backseat driving if she hadn't been at the wheel. Instead, I reached back to open the rear door. "All right, damn it. Hop in."

Alex didn't respond. He just kept creeping along, staring at his feet as if they were trying to tell him something. The song "Inchworm" floated through my mind. I checked the time. It was 8:45.

"C'mon, get inside." I gestured invitingly with one hand.

He shook his head, a slow pivot back. And forth.

"This is taking too long," muttered Jane. She honked the horn.

It didn't faze him. He'd almost covered a sidewalk square by now, moving even slower than before. At this rate, he'd arrive at school sometime in the afternoon.

"Michael, you've got to do something."

Ah, so now I was the power figure again. I rubbed my jaw—I do *not* have a weak chin—and decided to act. I stepped out of the car. "All right, Alex. This is it."

He inclined his head toward me ever so slightly, pouting. "What do you mean?"

"You either get in the car now . . ." I waved my hands like a magician about to make an entire cabinet vanish ". . . or else no TV for a week."

"*No . . . !*" His pout collapsed into a crater and he stopped creeping forward. "No fair!"

"Alex, it's perfectly fair," called out Jane from behind the wheel. "Just read the contract."

That brought him up short. When Mommy and Daddy actually agreed on something, it was serious. Still, that didn't immediately propel him into the car. He had to save face.

"But I'm doing what Daddy told me to do. I'm walking to school."

I crossed my arms. "Fine. You've shown you can do it. Now get in."

"But I—"

I reached out to grab him, the last parental resource, but he jerked away.

"It's not right! I don't want to go with you, and you can't make me!"

A Ford Explorer glided slowly by, the driver's window open. Was someone going to report us? I yanked Alex into the back seat, but not before the brat kicked me. I clamped down on his wrist till he squealed.

We drove to school with the prisoner sentenced to seven days of no television. I signed him in at the principal's office, where he needed a note. He didn't thank me. I left him inching toward his classroom. Why do so many people say, "We're staying together for the sake of the kids" when children seem to be a major reason for divorce? By the time I got back to the car, Jane was clawing at her watch.

"I'm going to miss my train, damn it." She looked hard at me. "Why did you tell him to walk, anyway?"

"Lay off. And move over. I'll drive you to the station." Luckily, she'd brought her briefcase. I deposited her near the platform just as the train was pulling in, and watched her fly up the ramp as if she were about to take off. I drove back in her careening chariot style, rumbling into the driveway just in time for my first patient of the day. At 9:05, I opened the door to find R, slumped in one of the bowl-like wicker chairs and reading an old *New Yorker*.

R stared up from her magazine. "You're late."

"I know," I told her as if it were intentional. "How do you feel about that?"

"A little betrayed, if you want to know." She arose from the depths of the seat, showing some thigh as she got up. As the spring weather settled in, she was dressing more provocatively. Today she was wearing an off-white sleeveless blouse displaying her firm upper arms, along with a short brown skirt that showed off what fine legs she had. I don't know why I never noticed before—though I'm quite careful about countertransference. It's one thing for patients to project onto you, and they do it all the time. I come across as a parent figure or a sex object, and that's how I figure out that they hate their mother or miss their father. It's quite another matter for you as the therapist to see them as your friend or beyond.

All right, I confess: I've always known about the flip side of mousy R, how attractive she could look if she just took some pains. Whenever she did, her hair appeared less auburn. She'd had it cut recently, and now it looked flame-red. Or maybe just today, especially after what had happened with Jane, I was transfixed by the sight of R.

"Betrayed?" I echoed as I ushered her into my sanctum. "How do you mean?"

"You know how Dwight keeps me waiting whenever we're out together." She sat down again, this time in the consultation chair, now showing the full sweep of her thighs. I tried to stay away from that area, but realized I was staring at her breasts. Her nipples were erect. As if in displacement, my jaw began to throb again. In the fuss over Alex, I'd had no time to put any ice on it. I half-covered it with my left hand, as if it were an aching groin.

"You've said something about that, yes." What she'd said was that Dwight would excuse himself to go to a public restroom and then not return for a while.

"Well, I get tired of hanging around. It makes us late, yet somehow he blames me." She attempted a smile as she leaned backward, her bra pulling tight and suspending her perky breasts for my inspection. So I contrived to look down at her thighs. Christ, did my jaw hurt.

R went on to talk about how insensitive Dwight was to her feelings, but I realized in that juncture just how furious I was at Jane. I'd held it off this morning—or for days, weeks—and now I realized what I had to do.

You should leave, Snoggs mumbled. *It's about time*, Martin intoned fussily. If they agreed on something, it was time to heed them. I barely remember the rest of the session, except that after I got up to show R out, I left the house at once to get some air. As soon as I passed our driveway, my jaw stopped hurting so much. The weather had turned cool and clear after a rainy spell, with April in the air: budding trees and a faint whiff of cut grass. Striding up Garner Street, with the slightly ridiculous gait of a race-walker, was a man in gray-slacks cutoffs. Another harbinger of spring? He seemed familiar, though he kept his head down as he passed. Was he a stay-at-home parent I knew from Ridgefield? Should I have said hello? Funny how you can ignore the people in your area, even if they live a block or two away. Frightening, too. In the city, anonymity is almost a right. But in the suburbs, citizens are supposed to be neighbors. Shuffling across our lawn, I stared back at his retreating figure until he rounded the curb.

When I finally turned around, I got a mouthful of gorse. I realized with a start that I'd drifted and was now on Steinbaum property. The impregnable hedge was what had stopped me. Only this time I noticed a break in the green wall: about waist-high, as if an animal the size of a six-year-old child had burrowed inside. Curious, I bent down to crawl through but got caught on the broken-off branches. When I tried to back up, they clawed at my face. One stick-end nudged at my sore left cheek, and I howled in pain. Time to get back and maybe grab some ice for myself. I yanked myself out, scratching my face in the process, and lumbered back to therapy.

The office was locked. I rattled the knob hopefully, then kicked it, but it was one of those doors that shoots its bolt automatically whenever you close it. Usually I left it ajar for my patients or kept a key in my pocket, but I'd been fiddling with it on the desk, then left in a big hurry after R. Let's just say I was preoccupied. And the house, where I had a spare set of keys, was also shut tight. The emergency key stashed in the garage—no, the babysitter still had it. I was wondering how to get in when S showed up and saw me outside rather than inside.

"Hey, what gives?"

The analyst should always level with his patients. "I'm, uh, locked out. You don't have any skeleton keys on you, right?"

S scratched his head. "No, but I got something that might work. Not a dead-bolt, is it?"

"No, snap-lock."

"All right. Hold on a minute." He walked back to his car to get something from the glove compartment that looked like a credit card, but thinner and made of some springy metal. Inserting it into the lock area, he managed to spring the door-catch.

"Neat trick." I didn't even ask him what he was doing with a tool like that. Instead, I apologized, thanked him, and said, "Tell you what—I'll give you this session for half off."

That seemed to cheer up S immensely. He sat buckaroo style in the armchair and chatted for a while about an impending promotion he'd been gunning for, executive vice president. Of course, given his competitive nature, it had to be at someone else's expense, a milquetoast named Crawford who just didn't have enough umph. Or maybe it was just how the corporate world worked. Was this how Jane thought? For the hundredth time, I wondered whether I had enough drive for her. Or whether we were even driving the same vehicle. My jaw felt swollen and tender.

S wound down soon enough, and we left it at that. As soon as he departed, I rushed out the door to put some ice on my jaw—and remembered just too late that once again I'd left the key on my desk. I ran back just as the door shut in my face.

I pounded on the door, but it was no use. I was locked out again. It was doubly frustrating, considering what a careful person I usually am. Sometimes the unconscious works in strange and subtle ways. Other times, it's as obvious as a smack in the face. Okay, okay, so some part of me was telling me I didn't belong here anymore. *Should you leave?* cackled Snoggs. *What choice you got?* But that was for the long-term and didn't affect the immediate situation: I had one last patient arriving at eleven, and no place to see her. I checked my watch: 10:52. She was the woman who I still thought of as my new referral, though I'd been seeing her for two months already. She was so much in the mode of the Woman Executive that I'd mentally tabbed her W.E., or just "WE."

Call a locksmith? Sure, if I could get to a phone, and even then, it would take a while. Break into the office? Given time, maybe. Tape up a sign that read, "Sorry—called away on urgent business"? That would be cowardly, and besides, where would I get the paper and tape? I doubted that Jane had ever faced a crisis like this, nor would she be particularly understanding. She'd make some comment, wouldn't she, about professionalism. I was just standing at the edge of the lawn, wondering what the hell else to do when WE showed up in her white BMW. She parked curbside effortlessly and stepped onto the path in a gray tailored suit.

She was startled to see me loitering on the grass. I waved pleasantly, inhaling the scent of unfurling leaves. In fact, the day was so inviting, I really shouldn't be cooped up in an office—and that gave me an idea. "You know," I began, "it's such a nice day, I thought we'd go for a walk."

"Excuse me?"

"I mean, conduct our session outdoors." I waved my hands expansively: my couch is the grass, the sky my ceiling.

"Oh." She took a step backward. "Well . . . ."

Christ, she probably thought I was going to put the moves on her. I needed to add something. "I mean, the painters are here this week, and the office is a mess. So's the house. Carl Rogers and others have advocated a . . . perambulistic approach to therapy, and I thought . . . why not?"

She wrinkled her nose, but attractively. "Is this really orthodox procedure?"

"Let's just say it's a promising idea. Sometimes you need to hit the road." I jerked my thumb toward the crowned asphalt. *Michael "Kerouac" Eisler*, proclaimed Martin.

"Well, all right. But let me put on my running shoes." She pivoted on one dress-shoe toe. "They're in the trunk."

She came back with carbon-black Nikes laced over white cotton anklet socks. The lawns of Fairchester beckoned like a bejeweled green sea, the overhanging tree branches tracing patterns against the cloudless sky. In a minute, the two of us were scudding north along Garner Street. WE walked remarkably fast, as if trying to get in her exercise regimen at the same time as her therapy session. The air felt silken against my face, and my jaw was still swollen but no longer throbbed.

WE was talking about her own marital difficulties, and I had to pay attention. The affair she'd been thinking of conducting had turned into a fling and then wound down, only now she was faced with guilt and letdown. Her husband, an unassuming type named, of course, John, might have been understanding, though that was simply a hypothesis, since she hadn't told him, and I hadn't advocated such a course.

"And your daughter . . ." I murmured. WE had a girl named Ellen in first grade.

"There's nothing for her to know. She's only six."

Was it my imagination, or had WE speeded up at this point? I rounded the corner of Grove Street with her only by picking up my pace, maybe because I was on the outer track. I was about to comment loudly on the matter of guilt when we passed another walker going in the opposite direction. It was the same man I'd seen earlier, arms fluttering like some mad bug. Slightly creepy. The hint of a tan otherwise pallid skin, but he still looked like a grub. I gave him a slight nod, which he mirrored back as he passed.

WE repeated her point about Ellen, and I accorded her a slight nod, as well.

"Anyway," she continued, "what's bothering me is the situation with John."
When I mentioned guilt, she frowned. "Sure . . . but that's not the problem.
It's the whole relationship. It used to be comfortable, but now it's just
boring. And we aren't getting along. I have these fantasies of escape . . . ."
She slowed down as we came into the home stretch of Garner and Somers
and stopped in front of our house. I was prepared to start another circuit,
but she reached out, her fingertips grazing my shoulder. "Here's your home.
Don't *you* ever think of leaving?"

The question was as unexpected as her touch. *Hey, who's the patient
around here, anyway?* grumbled Snoggs. Martin merely sniffed as I scrabbled for a reply. "I'm not . . . sure I should bring myself into this situation. What I can say is that I understand." Her hand dropped down to my
biceps—preparatory to sliding off or squeezing? I'd never know, would I?
I drew myself up, and her arm retracted to her side. "We all have fantasies.
Acting on them is another matter. As you know."

The two of us discussed ways of repairing decayed relationships,
from reinjecting romance to rediscovering family life, but none of them
sounded too convincing. After going around in circles two more times,
I left WE at the curb. "I have an essay that I think you should read," I
told her, thinking of Kierkegaard's "Rotation Method": marriage as a field
that needs tillage and an occasional change of crop, maybe even a fallow
season. It might help. She nodded hopefully, and I said I'd give her a copy
next week.

Screw Kierkegaard, proclaimed Snoggs as soon as WE disappeared in
a BMW-colored plume of exhaust. It was true: old Søren hadn't done much
for me, despite a period when I thought he had the answer to my problem.
Remaking yourself means you're unhappy with the way you are, but what if
the problem is the other person? Or let's be fair, since Jane had composed a
list of complaints similar to mine: the problem was the condition that we'd
created. The only way out at this point was to leave. Maybe. Yes. Now that
it was upon me, the decision bulked too large for me to hold entirely in my
mind. It bulged and oozed into everything, darkening the grass and bending
the air around me. Male that I am, I groped toward food as a cure. I made
my way back to the house, hungry for lunch.

It came to me that I was still locked out. I kicked impenitently at the
back door, a dull thud against an unyielding surface. But since it was almost
noon and I had no commitments until the afternoon, I could think this situation out. I had to gain access to the office to get my keys, that much was
obvious. Since not even a half-open window was available to crawl through,
I'd have to break in somehow. The upper part of the patients' door had three

glass panels: break one of those, and I'd be able to reach the inner door knob. But I couldn't just smash it with my fist, or I'd be picking glass shards out of my hand. Man is a tool-wielding animal, and I needed a crowbar or something. I decided to settle for a rock, but the white pebbles in our driveway were too puny. When I was young, you could find a decent-sized rock in most yards, but today's suburbs had no use for them. Now where had I seen a whole row of small boulders recently?—all along the interior of the Steinbaums' mammoth hedge, that was it.

I trotted back to the topiary wall, looking for the opening I'd seen. There it was, though it looked as if it had shifted contour somewhat—but of course it had. Since I'd pushed my way in and out a couple of hours ago, it was now the shape of a suburban psychiatrist. A few broken twigs marked my previous exit. I pushed my way through tenderly. And there they were within arm's reach, the size and color of ostrich eggs. I didn't even have to pass all the way through, and in fact my legs still protruded from our side of the hedge as I reached for one smooth white beauty.

In a minute, I was at my office entrance, bashing the rock against the leftmost door-pane. It made a louder noise than I'd anticipated, especially since a small hole wasn't enough. I had to smash through the whole section of glass. It took five tries, but I did it. I was just reaching gingerly around to fiddle with the inside doorknob when a blue jay's squawk made me jerk backwards, cutting myself on a jagged shard. After I slid the key into my pants, it looked as if a ketchup bottle had nuzzled my pockets. I changed into another pair of pants after using up three Band-Aids in front of the bathroom mirror and finally going at it with gauze and surgical tape. In the next half hour, I made and consumed a turkey and lettuce sandwich, wrote a note to myself about calling a glazier to fix the office door, and returned the borrowed white rock by throwing it over the hedge. I taped a piece of cardboard over the gap. My afternoon patients politely said nothing about it. Then I climbed into the Subarau and drove to Home Depot with the idea that I could do the repair job all by myself. I got lost amid all the materials available in one aisle alone. Roofing shingles, molly bolts, toilet fixtures . . . by the time I resurfaced, it was past 5:30.

Alex!

You shouldn't roar down suburban streets, and by the time I turned onto Garner Street, I could see the aquamarine minibus pulling up to the curb outside our house. Alex got out, but the bus hesitated: you weren't supposed to drive away until an adult at home had taken charge. I accelerated the last hundred yards and then braked hard, parking right behind the bus. I popped out, singing, "I'm home!" The bus gratefully slid away.

But Alex had already turned away from the house. He frowned. "You're late."

"No, I'm not." I looked at my watch, which read 6:02. Once again, I had the feeling of being technically in the wrong but morally vindicated. I was the Good Daddy, the one who would soon be regretfully departing. "Do you know how fast I had to drive to get here?"

"No." Alex looked dubious. "How fast?"

"Over fifty. Just to reach you in time." I patted the hood of the Subaru as if it were a faithful horse.

"Hmm. And if you weren't here?"

This wasn't unthought of. In fact, Jane had rehearsed him on this. "C'mon, you know."

"No, I don't."

"But Mommy told you. Several times."

"I don't remember."

I sighed. Not the pleased sigh or the totally exasperated sigh but a sigh of acceptance, maybe. "Alex."

No response. He was examining the zipper on his backpack.

"Alex!"

"*Yes*, Daddy." Was he being sarcastic?

"You're supposed to wait ten minutes for me, and if I'm not home by then, go across the street to the DiSalvas." Jane had set up a reciprocal arrangement with Louise DiSalva for her kids, though it involved me rather than Jane because I was the one who'd be home. Like most good executives, Jane was a whiz at delegating responsibility. Anyway, after I rehearsed Alex twice on this point, I let up. "But I'm home now." I fished out the jewel from my pocket, the house key that I'd now separated from the rest of the bunch. "Here, you can open the door."

"Can I?" Alex grabbed the key and bounded up the flagstone path. Amazing how excited kids get from mundane chores. Unless he was making fun again. He was almost there when he tripped on the steps and went flying. He sat there, rubbing his knee. I asked if he was okay. "I . . . guess so."

"Good. So how about opening the door?"

He shrugged. "I don't have the key."

"What do you mean? I just gave it to you."

"No, you didn't."

"*What?*" Given the recent importance of keys in my life, maybe I over-reacted. I picked him up and shook him a bit, just to get him focused on me. "My key!" I might have held him upside down if I'd thought a piece of metal would fall out from somewhere. All I got was a terrified child. But I couldn't stop myself. Snoggs was in control. *"Where is it?"*

"I—I d-don't know . . . ."

"But I did give it to you, right? Right!"

He wouldn't look at me, but I had to make him know who he was dealing with. I pressed his cheeks with my hands and forced him to look at me. When his eyes slid elsewhere, I squeezed harder. "Now you listen to me—"

He was sobbing now, and I had to let him go, but as soon as I did, he looked so awful that I took him into my arms. He didn't pull back. Instead, he butted me with his head. Right on the jaw, which hurt like hell. "Why are you so nasty?"

I dropped him on the steps. "Because you never listen to me!"

"Because you're so mean!"

I clutched my jaw, which felt doubly tender. Family gives it to you both ways. But I wouldn't swat him. Instead, I shouted, "I act that way because you never do what I say!"

"But that's because you're mean!"

I was about to reply the same way when I realized we could circle this way forever. "All right, enough. I'll stop if you stop, okay?"

He muttered something. The kid's recovery was amazing.

"Look," I told him, "I know I gave you the key. You were running to the door. What happened?"

"I fell." He pointed to his knee. "It still hurts."

"I'm sorry. But what happened to the key?"

He shrugged, but fearfully. "I lost it, I guess. It was an accident." Which was as close as I'd get to an apology. So we searched for the key by the path, just beyond the steps, in the bushes . . . we couldn't find it anywhere. Ridiculous that we couldn't locate the damned thing. And my jaw was throbbing again. But far more painful was the thought that I'd better leave before Alex and I destroyed each other. I'd told myself that Alex was a reason to stay, not leave, but I wondered whether I wasn't fooling myself. I raked through one last patch of grass for the key but came up empty-handed.

Maybe the kid swallowed it, said Snoggs. I found that improbable, but I asked Alex anyway. He denied it. So after twenty minutes of looking around, we stood glumly on the path.

"I give up." I shook my head in defeat.

Alex looked up at the trees. "Maybe . . . maybe the key was carried away by a squirrel."

I told him that was unlikely. He proposed the same hypothesis about a sparrow. I said the point was moot. He asked what *moot* meant. I explained, and then he wanted to know about dinner.

"Well, it looks like we may be eating out tonight." I checked my watch: 6:30 already, and Jane was due back around 8:00. Only her car wasn't at the station, so she'd need to be picked up. She might have left a message on the answering machine, but I couldn't get into the house. Not that I felt like being accommodating to my spouse, but this wasn't her fault—unless everything was. Not to mention Alex, who was currently driving me crazy. Annoyance followed by guilt followed by atonement, that was family life lately. Why should tonight be any exception? I wasn't going to be around here much longer, anyway.

"Tell you what." Alex flinched when I clapped him on the shoulder. "Let's eat at McDonald's."

"Really?" He knew I hated the place.

"Yeah, why not?"

He was so grateful that I felt guilty all over again. *Why do you deny your child the most basic pleasures?* inquired Martin. I had no answer, except the fast-food reek that I knew would greet us as we drove up to the golden arches. With its strict zoning regulations, Fairchester didn't even have such a place, but forced it to set up in neighboring Greenwood.

I didn't even feel much like eating, but Alex had a double cheeseburger and large fries and Coke, followed by an individual apple pie. The dinner crowd looked habituated, as if they'd eaten there more times than they could count. I finally ordered a fish sandwich because I thought it would be soft. My jaw. When I stole a sip from Alex's Coke, it stung the inside of my cheeks. We sat there awhile, killing time until Mommy came home, as usual. This McDonald's had a plastic playground set up next to the dining area. The kids climbed up and slid down tubes and slides and ramps and ladders, showing boundless energy, which they no doubt extracted from their parents. A lot of mothers were nursing cups of coffee as they watched their kids with half an eye.

Alex was getting too big for this sort of frolic, but he went down the corkscrew slide a few times, anyway. His shirt rode up each time, exposing his belly like some kiddie erogenous zone. A large, gray man seemed to be surreptitiously watching the proceedings while reading his newspaper. Or maybe I was just overreacting. Finally I told Alex it was time to go.

"My stomach hurts," he complained as we left. "Can you fix it for me?"

"Hmm . . . ." I reached down to give him a tummy rub, something he hadn't asked for in a while. I roamed up to his nipples, no more than twin pink imprints, and almost down to his hairless groin. Children's flesh is such smooth perfection. I made a whorl around his taut little belly button. He sighed contentedly.

We had to hurry to reach the station, if Jane had taken the 7:09. I tried to drive in her Roman charioteer style, but too many other cars blocked the roads. By the time we reached the station, Jane was already standing by the platform, briefcase tucked under her arm. I felt a little lift at seeing her from a distance, as I always do until we start talking and ruin the spell. Usually she didn't need me to pick her up, anyway. But would she come home earlier to make Alex his dinner? I planned to be unavailable for a while after I left.

When she saw our car, she nodded as if in confirmation. She slid into the front seat, and I started off. Unable to mind-read, she acted as if nothing had happened. Alex sat in back, reading a mystery book we'd brought with us: *The Secret of the Old Homestead*. On the way home, I explained that we'd lost the house key and eaten out already. I didn't see any need to go into the ludicrous details.

Jane said she wasn't too hungry but rummaged in the fridge. Alex got into bed soon afterwards. It was a subdued evening—maybe they both sensed something. The quiet was almost unnatural, especially after Alex went to sleep. But when I unfolded the *Guardian* left on our steps that afternoon, the headline opened a hollow somewhere around my sternum. "LOCAL SEX OFFENDER SOUGHT IN RELATED INCIDENTS." A guy who liked to play with kids, it sounded like. Jesus, I'd sent Alex walking to school alone that morning. But Jane rarely read the *Guardian*—should I even tell her? It would just be one more instance of Jane triumphant. Maybe I looked guilty at this point, or possibly Jane could now read my mind like an open newspaper.

She came over to me. "What are you reading?"

"Here, you might as well see this."

Jane is an expert skimmer, and it didn't take her long. She dropped the paper as if it were lethal. "I can't believe you let Alex walk to school today!"

"I know, I know . . . ."

She picked up the front page again, this time scrutinizing it. "It doesn't give too many details. You'll just have to be a lot more careful."

What about you? I almost asked but didn't. *You'll be the one seeing him off every day.* But since I didn't say anything, Jane didn't answer me. She just went on.

"Did you watch him at McDonald's? I've heard that's where certain types hang out. He shouldn't be eating that kind of junk anyway."

"So *you* make his dinner, damn it!" I tried to shut my mouth over the words that Snoggs had just uttered, but they were already out.

Her head rocked as if I'd slapped her. Her face flushed. "I—I can't, not with the job I've got. We've had this discussion before—"

"Don't I know it."

"Then add it to your stupid list, okay?"

Repression's an odd mechanism, mostly seen as constrictive by our tribe of therapists but in fact not always a bad thing. Some things *should* be bottled up, at least for a while. Together but alone in bed, I stared out the window, unable to sleep. The moon, large and intrusive, forced its way through the window and illuminated everything I wanted to forget, from the dumb, domestic furniture of our lives to the graceful crescent of my wife, curved away from me and asleep under our shared Amish quilt. My attempts to please her all seemed ridiculous in this light. Or maybe an exacting woman like Jane could tolerate only herself—now there was an idea I hadn't tried. *Be* Jane.

I saw myself mimicking all her mannerisms, from her toe-tapping and finger-drumming to her work and dress habits. Alex would have two parents who treated him maddeningly alike. And what would our sex life be like? I squirmed, imagining a copycat scene in bed. In her sleep, Jane obligingly turned toward me, but who knew what she was dreaming about? Dreams are difficult to interpret anyway, especially when someone's withholding.

No, I had to leave before everything turned to bitterness. So why hadn't I told Jane yet? Why was I just lying there? Prompted by the urge to do something, I rolled noiselessly off the bed and padded downstairs to where Jane had left her pocketbook. I removed the house key from her coiled cable key chain. Back upstairs, I slid it into the right front pocket of my pants, draped over my bureau. The moon was already losing altitude, half obscured by a thatch of maple leaves from the tree in our yard. Years ago, I'd developed the knack of waking at whatever time I needed to get up, just by setting my mental clock. Surely a locksmith would be open at six in the morning. I shut my eyes and set my interior alarm for five-thirty. I still couldn't sleep, but at least I knew when I'd be up and around.

Chapter 14

Typing a message to the Modesto employee listserv about the importance of data backup, Ted wasn't in the mood to work. The print on the
screen flickered in and out of focus, the words more a collection of random
letters than anything meaningful. When he got up to refill his Tintin Mug for
the third time that morning, another worker waylaid him with a story about
two women in a hot tub, and Ted tried on a smirk. It didn't suit him. *Let
me tell you the one about the eight-year-old boy and his daddy,* he felt like
saying, but didn't. Back at his cubicle, he could hear Joan clack-clacking
away, her inch-long nail extensions sporting little butterfly patterns this
morning.

At lunch time, he'd head for some fast-food place where he could do a
little sightseeing. Lately, he felt a craving for boy-flesh so strongly that he
masturbated three or four times a day, including a couple of sessions in the
restroom at Modesto. It wasn't what he wanted, but live sex would have to
wait until he found some way to get that. "Means of access," a standard data
recovery phrase, kept nudging at him.

Take a Thai vacation, CRater had advised him. *I got addresses.* Maybe
he'd try that one day, but really what he wanted was to make local contact.
Walk around and make friends with some of the school-age boys. Fairchester
was a rich, respectable community, but with bulging family needs. Maybe
he should start a babysitting agency—he giggled at the thought, and Joan
wanted to know what he was laughing at.

"Private joke," he murmured, and when she persisted, he told her the
one he'd heard about the hot tub. She cackled loudly and told him another
that was more obscene. So the mornings trailed into early lunch breaks, and
the afternoons seemed equally empty. He wanted a little boy. The suburbs
were full of them, but they all had invisible "DO NOT TOUCH" stickers on
them. He was beginning to feel as if he had one plastered on himself: "DO
NOT APPROACH."

Evenings were spent in increasingly unsatisfactory sublimation, from
videos and cyber-chat to neighborhood walks and dungeon workouts.

Leaving his apartment one day, he'd actually had a five-minute conversation with the Asian woman in apartment #1: she worked in a bank but was thinking of quitting. The guy in apartment #5 exchanged curt nods with him when they passed. More important, through his daily walks, Ted had acquired a thorough knowledge of the Ridgefield district streets: the core of big houses ranging from Plymouth Avenue to Canterbridge Road, ringed by more modest dwellings that still had to cost a fortune, along Sycamore Street and Jefferson Lane. His favorite spot for sightseeing remained the Ridgefield schoolyard, though these days he was rarely around during peak usage hours.

Today, he got home around six, navigating the last few streets with the practiced ease of a long-term resident. Since he hadn't worked out that morning, he got into his walking gear at once and put in three miles before dinner. Shower, a brief thought of the slurpy seat, but in the end no Dungeon. Half-sick of Spaghetti-O's, he cooked two hamburgers in a frying pan he'd bought for just that purpose. After dinner, he once again put off calling Myra and instead settled in to surf the Web. These days, he found himself gravitating to sites he'd visited before, such as the Ridgefield Elementary School Web pages. The second-grade links in particular had mushroomed into a maze of photos and lists, presentations and bulletin boards. Nothing fancy, no 3-D graphics or flashing HIT buttons, just bright blocks of color and some enchanting kid-poses. A human pyramid built of six solid boys, he saved in his pic files and stared at repeatedly. Some school areas were accessible only with codes, but they were easy to crack. The passwords usually turned out to be the teacher's name. Right now he was most interested in Ms. Celia Hardin's class, which happened to include the boy from Garner Street.

Today he came upon a new link called "BY INVITATION ONLY," so naturally he was interested. It took a moment to get in, but only because he'd accidentally typed "Hardon" instead of "Hardin." Inside, he found a birthday invitation for ten boys at the Derby Roller Rink. Billy McCabe was turning eight. Boys only. Cute eight-year-olds a little unsteady on their skates, bumping into each other in the noisy semi-darkness.

The date was a week from this Thursday at four o'clock. It was all Ted could do to stop himself from clicking on the "RSVP" button, a yellow oblong bordered in red that looked almost edible, like a hot dog smothered in mustard. Before he logged off, Ted memorized the time and place.

*

A week passed, and still I hadn't told my family that I was going to leave. April rained into May. The suburban sex offender was monopolizing everyone's attention. Still on the loose, he provided the *Guardian* with a steady supply of speculation. Wylene at Between the Covers put up a display of "child-protective" literature, as she termed it: everything from the picturebook *Are You My Mommy?* to *Alice in Wonderland*, for some reason. Or maybe it was updated for our era of abduction: "Do not, for any reason, go down a strange rabbit-hole. If something says, 'Eat me,' read the ingredients first."

Principal Levy at Ridgefield issued a few empty soundbites about making children feel secure. "If concerned individuals will simply report any suspicious incidents," he murmured in a memo sent to all school parents, "we can overcome this menace together without creating our own phantom of paranoia." I gather he was worried about parents calling his office to advocate steel shutters over the classroom windows or militia with stun guns. Yet Frances Connolly, always thinking of suing the school on the grounds of something or other, reported seeing a big man in a suit-uniform patrolling the playground around recess time. He turned out to be a security guard on loan from Gianni DiSalva, who donated him as a favor to an anguished parents' group. Gianni had made his pile in the construction business, I'd heard, and I didn't want to know more than that. Levy publicly thanked the DiSalva family but said that such surveillance was contributing to a climate of fear. The kids seemed alternately disturbed and excited. I'd heard that a bunch of tough fifth-grade girls at Pinewood had started a game in which one of them pretended to collapse onto the pavement, and then two other girls would yellow-chalk a victim outline around her. Samantha was one of them. They'd even made up a jingle about the sex offender:

> Chester the Molester,
> Don't you pester
> me!
> See?

It somehow made it onto the Ridgefield Web site for a day before it was taken down.

Meanwhile, I walked Alex to the bus stop every morning and waited until he got on. I wasn't the only one: among the score of kids was a supporting crew of at least a dozen worried mothers and a handful of deputized fathers. I even saw Ellen Ottoway there, her hands around a frail-shouldered James. He was out of the hospital again, though he didn't look as if he should be. When I asked Alex about his friend that afternoon, he looked away.

"He doesn't feel well," Alex said finally. "He says he's tired all the time."

During the day in my office, I counseled semi-well adults, the neurotics among the rest of us maladapts who felt sick enough to seek help. Most didn't want to leave their families. But then I heard from Jerry that Mavis Talent and Arthur Schramm had split up.

"Tell me you're kidding," I begged him. I felt not exactly insulted but unconsulted. And we'd known them for—what?—okay, just three years. But it seemed like forever.

"No, Arthur's sleeping in his office until he can find a place in the city. Mavis is still here with the three kids."

I tried to picture the new domestic arrangement, wondering whether it didn't suit them better. Both Mavis and Arthur owned egos too big to include a spouse and three children. Three, imagine that, and I was struggling with only one. I thought about the wrenched-open window that I'd finally shut on Dalton and hoped I'd done the right thing. I'd put the knapsack outside the window beforehand. Maybe I should have tucked a one-way bus ticket to Canada inside.

The rest of the call was a typical Jerry lunch-hour message, time for catching up on news. I told him the latest about the Connollys: Someone had spotted Frances getting out of a car with an unidentified man at the White Plains Daisy Inn, nicknamed the No-Tell Motel.

"Really? I'd heard that it was Fran*cis* with a strange woman."

We speculated juicily and moved on to professional matters. Jerry particularly wanted to know how his woman executive referral had panned out, and I told him about my power walk with WE.

"I've been thinking about something like that. Sort of suburban therapy." Jerry's book was almost finished, but he was still working on a conclusion.

So was I. My office door still lacked a new glass panel: the glazier had never shown up, and I kept meaning to call again. I wanted closure, but I'd also overslept the morning I wanted to make a new key, so I'd had to ask Jane's permission. The whole story came out, and she laughed, sort of. "How Freudian," she remarked.

I still found daily life with Jane damned awkward. She'd seen my list of grievances, and we'd fought bitterly over it. When I replayed the scene in my dreams, sometimes I was the one who clocked her. These days, whenever I spoke to her, it made for irritation.

"Here, have some more chicken."

"No, it's too dry."

"But you like it that way."

"Not the way you made it."

Alex would hear and start acting poisonous himself. If you asked him to clean his room, he'd say no, and if you threatened him with no dessert or TV, he'd sing an increasingly familiar refrain: "I don't care." At least I could influence his behavior, or try. He was still afraid of Big Daddy. But mostly we didn't get along. "Daaaaady," he'd whine, and I'd reply by imitating him: "Aaaalex." At one point, I shut him in his room for a whole hour, after which he tried to hit me, but I was too fast, pinning his arms as he flailed out. I wasn't going to be the punching bag for my entire family. Then I punished him for that, too, and he came up with a new refrain: "I hate you, I hate you, I hate you."

"Well, *I* don't hate *you*," I told him after listening to his chant for a while.

"You don't?" He glanced up in spite of his resolve never to look at me again.

"No, I just find you immensely annoying at times."

"You're mean!" He ran out of the room.

"No," I told Alex's empty bedroom, which seemed an accomplice to these conversations, "I've just had it." Snoggs was in the ascendancy. At times, I just wanted to exit by the front door and not look back. Only I didn't want to leave such a bad image behind. Mean Daddy, hateful man. Undeserved guilt, that's the worst part about being a parent. So when Billy McCabe invited all the boys in his second-grade class to a roller rink party a few Thursdays from now at four, I grabbed it as a chance to redeem myself. I canceled my last Thursday afternoon session, pleading a family obligation. This party was more important. My own skating was so bad it was comical, but I'd accompany Alex there, I'd act the model father, I'd be kindness itself—something for him to remember. If I had time, maybe I'd do the same for Jane.

Two weeks before the party, the sex offender was arrested. The staid *Guardian* was almost jubilant in its front-page coverage. They cops had caught him in Greenwood. They had some DNA matches and what sounded like incriminating testimony. It looked like he was going to be in jail for a while. The whole town of Fairchester breathed a sigh of relief. Even the hedges bordering the Steinbaums' property seemed to bristle less. Oddly, only after the arrest of the sex offender did I have a nightmare that someone had snatched Alex. In my dream, the incident morphed into a kidnapping, with Jane and me arguing over the ransom money. I wanted to pay in Monopoly money while Jane kept insisting that only Haldome stock would do. Eventually, Alex grew disgusted and escaped by himself, flying home on gauzy wings in time to watch the TV programs he'd missed.

*

At 3:50, Ted found a lovely parking space right near the entrance of the Derby Roller Rink. He killed the engine and sat there for a while, idly flipping through an issue of *Disaster Recovery Management*. "Reaching Out to Your Support System," read the title of one article, with a smiling woman's face on which Ted mentally superimposed Don Feinstein's features. From time to time, he wondered about Don, but the two e-mails he'd sent had gone unanswered. Still, he remained interested in contingency planning, and his boss at Modesto had hinted that the company could use that kind of assistance. Today he had called in sick, so the company would just have to do without him. "What's Your Preparedness Factor?" asked another piece, but Ted shut the magazine. Children were arriving. They slammed car doors and trudged toward the rink entrance, a green-rimmed set of double doors with "IN" and "OUT" marked in faded gold. The building itself looked like a collapsed cake, its flat roof frosted in red and white.

Ted waited until eight boys had entered, by which time it was 4:03. He recognized many of the faces from having studied the class photo. At least 60% of them were cute, with the bumbling, puppyish look that would soon disappear as muscles hardened and bodies grew taller. In most cases, the boys were accompanied by their mothers, though an awkward-looking father or two were also part of the crowd. Spotting a Bobby type slamming the door of a Chevy Tahoe, Ted felt a tightening in his groin. He got out of his Sentra and walked catlike to the entrance.

Inside was a double railing separating the entrance from the exit. Halfway down the corridor was a ticket booth in which a fat man sat, chewing an unlit cigar. Loud canned rock music came from beyond the booth. Ted hadn't been to a roller-skating rink since he was a child, if then—maybe he'd just absorbed the experience from photos and TV. All he really recalled was a rusty pair of skates that adjusted with a metal key. You trundled up and down the block in them, moving even slower than walking. Then Daddy came home, and he put them in the hallway. Then came a scene after dinner, Daddy tripping on a skate, then no more skates. So many parts of his childhood had ended that way. He felt a familiar black haze hovering at the edges of his vision and shook his head to clear it.

But now he was in front of the booth. The fat man looked at him without interest. Adults were six dollars, stated a sign behind the man's head, so

Ted dug into his wallet and paid up. He hadn't thought much about how he'd explain himself—the father of an absent boy? a guy out to relive his youth?—but the fat man didn't ask. He stamped Ted's hand with a red derby logo and waved him inside. The music grew louder the closer he got.

The first sight that hit him was a row of video games, all lit up but mostly unused. Alongside the games was a cheap refreshment stand, including popcorn and cotton-candy machines. The sign in back listed sodas and slush puppies. The children were mostly near the side, sitting on molded plastic benches in cafeteria colors while putting on their skates. The parents were milling around a trestle table as one woman sailed a tablecloth over it and started setting out paper plates and napkins. What was the name of the birthday boy again? Billy Something.

Luckily, Billy's party wasn't the only activity in the place. Other children were out on the rink, a huge painted concrete oval enclosed by a waist-high railing. A few looked like young adolescents, and one torpedo-shaped girl in particular skated damn fast. The rock music chugged from two giant overhead speakers in the low ceiling. As Ted's eyes adjusted to the dim interior lighting, he noticed that another party was taking place on the other side of the refreshment stand, a younger set of kids halfway through a gooey sheet cake.

But Ted was after the second-grade boys, so he approached the benches obliquely. He pretended he was observing Torpedo Girl in the rink. In fact, she glanced at him more than once as she skated circles around a few slow-pokes. She must have been about twelve, blonde and determined, and it struck him that he could have been her father. Such a thought had never occurred to him before, and it made him feel weak in the knees. He had to sit down for a moment on one of the plastic benches. By the time he got up and made his way to the boys, the light panels in the ceiling had shifted from dull yellow to red, green, and blue, and the speakers had changed to something from the Bee Gees.

Like a flock of starlings, the boys all took off as Ted arrived. They crowded onto the rink, bumping up against one another and giggling. They made it hard for real performers to navigate, reducing Torpedo Girl to short, frustrated bursts of speed. Once the kids had evacuated the table area, most of the parents sat down to chat, shouting over the swell of the music. But a few wandered over to the railing to watch, and Ted joined them. Boys glided by, their arms held out for balance. Ted yearned to step out onto the rink and blissfully collide with all those bodies. Any moment now.

*

We got to the party late—because of Alex, naturally. When I picked him up at the Y, his knapsack was nowhere to be found. One of the staffers finally found it under a bench. Then we were all set to go when Alex had one of his scenes, in this case about his after-school snack. "Not today," I told him, "because you're going to eat a lot of junk at the party."

"That doesn't count. I want my pretzel sticks."

To make a long tantrum short, he finally got into the car, but not before we'd hashed out a few rules for special occasions. He muttered that I was evil, and I said not half as much as I could be, and that shut him up for most of the ride. Neither of us was in the best of moods when we arrived. Alex, who had his own pair of rollerblades, ran to the entrance without waiting for me to get out of the car. By the time I passed through the green doors, he was already inside. A seedy gentleman mouthing a stogie looked up briefly when I passed. When I said I was with the McCabe party, he nodded and stamped my hand. It was noisy, and I could feel an incipient headache as I entered the main area.

The kids were already in the rink, some zooming, others coasting to a puzzled standstill. Too bad James couldn't make it. I'd heard he was back from the hospital but languishing at home. Leukemia, which I hadn't mentioned to my son. Alex was hunched over on a red plastic bench, trying to get his skates on. A herd of parents milled around nearby—mostly stay-at-home moms, I couldn't help thinking. They were nice, and always happy to talk with a man, but their main topic was child-rearing, like a bunch of lawyers who can't stop talking shop. One of the mothers, a short, wide woman in comfortable jeans, was spreading a paper cloth decorated with race cars over a long table. Then came paper plates with the same design, obviously Billy's choice. She looked up and smiled in automatic greeting as I neared the table.

"Hi. You must be Alex's dad."

I nodded. "Hello, Billy's mom." I placed the present I'd brought—Alex had left it in the back seat—alongside a small mountain of other gifts rising from a blue plastic bench. It was fortuitously a model car kit, picked out from Fairchester's Toy Boutique earlier in the day. The wrapping job alone, featuring gold cars chasing each other over mountains and deserts, was probably worth five dollars, but I hadn't had time to visit one of the huge discount warehouses outside our town limits.

"I'm done!" Alex stood up, almost slid out, but managed to hold on to the bench.

"Careful . . ." I warned parentally.

"Leave me alone. I can skate." To prove it, he pushed hard away from the bench, gliding toward one of the breaks in the low wall enclosing the rink. A short line of parents leaned against the railing like bettors at a horse race. Only a few were men, and one of them wore gray pants with mismatched green socks. He looked familiar, but the overhead light panels had started flashing in multicolor, so it was hard to make out more details. I tried to join the spectators' line, but when Alex saw me on his first circuit, he waved me away. Some send-off. A tall woman in heels who I recognized as Juan's mother leaned forward to take a picture with a disposable camera. I trudged back to the table, where Billy's mom was removing a three-foot-long cake from its flimsy white cardboard box. Flanking her, three tired-looking women were discussing family vacations, or at least that's what it sounded like. The noise level had risen with the latest amplified song, something else from the golden era of disco. I knew one or two of the women from school events, and we helloed each other. Over in the corner, by an out-of-order video game, another mother shouted into a cell phone.

Meanwhile, Alex was rolling around during one of our last afternoons together. So much for father-son bonding. Jane apparently skated with him during these parties, but I hadn't been on skates since I was Alex's age. At the end of the video-machine corridor was an equipment rental booth, marked by an orange light overhead glowing like a guilty reminder. The three mothers had moved on from vacations to clothing outlets. I could have joined in. Or I could have sulked like Alex. My son, all too much like me in uncomfortably recognizable ways. All right, damn it. As the sound system started playing the theme song from "Saturday Night Fever," I headed toward the rental counter for a set of wheels.

*

After waiting for the right interval, Ted took a squeaky-shoed step onto the rink. A chunky boy wearing knee pads had just pushed by, opening a gap between him and a clump of three other boys elbowing each other as they advanced. They saw Ted in time and swerved. Two veered toward the inside while the other headed for the rink wall and collided with a dull thud.

"Sorry," offered Ted and reached out a helping hand to the boy. The kid was red-haired and freckled, gawky without being tall. He wore a goofy grin even when splayed out on the rink floor. But he grabbed the hand Ted extended and was upright before Ted even had a chance to be pulled down. With a brief thanks, he pushed off the wall and zoomed ahead to join the two other boys. Ted watched the whirl of kids, pondering what to do next.

Beyond encountering a lot of little boys, he hadn't thought much about a plan. His methodical manner deserted him in these situations, his mind filling haphazardly with soft flesh and a tangle of limbs.

Another try. Swiveling his head as if looking for a stray child, he advanced into a lane on direct collision course with a flying wedge of approaching boys. Torpedo Girl came around the pack as if propelled from behind, scowled at him, and skated right by with an inch to spare on the right. A second later, the wedge of boys split magically into two, though not quite all of them. One of the last kids sailed right into him. Ted loved the fleshy impact, the windmill arms out to greet him. "Sorry, *whoops!*" he cried, executing a half turn so that the two of them were almost dancing together. When he pressed himself against the boy's body, he could feel a gentle squirming that was nearly too much to bear. After a slight squeeze that he hoped would go undetected, he sent the boy on his way with a heavy pat on the rear. The lighting was dim, the noise high—what the hell. This was heaven.

He had done this two more times, almost straddling his last boy, when a woman coasted by and shouted something at him. Ted shook his head to indicate that he couldn't hear.

"I said, you're not supposed to be here without skates!" She pointed accusingly at his sneakers as she passed. He was inclined to ignore her, but she looked darkly back at him—and knocked into a boy stubbornly skating clockwise. The way they clutched each other for support gave Ted an idea: he could collide even more accidentally on purpose if he were rolling. That way, he'd have a good motive. Brushing by one last eight-year-old, he exited the rink with a sigh. He'd be back soon, though—rolling along.

*

I remember the few times my mother took me ice-skating at a rink with a changing room that smelled of wet wool. She used a metal hook to pull the laces tight, grimacing as she did. The rink from bygone days featured organ music, not disco, while people glided around. Sometimes they slid, like me. I had weak ankles or something. At least these new rental rollerblades didn't require a hook. Like ski boots, they closed with three adjustable plastic latches. One, two, buckle my skates.

Still, when I stood upright, I felt the tremor of youth. The slightest motion sent me forward as I scrambled to regain my balance. I grabbed onto the railing and watched the bodies skim by. "*Are you ready . . . ? Now, one-two-three!*" boomed the rock music from the giant ceiling-amplifiers, perched as if they might fall on my head. My reason for embarking on such foolishness was to be with Alex, to show him I wasn't such a drip. A few other adults were whizzing around, though one woman in black stretch pants was emitting little shrieks every ten feet. An adolescent girl with big thighs moved down the straightaway like a guided missile. *I can do this,* I told myself, echoing a phrase from the one psychiatric support group I'd ever led. *Prove it,* sniped Snoggs. I entered the arena just after a rush of children and gamely pushed off the railing. Not so bad—except when I tried to turn and my blades began to cross. I managed not to fall by spreading my arms outward as if trying to fly. I slid to a stop, becalmed in the middle of the rink. I shuffled my blades and got going again, this time with more assurance. Others were passing me, perilously close to cutting me off, but I hadn't fallen yet. *"Now pick it up!"* taunted the rock song electrically. *"Four-five-six!"*

I moved on with the latest clump of kids, though slowly drifting behind. The lights flashed green and yellow as I looked for Alex.

*

Ted was surprised at how comfortable he felt, gliding by with the slightest of kicks. The metal skates he remembered had been far clunkier, and he'd had to trundle along. Maybe it was all the walking he'd been doing recently—more in control of his body or something. Slipping in at the far entry, he joined the stream of skaters and at first concentrated on simply keeping up speed. The rhythm of the disco music, "I *want* to find *some*place to *be* . . . I *want* to find *some*one like *me*," matched his stride. Right push . . . glide . . . left push . . . skim along . . . . After a few laps, he found himself gaining on a throng of boys, their legs straddling the air as if they were riding sawhorses. He fantasized bending backwards in a limbo move and gliding under their groined arch. Or sliding right through their bodies and emerging fulfilled on the other side. As he slowly passed them, individual identities began to emerge: the goofy red-haired kid, a blond pudge-belly, a wiry kid whose arms were furiously in motion. He tried to inhale their essence, but instead breathed in the stale popcorn smell from the refreshment stand. "NO STOPPING," cautioned a poster on the far wall. As he skated about with increasing confidence, the painted cinder-block walls began to blur.

*

Since I can't skate well, let alone fast, I decide to let Alex pass me rather than try catching up to him. The colored lights make for poor visibility, but I think that's him in the gray shirt on the other side of the rink. He's not a smooth skater like some of the other boys, but he's making steady progress. I wish I could say the same for me. Every time I push off from one skate, I lurch in the other direction. The damned music isn't helping matters—*"Falling, falling, I think I'm falling . . . in love!"* The kids instinctively know to skate around me.

I can't look back and keep my balance, so all I register is a gray blur from behind. "Hey, Alex!" I call out. When he's abreast of me, I reach out to tap him on the shoulder. I end up leaning on him as he tries to shrug me off.

"You're gonna make me fall." He moves faster, my hand now trailing from his body like a tail. One of the other boys looks back and grins.

"I thought I'd skate with you." I feel pathetic. When he pushes away, I'm still holding on. But his burst of speed pulls me off balance. I grab out for something, which happens to be my son. *Falling, falling*—down we go, in a confusion of arms and legs, with Alex somehow pinned beneath me. I've bashed my knee. That concrete floor is hard as concrete. I slither away, favoring the other leg. I could be a snake on skates. The girl like a missile shoots right between us, scowling.

Alex scrambles to his feet. (How can he do that on skates?) He doesn't seem hurt, just terribly annoyed. "Are you okay?" I ask, like concerned parents everywhere.

"Leave me alone." Without waiting for me to right myself, he skates away. *"It's nothing, nothing at all,"* the speakers overhead reassure me. *"Nothing to say or do . . . ."*

"Wait!" But he won't, so instead I'm the one who waits, coasting slower and slower until I'm almost at a standstill by the railing. He'll come by soon—that's the great thing about circularity. Unless he decides to skate in some new direction, which would be just like him, wouldn't it? My son defines the term *idiosyncratic*. In fact, I miss him the next time around, probably because he's flanked on both sides by other boys. So I half-skate, half-hobble, to just after one of the long stretches, where the oval starts to curve. An electric sign on the wall grabs my attention:

ALL SKATE, REVERSE, GAME
ADVANCE, COUPLES, TRIOS
WALTZ, SPECIAL, BACKWARDS

"ALL SKATE" is lit right now. I try to imagine waltzing on skates and come up with collision after collision.

Now comes my second chance: Alex is coming into the stretch, pushed by centrifugal force toward the outside. The truth is, he can't turn that well—he's only eight, after all. And he's not that well-coordinated. A red-haired kid from his class and some fat blond boy are handling themselves as if they've taken a course. It's just like on the soccer field, when I see someone Alex's age execute a perfect goal and wish I were the kind of father who kicked the old pigskin (or is it thrown?) in the backyard with his boy. Anyway, I figure I'll slide alongside and do a lap or two with him. As he glides toward me, I push off to build up some speed.

But the flashing of the pink-yellow-green lights throws me off. What I thought was an open space turns out to be a boy wearing a green shirt, and he plows into my legs. I manage to stay upright, but the boy falls. I can't stay to help him up—I have to be with my son. "Sorry . . ." I tell the boy on the floor and push off to merge with Alex. Here I am, trailing parallel to him as we go into the first curve. I wave in an arc wide as a windshield wiper, but he doesn't wave back.

"C'mon." I reach out for him. No response. I grit my teeth, longing for what all fathers desire. I want to give him a hug, I want to smack him, *I want him to heed me*. But when I get to within a breath of him, he takes a turn toward the middle of the rink. "Hey!" I reach out for him, but he's too far away already.

Just before he rejoins the circle on the other side, he looks back. "Go away!" he shouts over his shoulder. "You're not my daddy, anyway!"

*

As Ted skates about with increasing confidence, he begins to take greater notice of his surroundings. On the far wall is an old sign that reads, "HOCKEY PLAYED HERE," with a game board listing "PLAYER, PENALTY, ROTATION STATION, HOME, PERIOD, GUEST." Hockey is a sport he never tried. It was for real bruisers who didn't mind losing half their teeth. Will some of these boys turn out that way? It's hard to tell, though one of them, a husky, mop-haired kid with a scowl, already dives ahead as if he held a stick in his hand. Another skates as if reading a book in front of him, always unprepared for the turns. Occasionally he realizes how far behind he's fallen and veers across the oval to catch up. He's wearing a gray shirt and looks familiar, but only after Ted has passed him twice does he recognize him as the strange boy from the bakery.

On skates, Ted has managed to bump only a few boys satisfyingly. At this speed, seemingly accidental groping is too difficult, and outright collisions are too unpredictable. *"Only the lonely . . ."* wail the speakers

above. When he encounters the bakery boy for the third time—Alex, isn't
it?—he decides to keep pace with him. It isn't easy, since the boy's erratic,
but Ted manages. Alex really doesn't seem focused on what he's doing, as
if replaying a different scene entirely in his head. But the kid is undeni-
ably cute, with chipmunk cheeks and that groin-stiffening pout. After one
and a half circuits paralleling him, Ted's thinking of drifting off to shadow
another boy. Then around the next curve, Alex's skates keep straight instead
of turning. He tries to veer too quickly and is about to skid out when Ted
steadies him around the waist.

"There you go." He lets go after a pause and pats the boy on the head.
Nothing to misconstrue there.

"Thanks." Alex skates straight for a moment before looking over at his
helper. "Hey, aren't you the man from the bakery?"

Ted nods. *Yeah*, he doesn't say, *and you're the boy who licked me*. Instead,
he waits for something to distract Alex, to draw him in another direction,
though of course they're circling the same way. But something about the boy
is troubling, if alluring, like poisoned fruit. "*Only the lonely . . . can play . . .*"
the music whines overhead. The lights flash purple and rose.

Alex breaks the noisy silence. "Do you come here often?"

The question is so unexpected that Ted laughs, then quickly stifles himself when he sees how serious the boy is. "Me? Here?" He decides to pose
a question himself. "Why do you ask?"

"Because . . ." Alex executes a faulty turn and nearly collides into Ted's
waiting arms ". . . you skate really well."

Ted dismisses the compliment with a wave of his hand, incidentally
brushing Alex on the shoulder. "Nah. I learned when I was a kid, but I
haven't skated since. I guess it just comes back to you." The shoulder is
warm to the touch, the boy overheated from exercise.

Alex takes in this news gratefully. "I hope it'll be that way with me.
When I get it, I mean." He skates another ten yards before he asks, "Are you
here alone?"

Ted almost loses his balance at that. "Yes," he finally replies. "I'm
not—" *I'm not a daddy*, he thinks—"I'm not with any other boy."

"That's good." Alex seems to be narrowing the half-foot between them.
"I'm here alone, too."

"Really?" Ted takes a quick look around, not that anyone can see much.
He supposes it's possible: kids car-pooling or something. "So where are
your parents?"

"They're in Arabia."

"What?" The sound system has just shifted into high gear, with a new song that seems twice as loud as the previous one. "*Woo hoo hoo . . . !*" echoes in Ted's ears. Meanwhile the lights have started to strobe, which makes him feel as if he's skating through a series of stop-time photos. Each moment is colored yellow, red, or blue. Torpedo Girl whizzes by, looking like three people.

Alex repeats what he said, shouting this time. He explains that his family has abandoned him, but he's still going to school. Ted catches most of it and expresses loud sympathy. He isn't sure what to make of Alex's story, and anyway, it's hard to think with the light-and-sound band playing in his brain. The fuzzy edges of a blackout flirt with his vision.

By now, Alex is quite close to Ted, so when he hollers, "I want to go now!," Ted hears every word. Since Ted doesn't react, Alex repeats his sentence and reaches out a hand. After a moment's consideration, Ted takes it.

*

Just because my son has disavowed his parentage doesn't mean I've forsaken him, though it's tempting. I wonder how many people heard Alex yell that I'm not his father. I should have shouted right back, "So find a ride with someone else!" I should have hauled him back by his shirt and made him eat those words. I should have worked on his sense of guilt, if he has one, and I'm sure he must. I shouldn't be skating—or fumbling—around this rink, trying to relocate the boy. It's as if he's hiding again, only this time in the open. The blinking colored lights don't help. For some reason, the music's grown louder, too. Goblin rock or something, with a refrain that sounds like "*Hoo hoo hoo!*"

Damn it, if I'm not his father, who am I? And why would I be going to all this trouble? I tell myself I'll miss him and try to believe it.

After a few pratfalls, I realize that my best bet is to anchor myself somewhere and wait for him to pass. But when I reach out for support at the far end, it's just a trompe l'oeil railing painted on the high cinder-block wall, and I fall again. A pink-red captioned sign, "NO STOPPING," reprimands me three yards ahead. The hell with that. I stumble over to where the real railing ends and post myself there.

Is that him coming along the inside? I'm about to make what the police call a positive ID when the overhead panels become strobe lights. Everything gets reduced to flickers, and I almost lose my balance again. By the time I've got both hands on the railing again, the gray shirt is gone.

"*Not me or you . . . hoo hoo hoo . . . !*"

Next time, I'll get him for sure. By blinking rapidly, I can sort of see in synch with the strobe lights. Waiting . . . waiting . . . coming around the bend . . . but who's that with him? Looks like an adult.

"Alex!" I shout, but the music blocks my voice. I yell out his name again.

*

Threading his way through the thick skein of skaters, Ted leads Alex toward the break in the railing near the restrooms. Or maybe Alex is leading him—it's hard to tell. The small hand in his tugs at him, but which way? As they emerge at the far end, a mirrored ball in the center of the rink starts to turn, casting giant orange Cheerios on the floor and walls. But outside the rink, all the colors flatten out, and the two of them are left standing between a karate video game and an out-of-order pinball machine.

"Do you have a car?" asks Alex, disengaging his hand.

"Um, yeah." Ted is still trying to gauge how far to take this. It seems too good to be true. Not to mention dangerous. He thinks briefly of urging Alex toward the men's room.

Alex plants his hands on his hips. "Can we go now?"

Ted gestures downwards. "What about your skates?"

"Oh, yeah . . . ." Alex looks sheepish. He bends down and starts to unbuckle them, but then looks up. "Wait, can't we just skate out of here? That would be so neat."

"Maybe." A vision of them both skating out the exit floats into Ted's mind, replaced by a cigar-chewing fat man chasing after them. "But these aren't my skates." He places both hands on Alex's shoulders, gently massaging. "Look, I've got to return them at the booth and get my shoes. Where are yours?"

"Never mind. I want to skate to the car."

"Suit yourself." He pats Alex on the back. "But stay here till I get back. I'll be quick, okay?"

"O . . . kay."

Ted glides over to the rental booth and unlaces his skates. The kid behind the counter is reading a hot rod magazine and doesn't even look up for the transfer of shoes and skates. His face is briefly obscured by a floating orange halo reflected from the mirrored ball. The sound system's pounding out a heavy bass line with a lyric that sounds like "*Gimme gimme gimme.*" Grabbing his loafers as they change from orange to green, Ted doesn't even take the time to put them on but pads right over to where he's left Alex.

Time to get new socks, he thinks, as a hole in the right big toe snags on something.

The boy's right where he left him, impatient to leave. "What took you so long?"

"Nothing." Ted checks his watch as he slips on his shoes. "One minute and thirty-three seconds, that's all."

"It seemed like ages." Alex gets to his feet and rolls gently toward him. He sticks out his small hand against Ted's waist to stop himself. "Let's go."

*

This music feels like it's boring a hole in my ear. And these colored lights—the more they flash, the less I can see. The rink operator must've decided the kids weren't having enough fun or something. I wait three whole circuits, and I still don't see him. I can't locate that gray shirt anywhere, not when everything's suddenly green or pink. When I shout out "Alex!," the sound system bats back "*Ally-ally-ally-oop!*" Now I'm getting worried. I know he's out there, but I also know Alex. My annoying son, who likes to hide.

The bathroom. I'll bet that's where he is. Little brat, does he know how frantic this makes me? Probably standing stock-still by the toilet stall, daring me to find him. The sign for the men's room glares in fluorescent orange near the exit, untinted by the light show. I skate over there, nearly running over that man in mismatched green socks—odder now because he's not wearing any shoes. We're both in a hurry, but I swerve, skidding out the last ten feet. "Alex!" I yell, clack-clacking sideways into the bathroom. "I see where you're hiding, so come on out!"

A pair of skates sticks out from the bottom of the cubicle divider. I bang heavily on the side. The toilet flushes rapidly. "My name's not Alex, it's Jimmy," squeaks an indignant voice.

Shit. I should've known—those aren't even Alex's skates, anyway. I apologize and lumber out. *So where is he?* I skate over to the birthday table, where Billy McCabe's mother has just set out the drinks. I steady myself by reaching out for the table.

"Have you seen Alex?"

"No," she replies brightly, "but the food's ready. I'm going to call them all in now."

I slide-glide-skid over to the railing to watch the kids troop in. First comes the birthday boy, Billy McCabe, a mop-haired chunky kid already

acting like a world-weary eight-year-old. A dirty blond kid wearing a
"SKOOL DAZE" shirt follows so close on his heels that he almost trips.
Then come seven more kids, a few of whom I know from afternoons in the
park. Not one of them is Alex. I ask the last one off the rink, a shrimp of a
kid with purple Magic Marker on his hands, if he's seen Alex. He shrugs
purply.

The music has risen a level in noxiousness. "*Be me, be me, be . . .
yeah!*" Plenty of other kids are still skating around, but I can't see a goddamned thing with all those lights flashing in my eyes. The only way is to
get out there and pass through them all. I take a deep breath, shove off from
the railing, and turn to where I'm facing an onslaught of kids. Five or six
at the most, but they keep changing colors, and none of them is my son.
"Alex!" I shout, waving my arms like a mad windmill.

*

Ted takes Alex's hand and starts to lead him down the entry ramp like
a mannequin on castors. As they pass the booth, the fat man looks up, notes
the kid is wearing his own skates, and shifts his attention back to the TV
set by his stool. Outside the exit, the sudden absence of music and colored
lights clap them in the face.

"I can hear again," marvels Alex.

"Yeah. It was kind of loud." Hand in hand, half skating, half walking,
they emerge in the parking lot. Ted looks four or five ways as if waiting to
cross an impossibly complex intersection. No one around. "C'mon." He
hustles Alex toward the Sentra and unlocks the passenger's side for him.
"Get in."

"But my skates—"

"They'll fit."

With a little push from Ted, Alex reluctantly gets in and automatically
fastens his seatbelt. His skates make short runs on the carpeted interior.
"Where are we going?"

Ted looks curiously at his prize. "Home."

*

The only way to rake through this crowd is to skate backwards. But I
can't see much. It feels like the mirrored ball in the center of the rink is spot-
lighting my forehead. I grope a few boy bodies. No Alex, no Alex—God
damn it, where *are* you? If you show up now, I'll forgive you till next week.

If you show up later, I'll make you sorry you were born. I'm halfway around the oval by now, dizzy and seeing stars on the wall in blue and gold. No, those *are* stars painted there, floating above an American flag. The music bops my ears: "*Want to find someone like you, wish that I could fly, too . . . .*"

More boys, and some cries of "Hey!" and "Watch it!" Alex has gone, he's skating home just to spite me, he's left for the moon. I've got to get out of here. Red-blue-pink and back again. I sway leftwards, heading for the railing. I'm just about to leave the rink when *whoompf*—that girl shoots right into me. We go down in a tangle of limbs, and I get a mouthful of thick thigh.

"Why'ncha watch where you're going?" she barks, levering herself up.

"I'm trying to find someone."

She jerks a thumb toward the exit. "Ask Al in the booth." She skates off.

Okay, I'm out of the rink, and the booth is right ahead of me. As I skate by, the fat man leans out the window and yells at me. "Hey, pal, the skates!"

I skid to a stop an inch from his nose. "Have you seen a little boy . . . blue skates . . . gray shirt?"

The man nods, pointing with his unlit cigar. "Yeah, he left a few minutes ago. With someone else."

"With who?" I practically grab the guy by his shirt. "Where'd they go?"

"Just a man. Look, I can't keep track of who comes in here with who. You want me to call the cops?"

"No. Yes! What did the guy look like?"

He scratches his head maddeningly slowly. "I dunno . . . I think he was wearing green socks."

The rink starts spinning, and my skates slide out from under me. I end up clutching the fat guy's shirt as he reaches for the telephone. I want to stop the planet, reverse time, make it so it never happened, but I settle for 911. The police will be right here, any day now.

When the cops come, I'm back at the party asking questions, but no one knows a damn thing. All I have left are Alex's empty shoes.

Chapter 15

"My God, how could you leave him alone like that!" Those were the first words out of Jane's mouth.

"I couldn't help it, okay?" I'd been pressing the receiver so hard against my ear that it hurt, and then I wanted to throw it under the sink. "It was dark in there! The music was deafening."

"What's the music got to do with anything?" She paused, and I could hear another phone ringing in her office. The sound seemed to snap her into another direction. "I'm sorry, I didn't mean that. But what did the police say? Where do they think he is now?"

"*I don't know.*" The Greenwood detective I'd talked to had kept refer-ring to "an abduction situation." He was still here with another policeman, poking around upstairs—what the hell was that thump? I couldn't think, could barely speak except in short sentences. "They've issued an alert. They're doing a search. They're checking out the house."

The detective, Ferrara was his name, loomed in the doorway. He held out a hammy hand. "Maybe I should talk to her, sir."

I gave him the receiver and watched him go through a yes-and-no series, mostly no near the end. Finally he handed the phone back to me.

Jane was brief. "I just can't—I can't *believe* this. I wish—I'm coming home *right now.*"

And she hung up. That had been twenty minutes ago. The police had left shortly afterwards, telling me to sit tight. If I left for any reason, I was to make sure someone stayed home and check in for messages. Now it was a quarter to seven. I was pacing around the kitchen in large, sloppy loops that had me bumping into chairs. Voices were beginning to get at me, weird tones I'd never heard from Martin or Snoggs. *Alex is missing*, I know, *Alex is gone*, shut up already. *It was all your fault, you never should* knock it off, goddamn it. I rounded another corner and kicked viciously at the pots-and-pans cupboard. *Where the hell was he?*

The police had asked a lot of questions, but half of them I didn't like. "What was your last contact with him?" "Did the abductor use force?" I told them all I knew, but that included my argument with Alex. I didn't mention those awful words, "You're not my daddy, anyway!" Yet the guy in the booth at the rink was a witness to how peaceably they'd exited. The cops even thought he might be hiding somewhere in the house, for Christ's sake. Or had run away somewhere. They'd put out an all-points bulletin, but obviously the guy was indoors somewhere—I could *feel* it.

I heard the sound of a motor thrumming down the road, so I ran to the front of the yard to see it, but it was only a van passing by. No arm from the front window tossing a ransom note tied to a brick. Not that I thought it would happen. I glared at the stupid vehicle passing out of sight. Maybe because of the sex offender they'd caught last week, the idea of kidnapping never entered my head. Jane hadn't mentioned it, either. "WE HAVE YOUR LITTLE BOY. LEAVE $100,000 IN SMALL, UNMARKED BILLS BY THE THIRD OAK TREE IN THE PARK OR YOU WILL NEVER SEE YOUR SON AGAIN." But this seemed unplanned, a casual pickup. But they'd already caught the guy—but was there some rule, only one molester per suburb? I kicked the cabinet so hard I split the wood. This was *another* guy, idiot.

I could almost see him in my tortured mind's eye: gray slacks and mis-matched green socks. That was what the fat man in the booth remembered. Not only that, but I could have sworn I'd seen the guy elsewhere. I'd told Ferrara all that, and now what was I supposed to do? I glanced up at the trees to obliterate the scene of the rink before my eyes. When the spreading branches began to resemble arms reaching out, I looked away. I went inside, shut the door, and returned to the kitchen. If I paced long enough, I'd wear a circular groove in the linoleum.

I want my son.

I ran outside again, despite my instructions. Suddenly I was on the sidewalk. I trod up and down the block, peering at everyone's windows. But it was close to sunset, and the reflected glare made it impossible to see inside. Should I start knocking on doors? I had the feeling that whoever had gone off with Alex was local, that if I walked around Fairchester long enough, I'd come upon them. Were the police searching that way in their patrol cars? My description of the abductor wasn't too detailed, though I knew him from somewhere. Average height, average face, nerdy-looking. The kind who'd blend into any crowd. Except for those mismatched green socks. "*Attention, all cars: be on the lookout for a man with green socks, not matching, repeat—not matching.*" Shit. No one would report on his car because he hadn't done anything when he parked at the rink. "*Oh, yes, officer, I know the vehicle you mean. License plate looked mighty suspicious. "* Even when he and Alex got into his car, they probably seemed like father and son. That really galled me—Alex was mine.

Come back, and I'll never leave.

"Daddy!"

I glanced over to the right, but it was another kid, wanting his father to throw the ball. Alex would have pretended it was a bomb, and ducked. *Play ball with me, sonny, and I'll ball you.* I shook my head to clear it again as the baseball hit the kid's mitt with a smack. The kid was tall and blond and looked nothing like my son. Should I tape posters on all the telephone poles?

At least my description of Alex would help: light brown hair, blue eyes, elfin face, slightly built, 4'0", 54 lbs., not to mention the wallet snapshot I'd given to Ferrara. It happened to be an old photo from a year ago; still, it was unmistakably Alex. But again, they'd be indoors by now, so what was the purpose of that?

As if to emphasize my point, the man and his son went inside their fake Tudor house and closed the door. They left no evidence of what they'd been doing. And how could you tell what was going on indoors? The blinds would be shut. Even a boy's piercing scream might be muffled by the surrounding walls. Past Emory Street, I started jogging, then broke into a run, but stopped at the next block. What the hell was I doing?

I walked swiftly home: no Jane. No ransom notes on the lawn, no messages on the machine. Nancy McCabe, the birthday boy's mother, had already phoned twice, but the second time I just thanked her curtly and hung up. No one at the rink had been much help, though they offered to do anything—put out the word, hold our hands, set up a neighborhood watch. One of the mothers told me her husband had FBI contacts. Another offered to cook for us. Maybe later, maybe now—I couldn't think. I was starved but didn't feel like eating. I grabbed a handful of Alex's pretzel sticks and almost choked on them. Being alone wasn't good for me right now, and I longed for Jane. It was 7:45.

An unknown car pulled up to the curb. A black limousine with a T&LC license plate. Jane scrambled out, dropped her briefcase, picked it up, and the car glided away. Before she could take out her key, I swung the front door wide open. Her face looked ravaged, clawed.

She dropped her briefcase on the foyer table and gave me a long, hard hug. While it lasted, I felt secure, her strong arms holding me firmly against her.

"I came home as fast as I could—I took a car service. Look." She opened her briefcase and extracted a thick sheaf of downloads. "I had Bryce print out the profiles of all the known sex offenders in the county. Fairchester actually has a few."

"The rink's in Greenwood."

"I know, but I've got other towns in here. They say these crimes are often local."

"So you don't think it's a kidnapping, either." I kicked at the floor.

"No! I don't know." She bit her lip. "I wonder if they even caught the right suspect last week."

I held up the list. "So what are we going to do, knock on all their doors?"

"*We have to do something!*" Her face crumpled, and I could see that the runnels on her cheeks were where tears had sluiced through the makeup. When she sagged, she was shorter than me.

I reached out to support her. "Okay, but what? I just looked around the neighborhood. Want to get in the car and drive around?" I rolled my eyes. God, was I tired. "I have no idea where to start."

"Have you phoned the police again?"

"No, but they said to check in around eight."

"I'm going to call right now. What's the number?"

I recited it from memory. "But it's Greenwood, not Fairchester."

"Okay." She grabbed the cordless from beside the refrigerator and punched in the numbers. "Who'd you speak to?"

"The same guy who talked to you. A detective named Ferrara."

In a remarkably short time, Jane was hooked up to someone answering her questions. "No . . . yes, I *know* all that." She swung her head as if she wanted to club something with it. "But he could be *hurt* . . . . All right, all right, we'll make a list." She grabbed the pen and notepad stuck to the refrigerator door and began jotting things down.

What was I doing? Sloshing some gin into a dirty cup from the sink. Then I thought better of it and poured it out.

When Jane got off the line, her face was flushed. "I told Ferrara we'd give him the numbers of all Alex's classmates. They might know something. Maybe they've seen this guy before."

"Maybe *I* have. Or *you*. Maybe he hangs out at roller-skating rinks." I blinked hard against the scene of the rink coming back to me, the colors flashing. "Damn it, I'm almost sure I've seen him somewhere else."

"*Almost* sure? *Where*, Michael?" Jane leaned forward, her eyes focused horribly on me.

I backed away till I was against the sink. "I don't know . . . maybe I'm wrong. It's hard to see in that lousy rink. And I wasn't looking for anyone in particular."

"That's not helpful!"

"It's not my fault. We had a little argument, but so what?" I could smell the burnt odor of blame in the air. "Usually *you* take him there."

"I wish I had. Then none—"

"'None of this would have happened,' is that what you were going to say?" I came forward again, fists clenched. "Don't second-guess me on this."

"I'm not guessing. When I take him there, I skate with him for a while."

"Then let *me* guess. After that, you find some quiet corner where you can whip out your cell phone."

"So what?"

"You check your voice mail for any messages. The amps are blasting Kiss, and you're trying to get in touch with Harry Whatsisname—"

"Stop it!" She clapped her hands over her ears, as if trying to block out my accusation along with that awful music. She looked scared around the eyes, which flickered and couldn't meet mine.

"It could have happened with you, too. Don't throw it all on me." I began to pace again, freed from my position by the sink. Each time around, the kitchen looked more like a cell block. "Let's *do* something." I picked up the phone. "Why don't you start getting those phone numbers?"

"Okay." She reached for the receiver, dropped it, picked it up, rummaged in the nearby cabinet drawer for the local phone book and a pad and dropped them, too. "Jesus, I can't hold on to anything." She extended a hand and we gripped each other so hard it hurt. "Tell me he's all right, wherever he is."

"I—I hope so, too."

Jane bit her lip. "I'll call Ms. Hardin first. She's got all the names. Besides, she might know something."

"Does she live in Fairchester?"

"Damn." Jane looked around fixedly, as if hoping to find Alex's teacher within hailing distance. "I'll call Information in all the surrounding towns. I think her first name's Celia."

"The cops could get it for you. Maybe she doesn't even have a listing."

She half-sighed, half-snorted. "All right, I'll call Ferrara again. What are you going to do?"

"I'll think of something." *Better hurry, he's your son* shut up. *He could be spreadeagled on a bed somewhere with his*—I slapped myself this time. It helped for a moment.

Jane didn't notice. What were her demons like? She pointed at the printouts. "Why don't you look through these? Maybe you'll recognize the guy."

I took the sheaf of paper to my office, where I could focus, because Jane was dialing away in the kitchen. Being apart right now didn't seem right, but what was I supposed to do, hold the receiver for her? The two of us in that kitchen just might combust. If the abductor were in the same room, what would Jane do? I visualized her tearing him limb from limb. Then I kicked the remains.

I looked at the papers. The printouts were of registered sex offenders in Dover county: name, place of residence, race, sex, crime committed . . . each with a mug shot. Phrases like "criminal sexual contact" and "endangering the welfare of a child" jumped out at me. These people were repeat-offenders who had to register with the local authorities every 90 days. Darryl Hissel, age 34, black, male, residing at 2023 Crescent Drive in Greenwood, convicted for criminal restraint. "Criminal restraint"? "If the victim is less than 18 years of age and the offender is not a parent or guardian." Jane—or Bryce—had printed out a glossary of terms from a sex-crime Web site that defined everything. If the perpetrator was related, did they just call it family matters? I flipped shakily through more profiles. "Child luring," what was that? The next two were sodomy charges.

At the clinic where I used to work, we had a few sex offenders, including a molester I was assigned to, though he didn't stick around long. A nerdy guy in his thirties who spoke drably, got excited only when describing little boys. But we'd talked for a while: where he lived, his colorless job, why he didn't like his neighbors, his anger at his father. Details came back to me: his refusal to meet my eye, his fluttery hand gestures that never matched what he said. His specialty was playground slides.

I pushed aside the rap sheets and stood up. All sorts of people committed sex crimes, but the man with the gray slacks seemed like a type I knew. Now what? My mouth felt dry, and I could have used that gin I'd poured out. Instead, I wandered over to the couch and lay down, whispering, "Help me." I was dead tired but so keyed up I could have punched a hole in the ceiling. With its wormhole acoustic tiling, it now looked sinister as a dungeon wall. All those neurotic sounds trapped in there, waiting to fall down on my head. *Was Alex in a place like this?*

I tore my mind away from that path, but then I floated down roads with big suburban houses on small lots, maddeningly smug. The kids and their over-programmed after-school activities, the adults and their job-job-jobs. Bunch of egotists thinking they deserved the best. Would the kids grow up that way, too? I thought of Juan the castoff kid, Mark the soccer star, Samantha the juvenile delinquent, the Connollys' perfect children, and Mavis and Arthur's screw-ups. James, now there was a saintly child, but James was almost dead.

Little angel.

Not a good direction to think. I shut my eyes and desperately tried to recall where I'd been with Alex recently. Not too many places. I dragged him on errands, and he resented that. The rink kept coming back to me in all its noise and colors, as if I were imprisoned in some hideous echo chamber: "*Are you ready? . . . now, one, two, three . . . .*" I dug my head into the triangular wedge of a pillow. "I *want* to find *some*place to *be* . . . I *want* to find *some*one like *me* . . . ." A hairy hand from my unconscious reached out to grab me, and I bolted upright.

Alex, come back.

For a brief, mad moment, I saw myself climbing upstairs to find him hiding under his bed. Or in the furnace room. I was headed to the basement before I knew what I was doing.

The bulb was out, so I left the door open as I descended the stairs. Below, the slate-green furnace loomed like a locomotive in the shadows, the cracked linoleum a track to nowhere. There was no evidence that Dalton Schramm had returned. The knapsack I'd left outside had vanished. Wait, hadn't Mavis told Jane that Dalton was now at some private school in Vermont? That much closer to Canada. Where was my son headed? *Where was he at this very instant?*

For some reason, I hadn't tossed out the worn beige blanket, which huddled in the corner. It looked as if a little boy might be hiding inside, and I yanked it upwards the way a magician might pull a cape off a trick cabinet to reveal—nothing. The dust on the fabric made me sneeze as its folds shook out. But I gathered it around myself anyway, the way Alex had. There. I was the crown prince of Arabia. I was the boy-assistant to Oscar the Wizard, who stuck swords into my body from behind the drapery without so much as a scratch. I was the long-lost son of a reclusive scientist who had invented time travel. Press the button, and we could go back to the day before all this happened.

I climbed back up the stairs, almost tripping on my improvised robe. From the kitchen, Jane's telephone voice throbbed. "He was wearing a gray-striped shirt, at least that's what Michael remembers. No, I've *told* him that before." Her voice had lost its vibrancy, repeating the same message over and over. She gripped the cordless phone in her left hand as she jotted down notes on a legal pad. Her broad shoulders were hunched, her head bowed. The skirt of her dress suit was hiked over her thighs, but she hadn't bothered to rearrange it. She'd taken off her jacket, her tennis arms protruding from her short-sleeved blouse. "Well, anything you can think of. It doesn't matter how small. Thanks." She punched the OFF button and stared hard at the pad. Then she noticed me.

"Hey." She got up from the table, her arms spread. I recalled a time when that was a prelude to a hug. "No one knows a damn thing. Did you get anywhere with that list?"

"No, nothing rang a bell. Maybe I should go back to the rink. See if that'll spur anything."

She half nodded, half shook her head, then looked more closely at me. "What's with the blanket?"

Had I never explained to her about Dalton and his home-away-from-home? Was now the time to say something? Or would it just be chalked up to more negligence on my part? "It's a ratty old blanket I found in—the diSalvas put it out for curbside pickup. Alex—Alex thought it made him look like royalty, so we kept it." I could actually see my son draped in the blanket, the frayed hem sweeping the floor, as he proclaimed himself Little Lord Fairchester. *Where was my little prince?* A nondescript man was leading him away. I caught a rearward glimpse.

When Jane came toward me, I wrapped us both inside. She held me and I held her. For a moment, the world was beige, and I could feel our two bodies almost becoming one. Hold me forever. This was the woman I'd loved, the wife who had given me Alex. We needed each other. Why had I ever thought otherwise? Finally I looked up and noticed the kitchen chairs bunched nearby like an impatient audience, and the clock by the refrigerator that showed how late it was getting. The chair in the middle was where Alex always sat, his legs not quite reaching the floor. An image from weeks ago was coming into focus.

For the tenth time, Jane begged, "What can we *do*?"

"I—" I began, and stopped. The blanket had slipped from our shoulders onto the floor, and a few feet to the right of it, Alex was seated in his chair. He was reaching for a cinnamon bun offered by a man in gray slacks. *That's* where I'd seen him before—Price's Bake Shop. He'd been pretending to read the newspaper, but his eyes had kept shifting away from the pages. This was a lead! But if no one had recognized him at the rink, why would anyone know him at the bakery?

"What's the matter?" Jane moved toward the table, stepping around the blanket as if it were a puddle.

"I'm trying to remember something." I kicked the blanket between the table legs for the moment. Maybe the bakery staffer would know something, but who had that been? If I called the owners, wouldn't they have some list of who worked what shift? When was I last there with Alex? I closed my eyes, the better to see. There *had* been someone regular at the bake shop, someone Alex knew, too . . . . I shook my head furiously, trying to cast off fatigue. Why, when I needed my mind to be a steel trap, was it like a steel sieve?

"Can you think of anyone I haven't called?" Jane was back in my face, thrusting the yellow legal pad at me. "Here's the list."

"I don't want the list." I needed to close my eyes again. There she was, in back of the counter, exposing a spider tattoo—of course! "I want Steffie!" I bellowed, knocking away the pad as I got to my feet.

"You *what*?" Jane looked like a woman betrayed.

"Steffie Salter—isn't that her last name?"

"You mean the babysitter? The one you shared Cheetos with?" Jane glared. We had never talked that out, I recalled.

"I told you, it was just a game. Anyway, that's not the point." I looked around for the phone. "I think she might know something about the guy who—who took Alex."

"Then call!" Jane thrust the receiver at me so fast, it clobbered me on the chin. Why was I always getting hit by my family? But I held the receiver out like a microphone and prepared to dial.

Wait. "What's her number?"

"973-2367," recited Jane. She straddled one of the kitchen chairs Marlene Dietrich style and watched as I punched in the digits. I was so nervous I did it wrong twice, the first time ending in a recording that told me I'd dialed a non-working number. When I hung up and tried again, I was connected to an old woman who asked plaintively if I were Jamie.

"No," I told her. "Is, um, Steffie there?"

"Ain't no Steffie *here*. Now where's Jamie?"

"Sorry, wrong number." The next time, I stabbed each button slowly and precisely and got it right. A man's voice picked up. I asked if Steffie were available.

His voice grew harsh. "Is this Chad?"

"No, this is Michael Eisler. I'm Alex Eisler's father—we've used Steffie as a babysitter before. I need to ask her a few questions."

"I'm sorry, she's not here right now."

"When do you think she'll be back?" I could see Jane gesturing frantically. In a minute, she would yank the phone from me and hector him herself. "It's important."

"Tell him what the hell's going on!" Jane wrenched herself from the chair and strode toward me, but I danced away. I had to ask Mr. Salter to repeat what he'd just said, which was that she might be back late.

"Look, our son is missing—no, nothing to do with Steffie. But she works at a bakery where the man—the abductor, I think she might have gotten a view of the man who—who drove off with him."

Mr. Salter instantly grew accommodating, like all the people I'd talked to since the incident. I could have been wearing a button: "BE NICE TO ME: MY CHILD'S BEEN ABDUCTED." But there's a limit to what the parent of a teenager can do. Mr. Salter sucked in his breath. "I'm sorry, she could be anywhere. I'll phone a couple of her friends; call you right back if anyone knows where she is."

"Doesn't she have a cell phone?" called out Jane from a foot away.

"Yeah," said Mr. Salter, and gave me the number—"but she keeps it switched off, unless she's expecting a call from her boyfriend."

I thanked him, disconnected, and tried the number at once, but all I got was Steffie's voice mail greeting. I left as urgent a message as I could without scaring her off. I called Ferrara to tell him this lead, and he said he'd see what he could do with it. "Anyone else in the store who might have seen this guy?" he asked, but I just couldn't think. Images of the rink blocked out everything else. He told me again to sit tight, and I hung up. Then I turned back to Jane, still hovering a foot away.

"That's *it*?" she demanded. "*Now* what?"

"We wait, I guess." That's what we'd been doing all night. I checked the wall clock: 9:40. I should have been ravenous. I felt nauseated. Alex's pretzel sticks sat on the counter, but I couldn't touch them again. What I wanted more than anything else was to see Alex in his chair, fussily arranging his snack. But the chair remained empty, so I turned toward the refrigerator. "You want anything to eat?" I asked tonelessly.

"Are you kidding? I feel like I've been kicked in the stomach."

"Me, too."

"If it were a kidnapping, we'd have heard something by now."

"I guess. Ferrara didn't think it was likely." But when I'd asked him what *was* likely, he refused to speculate. *We can't know until we catch the guy*, he'd said, looking away from me.

I put the dishes in the sink. Jane got up to pound the wall. "*I want my son!*"

I went over to where Jane was howling and put my arms around her. She struggled and I bit her. She told me she loved me no matter what. Nothing and everything we did that night made sense. Somehow we ended up on the couch in the TV room, staring at the blank screen, like a gray portal behind which lay something mindless and evil. Soon I got up and started pacing again. "Want to drive around Greenwood? That'd be better than just sitting here."

"What if we put up signs? With a picture of Alex—maybe someone saw him. Offer a reward."

"Sure, but it's almost ten. No one's going to see them now."

"I'll—I'll find a photo." Jane went upstairs, leaving me more alone than I'd been before she'd come home. I wanted her next to me again. While she was gone, I tried to think null thoughts, but Alex was in all of them. And increasingly, a man with gray pants. Okay, we'd put up some posters in Greenwood, and maybe post one on the Web, as well. Some folks, Ferrara had remarked, took matters into their own hands. Were the police working around the clock? What could you do at midnight, other than catch a mailbox-whacker? How did they propose to catch him, anyway? Follow up leads—what leads? My son could be in a field, in a basement, in a bathroom with the door taped shut. Was he hurt, was he drugged? It was way past his bedtime, I thought idiotically. Maybe he was digging a tunnel through the floor with a spoon. What would happen if the man said, "Do this," and Alex said, "I don't *want* to"?

What if Alex didn't come back?

This last thought was so appalling, it didn't lead to more worrying but just ended there. I ran upstairs and met Jane coming down. She'd printed out the same photo of Alex again and again on a stack of printer paper, along with a message that began "MISSING."

Neither of us could stare too long at the photo, which was a bit clownish and heartbreaking. He had his mouth open. His ears stuck out like open car doors. He had to be out there somewhere. Had to be. MISSING: ALEX EISLER, 8 yrs. old, 4 ft. tall. Please call police at once.

The phone rang. I beat her to it by an arm's length. "Hello? Yes, *thank you*. No, it's not too late. Listen, I need some information. No, not quite." It was Steffie, and her father had garbled the message a bit. Alex hadn't been kidnapped by a babysitter at a bakery. "But that's where you come in," I told her, ignoring Jane's frantic semaphores. Her wide hand rub-outs signified *You're not doing this right*. The finger pointed at her own nose meant *Let me handle this*. I performed my own pantomime: I shook my head.

With my back to both the television and my wife, I explained to Steffie that I was looking for a man whom I'd seen a few times at the bakery. "Kind of nebbishy-looking. He wore gray slacks."

"Um, that's *it*? I don't know . . . ."

"Wait." A frosted pastry floated in front of me, gradually settling onto one of the bakery's diminutive tables. "He bought cinnamon buns."

"Oh . . . wait, you mean Computer Guy?"

"Is that what he does? Anyway, I know he offered one to Alex."

"Is that a crime?"

"That's not the point. I saw him at the rink, and he walked off with Alex." Was she trying to protect him? "Look, what do you know about him?"

"Not much. He just came in to buy cinnamon buns. Sometimes we talked. He was kind of shy."

He was quiet, he was shy—why do people always say that? I shoved on the wall, which pushed right back. "How about his name? What kind of car did he drive?"

"I don't know, I don't *know* . . . . I'm sorry, Mr. Eisler, I really am. I never saw his car. He always walked. I think he lived pretty close by, if that helps."

"It might." I asked her a few more questions: What did they talk about? How did he act? What embarrassed him? It was painful—I didn't want to know this creep—but I felt somehow it would help, as if something would tip me off. I was about to hang up when she blurted out something she'd forgotten. She remembered that he worked in data recovery or something like that. I thanked her. I also told her she might be hearing from a Detective Ferrara. Then I called Ferrara again, who took down all the information, said it could be helpful, and told me to sit tight.

I spent the next five minutes relaying the information to Jane and hearing how I could have asked better questions. "Physical details," she insisted, even when I told her that he looked like a nobody. "But about his job—she means disaster recovery planning. It's mostly for big financial corporations."

"What is it, exactly?" I had a mental vision of someone hunkering down in a storeroom, waiting for a tornado.

"They're the people who know what to do in case the computer system crashes, or a fire burns some vital files. It's important—it's just not that interesting." She yawned as if to emphasize her point. It was involuntary. We were both exhausted yet couldn't sleep, maybe ever again. "They spend a lot of their time making rosters, running simulations."

"Huh." So he was a methodical type. He'd probably planned the abduction weeks in advance, staked out the place ahead of time. But what if Alex had kicked him in the shin, or screamed even louder than the amplifiers? *Go away!* Alex had shouted at me. Maybe he'd used something like chloroform—except that the fat man said he'd seen the two of them leaving together.

"And Steffie said he was local." Jane was jotting down points on her legal pad. "I think we should put up the posters here, not just in Greenwood."

I saw myself walking around town with a staple gun. Then I had an awful moment in which I saw Alex chained to the wall in some small white room. He couldn't move, he was beyond tears, and the man in gray pants was coming back any minute. I thrust away the list. How would any of that help with what was going on *right now*? I thought of *How to Cope with Suburban Stress* and wondered whether Jerry had squeezed in a chapter devoted to abduction. When Jane heard my sick snort, she asked what the hell had prompted it, and I told her.

She shook her head slowly. "That's not funny. But I know what you mean."

"You do?"

"Sure. You know, we think a lot alike."

It was true. It was one of the reasons we argued so much. Jane was a part of me, really. How could I not love Jane?

She held out her arms. "Please. I need a hug."

I swam into her embrace, holding her tight against the terrors of the night. She squeezed back. It was going to be a long time till dawn. Was that a shadow crossing our front yard? I glanced over her shoulder, looking out to the thick green blackness of the suburban night and wondering what else might be going on. A quiet murder, a polite case of arson. Fuck everyone.

"What's our plan?" I asked her when we finally broke from our clinch.

"Put up posters, check out some neighborhoods—I don't know, but we *have* to get out of this house."

"Someone has to stay here," I reminded her.

"Oh, no." She put a restraining hand on my shoulder. "We're going together."

I didn't debate the point. "All right. Who're we going to call?"

And that's how Jerry Mirnoff came to be speeding across town, knocking at our door fifteen anxious minutes later: my friend, my colleague, and someone who thought he knew all about coping with suburban stress. His face looked yellow in the porch light, as if he'd swallowed sodium vapor. We listened to his empty reassurances and tried to brief him as best we could. Then Jane thrust her legal pad at him with all the information on it, and we fled into the darkness.

Chapter 16

Ted drove back to Fairchester carefully, trying to watch the road while also keeping an eye on Alex. The boy sat securely belted in the front seat, his skates digging lazily into the beige carpeting. The drive was accomplished mostly in silence, since Alex seemed to have lost his penchant for chattering, and Ted really didn't know what to say. The medium hum of the Sentra's engine filled in any blanks. A bank of clouds scudded by on the April wind, heralding the onset of evening. The tail-end of rush hour crowded Route 1, but the other cars had their own destinations, floating away like bubbles at each intersection.

As they passed Douglas Street, Alex broke the stillness. "Can we stop at Price's Bake Shop? I'm hungry."

Ted stared at him. "Um, we can't."

"Why not?" Alex's lips set in a pout.

"Because—well, it's closed now. Anyway, I have some of their cinnamon buns at home. Okay?" He reached out to pat Alex's knee, which felt warm through the pants leg. His hand lingered for an extra few seconds before sliding away.

"All . . . right. I guess." Alex peered out the window. "When are we going to get there?"

"Soon." *And then what?* The enormity of what had happened was beginning to sink in. He steered slowly around the corner of Chester Street, feeling as if he were driving off a cliff. He needed a contingency plan, a fallback. He should have run a simulation. What if everything went horribly, awfully wrong?

He licked his lips and looked awkwardly at Alex, who was studying his skates. What if everything went right?

Ted reached the Fanshaw Garden Apartments opposite from his accustomed approach, first passing the no-name apartment cluster, not that it made much difference. He parked his Sentra farther in than usual so it couldn't be seen from the road. "We're *here*," he announced, with more emotion than he'd felt for the place since he'd moved in. This was his domicile and sanctuary. He got out and circled around to let Alex out, since he'd toggled the child-lock on the car door back at the rink. Alex refused his offer of an arm, though he was still in skates. When he tried to glide up the flagstone path, he tripped on the first cemented groove and would have fallen, but Ted managed to steady him from behind.

"I can do it myself," muttered Alex.

Ted pointedly said nothing, but Alex still wasn't watching where he was going. When Alex looked backward to add something, he crashed into the doorstep and went flying. He hit his knee hard on the gray concrete and started crying. The sound was disturbingly loud.

"You okay?" Ted crouched by Alex, reaching out to examine the rip in Alex's jeans. It looked like a bad scrape.

"It *hurts*!" Alex jerked away his knee, which must have hurt even more because he started wailing again.

"I've got Band-Aids and stuff inside." He carefully stepped around Alex, pausing only to pat him on the head, and drew out his key. As soon as he had the lock open, he thrust open the door and half-hoisted Alex inside, despite a howl of protest. His arms were full of squirming boy as he carried him to the chair in the hallway and dumped him there. Alex's face was red, but at least he wasn't crying anymore. "Just stay put!" Ted yelled over his shoulder as he retraced his steps back to the door and bolted it. Making his way to the medicine chest in the bathroom, he fished out an old metal Band-Aid box. He grabbed a hank of toilet paper and wet half of it at the sink, adding a little soap.

"Now this is gonna sting," he told Alex, just as his mother used to say to him. He tried swabbing the wound through the jeans, but the fabric got in the way. *What luck.* "But first, I need you to take off these pants."

"I don't want to . . . it'll hurt." Alex eyed Ted imploringly, who tried to look like an implacable parent.

"You have to. It'll get infected." First he removed the skates and lay them on the carpet. Then, with the gentlest of tugs, he slowly eased off Alex's jeans. The boy's pale thighs emerged first, their skin so smooth that they seemed almost out of focus. The calves had a doe-like vulnerability. All that was left were scuffed-looking white socks, which Ted peeled off, too, tossing them onto the skate-pile. He was curious about Alex's toes, which were just as he'd imagined them: pink little shrimp with a deliciously musty smell.

"Hey, why'd you take off my socks?"

Ted shrugged, absently tracing the boy's foot. "To make sure nothing else was scraped." He admired Alex's feet a little longer, each arch delicate as a Japanese bridge. He wasn't a foot fetishist like CRater, but he appreciated perfection when he saw it. And when he imagined these two feet nuzzling his armpits, the body of the boy overhead, he felt a tingling in his groin. It was all he could do to restrain himself from reaching out then and there, but the time wasn't right. Instead, he extended his hand for the soapy toilet paper and applied himself to the task at hand.

"Ow!" Alex squirmed as Ted dabbed at his knee.

"Hold still, hold still . . . ." Ted pulled Alex's leg over his lap, his left hand encircling the tender calf. The knee wound was just a scrape, the skin raw but the bleeding already stopped. He cleaned the area as Alex whimpered, which made Ted feel both sympathetic and masterful. From a certain vantage, he *was* Alex, staring imploringly upwards. The adult in him carefully patted the wound dry with some more toilet paper, savoring the feel of that unblemished skin. He pressed on a Mickey Mouse Band-Aid and drew back to admire his handiwork.

"There, that wasn't so bad, was it?"

"No . . . ." Alex examined the Band-Aid uncertainly, as if it had robbed him of something. He was half-lying on the couch with his legs and arms extended—on a magic carpet ride, or performing some awkward calisthenic. His white jockey briefs clung tightly around his thighs, the front flap concealing a tiny bulge.

Now what?

Ted licked his lips nervously. His hands fluttered at his sides. In fact, he felt dizzy. Or maybe it was just hunger. The time was after six, and he hadn't eaten anything since a slice of pizza at one. He got up without bothering to hand Alex his pants. "Listen, you want some dinner or something?"

"I want a snack." The boy's tone was peremptory, almost reprimanding.

"But it's already 6:20." He showed his Rocky and Bullwinkle watch-face to Alex.

"I don't care. I want a *snack*." Scowling, Alex sat up, his face compressed into three horizontal lines.

A smack, that's what I'll give you, said his father from somewhere. Ted tilted his head and the voice was gone, but the anger remained. Something in his usual poker-face must have betrayed this emotion because the boy wrapped his arms protectively around himself. "A snack," Ted echoed.

"Please," said Alex. He said it so unexpectedly and with such sincerity that Ted was charmed. The syllable hung in the air like a silver globe.

Ted got to his feet and moved toward the kitchen. "What do you usually have?"

"Seven pretzel sticks."

It was a near-miracle that Ted had bought a bag of Rold Gold pretzel sticks the day before—something to munch on while watching reruns of *The Andy Griffith Show*. "Come into the kitchen," he called back over his shoulder. "I've got just what you want."

"I can't." Alex giggled. "I'm wounded."

Ted reemerged with the bag in his hand. "Not that badly. You can walk."

"Can I skate?"

"Not in the house, no."

"Can I watch TV while I eat them?"

Ted saw the two of them wedged together in the overstuffed armchair: Alex was sucking lazily on a pretzel stick as he reached for the remote control, which was buried between Ted's thighs. "Yeah, okay," he said. "Let me just get a plate."

Alex pulled on his pants and followed Ted into the Blue Room, limping slightly and making sure that Ted noticed it. Alex wrinkled his nose. "Peeyew! Something smells in here."

Ted frowned. "I'm doing experiments with sea water."

"Really?"

"Uh-huh. Tell you about it later." He gestured for Alex to sit in the armchair, and the boy sprang into it surprisingly bouncily for someone with a hurt leg. When he offered the pretzel sticks, Alex scrutinized the bag.

"These aren't the right ones."

Ted fought the opposed urges of wanting to yank the boy's hair and desiring to stroke it. Instead, he took back the bag and pretended to examine it. "No, these are correct. What brand do you eat?"

Alex folded his arms. "Bachman."

"Well, that's the problem. You've been eating the wrong kind." He reached for the remote control and flicked on the TV. "These are better."

MTV, which Ted occasionally watched for its videos, came blaring onto the screen, filling the small room with a rock song about lost roses. They both watched a boy-man gyrating on the hood of a Corvette parked in a vacant lot, as Alex reached out for the pretzels. He crunched one experimentally. "Not bad."

Ted nodded as he perched on the padded arm of the chair. He pushed his hand into the bag nestled in Alex's lap. Rooting around a little longer than necessary, he plucked out one nubbly stick and put half of it into his mouth. He dropped his left leg onto the seat, and Alex said nothing. He was about to slide his right leg on, as well, when Alex stopped him with a peeved look.

"This is boring. Can we watch something else?"

So Ted flipped to Nickleodeon, where the Rugrats were torturing a babysitter.

"I've seen this." Alex reached for another pretzel stick. "Can I have the remote?"

"Sure." Ted was still half-annoyed and half-charmed by the boy's behavior. To sit on that bubble butt would be just as thrilling as to be sat upon by it. He edged both legs onto the seat, carefully keeping an inch of distance between Alex and himself. Alex was leaning forward, pushing the channel changer with concentration. On the screen, a horse chase blinked into a news commentator, which shifted to a house on fire and then another music video. A scene between a man and woman arguing at a dinner table lingered for almost a minute before Alex switched channels again. As he did so, he reached automatically for another pretzel.

Ted moved his thigh so that it gently nudged Alex's. No response. When Alex settled on *Rugrats* again, Ted began to take over the seat. If he did it stealthily enough, he thought, the boy might wind up in his lap. The chair cushion was squashy, useful for burrowing. Alex was over his left knee . . . shove a little more . . . now the thigh—but suddenly Alex broke his gaze away from the screen and seemed to notice Ted's presence as if for the first time.

"Hey, this is *my* seat!"

"There's room for two . . . ."

"Is *not!*" Alex shoved with his leg, and Ted shoved back with his. Normally it would've been no contest, but Ted allowed the boy to push against him until they were locked in the middle. They held that position for a moment until Ted raised his thigh—and Alex found himself sliding underneath. Soon he was half under Ted, who snaked his leg over to keep the boy down. The squirming under his weight felt delightful.

"No fair!" Alex pounded on Ted's buttocks, his voice muffled.

Ted's father had occasionally sat on his son when mock-wrestling or squeezed him in a scissors grip between his legs. There was no way out, just an unyielding sensation of big body against little body. It was one of the few times his father had given him his full attention.

Ted gazed down at Alex, pinned with his arms outstretched. Those hairless forearms emerging from the sleeves of the gray T-shirt, those defenseless armpits. Ted reached down and tickled the delicate hollows, which made the boy burst into tortured laughter.

"Stop, stop!" Alex tried to turn away but was held down. When he tried to cover himself, Ted eased up and went for Alex's belly. And when Alex slapped furiously at the hands crawling over his stomach, Ted slid down to his groin, squeezing the inner thighs and cupping the birdlike bulge between them. As Alex bucked and writhed, the room itself seemed to tilt, the upper half fading from sight. Ted shook his head and his vision cleared, but the dizziness remained. His hands had stiffened into claws, his weight a dead lump from under which Alex slowly crawled out. When he looked up, the boy was standing alongside the armchair, looking accusingly at him. When Alex spoke, his voice was clear and piercing.

"That wasn't right. How'd you like it if I tickled *you*?"

This was unexpected. Ted threw up his arms and allowed himself to be invaded. The little hands reached toward his shoulders and tunneled in. When Ted clamped his arms against his sides, the hands scampered up to his neck, with Ted shaking his head in mock-fury. The walls tilted again as Ted slid backwards, collapsing onto the floor. Alex followed him, clambering onto his hips to tickle his ribs. Ted let him have his way for a while, the heft of boyflesh bringing him toward ejaculation. But halfway there, he neglected to protest enough, and Alex lost interest. The boy hopped off Ted and announced he was bored. The television was back to *Rugrats*, where the twins had just gotten hold of Angelica's doll. They were carrying it to the kitchen and God knows what fate.

"My turn!" said Ted hopefully, reaching out. But Alex danced out of his reach, and Ted, who was still slightly dizzy, decided not to pursue it. Yet. He felt the premonition of a spasm.

Shoulda taken your meds.

Alex stood behind the armchair, arms crossed bossily over his chest. "I'm still hungry."

"Well, now it's dinner time." Ted got up shakily. He switched off the TV and motioned for Alex to follow him. "Spaghetti-O's."

"Really?" Alex sprinted past Ted, beating him to the kitchen. "We never have that at home!"

"Too bad. They're my favorite." Ted reached the food cabinet and elbowed gently past the boy. He plucked two familiar red-and-white cans from the upper shelf and smacked them down on the stove. With practiced motions, he applied a can opener to both and dumped the contents into a shiny one-quart saucepan. He adjusted the burner to medium-high and scrutinized it as if surveying a scientific experiment. "Sinner—I mean dinner— should be ready in approximately three minutes."

Alex sat expectantly at the kitchen table as Ted dealt out twin Donald Duck forks and Mickey Mouse bowls. Ted had never entertained visitors, except in his dreams. He stirred the glop from the cans with a wooden spoon stained pink from tomato sauce. Shifting from foot to foot, he hummed an old tune his mother had liked, "When the Red, Red Robin." He still couldn't quite believe this was happening.

Alex picked up his utensil and examined it. "Don't you have any other forks?"

"I might . . . ." Ted frowned. "What's the matter with that one?"

"I hate Donald Duck."

Ted looked hurt. "Really? I think he's cool." Ted also thought that Donald's sailor suit, with his white bottom and tail-feathers sticking out, made him cute as hell. But he rummaged in the drawer next to the fridge and found an old cafeteria fork. He held it out so that Alex had to take it from him. Those innocent little fingers wrapping around it, curling, squeezing. Since the molded plastic seat made the table chest-high for Alex, he knelt on the chair. In a minute, Ted poured out the Spaghetti-O's with gusto, making sure to equalize the portions. He sat opposite Alex and led off with a huge forkful of O's. "Mmmm," he mouthed.

Alex lifted his own forkful, scrutinizing it in midair. "My daddy makes black spaghetti."

"Huh. What's it taste like?"

"It's only the sauce, and it's just like the red kind." Alex jiggled his fork. "Looks funny, though."

"I'll bet. Eat up." Ted made three forkfuls disappear in quick succession. He was surprisingly hungry and felt he could suck up Alex's portion and Alex, as well. Alex, on the other hand, was a toyer, scooping up a catch of pasta only to let half slide off. Then he dribbled the remaining O's into his mouth one by one. A red mustache of sticky sauce soon covered his upper lip.

Ted calculated that he could lick off that mustache with one swipe of his tongue, but instead offered the boy a paper napkin from an open box on the counter. Alex shook his head. Then, as if listening to some internal cue, he added, "No, thank you."

Ted's mother had always made him say "please," sometimes even for a trip to the bathroom. "Please yourself," his mother told his father as he went out the door to drink and drive. Ted waited for Alex to finish, watching the food disappear into that little triangle of a mouth. At the end, Alex wiped half his mustache onto his sleeve, but Ted said nothing.

Alex shoved aside his bowl. "What's for dessert?"

"Well, I've got cinnamon buns."

"That's breakfast!"

"Nah." Ted rose from the table, licking his lips. "They're sweet and sticky, like you."

Alex scowled. "What do you mean?"

Ted wanted to rush the boy, pin him to the linoleum, and tug off his jeans. He did nothing of the kind but instead fixed him with a sly look. "You know what little boys are made of. Sugar and spice and everything nice."

"That's not it. It's 'snips and snails and puppy dogs' tails.' The other one's for girls." Alex drew out the last word as if it had three syllables.

"Maybe, but some boys are nice, too. Wanna play a game?"

"Okay. Have you got Monopoly?"

"No. Sorry." Ted's collection of juvenilia didn't include many games since his childhood hadn't, either.

"How about Yahtzee or Parcheesi?"

Ted sadly shook his head.

Alex looked annoyed. "Like what, then?"

Ted considered the question. He knew a few deliciously nasty games, including one called Suck Up, and another that didn't even have a name but which he played by himself in the Dungeon. No, they wouldn't do—not right now, anyway. Win the kid's confidence, Chomper always said, and then you can do *anything*—not that he necessarily knew what he was talking about. Or any of them. If even half of what CumAsUR mouthed was real, he'd be serving ten-to-twenty behind bars. Just thinking about this made Ted feel lightheaded again. What the hell was he doing entertaining a boy he'd picked up at a roller-skating rink? Even now, he could stop it, show the kid to the door and say it had all been a mistake. *Mistake, my ass*, HalfPint would say, because that's what he always said. Really, what could explain this if he stopped now? The boy said he was hungry, so I took him home and gave him some dinner. He was wobbly on skates, so I gave him a private lesson.

He looked over at Alex waiting expectantly for a game. He was leaning forward, his pert little buttocks pressed lightly onto the chair, pale arms perched on the table like an offering. How could he ignore such a gift?—something that had just dropped into his lap, or might at any moment. But no one would believe such a story.

"A game," prompted Alex.

"Right." Something from his own childhood, maybe. But whenever he reached down into the swirling black water of his past, he came close to drowning. It also prompted fuzz-out episodes. He tried focusing on a serene spot, maybe after his father had left, something in the beauty parlor. He was bored, and his aunt was entertaining him during her break. How about Wild-Child?—though maybe he shouldn't call it that. "Okay," he told Alex. "Ever play Beasts?"

Alex raised his perfect eyebrows. "I don't think so. How do you play it?"

Ted bent down so he was on Alex's level. "First, I imitate an animal. I make sounds, maybe move around like the animal. Then—"

"Then I have to guess what the animal is—I know that game!" Alex clapped his hands. "It's not called Beasts. That's Wild-Child."

"You know it?"

"Sure. I'll start."

"Yeah, okay." Maybe they should have some sort of forfeit system. First one to lose three times plays victim.

But Alex was already jumping up and down, scratching his armpits. His shirt hiked up as he grunted.

"That's easy. A chimpanzee."

Alex nodded, looking happy at being understood but also slightly disappointed to be found out so fast.

"My turn," announced Ted, figuring he should start easy. Cupping his hands sideways, he clapped them together and barked with an *orc-orc* sound. Alex looked puzzled, so Ted made his arms more like flippers and shuffled forward on his knees. In a second, he would enfold the boy and pretend it was all part of the imitation.

"You're a seal!" cried Alex, springing to his feet. "My turn again." He hung his head down with his arms twined together in front. Turning toward Ted, he came out with an amazingly loud noise that sounded like *herrrt, herrrt*. Ted scratched his head. But then Alex swept the floor with his clasped hands, and Ted smiled.

"Okay, you're an elephant. Now me again." He was already growing tired of this game, which seemed too childish for both of them. Time to end it, maybe with something really difficult. He stuck his neck out, peering toward the tops of the kitchen cabinets and crawling around stiffly on his feet and hands.

"Make a sound," said Alex after a moment.

Ted just smiled in a superior way and kept craning his neck, shaking his head once.

Alex frowned. "That's not fair."

Ted made a concession and arched his neck toward the Formica counter, where a dishrag hung from a hook. He opened his mouth and snagged the dishrag, chewing it as if it were a clump of leaves. *My, what a big mouth you have. Stick your head in there.*

"I don't think you're doing it right. What are you?"

"Give up?" Ted grinned horsily.

"No." Alex paused. "Yeah, all right."

Ted came loping forward, bending down, nosing into the crevice between Alex's shoulders and his head. He stuck out his tongue and gave a long lick up that tender shoot of a neck.

Alex squirmed and tried to push Ted away. "What *are* you?"

As an answer, Ted screwed his neck toward the lower foliage. He was mouthing the hem of Alex's gray shirt, pulling it away from the taut little belly. He nudged farther down and began nuzzling at the boy's groin. It smelled ever so slightly of fresh sweat.

"Hey, stop! I told you, I give up!" Alex fastened his hands on Ted's ears as if they were handles, tugging at the adult head twisted into him. He scrabbled at the linoleum floor with his stockinged feet but gained no purchase, like a cartoon character revving in place. Finally, Ted allowed himself to be pulled sideways, his head lolling on the floor, with an upward view of the boy as conqueror. Alex planted one foot on top of Ted's chest and shoved. "Get away—and say what you are."

"Me?" Ted reluctantly rolled away. All in good fun, no harm done, maybe more later. He opened his mouth wide. "A giraffe."

"Oh." Alex considered this piece of information. "Giraffes don't talk, do they?"

"Nope." *The secret sex lives of giraffes. And since you lost, your ass is grass.*

Alex stared at the beast. "Anyway, I'm tired of playing this. What about dessert?"

"What about it?"

"You said you had some."

"Well, some cookies, maybe." The real question was how long this could go on. And how to end it. But for right now, he located a half-empty box of Oreos and watched with delight as Alex pried open three cookies to lick off the cream. When the boy had almost finished, Ted was ready with some questions. "What do you usually eat for dinner?"

Alex shrugged. "Stuff like this."

"You live right around here, don't you?"

Alex started to nod, then shook his head vigorously. "My parents are in Arabia."

"A-ra-bi-a . . . ?" Ted savored the syllables. "That's right, you said that at the rink. What are they doing there?"

"Oh, that's where they work." Alex had somehow become focused on the refrigerator and wouldn't meet Ted's eye. He held on to his last cookie half as if it might fly away from him.

"Hmm." Ted knew he should back off but couldn't resist the impulse to needle. "What kind of jobs have they got?"

"Mommy's an executive. She works for an oil company." Alex was now gazing at the ceiling. "My daddy's a sand sweeper. There's a lot of sand in Arabia."

"Yup, I've heard that."

"I haven't seen them in a while."

"Why not?"

"Because," explained Alex as if going over a painfully obvious point, "they're in Arabia."

"Ah." Ted pretended to digest all this information. "But don't they—"

"Wait, what about *your* parents?"

"What do you mean?"

Alex was now gazing at him directly, a piercing blue-eyed stare that made it Ted's turn to look away. The boy put on his explaining tone again. "Where do they live? What do they do?"

"They're both dead," said Ted dully. He felt a bit woozy. This kind of conversation probably wasn't good for his mental equilibrium, with all those ghosts flitting across his brain. Still, he'd started it.

"Well, what did they do when they were alive?"

Ted breathed heavily. "My dad was . . . a carpenter, mostly. After he left, my mom worked in a beauty parlor." He reached into the Oreo box for succor and shoved one into his mouth.

Alex took this juncture to finish his last cookie. The two chomped in silence for a moment. Then: "What do *you* do?"

This was growing uncomfortable. It wasn't just the questions he was being asked but the implications. *I know your name and where you live and what you do for a living. I know what you eat for dinner.* Why hadn't he followed CRater's advice and interviewed the kid with a stocking-cap over his face? Or driven him to some deserted field? Just what the hell was going to happen when he let the boy go? Or would he have to keep him in this apartment forever?

"What do I *do*?" Ted echoed Alex's question. The point was that he had no plan. Think fast. "I'm a plumber."

"Oh." Alex's disappointment was obvious. "Is that all?"

"Hey, it's a full-time job." Ted became indignant on behalf of all plumbers everywhere. "Do you have any idea what it's like, crawling under the sinks, cleaning out the pipes?"

"No. It just sounds boring." Alex got up from the table and headed toward the living room. He was still in his stockinged feet but looked tousled and only half-dressed. "By the way, I have to go home soon."

"Wait!" yelled Ted, but could think of nothing to follow it up with. He propelled himself forward and caught up with Alex by the couch. "Um, I thought you lived in Arabia."

"My *parents* live there. *I* live in Fairchester." Alex placed his hands on his hips, looking delightfully stern. "I don't know about plumbers, but *some* people have homework to do."

"I see. All right. Sure." Ted checked his watch: 8:15 already. That this boy was going out of his life so quickly appalled him. "Look, I'll drive you home if you want, but first—" he gestured toward the Blue Room "—how about a little fun on the computer?"

"Hmm. You mean games?"

Ted nodded. He had amassed a collection of animated adventure-quests, all featuring characters in mid-boyhood. "I've got Scorpio, Blue Legend, and Kick-Box 3. Some others, too." He held out his hand. "C'mon, let's go back to the TV room."

"O . . . kay." Alex followed him through the doorway, but lagged as if traveling through some medium denser and stickier than air. He looked all around himself, as if noticing the apartment for the first time.

Inside the Blue Room, Ted whisked the dust cover off his computer and booted it up. "This'll take a little while. And then I've got to load the game." He sat down in his swivel chair, resting his feet on the makeshift desk. There was only one seat, but they could share. A few bouts of Scorpio, following two seductive boys in the desert, and then what?—that was the problem. He couldn't think ahead on this contingency: no numbers to call, no ditch plan.

"I have to go to the bathroom," Alex announced.

"Yeah, okay." Ted gestured vaguely with his left hand. "Through that room and take a right."

The boy disappeared from his field of vision as Ted frowned at the screen. "ERROR, NON-SYSTEM DISKETTE. PLEASE REMOVE AND PRESS ANY KEY TO CONTINUE." Stupid, he'd left a floppy disk in the drive from last night. He punched the eject button, yanked out the disk, and pressed the space bar. Now the machine started cooperating. In a minute, he slid the Scorpio game into his CD player and waited for the familiar sky-high graphics and earthquake rumbles. Akbar the boy wizard appeared on the left, charming a snake. On the right in a dust cloud floated Ali, Akbar's cousin and sometime-enemy. Both were naked to the waist and sported desert tans. The purpose was to use any means possible to vanquish one's opponent, from hocus-pocus to flying-V kicks—though sometimes the purpose was just to masturbate, a goal the game-builders seemed to have anticipated with their explicit and humiliating action scenes.

Ted waited for the opening to finish in a crescendo of Arabian horns. "Alex, you ready?" He reached back absently, his hand wishing for a connection.

No one else was in the room.

"Alex!" He got up grumpily and headed toward the bathroom adjoining his bedroom. Maybe he could just knock and enter at the same time—that way, he might see something. "Are you in there?" he asked the door. When the door refused to reply, he turned the knob and barged in.

No Alex.

"All right, where are you?" He hustled back to the hallway, where Alex's skates lay askew by the chair. He checked the outside door, but the lock was still on. He wasn't in the kitchen, either, unless he was hanging from the ceiling, and Ted checked there, too. "C'mon out," he told the apartment. Then he started checking behind, under, inside: the armchair, the curtains, the closet, even the cupboards. He was on his way back to the bedroom to look under the bed when he thought he heard a slight creak from somewhere.

The door in the middle of the corridor. The Dungeon. He headed for the entrance, a thousand thoughts crowding his brain. Finally, a guest suitable for the equipment, the ghosts of his imagination to be replaced by solid flesh. Christ, you've got to get that kid out! What the hell was he doing in there, anyway? Oddly, Ted felt violated, as if someone had pried open a secret abscess. But don't spook the boy, right? He pushed right in, calling with forced gaiety, "Come out, come out, wherever you are!"

No reply. And it was dark. He flicked on the overhead fluorescent light with a sound like an electronic bumblebee. An undersea glow shimmered to life. As he glanced about the confines of the room, the white porcelain surfaces of the sink, the toilet, and the bathtub stared back at him. He took a step forward.

A layer of green-black ooze coated the inside of the bathtub. Play-Slime, from a packet of colored powder he'd bought in a Manhattan shop called 4 KIDZ with simple instructions: "Just add water." He'd had fun with it a few days ago, pretending that the Creature from the Black Lagoon had tied him up and was going to squelch him in a soggy embrace. But Alex wasn't in the bathtub. He peered around. Alex wasn't in the slurpy seat, either, which had been splashed with some of the slime and looked as if a child had experienced an embarrassing accident close to the toilet.

Ted frowned. "If you don't come out, I'll—." He paused. What *would* he do? "If you do come out, we can play that computer game. If you don't, I'll just have to lock you up in here." He turned. Not a sound. Maybe the kid wasn't in the Dungeon. One last chance, something his father had done. "Tell you what. I'm going to shut my eyes and count to ten. And when I open them, you'd better be here.

"Okay? One . . . two . . . three . . . ." This better work. "Four . . . five . . . six . . . ." He was almost up to nine when he heard a footstep. He slit his eyes and saw a small leg appear from behind the door. By the time he counted "ten," the boy stood in front of him, looking more pleased with himself than frightened.

"You couldn't find me."

"Where were you?"

Alex shrugged. "Around. Hey, what is this place, anyway?"

Ted took a deep breath. "You really want to know?"

"Sure."

"It's a dungeon. You know, where they used to lock up—"

"I *know* what a dungeon is." He placed his arms akimbo, looking like a dwarfish dictator. "But that was a long time ago. What's this one for?"

"People . . . still need to be punished." Ted licked his lips. "Especially little boys."

Alex looked around as if searching for other miscreants. He backed up until his legs brushed the slurpy seat. "Why me?"

"You were hiding." Ted reached back to shut the door firmly, putting on the snap-lock. "When I called, you wouldn't come."

"But I *did*. You counted to ten, and I came out."

"Too late." It was Ted's turn to put his hands on his hips. This was too ripe an opportunity to be missed. Whatever happened would look like a lesson. Somewhere in his mind he knew it might not seem that way in retrospect, but there was no retro yet. Only the here and now mattered in this room, though the contours of objects were growing a little hazy. He blinked and shook his head to set things right again.

"If it was too late, why did you count?" Alex was pouting now, the kind of expression Ted's father could wipe off his son's face with the back of his hand. But Ted wanted the pout to stay, with a vision of it brushing lightly up and down his body. Push the small brown-haired head back and forth. Then it would be his own turn.

"*You* said we were going to play on the computer."

"I did?" A hazy curtain hung over half his memory. "Well, no more games. This is for real."

Alex stamped his foot. "What's the point?"

"Point of what?" He had drifted again.

"Oh, never mind." Alex touched the slurpy seat gingerly. "What *is* this thing, anyway?"

"I can show you." He lurched forward, and Alex danced to one side. "Maybe it'll be part of your punishment."

"It's not fair." The slurpy seat was between them now, looking like a diseased throne. "I didn't do anything. *You're* the one who should be punished."

For the first time that evening, Ted smiled—a rare, wide smile that took in the boy and the room, his unhappy childhood and the brother he'd never had. "Okay," he said softly. "We'll take turns. But you first."

In a minute, Alex was dangling over the bathtub, held tight by velcro straps at the wrists and ankles. He had struggled a bit, but stopped abruptly when Ted clamped down hard on him. "Is this going to hurt?" he asked, looking away.

"Not much." Ted wasn't even sure what he was going to do, but the expectation that something was going to happen had given him an enormous erection. The boy was hanging in front of him, all his tender parts available. It would be fun to make him squirm. But maybe start out gentle. Ted reached out with a probing forefinger and hovered for one dramatic moment while Alex writhed in anticipation. Then he lifted Alex's shirt and inserted his finger into the boy's belly button. "Death by tickling," he intoned.

Alex tried to turn away but was held fast by the restraints. He started giggling madly. "S-stop, stop!"

Ted forced his thumb between the boy's thighs and rubbed gently.

"Ah, ahhh!" Alex couldn't press his legs together because the restraints had stretched everything apart. All he could do was dangle helplessly as Ted poked and prodded.

Ted kept it up for a minute before announcing, "Okay. It's your turn." He reached down to rip off the velcro.

By this point, Alex was red-faced and angry, which was fine with Ted. He still felt lightheaded, but not so much from the black fog as from thousands of foamy bubbles scudding about his brain. He was ready for surrender to almost anything.

Alex didn't bother with the restraints but simply commanded Ted to lie down in the slimy bathtub. Then he sat on him, his rear planted firmly on Ted's chest. He held down Ted's arms with his hands fastened to Ted's wrists—but then he couldn't move much without letting up. So he dug his

toes into Ted's armpits and watched in satisfaction as Ted writhed underneath him, hair and backside matted with slime.

Finally Ted sat up, breaking his invisible restraints to proclaim that the
time was up. "My turn again." Alex lay toppled by the edge of the tub. "Go
sit in that chair."

"But it's got gunk on it!"

"So what?" Ted passed a hand through his hair and came away with
green-black fingers. "You made *me* lie in it. Anyway, it's just Play-Slime.
Tell you what—better strip first."

"O . . . kay." Alex tugged off his jeans and shirt. Those perfect legs,
the hairless armpits. The nipples that were tiny red seeds. Alex removed
his underwear. A cute little pecker, smooth as a flesh-tone mushroom. Ted
blinked furiously to keep the haze from overwhelming him, and when he
opened his eyes, Alex was still there, right in front of him. Alex padded over
to the slurpy seat, looked carefully at the chair surface, and slowly sat down.
He looked like a boy on the toilet.

Amazing. Ted shook his head. Just as in his fantasies. So. Now or never.
Go for broke. Take the bull by the horns, said his father, taking it. He got
down on his knees and crawled toward the seat.

"Wait!"

Ted looked up warily.

"No fair!" Alex was frowning. "You have to take off your clothes,
too!"

Gray slacks, blue shirt, and Fruit of the Loom underwear went flying
into the corner of the room. Then Ted advanced. Snakelike, he slid between
the front legs of the chair, twisting about so that he lay on his back. The
slurpy seat revealed all. Above him hung a curved ceiling of boyflesh, thighs
blending seamlessly into poised buttocks. And hanging in the middle—

Ted lifted his head and gave an exploratory lick. Little stalk, it tasted
only of salt. Alex squealed and clamped his thighs together.

Didn't come so far to get locked out here. Ted butted his head between
the boy's thighs, but the legs wouldn't spread. *Open sesame*, he chanted in
his mind and tried a different approach, extending his tongue to probe the
delicate cleft that now hid the scrotum. He was both the flesh and the vio-
lator, he was a giant penis and a boy sitting on a toilet seat, so long ago. He
extended his tongue and gave a long lap.

"Hey!" cried Alex, his thighs springing apart. The green-black snake's
head emerged from below, its tongue lashing about. He hitched sideways,
but the head was upon him, the mouth bearing down. He was half inside the
mouth—the snake was going to eat him! He tried to push away the head,

but it forced its way upwards. It made an awful slurping sound, the eyes all white. "Stop it!"

But there was no stopping.

Ted was bobbing up and down. He squeezed an arm through the opening and was reaching out to hold Alex around the waist. But when he drew back for air, Alex jerked around and shinned him in the mouth.

"Ow, you little shit!" He reared back, his mouth suddenly numb. Alex scrambled off the seat as Ted spat out some blood. The boy ran for the door, but the snap-lock was on, and in the moment it took him to undo it, Ted caught up with him, tackling him to the floor. "I'll teach you to kick me!" came a voice from somewhere in Ted's head.

"Let me go!"

Ted flipped the terrified boy over on his belly and crawled on top of him. His limbs began to spasm, making it difficult to bend. The haze was coming from the ceiling now, the sky descending as he gripped the boy hard—

and woke up sprawled on the floor. The dungeon was empty. His head was throbbing, the way it always did after an attack, and the rusty taste of blood sat in his mouth. He rubbed his jaw, which was coated with slime. How long had he been out? He slowly looked around. Something was missing.

The boy. What had happened, and where was the boy? He couldn't even remember much beyond a minute ago. He got unsteadily to his feet and called out. "Alex!"

No response.

Was he hiding, was that it? He had hidden before, and then Ted had chased him down, right? Here in the Dungeon. And then what? Something to do with games. And after that?

As full consciousness slowly returned, his torpor grew fluid-filled with panic. He had to locate the boy—worlds depended on it. "Alex, where are you?" he cried as he started searching the apartment. The bedroom, the kitchen. Hadn't he done this before? "We haven't finished!"

The computer was on in the Blue Room. The skates were still by the chair. He strode through the hallway. Hadn't he bolted the door? It was open now. He was about to rush outdoors when he realized he was naked. He found his clothes back in the Dungeon. Cursing softly, he shoved them on, not bothering to clean himself up first. What time was it, anyway? For some reason, his watch was in his pocket. 10:50. By now, the boy was probably—where? Roaming the streets, cowering in someone's back yard? He had to find him before, before someone else found him so, so he could do, do what exactly?

Here, you forgot your skates. Stupid excuse, but it might work.

Alex could be anywhere. But he would know what happened. Then maybe they could make up some story together. Parents in Arabia. Ted shook his head. The fuzz was still there but clearing slowly. All his muscles ached, and his tongue felt swollen.

Search the neighborhood. He rubbed his eyes, feeling an immense weight above. It made him want to sit down, but he had to get moving. In a few minutes, he was ready. He locked the door behind him, carrying the skates, and hurried toward the car.

Chapter 17

Where can you go in the suburbs on a Thursday night? Ted zoomed up Winfield Avenue and across to Bromley, the turn marked by a clapboard house that looked like a collapsed hat. Straight for three blocks, then right on Sycamore, where they were fixing the sewer system, and three orange traffic cones outlined a manhole cover in the dark. Alex wouldn't have crawled inside there, would he? Ted slowed down to peer at the construction site but didn't stop. He topped the hill three blocks down (what was it about threes?) and decided to turn on Fenley Lane, a street bordered by tall maples whose leaves reached out like hands. Past a triad of houses—looking for what? A small boy scurrying along the sidewalk? A sock dropped on the pavement?

He slowed down five blocks later, his adrenaline rush draining into a vast unease. He stopped at the curb, next to an old house with three terraces on a sharp incline. He had no idea where he was going. He was now—what?—about a mile from his apartment? A map of Fairfield and the surrounding suburbs was folded in the glove compartment, but he wasn't exactly lost. He had lost the boy. He had to get him back.

But why? He should be running, hiding, driving the hell out of Fairchester. The boy knew where he lived, and this was going to hit home. The maple tree leaves quivered in agreement. Though he couldn't recall just what he'd done, Alex would. The breeze picked up. Even if it had felt great, it wasn't going to look good—maybe he should be thinking about this while heading toward I-95. He started the ignition, zoomed forward, and made it all the way to the access road for the expressway before slowing down. A vision of his father's dirty white pickup truck rumbling farther and farther away from their house kept blocking his vision. At the last possible moment, he made a U-turn and started back. Through a sort of homing instinct, he found himself right back at Winfield Avenue and turned into the apartment lot, where he killed the engine. It was almost 10:30 now.

Where to start? Too many questions and no good answers. He rested his head against the window, staring into the semi-darkness. A dim crescent

moon hung low in the sky. The street light on the corner hummed as if
it knew some secret it wouldn't share. An awful taste of rubber curdled
in his mouth as if he'd chewed something back in the Dungeon. His jaw
was swollen, too. He rolled down the window and spat. He looked half-
hopefully down the street, as if expecting a sign of some kind, any available
data. An evening breeze tousled the maple leaves, that was all. Too bad
he wasn't looking for a tree—Fairchester was lousy with them. The town
also grew lots and lots of boys, but they were probably all in bed by now.
He shut his eyes against the night, trying to see beyond Winfield Avenue.
Contingency planning had helped him project. Where would *I* go, what
would *I* do, if—?

If some man came up to me in the skating rink and took me home.

An unpleasant recall surfaced like a sour burp: his father and his uncle at
the bowling alley when he was five, forgetting all about him as he crouched
by the men's room with the lollipop he'd been given. He'd focused on the
X's and slashes on the overhead scoreboards, the drone of the rolling balls
and the bone-breaking sound of flying pins. He was the ball, then the pin
on the farthest right, the one they kept missing. He kept waiting for them to
look in his direction, but they never did. They finished their game and left
without him, though they came back later and pretended it was all a joke.

I wish someone had taken *me* home. Anyone.

He shook his head to clear it. The memory dissolved in a dull mist. A
collapsed past and a doomed future. What would he do if he found the boy,
anyway?

The question paralyzed him. He sat stock-still, gazing through the windshield without seeing anything. How could he act when he had no plan? The
engine was still running for a trip to nowhere. With a great effort of will, he
squeezed his eyes shut again, and once he'd blocked out the world, he could
see more clearly. Slowly, he outlined the contingencies, with appropriate
actions for each option.

1. He would run into Alex before he'd gone too far, and he'd—what?
*Drag him back to his apartment and tie him to the armchair? Buy him an
airplane ticket to Arabia?*

2. He would encounter Alex, but not before Alex had been found by
others. *Would Alex lead them back to his apartment? Maybe he should sleep
overnight in his cubicle at Modesto.*

3. He would never find Alex, who would never see him again, either.
Case closed. *But what would he do for the rest of his life?*

Shit. He opened his eyes to face Fairchester again. The problem was
that the incident had occurred before any safety plans were in place. Maybe

it would be worse to meet Alex again, but he was genuinely worried about him now, in case something really bad had happened to Alex.

Where would you hide if you were a little boy on the run?

I still am.

Go home. Maybe that was it. But that was just as bad since soon Alex would put out an alarm or something. If he hadn't already.

On the other hand—shit, there were so many hands—he couldn't just leave the Dungeon the way it was, and he had to take some clothes and stuff with him. He emerged stiff-legged from the driver's seat and opened the trunk. Space enough to bring necessities and leave the rest. Anything incriminating he'd have to ditch in the big green dumpster down the block. In a moment, he was inside his apartment, fumbling toward the Blue Room.

At first, he began sorting through the cardboard boxes, creating a pile of some uncensored videos from God knows where, a few sniffy clothes, and some cute pix. But the deciding took too long, and soon he was just heaving stuff into one big box. Now that he was ruthless, he worked fast and efficiently. Taking a deep breath, he smashed apart his Dungeon apparatus till it was unrecognizable and hauled the wreckage to the car. He loaded up and emptied three times, figuring the dump truck would come by in seven hours or so. It was a calculated risk, like the rest of his life.

He left his bedroom intact, except for the clock and a poster or two. From his underwear drawer, he extracted a thick wad of cash and a bankbook. Almost done. He checked his watch: 11:05. More work to do. Back in the Blue Room, he hoisted the television and staggered outside. A low-hanging cluster of maple leaves smacked him in the face, and as he brushed them aside, a jagged crack in the concrete path sent him sprawling to the ground, the television still clutched to his chest. The casing sprang open with the crack of breaking plastic. But he was more occupied with his knee, gouged on the concrete and beginning to throb. Christ, it hurt. When he unbent his leg and stood up, it felt a little better, but he cursed all the trees and paths in the neighborhood—no, in this whole goddamned suburb. Retrieving the television in the dark, he tried to judge the extent of the damage, but it rattled when he shook it. His knee was bleeding onto the pavement.

Make a list of medical personnel to call in case of an emergency. Always have a back-up system.

To hell with contingencies. Clutching the dead television as if it were a damaged child, he limped forward. The pain helped focus him, but mostly his mind was now racing without anything catching, like gears too far apart to mesh.

What was he forgetting? Something important, but he was in panic mode now. He scrambled back to the ex-Dungeon, which once again looked like a beaten-up bathroom, and found a Band-Aid from his kit in the medicine chest. Hands trembling, he peeled it onto his knee. About to leave, he spotted a pair of boy's underwear in the corner of the hallway—must've fallen from one of the boxes as he was hurrying out the door. Tweezing it between thumb and forefinger, he brought it outside. For one rapturous moment, he buried his nose in the crotch. Then, spearing it with his pinkie and pulling it back by the elastic waistband, he slingshot the underwear into a bush, where it half disappeared. Fuck Fairchester.

He checked his watch: 11:15. With a mock salute toward the center of town, he got into his Sentra and backed into the street. Around Montrose Street and across Plymouth Avenue . . . but he found himself making one last circuit around the park before he headed for the highway. Under the soft glow of the street lamps, the green benches sat like wide sentinels about the perimeter. The surrounding trees soared above, patchily blocking out the dim moonlight. From the giant slide to the ropewalk, from the sandbox to the swings, all the equipment was held in a lunar stillness.

Was that a child next to the second set of swings? He slowed the car.

No, just the shadow of a pole, thickened at the crossbar.

Was that a shoe over there, on the steps to the slide?

This time, he stopped the car and got out, half-limping toward the slide, to find only that: a child's dirty red sneaker, half unlaced, perched there as if just stepped out of. His panic subsided and turned to interest. He picked up the sneaker and fingered it, sniffing the inside curiously. Musty. Now who would leave a shoe at the playground? He gripped a side-pole of the slide for support, worn shiny and smooth by innumerable little hands. No children. No one at all. The playground after hours felt both comforting and awful, a ghost town with all the life temporarily drawn out, dispersed to homes lit by yellow squares across the way. But the houses might as well have been in outer space for all the distance between them and him.

Maybe he should call Myra. Maybe he should have called her weeks ago. Too late.

He limped across to a low-slung swing and sat down heavily, his bottom gripped by the canvas and rubber thong. Pushing away with his toe, he glided back and forth across a sandy divide. He was alone. His parents had never come to the playground with him, and he had been forced to figure everything out on his own. This is a seesaw. Don't play on it with Jimmy, who likes to smash your side down on the pavement. That time back in first grade gave you three stitches over your left eye. Here's the sandbox. Make something. The sand isn't for eating, even if Steve tries to shovel some down your mouth. And the jungle gym, with its skyscraper shape and hard iron bars: Ted had a vision of playing tag with a little girl named Angie as they swung around the bars. Who was it had her teeth knocked in that way? Or dangling from the third-story bars as Angie tickled your armpits, trying to make you drop onto the hard-packed dirt below.

At least they'd paid attention to him. In second grade, he'd befriended two bullies named Nick and John, who made him perform humiliating tasks—"Go ahead, lick the knob on the water fountain!"—and occasionally sat on him to torture him. Nick's slightly crooked face, framed by dirty black hair, hung over him. In his worst moments, he'd pretend he was up and Nick was down. He'd project himself into another boy's body or even a dog or a tree. It was a pattern, and patterns became behavior after a while, which caused more patterns to occur.

Slowly, then picking up speed, he began to pump on the swing. Skimming over the ground, yet held securely in place. He was Alex, small and neat. He had just come from the skating rink, where a nice man had taken him home. He'd fed him and played with him. And then—

But Ted's mind fuzzed out at that point. It was as if he'd been drawing a picture in crayon, and at the far left, someone had swiped at it with a pink gum eraser. The crayon hadn't been fully erased, but it had smeared all over.

He pumped hard, his legs splayed out, his throbbing knee temporarily forgotten. The sky revolved, the trees closing in from a funny angle. Their boughs seemed full of children. When the branches fluttered in the late-night breeze, their faces distorted and gaped, crying out soundlessly. It was an image from a recurrent dream, which he tried to whip away with a backwards fling of his head. When that didn't quite work, he jumped off the swing. He landed on all fours, his knee soaking up more pain, and he cried out.

"You think that's bad?" his father would say when he came back all cut up and bruised from the playground. He'd peer at Ted through a bushy cloud of beard, beer, and cigarette smoke. "You don't behave, I'll make it a lot worse."

His mother was vague about these times. "Your father gets irritable, so don't push him." She never said anything about Ted's cut lip or the extra bruise on his arm. Later on, after the old man had split, she just stopped talking about him. If Ted brought up the subject, she'd mutter something about his being away for a while. When it became apparent that he wasn't coming back, Ted cried for two days. He still owned a ratty little screwdriver that his father had used for fix-it jobs around the house.

Or had he thrown that in the dumpster?

He kept his stunted past in a blue cardboard box tied with twine: his mother's scissors, a lock of his aunt's permed hair, a few photos. Mommy, Daddy, and son in front of a motel on a trip they'd made out west; two portraits of his parents before they became Mommy and Daddy—faded happiness, or the appearance of it. He'd brought the box with him.

Ted crawled toward the wooden play station, which offered a split-level crawlspace ending in a rope bridge. For some reason, crawling hurt less than walking upright. He hauled himself onto the first platform, which was padded with some sort of outdoor foam rubber. The playgrounds of the suburbs, he'd noticed from a few comparisons, had less metal and fewer sharp edges than in the city. From a circular window cut halfway through the crawlspace, he could see the lush lawn of the school, the sand-colored brick building moored in the green expanse like a ship in an emerald sea. His fate to miss the boat.

He stretched out his legs, reaching his arms to the next level, and suddenly he was Alex again. He was small for his age, so the other kids beat up on him, and his father, the irritated-looking man in Price's Bake Shop, only made it worse. When he ran to hide, his father came after him. He spent a lot of time in his room, and when he tried the doorknob, he found that his father had locked him in. His mother was out. "Cut the noise in there!" his father yelled at him if he played too loudly with his toys. He made up stories, but he dreamed of escape. Ted shuffled his shoes back and forth. When he got an invitation to a skating party, he saw his chance.

He crawled through the tunnel, which ended in a ramp connecting to a level like a tree house. The children's faces swayed in the nearby branches like a hidden-picture puzzle, so he looked away. Down the other side was a rope rigging, buttressed with rubber. He spidered down the netting until he was almost at the other edge, but then his foot caught and pitched him forward. He lay face-down on the rope strands, just a few feet off the ground. He groaned, half in pain and half from humiliation. He wasn't Alex anymore, he was back to Ted, and he didn't belong here, not really. Alex was out there somewhere, certainly not at the playground, but, Ted guessed, still at large.

"Yeah?" said his father, not even looking up from his newspaper but clenching his hairy hands into fists. "So what're you going to do about it?"

Ted punched the empty air. The force of it pressed his bad knee into one of the ropes. Caught in hurt and self-pity, he just lay there, staring at the dirt below. When the knee began to twist away of its own accord, he dug it in harder. He had the sense that he ought to be punished somehow. Bad boy, bad man. Bad world, too. What the hell was he doing in the suburbs, anyway? He couldn't see much from his position, but he knew, without looking, the darkling houses all in rows, the respectability he imagined must reside indoors. What was the purpose of such an arrangement? The patterns were all wrong.

A good contingency planner didn't concern himself with motive. The point was to keep the system running. As a mist gradually takes shape, a question began to form. What would it be like if he had a son? He twisted about in the netting until he was on his back, staring at the sky. The half-moon was a face in profile, blurred with distance and time. Had Alex escaped to the moon? Maybe his son would also be that radiant and moody, company during the long hours: the two of them wedged into a chair, both reaching for the remote control at the same time. He'd scowl, the boy would make a face, and they'd both laugh uncontrollably. When it was time for lunch, he'd fix them both sandwiches that they'd eat in stages, picking at the cold cuts or biting the bread into odd shapes. They'd compare milk mustaches. And then what? Ted was vague on certain details, though he could almost feel the boy's thin but sturdy limbs, stroke one downy forearm to the crook of the elbow.

He turned and saw the boy from the back, his neck emerging from the collar of his gray T-shirt like the white shoot of a plant, his small head bent over a book, looking up occasionally to ask a question. *Daddy, what does "humongous" mean?* Ted, the ruler of his universe, could tell him that, and so much more. The boy would have his own computer, too, with a microprocessor so fast that any animated figure would practically vault off the screen. (Something nudged at Ted's brain at this point, but he pushed it back.) They'd play Karate Boy 3 and Mutant Man. At night, he'd tuck his son in bed and tousle his hair, soothe that squirmy body into sleep. Maybe they'd be in bunk beds.

Don't be ridiculous.

Ted blinked and his son was gone, a hole in the web where one of the strands had worn through. The moon slid behind a cloud, and life was sad. Slowly, painfully, he clambered down from the netting, careful this time not to snag his foot. He really had to do something about his situation, even if it was years too late. But when he stepped onto the dirt, he paused, unsure of which direction to take. His hand felt as if it should be grasping something—where was that shoe? After a minute of searching, he found it by the slide.

He began to caress the sneaker, rubbing the insole softened from use, running his fingers across the rubberized toecap. The feel of it created an achy tenderness, different from the usual stiffening. He'd never seen Alex's shoes, he now realized. These stupid bits of people he collected, from no one he knew at all. He needed a circuit-interrupter, a new code, a different algorithm to change the pattern of his days.

He was still holding the sneaker when the police cruiser swung by the far side of the park, its headlights almost capturing him in their beam. Jesus. He froze until the patrol car was past. Fifteen seconds later, he was in his car and accelerating. Driving up I-95, he hit 80 mph before forcing himself to slow down. He didn't know exactly where he'd end up, but he was heading toward Buffalo. In the front seat lay Alex's skates.

That's when he remembered the most incriminating item: his hard drive. After dropping the television set and hurting his knee, he'd forgotten the goddamned computer. Cursing softly, he peered ahead at the exit signs, looking for the nearest turnaround.

Chapter 18

We tore out of the driveway in the Volvo, Jane at the wheel, an accordion file of posters, a flashlight, and a roll of masking tape at my feet. The street was deserted, an ivy-black darkness hovering over the houses and lawns as if nothing would ever move again. But it wasn't going to stop my Jane. She careened around the corner of Garner and Somers, then slowed down as we approached the next intersection. "Wait," she said, "I don't even know where we're going."

She had a point. "How about if we start with some telephone poles around town?" I suggested. "Maybe some stores later."

"Sure. How about this one?" She braked at the corner, and I got out to tape up our first poster. Printing out fifty of them had been heart-rending, but slapping one on a pole made me want to cry. I tried not to look at Alex's face, but I caught his eye as I taped him five feet off the ground— taller than he was in real life. His smile was slightly off-kilter, and his ears stuck out. I muttered something that might have been a prayer if I were religious, and got back into the car. Jane gunned the car for another five blocks until we stopped again. We did that for a while until we approached Crest Hill, a.k.a. Dead-Dog Road. We were also supposed to be looking around, I reminded her.

"I know, but for what? A pair of gray slacks?"

I sighed. If we only had some better leads. When I tried my usual technique of introjection, I got only so far. It was really just putting myself in another's place, not so easy with a pedophile. Not just any pedophile—*that bastard, if I—*

"Did you say something?" Jane turned onto Sycamore Street.

"Just muttering to myself." I looked out the window, my eyes mostly adjusted to the looming shapes of Fairchester mansionettes. Now: if I were a computer geek with a fashion problem, I was probably socially maladjusted. I didn't own a house. That was for families. Maybe a rental, but where did the town offer apartments? I dimly recalled some sort of development between Bromley and Jefferson, some street that began with a *W*.

Time for another poster, at Sycamore and Montrose. When I got back in, it was time to call the house. Jerry answered at once but sounded disappointed to hear my voice.

"No messages, huh?" I could hear the TV blaring in the background.

"No. Sorry. Listen, I ate some cold pasta from the fridge—"

"Don't worry about it." Jesus, what preoccupies some people. I cut off Jerry explaining that he'd cook some more. As long as Jane's Nokia was still in my hand, was it too late to phone Ferrara? He'd given me a 24-hour number to call. When I got someone who wasn't Ferrara, I asked her for an update. Nothing. Since she didn't tell us to sit tight, I told him we were out to look around and gave her Jane's cell phone number.

I took a deep, jagged breath. "They're useless. They wanted to know if *we'd* heard anything."

"What's Ferrara done?"

"It wasn't him. Some woman in the family crisis unit. The kind who holds your hand during the crisis."

"What about Ferrara?"

"He'll be in soon. She told us to go home."

"Should we?"

"No."

Because we were near the downtown area, I hit the Food Emporium. Jane did Talbot's, and I did B. Dalton's—the outsides, anyway. We kept calling home: no messages. Then for a while we did telephone polls in residential areas: Pinewood, Dovecote, Highmeadow. Only once did some woman into neighborhood beautification yell at us, and she backed down when she read the notice.

"Oh." The woman looked at me getting back into the car. She had on black leggings and a white blouse, wearing big-frame glasses that belonged on someone else. She took them off, and her eyes blinked rapidly. "I'm so sorry. I mean, really, really sorry. I had no idea."

"Yeah." I started the car.

She put her hand to her breast and started to approach Jane's side. "I'm sorry. It's just that when I saw you, I didn't know what you were doing. You must be so, so—"

I rolled up the window. "Get us out of here."

Jane mashed the accelerator and the Volvo shot forward, almost running over the woman's foot. I looked back in the rearview mirror when we were half a block away, and she was still standing there, looking sorrowful.

But Jane was beginning to lose control. She drove two more blocks or so, weaving too much to the left, then nosed the Volvo to the side of the road and stopped. She put her head on the steering wheel and started to sob. "I just . . . can't think. I keep seeing Alex's face in front of me." Her face looked haggard, as if some elastic grid holding it up had sagged.

I had no response, but I had to say something. Her arms were wrapped around the wheel, her back bent forward as if she were praying. Her sobs began to catch in her throat, making her cough. In the end, I said nothing at all, but reached over to hold her. I pressed my chest against her back, and she slowly stopped shaking. A minute or two passed. As we sat in the parked car, I had a vision of us growing old on a side street in Fairchester, childless and alone, until they dug our bodies out of a rusting Volvo.

"I love you," I finally told her, as if that would make things all right. But it's what I felt.

She twisted to kiss my shoulder. "I—I love you, too. And I love my son." She started shaking again, her whole body racked with sobs.

I held on. In a while, the ivy-black darkness would retreat into whatever cave held it for the night, and an egg-yolk yellow would start to ooze from the eastern corner of the sky. When Alex was abducted, time should have stopped, but it kept cycling on, oblivious. Why couldn't I undo just a small segment of time?—that afternoon at the roller-skating rink? Give me the chance to press REPLAY, and I'd promise never to do it again.

Quit whining, commanded—was it Snoggs? Martin? A voice I didn't recognize. *You have to act. Now.* I nodded. "Let me drive," I said.

"What?" Jane's voice came out as a croak.

"My turn to drive. Okay?"

Jane got half out of the car to walk around. "Where are you going?"

"I'm not sure. Just a hunch." As soon as she got in, I piloted toward a dim region in my brain, projected onto this dim suburb. I thought about that development again as the headlights pierced the thick darkness. I pictured the man in the gray slacks again. He lived close to the park, I bet. We were headed for Pinewood when I sensed that was out of his area. I stopped the car at once.

"What's going on?" Jane canted forward against her seatbelt. "What do you see?"

"Nothing yet." We were on the other side of Plymouth Avenue again. "It's just a feeling. I think he might live around here."

"What are you going to do?"

Act now, urged the voice. "I—I don't know," I told Jane. "Skulk around." I opened the car door. "Maybe it's stupid, but I've got to try."

"How about the rest of the posters?"

"You put up some." I waved her on. "I'll meet you . . . how about at Montrose and Winfield?" Montrose was what Somers eventually turned into. Winfield was where my hunch was coming from.

"Okay, but when?"

I checked my watch. It was 11:30. "Give me till midnight."

"Please be careful." She was creeping along in the car as I trudged eastward. "Want me to come with you?"

She and I really felt like a team tonight, but I shook my head. This I felt should be done alone. It occurred to me later that a respectable couple walking along the street would be less obtrusive than a lone man skulking around, but I didn't think of that at the time. I couldn't think of much at all. Alex's scared face bobbed above the bushes while I was trying to concentrate on the man who'd taken him.

Shut up and do it, growled that voice. I closed my eyes to focus better, slowly opening them to the alienating homes of Fairchester. This guy must always feel like he didn't fit in, so why was he living here? Jane had driven ahead, her tail lights disappearing around the next corner. I paced along Montrose, but looking for what? A sign on the door, "CAUTION: MOLESTER INSIDE"?

I paused by a giant fir tree in someone's front yard, losing myself for a moment in the shadows. By now my eyes had adjusted to the dark, yet the noises from the rink kept haunting me—if only I could get that sound of roller-skating out of my ears. I shook my head to clear it, but instead the noise grew louder. I glanced up to see a teenage guy skateboarding by on the other side of the street, looking in the other direction. He was using a five-foot metal pipe to push himself along as if it were a ski pole. He had that rangy surfer-dude appearance, updated with a tattoo and pierced ears. I had no idea what he was doing—till he hoisted the pipe and swung it *spang* against the nearest mailbox.

The metal box crumped sideways, its bread-loaf shape half caved in. He quickly skated toward the next one and whacked it, too. Goddamn punk, I thought, maybe showing my age. All the fury I'd built up against the molester began to pull me across the street. He'd just stopped to admire his handiwork when I yelled out.

"Hey, what the hell do you think you're doing!"

He didn't even turn around to look back but jumped right on his skate-board and started to roll away, poling himself along. In a moment, he'd be gone, never there.

Before I knew what I was doing, I'd vaulted over the curb and sprinted after him as if I were still Tough Guy.

"Come back!" I was ten feet away and gaining.

"Fuck off, man!" He shoved away to widen the gap, and for an instant I thought I was going to lose him. He was traveling fast as a bicycle by that point, but I gulped in oxygen and kept at it.

I'd almost caught up at the next intersection, with him pushing away like mad, when the pole caught me in the shin with a *thunk*. It hurt a lot worse than being kicked by an eight-year-old soccer player, and it knocked me to the ground. By the time I scrambled to my feet, he was already halfway around the corner, disappearing into the darkness. I was sweating like crazy, my breathing was ragged, and my shin throbbed like a second pulse-beat. I loosened my shirt and took big gulps of air until I felt okay to move again. Never mind the leg. I had someplace else to be, *now*. I checked my watch: 11:40. I started loping toward Winfield, passing a trail of bashed mailboxes. I visualized something that looked like condo units, which for some reason loomed gray in my mind, just like the slacks. I had just rounded the corner of Bromley onto Winfield when I sensed flashing blue lights at my back.

In our fair town, the cruisers are white with "FAIRCHESTER POLICE" in thick red lettering on the sides, emphasized by blue speed lines around the words. They always look as if they've just come from a full-service carwash. As a law-abiding citizen, I usually don't mind seeing them around, but it didn't take much to realize this one was after me. Maybe the mailbox whacker had gone to the police, or the cops thought I was the guy—either way, I didn't have time for this. I sprinted forward about fifty feet, absorbing the pain, then cut into the bushes surrounding what looked like a group of cottages. That's when I saw him.

He was loading a computer into the trunk of a gray car that already looked packed. But when he moved toward the driver's door, I knew who it was: the man in the gray slacks. Even though he seemed to be limping, that walk was too familiar. And I damn well knew that face and those clothes. He was running away.

This time, I didn't call out, didn't wait. I ran forward and tackled him just as he was getting into the car. He toppled onto the seat, his head smacking the steering wheel. For a moment, he was stunned.

I shook him. "Where's Alex, you son of a bitch!" He just groaned. I yanked his head up by the hair and asked him again.

"I don't know . . . ."

"What do you mean, *you don't know*? You fucking drove off with him!"

He looked at me blearily, his eyes unfocused. "I . . . don't know. He was in the . . . the bathroom, and then . . . ."

"*And then?*" I got a tighter grip on his hair.

Then the patrol car glided into the driveway. No lights or siren, just suddenly there. Two policemen emerged from the car, one drawing his gun as the other lunged forward and yelled "Freeze!"

So I froze. The man in the gray slacks tried to twist around, but I held him tight.

"What's going on here?" asked the beefy cop, the one in the forefront.

"This man took my son!"

"He's not, I told you . . . he's not here." The guy tried to shake his head, but he was shuddering too much.

"Then where is he?"

The beefy cop stepped up to the open car door. "Look, I don't care what the deal is—let him go. Then maybe we'll hear the story."

I took away one hand, reluctantly. It took too damned long to get out what had happened, but soon one of the cops was speaking to headquarters, and in a minute another patrol car swung into the driveway. By now, a few of the man's neighbors had come out onto the lawn, including an Asian woman and a guy in a blue bathrobe. Two of the cops searched the man's apartment while another one asked the man repeatedly about my son. "Look, stand aside," said the cop. But I couldn't take it anymore, and I was just about to haul off and slug our suspect when his eyes rolled upwards and he really began to shake. If it wasn't an epileptic seizure, it was a damned good fake job. Before the cop could grab him, he smacked his head on the asphalt.

That's why, when Jane drove by to pick me up at midnight, she saw two cop cars and an ambulance by the curb. They had just loaded the guy, out cold, onto a gurney.

She stopped the Volvo short and jumped out. "What's going on here?" In another life, she could have been a cop. She certainly got more cooperation from them than I had, but no one could pry any information from the guy on the stretcher. Another cop was asking the neighbors questions, but of course no one had seen or heard a damned thing.

"There's some blood in the bathroom," reported the beefy cop. "But the kid's not around."

When Jane started to shout, he put his hand on her shoulder. "Look, we're doing everything we can to find him, understand?" Jane opened her mouth, but he kept his grip on her. "You need to go home, okay? Best place for you to be." He stepped back, surveying both of us. "Think you can do that?"

We complied with half the officer's request. We got back in the car—and took a lot of side roads home, stopping to bellow Alex's name on every street. He could have been anywhere, for God's sake. Halfway home, Jane hugged me hard for apprehending the guy. "I hope—I just want Alex to be okay."

I want my son, I thought. I want—*us*. I shut my eyes and imagined the scene between Alex and the man in the gray slacks. Alex came out with some smart-aleck comment that stopped the man for a while. Alex said he had to go to the bathroom and locked the door tight. He said, "Just a minute," and then somehow escaped.

Stubborn, that's my boy. Maybe it was a survival trait. Now he was out of the den of the molester and alone, maybe hurt. But the man in the gray slacks couldn't win. Please.

Jane was starting to weave again. We were just turning onto Garner when I told her to watch out, and she yelled, "All *right*, I can see!," wrenching the steering wheel, and that's when we hit the tree. It was suddenly right in the middle of the windshield, like some huge lumbering pedestrian who couldn't get out of the way. Then—*crump*, and I was flung forward. The seatbelt caught me, and the airbag inflated with a *paf*. All I could see was gray. I could barely breathe. One hand felt pinned.

Slowly the grayness receded. The honking stopped. I had a darkened windshield view of a sycamore a few feet ahead. We were half on the Steinbaums' lawn, flanking the cannon ball hedge. The hood of the Volvo was bent upward at a rakish angle. My left arm was attached to something. I was holding Jane's hand, or she was holding mine. Her driver's seat airbag had deployed, too, and was only now sagging like a punctured hot-air balloon. We stared at each other.

"Jesus." She let go of the steering wheel, breathing heavily.

"Yeah."

She eyed the tree. "That was too close."

I nodded. We weren't biting each other's heads off, playing the blame game, raking our talons across tender flesh. Instead, we just sat there, stunned. A light went on in the Steinbaums' house.

This is what we fight and die for, intoned Martin.

Bitch, muttered Snoggs.

Shut up, I intoned silently. I squeezed Jane's hand. "Are you okay?"

"I think so." She peered ahead. "But I don't know about the car."

We got out and explained the situation to Leo Steinbaum, who backed down immediately when he heard why we were out. He said he'd take care of it and call an autobody shop. I couldn't help thinking Alex would've loved the crash.

Give him back.

We stood in the driveway after our neighbor had disappeared inside. The accident obviously hadn't made much noise because no one else had come outside. Now what? We weren't holding hands anymore. We were facing a large house that happened to be our own, but it looked as inviting as an empty garage. The air had been thick with night when we'd left; now it was gray and cheerless. The pebbles in the driveway looked hard and unforgiving, every stalk of grass on the lawn a green blade. Inside the house, I knew, would be worse. And I didn't feel like talking to Jerry.

"Alex," I whispered so low that I might not have been talking at all. "Alex, please come back."

"It's not fair," Jane pronounced. Tears were leaking again. "It's not right! He's only eight."

I nodded stupidly. The danger from the crash had passed by now, leaving me limp. Absurdly, I thought of the magic marker and tape we'd left in the car.

We stood there contemplating the rest of our lives. I thought about how I'd trade anything for this never to have happened. My home lost, two fingers chopped off—I don't know, just something to barter with, only I had no leverage. I was so damned—unable. Finally I came to a decision. "I know Alex is out there somewhere. And I'm going to walk from door to door in Fairchester until we find him."

Jane looked at me half hopefully, half warily. "Okay. I'll help."

"But first I want to call Ferrara again." I asked for Jane's cell phone because I couldn't face inside just yet. This time, I got through to the detective at once. He picked it up on the first ring.

"Ferrara here." In the background, another phone rang.

"It's Michael Eisler."

"Right, I got back to you and left a message. Where were you? Where are you now?"

"In front of our house."

"Yeah?" He sounded as if he were frowning, his thick upper lip curling down. When I'd met him at the station, he looked like the kind of Italian who in an earlier era would have worn a handlebar mustache. But still the kind of guy who'd buy an ice cream for a kid on a hot day. "How're you doing, both of you?"

I considered the question. Our child was still missing, and we'd just suffered a car crash. Ferrara didn't have to know about that last part. "Not so hot."

"It's tough, I know. We're working on it . . . got the police report on the apartment . . . that guy . . . start right . . . ."

Ferrara's voice was fading in and out, so I started walking away from the Steinbaums' wall of shrubbery to improve the reception. I caught something about waiting for the guy to recover at the hospital. I told him about our poster blitz, and he said that was all to the good. Or all understood—the fuzz on the line was still there. I was halfway around the house by now, leaving Jane to chew her nails. She'd wandered over to the front path but also couldn't bring herself to enter the house yet. I looked back and almost tripped over the basement access as Ferrara was explaining the Omega Phi Sorority. Or was that "make it a high priority"?

I finally gave up. "I'm sorry, I can't hear you."

"I'm sorry, I can't hear you," Ferrara replied.

"I'll call you back from the house," I told the phone. "Give me a minute." And I flipped the phone shut.

That was when I noticed what had happened to my office. I'd been meaning to call the glazier again, but I hadn't gotten around to it. Instead, I'd taped a piece of cardboard over the gap, making my office look like an '86 Mercury up for quick resale.

Only now the cardboard had been pushed in, and the door was open a crack.

I backed away for a moment. I should have been outraged, disgusted, scared—how had he gotten by Jerry? What if the guy who broke in was still here? But I was too beaten-up for any of those reactions. *Just what we need*, I thought, *a burglary on top of a car crash and an abduction.*

I paused outside my office to listen. No sounds of smashing furniture. The blinds were shut, so I couldn't see inside. Whoever had broken in had probably left. I tried to think of what was worth stealing—no expensive art on the walls, no antique vases. My laptop computer, that was about it. I gently pushed the door halfway open.

The room lay in deep shadow, one gray sliver of light slicing into the far wall. It took a moment for my eyes to adjust. I saw no one at my desk, the laptop perched on top like a silent sentinel. The untrammeled rug, my Eames chair, the bookshelf. The couch. An extra shadow lay on it, and even from my vantage at the door, I could hear jagged breathing. What kind of burglar would break in and then try out the couch? Who the hell was this, Goldilocks?

I had nothing with me except Jane's cell phone, so I picked up *The Psychopathology of the Child* from the bookshelf, a big heavy volume, and advanced. If he turned suddenly, I could brain him with the book.

Now that's using psychology, crowed Snoggs.

I got within three feet of the couch, but the figure didn't jump up. Instead, the body reached out a hand and wailed something.

"Daddy."

Chapter 19

Alex lay curled on the couch, digging in like a shipwreck survivor embracing the beach. His hair was matted, his face blotchy red. I pulled him to me and hugged him so hard that I winded him. I wanted all of him—his boy's body, his arms and legs dangling, the elfin head burrowing into my shoulder. "You're back, you're back!" I kept repeating.

"*Unnh* . . . Da-*ha*-ddy, I can't—"

I loosened my grip but kept him close, patting him, feeling that he was real, as he regained his breath.

"Alex, my God, are you all right?" Jane had run to my office when I called out. She picked him up and kissed him all over, hugging him even harder than I had. He squirmed helplessly until she put him down. When I flicked on the lights, I saw that his pants were ripped, his shirt stretched out of shape. His hair had an odd greenish tint. We were half out of our minds with joy, but worries were looming. For the moment, we stood there, in between reactions.

"Mommy, Daddy!" He started crying. "Where *were* you?"

"Alex, Alex . . . ." I tried to soothe him with my hands on his shoulders. "We were looking all over for you."

Jane couldn't help herself. "*Where have you been?*"

Alex looked away, his breathing rough as a rasp again. When he turned, you could see a streak of something that looked like blood on his pants.

"Alex, we love you—we were very worried." I knelt to be on couch level. "We thought something had happened to you. That man—"

Jane reached out. "Did he hurt you?"

Alex shrank back against the wall. He said nothing and wouldn't meet our eye.

Jerry hadn't seen anything, we found out when we entered the house. "He must've crept back there, I swear. I had all the lights on. Why didn't he just come in?" He swung back to look at Alex again. "How're you feeling? You gave your parents quite a fright."

Alex mumbled something, but it didn't sound like English.

So we took Alex to the emergency room at the Fairchester Medical Center. I wanted to talk more with him first, but Jane insisted. Since he wouldn't move on his own, she scooped him up from the couch and put him in the rear seat of the Volvo. I called back Ferrara to tell him what had happened, and he arranged to meet us there.

If I had known they'd taken the man in the gray slacks to the same hospital, I might have—I don't know what I would have done. At the time, I was more preoccupied with my son.

Alex was sent to a pediatric specialist in sexual abuse, who administered a penis examination, took a rectum culture for STD, and looked around a lot with a probe. Alex shut his eyes a lot. Jane was so agitated that she bit her fingers instead of her nails. I attempted to stay calm by trying to soothe both of them, but it didn't work. *He's okay*, I repeated like a mantra, but the echo chamber in my brain just repeated, *Okay?*

Then we got the test results. They were suggestive. Traces of saliva around the groin, along with sweat and other secretions. The rectum looked red and irritated but not ruptured. An oral exam may not always detect the residue of semen in the mouth. The blood stain on his pants turned out to be from a scrape. He said he fell while skating. That might account for a few other abrasions. Another red stain, this one on his shirt, turned out to be tomato sauce. The green slime in his hair was some kiddie product. Only none of that was at the rink.

I thought of what questions the man in the gray slacks could answer. I imagined twisting his head off. Jane gritted her teeth, maybe thinking along the same lines.

"He seems to be intact," the gangly specialist informed me, peeling off his latex gloves. His smile was probably meant to be reassuring, but it looked more like a leer. Alex was back in the waiting room area with Jane, holding a giant Hershey's bar that we'd bought from the hospital gift shop to ease the situation. But he wasn't eating it, which showed how out of whack he was. He wasn't doing much of anything. Jane had told him brightly that it was all a special health check-up.

"Special for what?" he'd asked, looking at the chocolate as if it were a block of wood that someone had handed him. He got up as if to escape. I followed right behind. He was walking a bit funny, or was that just my eye?

"Because you're a special boy." It wasn't one of Jane's better lines. Ferrara had told us to level with our son as much as we felt comfortable doing. He introduced us to a mousy-haired woman in a beige cardigan who reminded me of my patient R. She was a psychiatric social worker who would talk with Alex about the incident, or whatever it was. She told Alex to call her Kathy.

Alex looked toward us. "What's this for, Mommy?"

"It's part of the exam." Jane aligned her hands as if she could invisibly guide Alex toward the truth. "We just want you to talk with her for a while."

Kathy led Alex into a room at the far end of the hall and shut the door firmly. Ferrara looked as if he wanted to go with them—his heavy mustache was practically twitching—but it was strictly a one-on-one affair. He soon excused himself and said he'd be in touch with us.

The wait was excruciating since we didn't know what was going on. Jane and I alternated between fidgeting and holding hands. It was a day later before we heard the tape. Kathy's voice starts off, asking Alex what he'd call dumb stuff, like his name and age. She glides on to his hobbies, which for him at that time were reading and collecting bottle caps. "Do you like roller-skating?" she interjects, and he pauses.

"Um, yeah."

"Really? Where do you go skating?"

"The Derby Roller Rink. It's in Greenwood."

"Hmm. When were you there last?" And on and on like this as she slowly comes around to the point. Which is: "Who took you home from the party?"

After a gap of about fifteen seconds, she gently repeats the question. And waits some more.

"There was a man." Alex's voice is barely audible.

"Did he offer you a ride?"

"Yeah. Sort of."

Kathy's voice grows harder here, springy only because it's made of steel. "What do you mean?"

"I told him . . . I told him I wanted to go."

"Why didn't you tell your daddy?"

He looks away at this point—I can practically see it. "Daddy never understands. And Mommy's not around."

"I see. So you went with this man?"

"Yes." *What is Alex's face like at this exact moment, I would like to know.*

"That sounds like an adventure. Where did you go?"

They went to his place, naturally, after which the tape wanders again. Something about games and a special room. But whenever Kathy veers towards particulars, Alex grows vague. He says that he and the man talked.

About what? He had something to eat there. *We should pump his stomach.* They watched some TV and played on the computer. *And what else?*

"Then I had to leave." A rustling sound comes through. "Can I go now?"

Kathy persevered, asking all the right questions, interspersed with some innocent ones. Was he nice? What did he look like? Did you have fun? Did he touch you a lot? Where? She also gave him some paper and asked him to draw a picture of the man, his car, the special room—but Alex can't really draw; it's not one of his talents. At one point, Kathy offered to play Hangman with him, asking him to choose a word that best described his experience. He agreed to play, but she never got the word he picked. *Pederast?* I thought furiously, *fellatio?* Alex's teachers all agree that his vocabulary is exceptional for his age. He told me later the word was *frolic.*

The awful question is what occurred after they left the rink. The man in the gray slacks didn't take my son home to play cards with him, did he?

No response. Usually when Alex doesn't answer, he's thinking about something else. When he doesn't answer Kathy, I get the strong feeling he's suppressing what he knows.

"How do you feel right now?" This question comes near the end of the tape, after most other avenues have been exhausted.

There. Is that a slight whimper? "I . . . don't know," he confesses. "Kind of strange. Like there's something on me I can't wash off. Can I go now?"

When he came out from the question-room, as he called it, he was withdrawn. Kathy walked back in lockstep with him. "Thank you, Alex. You were very helpful," she told him, I think for our benefit. "Can you go sit over there for a moment? I need to talk with your parents."

So Alex sat in the nearby waiting room, his legs dangling from the plastic seat as if he were a doll. Usually he'd have asked for something to read, but he just sat there with his hands folded in his lap. I kept glancing back at him as Kathy explained the situation. He seemed to be examining his fingers. And covering his crotch.

"I'm afraid we didn't come up with much." Kathy looked as if she were delivering a medical diagnosis. "He wasn't too talkative, and when we got to the central event, he pulled up short. Is he usually like that?"

"No." Jane waved her hand.

"Yes," I said at the same time.

Kathy looked back and forth between the two of us.

I tried for damage control. "I mean, sometimes he's that way."

"It depends on who he's talking to." Jane waved her other hand wildly.

"I see." Kathy tugged at her cardigan, as if that would straighten matters out. From the corner of my eye, I could see Alex getting up to walk around. He was headed toward the far wall to look at a poster about breast cancer. I'd have been more nervous, but the waiting room had only one exit, and we were standing by the door. A large nurse surveyed everyone from behind a glassed-in counter. The whole scene reminded me too much of the clinic where I used to put in time. Kathy pursed her lips. "It's hard to tell the extent of the trauma. The interview was taped, so you can listen to it yourself."

Jane shook her head in agitation. "But what do we do now?"

"I'd advise counseling. Do you want the name of a good specialist?"

I drew myself up. "That's okay—I'm a psychiatrist. I know some people."

Kathy's expression softened. "Fine. Here's my card if you need anything." In a slightly ridiculous moment, we all exchanged cards, including Jane's tri-color Haldome business one. It felt as if we'd just concluded a deal. Alex had finished with the breast cancer poster and was now staring at the large breasts of the nurse.

So we left the hospital. We'd hear the tape later, we were told. The results of Ted's questioning, too. He was up and aware, Ferrara told us, but not talking. By the time we got home, it was almost six A.M. The reality of Friday morning began to filter through. Jane called her office to say that, because of a family emergency, she wouldn't be in that day. I phoned Jerry and asked him to make some calls and cover for me. I hung up before I could get the full measure of his sympathy. No one wanted any breakfast, but we sat in the kitchen as if we might any minute, held in a sort of uneasy limbo. Alex looked worried. "Shouldn't I get ready for school?"

"Oh, no, you're sick." Jane exchanged a glance with me, over Alex's head. "I mean, you've been through a lot. We decided you need at least a day to recover."

"But this *feels* funny." Alex got up to walk around.

Jane got up, putting on a falsely bright smile. "I think I *will* have something to eat. Anyone else?"

I shook my head.

"Maybe a snack," said you-know-who.

Jane wheeled around. "Sure! Whatever you like."

My automatic reaction, so help me, was to pound the table at rewarding such behavior—what in the world was I thinking? I caught myself in the middle. Jane and Alex were looking at me as if I were an uninvited guest in my own home. "Never mind," I corrected myself. "Give him whatever he wants."

Alex put his head in his hands. "I don't want anything anymore."

Normally, Jane and I would have had a scene right in front of Alex. We'd shout recriminations at each other until I smacked her right on the face—in my mind. But that was before all this. I looked up at her as she reached out to stroke Alex on the back of his neck. She was the mother of my child, the woman I loved. Hadn't we just suffered through a car crash together? I patted Alex on the back—he was now cosseted by two parents—and took Jane's other hand, as in some complicated body-linking game. Everyone felt warm. And Alex actually smiled, which made us feel some hope in this world.

He stretched. "I'm hungry."

"So am I," said Jane and I in unison. Alex acceded to having a snack: a few carrot sticks. Jane and I ate what remained of Alex's pretzels, and he didn't seem to mind. It was after nine by then, and when I glanced out the front window, the lone cloud in the sky was vacating the premises.

"Can I go out and play?"

Jane and I looked at each other. Alex wasn't exactly an outdoors type. Healthier than watching TV, sure, but what had prompted this change?

"Play what, dear?" Jane was picking at her thumbnail.

"I don't know. Just . . . *play*." He looked fixedly toward the window onto the street, which turned into a dark alley in my mind.

"Why don't you kick a soccer ball with Daddy?"

"Me?" My shin ached in memory, but I'd have been happy to run around with him.

He shook his head. "I just want to go outside."

Jane was staring out the window as if the lawn harbored goblins. After a child's been traumatized, you have to reassure him that he's safe, that it won't happen again. But who could say that now? Anything could happen here. In the past few weeks, for instance, I'd seen a van entering certain driveways mid-morning, painted on the side, "Safe, Clean, Reliable Consumer Trash Pick-Up, Vietnam Veterans of America"—yet driven by some unshaven eighteen-year-old. And what about the teachers at school, or the man walking down Garner Street *right now* with his hands shoved into his pockets? I rushed to the bay window, but he was gone.

"What are you doing?" Jane frowned.

"Thought I saw something." The three of us stood there, forming a triangle with unequal sides. Finally, I sighed. "Look, let's all go out. Want to ride our bikes somewhere?"

Alex considered the possibility. "Where would we go?"

"I don't know, anywhere within reason."

"Where's that?"

"This side of craziness."

"Michael . . . ." But the tone of her voice was different from usual. Jane was pleading, not scolding. "How about if we bicycled to the park?"

"Maybe." Alex crouched on the rug, as if lying low. "Maybe we shouldn't."

The whole day was like that, though we did ride once around the neighborhood in a tired, cautious way. Alex lacked the energy to exert himself and by dinnertime was fighting off sleep. He wanted to shut his eyes, he said, but was afraid of nightmares. Jane and I came into his bedroom to reassure him.

I placed my arms across the blanket at waist-level, like a police cordon. "I won't let anything cross this line."

"And I'll keep away bad spirits." Jane caressed his head as if it held a crystal ball rather than the opaque boy's brain that neither of us could penetrate.

"Thank you," he told both of us solemnly. After turning out the lights, we sat for a while at the edge of his bed, but he clearly was still awake. Finally, I reached out for Jane's hand to hold, and then he seemed able to drift off. When I clasped her hand tightly, I loved the strong squeeze she gave back, though it didn't lead to anything. We spent the rest of the evening worrying silently and out loud about Alex.

We still had the weekend to contend with. We mostly did nothing in an aimless sort of way, with small meals and bite-size conversations. Alex remained uncommunicative, but he cheered up when he saw Jane and me working together: she chopped the onions for the ham omelets I was cooking, so he set the table. He still wasn't talking much, but rather than subject him to a barrage of questions, we adopted a wait-and-see policy.

Sunday afternoon, we were in Alex's room, playing Monopoly. Jane had just bought Boardwalk when the phone rang, and I left the room to pick it up.

It was Ferrara, asking how things were going.

"Okay. Still jittery. Hey, has he talked yet?" From Alex's room came the sound of dice rattling. How could they be playing without me?

Ferrara cleared his throat. "He's still not saying much."

"What's that mean?"

"All he claims is that he gave a ride to your son. The boy asked to leave with him. They played a bit at his place. End of story."

Like hell it's the end. A fiery tower of rage began to build inside me again. I shoved hard at the nearest wall, which shoved back. "So what's that, kidnapping?"

"Abduction. A lot depends on whether the kid was free to leave, but that's unclear."

Free? I took a deep breath. That son of a bitch. "What's next? Do we need to identify him in a police line-up? Does Alex have to get involved?"

"Well, he's saying he did it. You're pressing charges, right?"

"Not before Jane castrates him."

"What?"

"Just thinking out loud." Snoggs mentioned something nasty with an electrical cattle prod.

"Yeah, I heard that."

"Just a fantasy." I visualized a courtroom scenario. The bedroom bent under my warped gaze. "Wait, will Alex have to confront this guy?"

"Depends on the charges. I'm no lawyer. You'll need one." He talked for a little longer about what might happen, and told me to sit tight. I didn't point out that sitting tight is exactly what he'd advised when Alex disappeared. Hadn't we achieved another position by now?

I needed a moment to calm down. Slowly the room returned to its ordinary dimensions. Then I went back to the Monopoly game, which had gone on without me. I seemed to have landed in jail.

"We rolled the dice for you and moved your piece. You landed on Chance." Alex seemed pleased at his initiative. "The card said, 'Go directly to jail.'"

"I landed on your property," remarked Jane pleasantly, "St. James Place, but I don't think you get any rent while you're in jail. Who was that on the phone?"

"Ferrara." I jerked my thumb toward the hall. "I need to talk to you for a moment."

Jane got up from sitting cross-legged so fast, it looked like she was doing the kazatsky. "Honey, we'll be right back."

"Sure." Alex rolled the dice. "I'll let you know what happens on your turn."

I hustled us back into our bedroom. "Looks like that guy's not talking."

"My God. That son of a bitch." She leaned hard against the far wall, just as I had. Sometimes Jane and I are totally in synch.

I explained what I knew in as few words as possible. "The question is what's going to happen now."

"What do you mean?"

"We don't really know what went on, do we?"

"He damn well took Alex!"

"Yeah, but it was Alex's idea to go with him. That's what the guy said, anyway."

"Oh, so that makes it okay?" She walked forward, breathing heavily, arms upraised, soaring to goddess height.

I stepped back, afraid of another tennis smash. "Who said that? I just don't think it'll be easy." I thought again about the conversation I'd just had. "Ferrara mentioned getting a lawyer. Do you think Francis or Frances handle that sort of thing?"

Jane's nostrils quivered as if she were a horse, which is how I sometimes dream of her. She tossed her head and dug a hoof into the floor. "Give me the phone. I need to make some calls."

*

The procedures were hellish, but we had to go through with them. Ted Sacks, that was his name, was brought up for trial, and at one point we had to take Alex in for a videotaped testimony. By that point Alex was talking more and revealed a few details that still leave a nasty taste in my brain. We had a whip-smart lawyer named Hodgkins, whom Jane had hired on the recommendation of an attorney at Haldome. He specialized in childhood abuse cases and described a few until Jane told him to stop. We had the cooperation of the police, who held Sacks without bail until the trial, a month later. Hodgkins, who wore suspenders and a bow tie, had prepared a damning case, but in the end Sacks didn't put up much of a defense, nor did the state-appointed lawyer. Mostly, Sacks mumbled about how he was sorry and wouldn't do it again, as if that would be enough. I recognized him from the few times we'd crossed paths and kicked myself for not having done—whatever I could have done. And what about his neighbors? How can you tell that much from the outside? When the police searched his place, they'd found nothing interesting, except for an oddly wrecked bathroom. Apparently there was a computer he used, but somehow its insides had been rendered unusable.

On Hodgkins's counseling, Jane didn't look corporate the morning of the trial. "Dress like parents," he'd told us, so we appeared fairly casual, though that wasn't at all how we felt. Alex had been back in school since that first Monday, despite advice that any semblance of normalcy might undermine our case. I figured the longer we kept Alex away from Ms.

Hardin, the more awkward he'd feel. In fact, he was almost grateful when we dropped him off at Ridgewood. I felt like accompanying him with an armed guard. The court case started at nine. These kinds of stresses can wreck a marriage, but it had strengthened ours. Jane and I walked in that morning as a team.

"Hello," said Ted Sacks softly, as if he'd been expecting us. Which he had, of course, but the tone was half inviting, half menacing. Or maybe that was just my projection. He was dressed in a plaid short-sleeve button-down shirt and those gray trousers. Of course, he wasn't addressing us, but the judge. He had a small scar on his forehead, which must have been from when I pushed him down on the steering wheel.

"Morning," said the judge, a sour-faced woman in a wrinkled robe. When the testimony began, I figured it would be a long, gap-filled exchange, like a slow afternoon psychiatric session. I was wrong.

"Can you tell me something about Alex?" began Hodgkins, after establishing the facts of identity.

"He likes to roller-skate."

Hodgkins tapped his pen on the clipboard. "Really?"

"But he's not so hot at it." Ted smiled briefly.

"So that was you at the rink?" Hodgkins murmured this.

Ted looked mildly surprised. "I told them that. You already know it."

"But there's a lot we don't know." Hodgkins looked almost pleasant, an uncle sent to cajole a confession from an errant nephew. "You know, a lot of people were there, but they didn't see everything."

Another nod. "It's kind of hard to see in there."

Orange and yellow flashed in my head. "*Are you ready . . . ? Now, one-two-three!*" The 237th time I'd replayed it. By the time I shook the noise from my head, Hodgkins was asking about who'd been with Alex.

Ted said nothing. Jane and I directed a unicameral glare at Sacks. Finally, he volunteered some news. "He said his parents were in Arabia."

"And you believed that?"

Ted stared at the floor. Brown-purple socks. His shoes looked mismatched, though it was probably just the way he angled his feet. He could tell us things, I felt sure. I reached over to Jane and placed my hand over hers, firmly, lovingly.

"Arabia, huh? What else did he tell you?"

"That he wanted . . . he said he wanted to go home with me."

Jane's hand jumped like a grasshopper under mine, but I kept it covered. For my own sanity as well as hers, I began to stroke her fingers.

"Really? Where did you live?"

"Fanshaw Garden Apartments." He licked his lips—nervously? Lubriciously?

Hodgkins made a note. "When you got there, what did you do?"

"Talked."

"Really? What did you talk about?" Hodgkins leaned forward.

Ted frowned in recollection. "Different things. He's a bright kid."

Jane's hand wriggled—maternal pride?

"He likes patterns, same as me."

"What do you mean?"

"It's hard to explain." He gestured vaguely. "He wanted a snack, but it had to be pretzels, and in a certain arrangement . . . ."

At least we know he took the right kid—that was our son. What else had Alex demanded?

"You gave him a *snack*?"

I'd let my attention wander, and Jane had freed her hand from mine.

"He asked for it."

He likes to have a snack before dinner, whether he's hungry or not, I wanted to explain. *That's part of his game.*

But Hodgkins had asked something else.

"No, that wasn't one of the games."

"What games?" Jane and I silently asked this question in unison, but Hodgkins asked it out loud.

Ted looked away. "Nothing . . . nothing much. There's a game called Wild-Child." He gave a description pretty close to the version we knew. He spread his arms as if ready to play.

Then Hodgkins really hammered at him, but he couldn't get the guy to admit anything sexual. Finally he moved on. "When did he leave?"

"I don't know."

"You don't know?" By this point, Jane had her right leg wrapped around my left in a wrestler's hold, she was so coiled and ready to strike.

Ted hid his face in his hands. "I'm . . . not sure. I have episodes. It's a long story. I blacked out, okay?"

Nokay.

Hodgkins frowned.

"It's the truth."

"All right. What were you doing when you blacked out?"

"Playing, I told you."

The Q & A went on in that vein for a while. Sacks would talk about events up until the point when he claimed to lose consciousness. But Alex also hadn't gone much further. Were they both hiding something?

Browbeating them wouldn't pierce that veil, or whatever it was. Then again, neither would gentle probing. The famous psychotherapist Carl Rogers claimed to have once led a schizophrenic to clarity over a few months, but the tapes have silences of up to fifteen minutes each, and anyway, it's not clear that Rogers—or his patient—ever really got anywhere.

What I couldn't get out of my mind was Alex's expression when we told him the police had nabbed the abductor. He looked elated, surprised, terrified, and sad all at once. As for Sacks, at the trial I tried feeling sorry for him, but it didn't work. Jane confessed she had fantasies of skinning him with a blunt knife. We told none of this to Alex, who didn't ask.

The trial took only a few days. Sacks was convicted and sentenced to 5-7 years. That afternoon, we would pick up Alex from school. One day before I was sixty, we might all feel normal again. Just then, it was anyone's guess.

Chapter 20

By day 10, Ted was already sick of his uniform, though it was mostly gray. The dull routine that got him up at seven and in bed by nine was nonetheless reassuring. It meant he didn't have to think, and the pattern would simply continue over and over. He shared a cell with a round-shouldered guy named Fred who'd already done time once for burglary. Fred gave him some advice: Keep your nose clean. Stay away from guys who look as if they want to buy you. Or hurt you.

The second week in, he sent a card to Myra, who didn't answer.

He was back on medication but didn't like it. Twice a week, he had to go in for counseling, led by a therapist who treated them all like recovering alcoholics. Ted soon tuned him out. He came more to life with the exercise program, when he could walk laps in a gym as if he were headed somewhere. Egged on by a couple of the guys, he even tried the weights. He liked the repetitions and the way the effort cleared his mind for a long while afterwards. From time to time, he thought of boys, but he didn't have much to stimulate him. When he looked outside and saw that it was another lovely day, he felt a genuine pang of regret, but he didn't miss Fairchester.

A lot of the guys earned a small stipend manufacturing toy models for a company called SIG. But by the third month, Ted learned of a prisoner incentive program where he could do some kind of secretarial work. After passing a few idiotic tests, he started work as a reservations agent for the Gold Mine Travel Co. It was really trivial stuff, worse than data processing, but at least he was back on line. He'd missed the glow of the screen and the click of the mouse as if it were a phantom limb. Carefully, methodically, he planned to establish a new computer identity once he'd circumvented the security device on the machine. He went to sleep dreaming of re-establishing old connections, of accessing any boy he wanted via modem, of skating around and around an endless rink.

Chapter 21

The end. But of course it wasn't. How could it be? The longer I live, the more I appreciate Yogi Berra's "It ain't over till it's over." What he neglected to mention—maybe it was too obvious—is how painful matters could remain meanwhile. I could give you a list.

Ted Sacks was in jail. The counter intelligence at Price's Bake Shop reported no further gray slacks sightings. But anyone else could have taken his place. We managed to keep the story out of the *Fairchester Guardian*, which makes you wonder how much other news goes unreported. The tape from the hospital interview gave away little except that we didn't come across so well. A few suggestive details emerged in court. That's partly what Sacks was convicted on, along with abducting a minor. He said it was consensual. Alex claimed it was a game penalty.

For a while we didn't just watch Alex's every move; we analyzed it. When he looked out the front window at breakfast, was that an urge to flee? What did it mean that he started asking for corn chips as a snack instead of pretzel sticks?—was that something he'd been fed in the den of iniquity? Why did he spend so much time in the bathroom these days?—mostly reading on the toilet, I discovered, but occasionally lying in the tub without any water. I know because the door was left slightly ajar, and I peeked inside. The first time, I thought he'd pulled off another vanishing act, but he answered when I called out. That was a change right there. There he was, his arms and legs pressed tightly together as if he were tied up. His clothes had been flung onto the tiled floor, I noticed, and I'd make him pick them up later. Had he been playing with himself? I couldn't tell.

"What are you doing in the bathtub?" I demanded of him practically, patiently, parentally. He didn't answer—that was more like the old Alex—so I asked him again, this time leaning over the side of the tub.

"I'm trying to . . . get another perspective." *Perspective* was a word he'd learned last year, picked up from some grade-school book that mentioned Greek architecture, I think. But when I asked him what he meant, he just put his finger to his lips and shut his eyes. I thought of turning the tap on, but instead left him, as my father was fond of saying, to his own devices.

Did I mention the game he came up with at school called "Sit"? Each boy sees how long he can take being sat upon. Because of where the boys put their weight, some other kid labeled it "Buttface." We heard about it from Ms. Hardin, who called to express concern. Who knows whether Alex made it up or just passed something on? You're not supposed to confront children these days.

We asked his babysitters whether they noticed anything different about the way he behaved, but the answer was ambiguous.

"So how was he?" asked Jane the first night we finally agreed it was all right to go out and leave Alex. Mary was at the kitchen table, wistfully scanning a menu from Wok Heaven. We'd offered her Chinese takeout, but she said she was trying to lose weight.

"Pretty good. Alex rated it 7.5. How was your evening?" She got up, showing a crescent of belly between her jeans and shirt. It looked appetizing, and I wondered idly how it would feel rubbed against my cheek, what I was missing on my monogamous diet. Games that married men play.

"Oh, I'd give it close to a 10." Jane patted me possessively. We'd gone to Hunan Pavilion, which was my choice, followed by a chick flick (her choice) at what I called Cinema 1-2-Many at the local mall. Just another evening out in the 'burbs. But we'd both wanted to make it work, and for once we declared a moratorium on discussing Alex. For a few minutes at the restaurant, between the poured tea and the steamed dumplings, we didn't know what to talk about. We filled the gap, so help me, with comments on the weather. It was a bit like a first date.

Driving Mary home, I asked her a few more questions about Alex's behavior. Did he eat his dinner? Mostly dessert. What time did he go to bed? Earlier than usual. He suddenly seemed exhausted. And what about that game, Wild-Child?

"Oh, we're not doing that anymore." But I noticed she wasn't looking at me.

"Why not?"

"Someone plays a little rough." She rubbed her breasts as if they were tender. "Anyway, we switched to Monopoly. I let him take back moves."

I talked to Steffie, but at the bakery, since Jane's response to hiring our second-string babysitter for another evening was simple and succinct: "*Her?*"

"If it's a question of those Cheetos, we can stay off snack foods altogether."

Or just switch to Doritos.

"I don't think so." It was Saturday morning, two weeks later, and Jane was getting ready to play tennis. The threesome she played with was still intact, though somewhat distracted. Mavis had missed some matches while getting her life back together. Wylene was petitioning to block the opening of a Barnes & Noble superstore in the mall. And rumor had it that Frances had somehow acquired herpes in a threesome and Francis was suing the third party involved. Yet for a while they'd all been so solicitous of Jane that she wanted, she said, to stuff their mouths with tennis balls. "But I need these games," she told me. "And it's only once a week."

So I took Alex bowling, a fine, masculine activity, where our combined score was less than that of the powerhouse woman in the next alley. We had fun, sort of. But was he gazing at that rugged guy in a crew-neck shirt at the far table? When it was time to leave, Alex said he just wanted to sit there. I ended up half-dragging him to the car. When he called me a mean daddy, I told him no, I really cared about him.

I drove us home, avoiding odd patches of guilt on the roads: the black dog on Crest Hill now decayed into memory, the staid houses where I had run up and down the block, calling out Alex's name. The sewing machine sound of cicadas stitched together the mid-morning streets. The overarching trees had laced their fingers into a green canopy. It was mid-June, harboring a lull that occurs a week or so before school lets out. This summer, we'd planned on sending Alex to a heavily recommended day camp along the Hudson called Oswondegott. Now we weren't so sure. What was the security like? How thoroughly had they screened the counselors?

"Daddy, what does *incon—inconsequential* mean?" A word from the book he was reading in the back seat.

"It means without consequences. Do you know what consequences are?"

"I think so. Effects?"

"That's right." Bright kid, as everyone said. Next year he'd be asking me about transcendentalism. "*Inconsequential* means that something has no effects, that it doesn't matter."

"Okay. That fits." We turned onto Garner Street, where spring had disrupted the Steinbaums' topiary with all sorts of tufts that needed cutting back. The giant bowling balls on the side looked like unshaven monster heads.

When we got home, I had to coax Alex out of the car. "C'mon, it's a beautiful day," I told him, relying on the blandest cliché known to family life.

"So what?" His face was screwed up in displeasure. Bright sunlight made him wince.

"Let's go kick the soccer ball."

"*Daddy* . . . ." He said this with infinite weariness and a slight edge of irritation. Some people never learned. "It's not the right season."

So we ended up playing Monopoly again in his room, though I refused to let him roll the dice again when he got a bad throw. I know he'd been hurt, but we had to be careful about overcompensation. Monopoly was not a metaphor for life. When Jane came back an hour later, flushed from her tennis victory, I'd almost driven him bankrupt.

"Who's winning?"

Alex scowled. "Daddy is. I think he cheats."

I sat up at that. "I do *not* cheat. I just don't let—"

"Michael, can we talk for a minute?" Jane stood over the board, arms akimbo, one bronzed thigh almost at my cheek. She who must sometimes be obeyed. When I got up, she was still taller, that crucial half-inch. She led me into the hall for a conference. We could have been at Haldome, discussing business strategy before a board meeting. No, we couldn't have.

"Hey, it's your move!" Alex whined from the floor.

I poked my head back into the room. "Don't go away!" I told him in my best TV announcer's voice. "We'll be right back!" I retreated again to the hall. "I know what you're going to say."

"Look, I don't think it's a good idea for him to lose." Predictable, but arguable. If only she didn't look so formidable in that Lycra top. Her chest rose like an impossibly steep promontory. Haven't you ever wanted to ravish someone and push her aside at the same time? You haven't? Then you've never been married. Still, we were getting along a hell of a lot better. I think we'd recalled why we got married: we loved each other. We were *made* for each other. We just had to remind ourselves of that fact.

"You want me to throw the game, is that it?" *She just wants him to grow up with a healthy admiration for capitalism*, remarked Martin.

"I didn't say that." Jane pursed her lips. Kissable, disapproving. "But after all . . . that's happened . . . ."

Whatever that *was*. Snoggs shrugged from somewhere in my cerebrum. I made an Alphonse and Gaston gesture: no, no, after *you*. "Fine. How about if you take over?"

Jane frowned. "Why? What are *you* going to do?"

"Me? I'm going to take a walk."

And that's what I did. Jane assumed my position on the rug. Instead of taking my place, though, she just started from Go. Jane would roll for both

of us. I hung around long enough to see Jane move her marker and Alex
land on a property of mine with a hotel.

"All right, just this once you don't have to pay rent."

"But that's not the way to play! That's cheating, too."

"Okay, then. You can take out a loan."

I hustled downstairs as Jane began to explain the finer points of col-
lateral on rental properties.

*

It really was a beautiful day, the emerald world of the suburbs in June
reaching up towards the yellow and blue of the sun in the sky. The DiSalvas
across the street were putting in wickets for a croquet game. The List no
longer loomed large in my mind, no longer a great flapping *J'accuse* but
a piece of paper that I'd torched alongside Jane's list in a small ceremony
by the outdoor barbecue. Then we distributed the ashes by the base of the
maple tree in our back yard.

As I sometimes tell my patients in relationships, there are two kinds
of compromise: one where you and your partner meet in the middle, which
seems scrupulously fair, though in fact neither party is quite satisfied—and
one where this time you get your way completely, but the other person rules
the next time. In the case of R, I recommended the first kind, and in fact
she and Dwight had achieved a balance of sorts. He agreed to recognize her
needs, or at least pretend to do so, which meant acting less like a thug and
more like a sensitive male. He put the toilet seat down and had trained himself to say "honey." In return, she affected to giggle at some of his unfunny
jokes and bought a sexy nightgown.

With S, I'd advised the second type of agreement. It made for the kind
of immediate gratification S craved, from pork and beans for supper to
sex on demand. But when it was Sheryl's turn, he'd found out that all she
wanted was for him to clean up after himself and cuddle romantically with
her at night. "My arm falls asleep, you know?" S had gestured floppily. "But
she loves it. Go figure."

Most of my other patients were still trying to cope. I may never completely unravel T's narrative; Z will probably die before he remarries. WE
quit therapy in favor of a divorce.

And me? I wasn't sure where to go, but a walk has to start somewhere.
I headed off toward Grove Street, deciding on a zigzag pattern of left and
right turns. Children dancing across a sprinkler, the whine of lawnmowers.
At the corner of Delanor and Fenley, a giant maple had cracked the sidewalk

with its gnarled roots and almost tripped me up. I rescued myself with a splay-foot maneuver and stepped right in a pile of dog shit.

I spent the next minute at the curb, scraping brown gunk off my Nikes. The suburbs felt tainted after what had happened to Alex, though I suppose it could have happened anywhere. But a lot of city streets at least look sinister, whereas in Fairchester the lawns look virginal green. I remember, when we moved here, getting up at dawn because I couldn't sleep and seeing a new Eden, a look of controlled innocence to everything, from the manicured grass to the never-used fire hydrants. Only now the dawn reminded me of returning home childless and frantic, driving up and down these damnably bland streets. I thought about how Ted Sacks had described Fairchester, as a sterile nightmare with pop-up dolls instead of people, but he'd escaped all that.

Or not quite. He'd left a part of himself, spread along the gaps in the bushes and the sidewalk cracks. In my brain. As I took a left onto Sycamore and a right on Montrose, I saw a boy and a girl chasing a ball down the block. Alex would never be that carefree again—and we certainly couldn't feel that way about him anymore.

Wait till he starts rubbing against other boys in fourth grade, said Snoggs, whom I hadn't heard from in a while. *Or grabbing at his crotch like a pro baseball player.*

If only . . . remarked Martin.

I kicked a stone, which clattered morosely down the sidewalk. If only Alex hadn't pulled that tantrum before the rink party, or if I'd looked in the right direction at the right time, or put two and two together when I saw those gray pants, or called on my secret powers.

This kind of delusion is what Freud called magical thinking, the idea that you have the ability to govern events beyond your control. If you keep focusing on your daughter's airplane in the sky, she'll land safely at O'Hare. If only you hadn't directed bad thoughts at your boyfriend this morning, he wouldn't have broken his leg on his lunch break. It's illogical, but you can't help it.

I paused by a giant fir tree in someone's front yard, losing myself for a moment in the shadows. You can't undo the past, despite psychologists' claim in that direction. You *can* ease trauma—if only I could get that sound of roller-skating out of my ears. On a hunch, I turned down Winfield and headed toward the Fanshaw Garden Apartments. A FOR RENT sign was on the lawn by unit #3. I wandered over to check it out.

I plodded around the grass, not sure what I was doing there. To justify the term "garden apartments," each unit had a sapling, a flowerbed small as a grave, and a hedge. I was about to leave when something buried in one of the bushes caught my eye. It was dingy white and looked like a broken-backed bird. But when I came closer, the contours became all too clear. Jockey shorts, junior size.

Now what would an adult male want with those? I peered at the underwear without touching it. They looked like Alex's. But he'd come back with them on, right? Certain events from that night remained confused.

Maybe some kid had tossed them into the bushes.

And I'm the king of Arabia.

I entertained a few fantasies of breaking into prison and beating up the party involved. Then I took a deep breath and walked away. I didn't even snatch the underwear from the bushes because it was too creepy, and anyway, what would I have done with it? I couldn't prove a damned thing—nothing criminal, anyway.

I had just turned around for home when I heard skating from down the street, a sound that'll probably get to me as long as I live. On impulse, I ducked behind a tree to watch. But this guy was on a skateboard, pushing himself along with a tall stick and looking damned familiar. It was Chad, Steffie's punkoid boyfriend. He glanced in both directions and saw no one around. Then the son of a bitch whacked the nearest mailbox with his stick and began to wheel off.

Too bad the mailbox he'd whacked was right by my tree. I shot out with no warning and tackled him to the pavement.

"Shit, man, what'd you do that for?" His skateboard had gone flying into the curb, and I lay heavily on top of him. "Get off me."

"Ha! Gotcha." I eased up from the tackle hold, unsure of what to do next. My shin was throbbing a bit, but I barely felt it. "This is a citizen's arrest." Isn't that what you're supposed to say?

"You're crazy. I—*ow!*" Trying to stand up, he collapsed onto the pavement again. "Son of a bitch, sprained my ankle."

"I'm sorry to hear that." I'd never spoken with less sincerity. I looked toward the nearest house on the street, a white clapboard hulk with a sloping lawn. Two cars sat in the driveway. There had to be people in the house, and surely one of them would let me use the phone. "But if you can't walk, I'll bet we can get you a ride."

The old couple in the clapboard house were perfectly nice about our unannounced visit, especially when I explained the circumstances. In fact, the wife thanked me over and over for apprehending the mailbox whacker. After the police report had been filed, I walked home alone. It was unclear what the arrest would lead to, but apparently the U.S. postal authorities took a dim view of interference with federal delivery. Chad had ridden down to the station house in the back of a patrol car. His parents would have to pick him up from there. He had a sprained ankle that he couldn't walk on. I'd identified him as Steffie's boyfriend, though he angrily claimed he'd broken up with her a month ago. I wondered what kind of people his parents were, and whether the community would be blaming me for something Alex did when he became an adolescent. "If you think he's hard to handle now," Arthur Schram had warned me a while ago, "hoo boy! Wait till he's sixteen." Dalton had apparently escaped from school in Vermont once already. For that matter, Samantha Mirnoff had been found drawing over and over on the Pinewood playground, "MS. YANCEY IS A CUNT." So Jerry had sent her to a child psychologist—but no, that must have come first, since the therapist's name was Irene Yancey.

*

Back home, I looked forward to some sympathy and admiration from my wife and son, and I'm happy to say that I got it. Alex wanted to hear my description of the all-too-brief chase scene twice over. Jane said that Chad probably couldn't sue me for the twisted ankle, "But I'd defend you, darling." I received two sloppy kisses. Everybody loves a hero. Nobly, I rejoined the Monopoly game. Jane had amassed a pile in spite of starting late in the game. Alex happily handed me the dice, and I promptly landed on Electric Department, which he owned. I forked over some bills, and we kept playing as if I'd never left. You *can* go home again.

The family that plays together stays together. We started doing more activities together, riding our bikes together rather than riding each other into the ground. The turning point, if I had to identify one, came when Jane started getting home from work at a reasonable hour. She claimed it was because the Singapore division had been launched. Shortly thereafter, Harry Laker left Haldome. Go figure. Still, it was delicious seeing Jane sometimes as early as six. On certain evenings, we played Monopoly during dinner, which is why some of the property deeds have spaghetti sauce stains on them.

And then one day, I realized that almost a week had gone by without any nagging arguments. I mentioned it to Jane that night, after Alex had gone to sleep, but she wasn't so sure.

"Wait, what about breakfast on Tuesday?"

"That wasn't really an argument." We were both reading in bed, and I turned to look at her. "We just didn't have any bread left."

"But when I asked you to take care of it, you—"

So I kissed her. It was easier than talking and felt better. She kissed back. Her lips melted as I began to tongue her. Her hair smelled lightly of oranges—had she changed shampoo? After we surfaced for air, she nuzzled my neck with her lips. It felt like being tickled and eaten at the same time. When I squirmed, she reached around me with those round, bare arms and squeezed. Her grip was hard enough to make me feel lightheaded. We'd been side by side, but now somehow she was leaning over me. I fell softly onto her half of the bed, pulling her down with me, but she landed on top.

*

So everything returned to a semblance of normalcy, but what's normal, anyway? Everyone's always trying to cope, that favorite verb of Jerry's—it must be used at least a few hundred times in his book, which was published this fall and seems to have found a real niche market: all upscale couples who live in the suburbs. I shouldn't complain—it probably helps people with their problems, however simplistically, and it lists me in the acknowledgments.

Alex is in third grade now, though without a best friend. James Ottoway died over the summer, and his parents moved away, which puts this all in perspective. For a while, Alex retreated into a gray shell of lethargy, as if he were the one with leukemia. But time passed. Eventually he made friends with a girl named Judith, who wears tortoise-shell glasses and can play Bach on the piano.

Damn it, I should be grateful. James is dead. Alex is still alive. He remains maddeningly unresponsive. We never talk about his "incident" anymore. If we did, it would be like that old parent-child Q & A routine:

"Where did you go?"

"Out."

"What did you do?"

"Nothing."

As a psychiatrist, I know that nothing can be something. As a father, I don't know anything, or at least that's the way it seems at times. The therapist we took Alex to, a friend of Jerry's, got nowhere, and Alex hated the weekly sessions, so we eventually dropped them. His teacher this year, a gray-haired veteran named Mrs. Schultz, has called Alex a natural writer and encouraged him to start a diary. If he does, should I peek to see what unspeakable things he's written about me? What if he's revealed something about the incident there?

My patients' lives yank me out of my problems. R is pregnant now, due next April. S is contemplating an affair, due for trouble any day now. So after all that's happened—you think that change is possible? Change within limits, maybe. Character is destiny, said Freud, or was it "Biology is destiny"? Whichever it was, what about a little wiggle room?

Granted, some of these people are simply not my problem, as my old supervisor Briggs used to say about others' caseloads. The Talent-Schramm team is provisionally back together, Frances and Francis are into some sort of *ménage à quatre*, and Jerry's wife has had a colostomy—no connections implied here. Me, I want to *do* something, from working out on my abandoned Re-Flex to writing my own book—to solve something, or maybe that doesn't matter so much. And I try not to be so neurotic.

So, are you back for good? The lists of our grievances are scattered in ashes over the back yard. I've put down my milky mug of tea and wander over to the refrigerator, where Jane has scribbled a list of Things to Do on a Haldome Post-it. She's become bossier now that they've made her head of the Asian growth sector, but I made her squirm when we made love last night. Alex's card for Father's Day is still on the fridge, with "DADDY" in three different crayon colors—two of which I found later on the TV room wall, and they took forever to clean off. I enter the dining room and look out the front window. A DiSalva just knocked a bocci ball into the street. The Wallers have put their house up for sale. Is a better world out there somewhere? *Should you leave?* I ask Snoggs and Martin and anyone else listening, as I take in the limits of my world, from car and garage to sidewalk and lawn. The answer comes back in a voice I recognize as my own: *Don't kid yourself.*